Charles J. Lever, Hablot Knight Browne

Charles Lever's Novels

Volume 26

Charles J. Lever, Hablot Knight Browne

Charles Lever's Novels
Volume 26

ISBN/EAN: 9783337125868

Printed in Europe, USA, Canada, Australia, Japan

Cover: Foto ©Andreas Hilbeck / pixelio.de

More available books at **www.hansebooks.com**

HORACE TEMPLETON

" ' Who are you?' said the Countess."

HORACE TEMPLETON

BY

CHARLES LEVER

AUTHOR OF "CHARLES O'MALLEY

WITH ILLUSTRATIONS

LONDON

GEORGE ROUTLEDGE AND SONS

THE BROADWAY, LUDGATE

NEW YORK: 416 BROOME STREET

LONDON:
PRINTED BY WOODFALL AND KINDER,
MILFORD LANE, STRAND, W.C.

HORACE TEMPLETON.

CHAPTER I.

It is a strange thing to begin a "log" when the voyage is nigh ended! A voyage without chart or compass has it been: and now is land in sight—the land of the weary and heart-tired!

Here am I, at the Hôtel des Princes, *en route* for Italy, whither my doctors have sentenced me! What a sad record would be preserved to the world if travellers were but to fill up, with good faith, the police formula at each stage of the journey, which asks, "the object of the tour!" How terribly often should we read the two short words—"To Die." With what sorrowful interest would one gaze at the letters formed by a trembling hand; and yet how many would have to write them! Truly the old Italian adage, "*Vedere Napoli e poi morire,*" has gained a new signification; and, unhappily, a far more real one.

This same practice of physicians, of sending their patients to linger out the last hours of life in a foreign land, is, to my thinking, by no means so reprehensible as the generality of people make out. It is a theme, however, on which so many common places can be strung that common-place people, who, above all others, love their own eloquence, never weary of it. Away from his children—from his favourite haunts—

B

from the doctors that understood his case—from his comfortable house—from the family apothecary—such are the
changes they ring; and if dying were to be done often,
there would be much reason in all this.　But it is not so;
this same change occurs but once, and its approach brings
with it a new train of thoughts and feelings from all that
we have ever felt before.　In that twilight hour of life,
objects that have escaped our vision in the blaze of noon-
day become clear and distinct; and, even to the least
reflecting of minds, an increased power of perception and
judgment is accorded—the *viaticum* for the coming
journey !

I remember being greatly affected by the stories in the
"Diary of a Physician," when first I read them: they
were powerfully written—and *so real !*　Now this is the
very quality they want : they are altogether unreal.

Terrific and heart-stirring as the death-bed scenes are,
they are not true to nature: the vice and the virtue are
alike exaggerated.　Few, very few persons can bring
themselves by an effort to believe that they are dying—
easy as it seems, often as we talk of it, frequent as the
very expression becomes in a colloquialism, it is still a
most difficult process ; but once thoroughly felt, there is
an engrossing power in the thought that excludes all
others.

At times, indeed, Hope will triumph for a brief interval,
and "tell of bright days to come."　Hope ! the glorious
phantom that we follow up the Rhine—through the deep
glens of the Tyrol, and over the Alps !—Only content to
die when we have lost it!

There are men to whom the truth, however shocking,
is always revealed—to whom the lawyer says, "You have
no case," and the physician confesses, "You have no
constitution."　Happily or unhappily—I will not deny it
may be both—I am one of these.　Of the three doctors
summoned to consult on my health, one spoke confidently
and cheeringly ; he even assumed that kind of profes-
sional jocularity that would imply, "the patient is making
too much of it."　The second, more reserved from
temperament, and graver, counselled caution and great

care—hinted at the danger of the malady—coupling his fears with the hopes he derived from the prospect of climate. The third (he was younger than either of the others, and of inferior repute) closed the door after them, and resumed his seat.

I waited for some time expecting him to speak, but he sat in silence, and seemingly in deep thought. "And you, my dear doctor," said I at length, "are you equally confident as your learned colleagues? Will the air of Italy —— ? " He lifted up his eyes as I got so far, and their expression I shall not readily forget—so softly tender, so full of compassionate pity, did they beam. Never did a look convey more of sorrowing regret, nor more of blank despair. I hesitated—on *his* account I feared to finish what I had begun; but, as if replying to the expression of his glance, I added, "But still you advise me to go? You counsel the journey, at least?"

He blushed deeply before he could answer. He felt ashamed that he had failed in one great requisite of his art. I hastened to relieve him, by saying with a joyous air, "Well, I will go. I like the notion myself; it is at least a truce with physic. It is like drawing a game before one has completely lost it."

And so here I am—somewhat wearied and fevered by the unaccustomed exertion, but less so than I expected.

I sincerely hope it is only the fastidiousness of a sick man, and not that most insufferable of all affectations —exclusiveness; but I will own I never disliked the mixed company of a steam-boat so much before. It is always an unpleasant part of our English travelling-experience, that little steam trip from our own coast to the French or Belgian shore. The pleasuring Cockney, only sufferable when sick—the runaway bank-clerk—the Hamburg Jew—the young lady going to Paris for spring fashions—the newly-married barrister, with his bit of tawdry finery from Norwood, silly, simpering, and fidgetty —the Irish landlord, sulky and familiar by turns ; all, even to the *danseuse*, who, too refined for such association, sits in her carriage on deck, have a terrible sameness when seen, as I have done them, something like fifty times; nor can I suppose their united attractions greatly heightened by the figure of the pale gentleman, who coughs so incessantly, and whose wan cheek and colourless eye are seen to such formidable contrast with the bronzed and resolute face of the courier beside him.

Yet I would far rather think this want of due tolerance for my travelling companions was a symptom of my malady, than of that truly English disease—self-importance. I know of nothing that tracks our steps on the Continent so invariably, nor is there any quality which earns for us so much ill-will.

It is quite a mistake to suppose that these airs of superiority are only assumed by persons of a certain rank and fortune—far from it. Every denizen of Cheapside and the Minories that travels abroad, deems himself immeasurably above "the foreigner." Strong in his City estimation, and charged with the leader in the *Times*, he struts about like an upstart visiting the servants' hall, and expecting every possible demonstration of respect in return for his condescension. Hence the unhappy disparity between the situation of an Englishman and that of any other native abroad. Instead of rejoicing at any casualty which presents to him a chance meeting with a country-man, he instinctively shrinks from it. He sees the Frenchman, the Italian, the German, overjoyed at recognition with some stranger from his own land, while *he* acknowledges, in such a contingency, only another reason for guardedness and caution. It is not that our land is wanting in those sterling qualities which make men respected and venerated—it is not that we are not, from principle and practice, both more exacting in all the requisites of good faith, and more tenacious of truth, than any people of the Continent;—it is simply that we are the least tolerant to everything that differs from what we have at home, that we unscrupulously condemn whatever is un-English; and, not satisfied with this, we expect foreigners to respect and admire us for the very censure we pass upon their institutions.

There is, therefore, nothing so compromising to an

Englishman abroad as a countryman; except—*hélas* that
I should say so!—a countrywoman!

Paris is very beautiful in spring. There is something
radiant and gorgeous in the commingled splendour of a
great city, with the calmer beauties of leafy foliage and
the sparkling eddies of the bright river. Better, however,
not to dwell longer on this theme, lest my gloomy thoughts
should stray into the dark and crime-trodden alleys of
the Bois de Boulogne, or the still more terrible filets de
St. Cloud! How sad is it when one's temperament
should, as if instinctively, suggest the mournful view
of each object! Rather let me jot down a little incident of this morning—an event which has set my
heart throbbing, and my pulse fluttering, at a rate that
all the prussic acid I have learned to take cannot calm
down again.

There come now and then moments to the sick man,
when to be well and vigorous he would consent to be
poor, unfriended in the world—taking health alone for
his heritage. I felt that half an hour ago—but it is gone
again. And now to my adventure, for, in my unbroken
dream of daily life, it seemed such.

I have said I am lodged at the Hôtel des Princes.
How different are my quarters from those I inhabited
when first I saw this city! This would entail a confession, however, and I shall make it some other day. My
salon is No. 21, the first drawing-room to the right as you
turn from the grand staircase, and opening by the three
spacious windows on a balcony overlooking the Rue de
Richelieu. It is, indeed, a very splendid apartment, as
much so as immense mirrors, gilding, bronze, and ormolu
can make it. There are soft couches and chairs, and
ottomans too, that would inspire rest, save when the soul
itself was restless.

Well, I lounged out after breakfast for a short stroll
along the Boulevards, where the shade of the trees and
the well-watered path were most inviting. Soon wearied
—I cannot walk in a crowd—I returned to the hôtel;
shortly toiled up-stairs, waking the echoes with my
teasing cough; and, instead of turning to the right, I

went left, taking the wrong road, as I have so often done in life ; and then mistaking the numerals, I entered No. 12 instead of No. 21. Who would credit it, that the misplacement of a unit could prove so singular?

There was one change alone which struck me. I could not find the book I was reading—a little volume of Auerbach's village stories of the Schwartz-Walders. There was, however, another in its place, one that told of humble life in the provinces—not less truthful and heart-appealing—but how very unlike! It was Balzac's story of "Eugénie Grandet," the most touching tale I have ever read in any language. I have read it a hundred times, and ever with renewed delight. Little troubling myself to think how it came there—for, like an old and valued friend, its familiar features were aways welcome—I began again to read it.

Whether the result of some peculiar organization, or the mere consequence of ill-health, I know not, but I have long remarked, that when a book has taken a strong hold upon me—fascinating my attention and engaging all my sympathies, I cannot long continue its perusal. I grow dreary and speculative ; losing the thread of the narrative, I create one for myself, imagining a variety of incidents and scenes quite foreign to the intention of the writer, and identifying myself usually with some one personage or other of the story—till the upshot of all is, I drop off asleep, to awake an hour or so afterwards with a very tired brain, and a very confused sense of the reality or unreality of my last waking sensations.

It is, therefore, rather a relief to me, when, as in the present case, the catastrophe is known to me, and all speculation on the future denied. Poor Eugénie, how I felt for all your sorrows !—wondrous spectacle of a heart that could transmute its one absorbing passion into another, and from love, the fondest and most confiding, beget a pure and disinterested friendship!

At last the book glided unnoticed from my hand, and I slept. The sofa where I lay stood in a part of the room where a deep shadow fell from the closed *jalousies* of a window, so that any person might easily have entered or traversed the apartment without noticing me. I slept calmly and without a stir—my dreaming thoughts full of that poor girl's love. How little does any first passion depend upon the excellence of the object that creates it! How ideal, purely ideal, are those first emotions of the heart! I knew something of this, too; for, when young, very young, and very impressionable, with a strong dash of romance in my nature, that lent its Claude Lorraine tint to all I looked at, I fell in love. Never was the phrase more fitting. It was no gradual or even imperceptible declension, but a headlong, reckless plunge; such as some confident and hardy swimmer, or very often a bold bather, makes into the water, that all may be quickly over.

I had been appointed *attaché* at Vienna, where Lord Newington was then ambassador—a widower with an only daughter. I was very young, fresh from Woolwich, where I had been studying for the Artillery service, when the death of a distant relative, who but a year before had refused to see me, put me in possession of a very large fortune. My guardian, Lord Elderton, an old *diplomate*, at once removed me from Woolwich, and after a short sojourn at his house near Windsor, I was introduced into what Foreign-office people technically denominate "The Line," and what they stoutly uphold as the only career for a gentleman.

I must some day or other jot down a few recollections of my life at Gortham, Lord Elderton's seat, where, with Grotius and Puffendorf of a morning, and old Sir Robert Adams and Lord Hailieburay of an evening, I was believed to be inhaling the very atmosphere of learned diplomacy. Tiresome old gentlemen, whose thoughts stood fast at the time of Fox and Pitt, and, like a clock that went down in the night, steadily pointed to an hour long bygone. How wearied I was of discussions as to whether the King of Prussia would declare war, or the Emperor of Austria make peace! whether we should give up Malta and lose Hanover! Pitt, must, indeed, have been a man of "dark counsels," for whether he wished for an alliance with

France or not was a nightly topic of debate without a chance of agreement.

All these discussions, far from tending to excite my ardour for the career, served to make me dread it, as the most tiresome of all possible pursuits. The light gossip, too, over which they regaled themselves with such excellent relish, was insupportably dull. Who could care for the pointless repartees of defunct Grand Dukes, or the meaningless caprices of long-buried Archduchesses?

If, then, I was glad to escape from Gortham and its weary company, had I formed no very sanguine expectations of pleasure at Vienna.

I saw very little of the Continent in this my first journey. I was consigned to the charge of a cabinet messenger, who had orders to deliver me "safe" at Vienna. Poor M'Kaye, slight as I was, he left me very little of the small *coupé* we travelled in. He weighed something more than twenty stone, a heaving mass of fat and fretting: the great misery of his life being that Washington Irving had held him up to European ridicule, for he was the original "Stout Gentleman" whose heavy perambulations overhead suggested that inimitable sketch.

We arrived at Vienna some hours after dark, and after speedily traversing the narrow and winding streets of the capital, drew up within the *porte cochère* of the English embassy. There was a grand ball at the embassy—a sovereign's birthday, or a coronation, I forget which—but I can well remember the dazzling splendour of the grand staircase, a blaze of waxlights, and glittering with the brilliant lustre of jewelled dresses and gorgeous uniforms; but, perhaps, even more struck by the frequent announcement of names which were familiar to me as almost historical personages—the Esterhazeys, the Schwarzenbergs, and the Lichtensteins, when suddenly, with almost a shock, I heard my own untitled name called aloud, "Mr. Horace Templeton." It is, I believe, a very old gentry name, and has maintained a fair repute for some half-dozen centuries; but, I own, it clinked somewhat meagre on the ear amid the high-sounding syllables of Austrian nobility.

I stood within the doorway of the grand salon, almost stunned by the sudden transition from the dark monotony of a night journey to the noonday blaze of splendour before me, when a gentle tap from a bouquet on my arm aroused me, and a very silvery voice, in accents every one of which sank into my heart, bade me welcome to Vienna. It was Lady Blanche Newington that spoke—the most lovely creature that ever beauty and station combined to form. Fascinations like hers were new to me : she mingled gentleness of manner with a spiritual liveliness, that seemed ever ready to say the right thing at the right moment. The ease with which, in different languages, she addressed the various individuals of the company, employing all the little delicate forms of those conventionalities French and Italian so abound in, and through all, an unobtrusive solicitude to please, that was most captivating.

My whole occupation that night was to steal after her unobserved, and gaze with delight at traits of manner that my ardent imagination had already elevated into graces of mind. I was very much in love—so much so that, ere a few weeks went over, my brother attachés saw it, and tormented me unceasingly on the subject. Nay, they went further : they actually told Lady Blanche herself, so that I dreaded to meet her, not knowing how she might treat my presumption. I fancied all manner of changes in her bearing towards me—reserve, coldness, perhaps disdain. Nothing of the kind ! She was only more familiar and cordial than ever. Had I known more of the world, or of the feminine part of it, I should have read this differently : as it was, it overwhelmed me with delight. There was a frankness in her tone towards me, too ; for now she discussed the temper and character of our mutual acquaintances, and with a shrewdness of criticism strange in one so young. At last we came to talk of a certain Count de Favancourt, the secretary of the French embassy ; and as I mentioned his name, she said, somewhat abruptly,—

" I half suspect you don't like the Count ? "

" Who could ? " replied I, eagerly ; " is he not a '*Fat* ?' "

—using that precious monosyllable by which his countrymen designate a certain class of pretenders.

She laughed, and I went on, not sorry to have an opportunity of severity on one for whom I had conceived an
especial hatred—indeed, not altogether without cause,
since he had, on more than one occasion, marked the
difference of our official rank in a manner sufficiently
pointed to be offensive; and yet, the rigid etiquette observable to another embassy forbade all notice of whatever
could be passed over.

Like a very young man, I did not bound my criticism
on the Count by what I saw and observed in his manner,
but extended it to every possible deduction I could draw
from his air and bearing; winding up all by a very broadly-
hinted doubt that those ferocious whiskers and that deep
baritone were anything but a lion's skin over a very
craven heart.

The last words were scarcely uttered, when a servant
announced the Count de Favancourt. There is something,
to a young person at least—I fancy I should not mind it
now—so overwhelming on the sudden appearance of any
one on whom the conversation has taken a turn of severity,
that I arose confused and uneasy—I believe I blushed; at
all events, I perceived that Lady Blanche remarked my
discomfiture, and her eyes glanced on me with an expression I never observed before. As for the Count, he
advanced and made his deep reverence without ever noticing me, nor, even while taking his seat, once showed any
consciousness of my presence.

Burning with indignation that I could scarce repress, I
turned towards a table, and affected to occupy myself
tossing over the prints and drawings that lay about—my
maddened thoughts rendered still more insufferable from
fancying that Lady Blanche and the Count seemed on far
better and more intimate footing than I had ever known
them before.

Some other visitors being announced, I took the occasion
to retire unobserved, and had just reached the landing of
the stairs when I heard a foot behind me. I turned—it
was Favancourt. For the first time in my life, I perceived

a smile upon his countenance—an expression, I own, that became it even less than his habitual stern scowl.

"You have done me the honour, sir," said he, "to make some observations on my manner, which, I regret to learn, has not acquired your favourable opinion. Now, I have a strong sense of the *inconvénance* of anything like a rupture of amicable relations between the embassy I have the honour to serve and that to which you belong. It is, then, exceedingly unpleasant for me to notice your remarks —it is impossible for me to let them pass unnoticed."

He made a pause at these words, and so long that I felt bound to speak, and, in a voice that passion had rendered slightly tremulous, said—

"Am I to receive this, sir, in the light of a rebuke? because, as yet, I only perceive it conveys the expression of your own regret that you cannot demand an explanation I am most ready to afford you."

"My demand is somewhat different, sir, but, I trust, will be as readily accorded. It is this: that you resign your position as *attaché* to this embassy, and leave Vienna at once. There is no necessity that any unfavourable notice of this affair should follow you to another mission, or to England."

"Stop, sir, I beg of you; I cannot be answerable for my temper, if you persist to outrage it. While you may press me to acknowledge that, while half an hour ago I only deemed you a ' Fat,' I now account you an ' imbécile.'"

"Enough!" said the Count, passing down the stairs before me.

When I reached my lodgings, I found a "friend" from him, who arranged a speedy meeting. We fought that same evening, behind the Prater, and I received his ball in my shoulder—mine pierced his hat. I was recalled before my wound permitted me to leave my bed. The day I left Vienna, Lady Blanche was married to Count Favancourt!

Some fourteen years had elapsed since that event and the time in which I now lay sleeping on the sofa; and yet, after all that long interval—with all its scenes of varied interests, its stormy passions, its hopes, its failures, its successes—the image of Blanche was before my mind's eye, as brightly, joyously fair, as on the evening I first beheld her.   I had forgotten all that time and worldly knowledge had taught me, that, of all her attractions, her beauty only was real—that the graceful elegance of her bearing was only manner—that her gentleness was manner —her winning softness and delicacy mere manner—that all the fair endowments that seemed the rich promise of a gifted mind, united to a nature so bounteously endowed, were mere manner.   She was *spirituelle*, lively, animated, and brilliant—all, from nothing but manner.   To this knowledge I did not come without many a severe lesson. The teaching has been perfect, however, and made me what I am!   Alas! how is it that mere gilding can look so like solid gold—nay, be made to cover more graceful tracery, and forms more purely elegant, than the real metal ?

I have said that I slept! and, as I lay, dreams came over me—dreams of that long-past time, when the few shadows that fell over my path in life were rather spots where, like the traveller on a sunny road, one halts to breathe awhile, and taste in the cool shade the balmy influence of repose.   I thought of Blanche, too, as first I had seen her, and when first she taught my heart to feel the ecstasy of loving, breathing into my nature high hopes and longings, and making of life itself an ideal of delight and happiness.   And, as I dreamed, there stole over my senses a faint, thrilling memory of that young joy my heart had known, and a feeling like that of health and ardent buoyancy, which for years long I had not experienced.   *Her* voice, tremulous with feeling, vibrating in all the passionate expression of an Italian song, was in my ears—I could hear the words—my very heart throbbed to their soft syllables as she sung the lines of Metastasio,—

> "E tu. qui sa si te
> Ti sovrerai di me."

I started—there she was before me, bending over the

harp, whose cords still trembled with the dying sounds; the same Blanche I had known and loved, but slightly changed indeed; more beautiful perhaps in womanhood than as a girl. Her long and silky hair fell over her white wrist and taper hand in loose and careless tresses, for she had taken off her bonnet, which lay on the floor beside her; her attitude was that of weariness—nay, there was a sigh! Good heavens! is she weeping? My book fell to the ground; she started up, and, in a voice not louder than a whisper, exclaimed, "Mr. Templeton!"

"Blanche!—Lady Blanche!" cried I, as my head swam round in a strange confusion, and a dim and misty vapour danced before my eyes.

"Is this a visit, Mr. Templeton?" said she, with that soft smile I had loved so well; "am I to take this surprise for a visit?"

"I really—I cannot understand—I thought—I was certain that I was in my own apartment. I believed I was in Paris, in the Hôtel des Princes."

"Yes, and most correct were all your imaginings; only that at this moment you are *chez moi*—this is our apartment, No. 12."

"Oh, forgive me, I beg, Lady Blanche!—the similarity of the rooms, the inattentive habit of an invalid, has led to this mistake."

"I heard you had been ill," said she, in an accent full of melting tenderness; while taking a seat on a sofa, by a look rather than an actual gesture she motioned me to sit beside her: "you are much paler than you used to be."

"I have been ill," said I, struggling to repress emotion and a fit of coughing together.

"It is that dreadful life of England, depend upon it," said she, eagerly; "that fearful career of high excitement and dissipation combined—the fatigues of parliament— the cares and anxieties of party—the tremendous exertions for success—the torturing dread of failure. Why didn't you remain in diplomacy?"

"It looked so very like idling," said I laughingly, and endeavouring to assume something of her own easy tone.

"So it is. But what better can one have, after all?" said she, with a faint sigh.

"When they are happy," added I, stealing a glance at her beneath my eyelids. She turned away, however, before I had succeeded, and I could merely mark that her breathing was quick and hurried.

"I hope you have no grudge towards Favancourt?" said she hastily, and with a manner that showed how difficult it was to disguise agitation. "He would be delighted to see you again! He is always talking of your success in the House, and often prophesies the most brilliant advancement for you."

"I have outlived resentment," said I, in a low whisper: "would that I could add, other feelings were as easily forgotten."

Not at once catching my meaning, she turned her full and lustrous eyes upon me, and then suddenly aware of my words, or reading the explanation in my own looks, she blushed deeply, and after a pause said—

"And what are your plans now? do you remain here some time?"

"No, I am trying to reach Italy. It has become as classic to die there nowadays, as once it was to live in that fair land."

"Italy!" interrupted she, blushing still deeper. "Favancourt is now asking for a mission there—Naples is vacant."

This time I succeeded in catching her eyes, but she hastily withdrew them, and we were both silent.

"Have you been to the Opera yet?" said she, with a voice full of all its habitual softness.

"You forget," said I, smiling, "that I am an invalid: besides, I only arrived here last night."

"Oh, I am sure that much will not fatigue you. The Duc de Blancard has given us his box while we stay here, and we shall always have a place for you ; and I pray you to come ; if not for the music, for my sake," she added, hastily : "for I own nothing can be possibly more stupid than our nightly visitors. I hear of nothing but ministerial intrigue, the tactics of the *centre droit* and the opposition, with a little very tiresome gossip of the Tuileries ; and Favancourt thinks himself political, when he is only prosy. Now, I long for a little real chit-chat about London and our own people. *Apropos*, what became of Lady Frances Gunnington ? did she really marry the young cornet of dragoons and sail for India ?"

"The saddest is to be told : he was killed in the Punjaub, and she is now coming home a widow."

"How very sad !—was she as pretty as they said ?—handsomer than Lucy Fox, I have heard ! "

"I almost think so."

"That is great praise from you, if there be any truth in *on dits*. Had not you a kind of tenderness in that quarter ?"

"Me ! "

"Nay, don't affect surprise; we heard the story at Florence, and a very funny story it was : that Lucy insisted upon it, if you didn't propose for her, that she would for you, since she was determined to be mistress of a certain black Arabian that you had; and that you, fearing consequences, sent her the horse, and so compromised the affair."

"How very absurd ! "

"But is it not true ? Can you deny having made a present of the steed ?"

"She did me the honour to accept of a pony, but the attenuating circumstances are all purely imaginary."

" *Si non è vero è ben trovato.* It was exactly what she would do ! "

"An unfair inference, which I feel bound to enter a protest against. If we were only to charge our acquaintances with what we deem them capable of——"

"Well, finish, I pray you."

"I was only about to add, what would become of ourselves ?"

"Meaning you and me, for instance ?"

I bowed an assent.

"' *Qui s'excuse, s'accuse,*' says the adage," rejoined she, gaily : "*I* neither do one nor the other. At the same time, let me confess to one thing of which I am capable, which is, of detesting any one who in this age of the world affects to give a tone of moralizing to a conversation. Now I presume you don't wish this. I will even take it for granted, that you would rather we were good friends, as we used to be long ago.—Oh, dear, don't sigh that way!"

"It was you that sighed."

"Well, I am very sorry for it. It was wrong of *me*, and very wrong of *you* to tell me of it. But dear me! is it so late? can it really be three o'clock?"

"I am a quarter past; but I think we must both be fast. You are going out?"

"A mere drive in the Champs Elysées, where I shall pay a few visits and be back to dinner. Will you dine with us?"

"I pray you to excuse me—don't forget I am a sick man."

"Well, then, we shall see you at the Opera?"

"I fear not. If I might ask a favour, it would be to take the volume of Balzac away with me."

"Oh, to be sure! But we have some others, much newer. You know 'Le Recherche de l'Absolu' already?"

"Yes; but I like 'Eugénie' still better. It was an old taste of mine, and as you quoted a proverb a few moments ago, let me give you another as trite and as true,—

'On revient toujours.'"

"'A ses premiers amours,'"

said she, finishing; while with a smile, half playful, half sad, she turned toward the window, and I retired noiselessly, and without an adieu.

Heigho! how nervous and irritable I feel! The very sight of that handsome barouche that has driven from the hôtel, with its beautiful occupant lying listlessly back among the cushions, has set my heart a-beating far, far too hurriedly. How is it that the laws that govern material nature are so inoperative in ours, and that a heart that never felt can make another feel? Heaven knows! It is not love; even my first passion, perhaps, little merited the name: but now, reading her as worldliness has taught me to do—seeing how little relation exists between attractions and fascinations of the very highest order and any real sentiment, any true feeling—knowing how "Life" is her idol, how in that one idea is comprised all that vanity, self-love, false pride, and passion can form —how is it that she, whom I recognize thus, that *she* can move me? There is nothing so like a battle as a sham fight in a review.

CHAPTER II.

I must leave Paris at once. The weather is intolerably hot; the leaves that were green ten days ago already are showing symptoms of the scar and yellow. Is it in compliment to the august inhabitant of the palace that the garden is so *empressé* to turn its coat? Shame on my ingratitude to say so, for I find that his Majesty has sent me a card of invitation to dine on Friday next. Another reason for a hurried departure! Of all moderate endurances, I know of none to compare with a dinner at the Tuileries. "Stay!—halt!" cries Memory; "I'll tell you of one worse again—a dinner at Neuilly!"

The former is sure to include a certain number of distinguished and remarkable men, who, even under the chill and restraint of a royal entertainment, venture now and then on some few words that supply the void where conversation should be. At Neuilly it is strictly a family party, where, whatever ease may be felt by the illustrious hosts, the guests have none of it. Juvenal quaintly asks, If that can be a battle where you strike and I am beaten? so one is tempted to inquire if that can be called society where a royal personage talks rapidly for hours, and the listener must not even look dissent? The King of the French is unquestionably a great man, but not greater in any thing than in the complete mystification in which he has succeeded in enveloping his real character, mingling up together elements so strange, so incongruous and seemingly inconsistent, that the actual direction or object of any political move he has ever made will always bear a double appreciation. The haughty monarch is the citizen king; the wily and secret politician, the most free-spoken and candid of men: the most cautious in an intrigue, the very rashest in action. How is it possible to divine the meaning, or guess the wishes, of one whose nature seems so Protean?

His foreign policy is, however, the master-stroke of his genius,—the cunning game by which he has conciliated the party of popular institutions and beguiled the friends of absolutism, delighting Tom Duncombe and winning praise from Nicholas. Like all clever men who are vain of their cleverness, he has always been fond of employing agents of inferior capacity but of unquestionable devotion to his interests. What small intelligences—to use a phrase more French than English—were the greater number of the French ministers and secretaries I have met accredited to foreign courts! I remember Talleyrand's observation, on the remark being made, was, "His Majesty always keeps the trumps in his own hand." Though, to be sure, he himself was an evidence to the contrary—a "trump" led boldly out, the first card played!

So well did that subtle politician comprehend the future turn events must take, that on hearing, at two o'clock in the morning, that his Royal Highness the Duc d'Orléans had consented to assume the crown, he exclaimed, "And I am now ambassador at St. James's!" It must have been what the Londoners call "good fun" to have lived in the days of the Empire, when all manner of rapid elevations occurred on every hand. The *commis* of yesterday, the special envoy to-day; a week ago a corporal, and now gazetted an officer, with the cross of the Legion—on the *grande route* to become a general. A General! why not a Marshal of France—ay, or a King?

We have seen something of this kind in Belgium within a few years back—on a small scale, it is true. What strange ingredients did the Revolution throw up to the surface! what a mass of noisy, turbulent, self-opinionated incapables, who, because they had led a rabble at the Porte de Flandre, thought they could conduct the march of an army! And the statesmen!—good lack! the miserable penny-a-liners of the *Indépendant* and the *Lion Belge*, that admirable symbol of the land, who carries his tail between his legs. The really able, and, I believe, honest men were soon overwhelmed by the influence of the priest party—the vultures who watched the fight from afar, and at last descended to take all the spoils of the victory.

Wandeweyer and Nothomb are both men of ability, the latter a kind of Brummagen Thiers, with the same taste for intrigue, the same subtle subserviency to the head of the state, and, in his heart, the same cordial antipathy to England. But why dwell on these people? they will scarce occupy a foot-note in the old "Almanach."

The diplomatic history of our day, if it ever be written, will present no very striking displays of high-reaching intellect or devoted patriotism; the men who were even greatest before the world were really smallest behind "the fact." We deemed that Lord Aberdeen and Lord Palmerston, and Messrs. Guizot and Thiers, and a few more, were either hurrying us on to war or maintaining an admirable peace. But the whole thing resolves itself into the work of one man and one mind; neither very conspicuous, but so intently occupied, so devotedly persevering, that persistence has actually elevated itself to genius; and falling happily upon times when mediocrity is sublime, he has contrived to make his influence felt in every state of Europe. I speak not of Louis Philippe, but of his son-in-law, King Leopold.

"Let me make the ballads of a nation, and I care not who makes its laws," said the great statesman; and in something of the same spirit his Majesty of Belgium may have said, "Let me make the royal marriages of Europe, and any one who pleases may choose the ministry."

Apropos of the Roi Leopold, is it not difficult to understand a Princess Charlotte falling in love with his good looks? There is no disputing on this point. The most eminently successful man I ever knew in ladies' society was Jack Beauclerc—"Caucasian Jack" we used to call him at Brookes's. Everybody knows Jack was no beauty. Heavy beetling brows, a dark, saturnine, ill-omened expression, was ever on his features. Nor did his face light up at times, as one occasionally sees with such men; he was always the same sad misanthropic-looking fellow. Neither could one call him agreeable—at least I, meeting him very often, never found him so. But he was of a determined, resolute nature; one of those men that appear never to turn from any object on which they have set a strong will. This may have gone very far with ladies, who very often conceive a kind of esteem for whatever they fear. He said himself that his secret was, "always using them ill;" and certainly, if facts could bear out such a theory, one might believe him. Probably no man ever cultivated these tastes with such assiduity—these, I say, for play and duelling were also passions with him.

He was *attaché* to our mission at Naples before he was sixteen, and had the honour of wounding the old Marquis d'Espagna with the small sword at the same precocious era. The duel originated after a truly Italian manner; and as there are at Naples many incorrect reports of it, I will take the trouble to give the real one. The Marquis was an old man, married to one of the most beautiful women in Italy. She was a Venetian, and if my memory serves me right, a Guillardini by birth. She married him at eighteen to escape a convent, he being the richest noble under the rank of the blood royal at Naples. Very unlike the majority of Italian husbands, the Marquis was excessively jealous, would not permit the most innocent freedoms of his young and lovely wife, and eventually secluded himself and—worse still—her from all society, and never appeared except at a court ball, or some such festivity that there were no means of avoiding. It was at one of these festivities that the King, who liked to see his ball-room put forth its fairest aspect, bantered the Marquis on the rumour that had even reached the ears of royalty, as to his inordinate jealousy. The Marquis, whose old spirit of courtiership predominated even as strongly as his jealousy, assured his Majesty that the worthy people of Naples did him great injustice, and that, although conscious of the Marchesa's great beauty and attractiveness, he had yet too high a sense of the distinguished place he and his family had always held in the esteem of his sovereign to feel jealous of any man's pretension; adding, "If I have not admitted the conventional addition of a *cavalière servante* to my household, I would beg your

Majesty to believe it is simply because I have seen no one
as yet worthy to hand la Marchesa to her carriage or fold
her shawl."

"Admirably spoken, Marquis!" said the King; "the
sentiment is quite worthy of one who has the best blood
of Sicily in his veins. But remember what an artificial
state of society we live in; think of our conventional
usages, and what a shock it gives to public opinion when
one placed in so exalted a position as you are so palpably
affronts universal and admitted custom; recollect that
your reserve involves a censure on others, less suspicious,
and, we would hope, not less rigidly honourable men, than
yourself."

"But what would your Majesty counsel?"

"Select a *cavalière* yourself, as little likely to excite
your jealousy as you please; as little agreeable as possible
if you prefer it: but, comply at least so far with the
world's prescription, and do not shock our worthy Neapolitans by appearing to reflect upon them. There, what
say you to that boy yonder? he is only a boy—he has
just joined the English mission here. I'm sure he has
formed no tender engagements to prevent your adopting
him, and you will at least seem to conform with the
usages of your neighbours."

"If your Majesty commands——"

"Nay, Marquis, I but advise."

"Your Majesty's wish is always a command. I feel
proud to obey."

"Then, I am very happy to say I wish it," said the
King, who turned away, dying to tell the court-party how
miserable he had made the old marquis.

Such are *débauché* kings; the glorious prerogative of
power becomes the mere agent of perverted ingenuity to
work mischief and do wrong!

The poor Marquis lost no time to follow out the royal
commands, and at once made acquaintance with Beauclerc—only too happy to be noticed in such a quarter. I
know not whether the lady was much gratified by the
result of this kingly interposition in her favour: some
said, Yes, and that the youth was really gifted and

spirituel, with a vein of quiet, caustic humour, most amusing; others, and I half incline to this notion—pronounced him dull and uninteresting. At all events, the Marchesa enjoyed the liberty of appearing often in public, and seeing more of the world than heretofore. She usually visited the San Carlos, too, twice a week; a great improvement in her daily life, as previously the Opera was denied her.

Immediately over the Marchesa's box was the large box, or rather *salon*, belonging to the club of the Italian *nobili*, who frequented the theatre far less for the pleasures of the opera and the ballet than for the more exciting delights of *faro* and *écarté;* and here, nightly, were assembled all the most dissipated and spendthrift youth of a capital, whose very gravest and most exemplary citizens would be reckoned "light company" anywhere else.

High play, with all its consequences of passionate outbreaks, ruin, and duelling, were the pastimes of this ill-fated *loge;* and, notwithstanding the attractions the box underneath contained, Jack Beauclerc was far oftener in the second tier than the first. He was, indeed, a most inveterate gambler; and the few moments which he devoted to attending the Marchesa to her box or her carriage were so many instants of pregnant impatience till he was back at the play-table.

It was on one evening, when, having lost a very heavy sum, that his turn came to deal; and, with the superstitious feeling that only a play-man can understand, he resolved to stake a very large amount upon the game. The attention of the bystanders—never very deeply engaged by the *scène*—was now entirely engrossed by the play-table, where Beauclerc and his adversary were seated at *écarté*. It was that critical moment when the cards were dealt, but the trump not yet turned, and Beauclerc sat enjoying, with a gambler's "malign" delight, the eager anxiety in the other player's countenance, when suddenly a voice said:

"Ha, Beauclerc! the Marchesa is rising—she is about to leave the theatre."

"Impossible!" said he; "it is only the second act."

"It is quite true, though," rejoined another; "she is putting on her mantle."

"Never mind our party, then," cried Beauclerc's antagonist; "I will hold myself ready to play the match out whenever you please."

"I please it now, then!" said he, with a degree of energy that heavy losses had, in spite of him, rendered uncontrollable.

"Il Signor Beauclerc!" said a servant, approaching, "the Marquis d'Espagna desires to see you."

"Tell him I am engaged—I can't come," said Beauclerc, turning up the trump-card, which he held out triumphantly before his adversary, saying, "The king!"

At the same instant the old Marquis entered, and, approaching the table, whispered a few words in his ear. If an adder had pierced him with its sting, Beauclerc could not have started with a more agonised expression; and he sprang from the chair and rushed out of the theatre, not by the door, however, where the Marchesa's carriage was yet standing, but by a private passage, which led more easily towards his lodgings.

"What is this piece of news, that all are so amused by?" said the King, the next morning, as he was rising.

"Your majesty alludes to the Marquis d'Espagna, no doubt," said Count Villafranca. "He challenged the young English *attaché* last night, at the theatre, and they have been out this morning; and, strange to say, that the Marquis, the very best swordsman we have ever had here, was disarmed and run through the side by his antagonist."

"Is the wound dangerous?" said the King, coolly.

"I believe not, your Majesty. Beauclerc has behaved very well since it happened; he has not left the Marquis for a moment, and has, they say, asked pardon most humbly for his offence, which was, indeed, a very gross neglect of the Marchesa no husband could pardon."

"So I heard," said the King, yawning. "The Marquis is very tiresome, and a great bore: but, for all that, he is a man of spirit; and I am glad he has shown this young foreigner that Italian honour cannot be outraged with impunity!"

Such is the true version; and, let people smile as they like at the theory, I can assure them it is no laughing matter. It is, doubtless, somewhat strange to our northern ideas of domestic happiness that a husband should feel called on to punish a want of sufficient attention to his wife, from the man whom the world regards as her lover. We have our own ideas on the subject; and, however sensitive we may feel on this subject, I sincerely hope we shall never push punctilio so far as the Neapolitans.

Such, without the slightest exaggeration, are the pictures Italy presents, far more impressive on the minds of our travelling youth than all that Correggio has touched or Raphael rendered immortal. Will their contemplation injure us? Shall we become by habit more lenient to vice, and less averse to its shame? or shall we, as some say, be only more charitable to others, and less hypocritical ourselves? I sadly fear that, in losing what many call "our affected prudery," we lose the best safeguard of virtue. It was, at the least, the "livery of honour," and we showed ourselves not ashamed to wear it. And yet there are those who will talk to you—ay, and talk courageously—of the DOMESTIC LIFE OF ITALY!

The remark has been so often made, that by the mere force of repetition it has become like an acknowledged truth, that, although strangers are rarely admitted within its precincts, there exists in Italy and in Italian cities a state of domestic enjoyment to which our boasted home-life in England must yield the palm. Never was there any more absurd assertion less propped by fact—never was the "*ignotum*" so easily taken "*pro beatifico.*"

The domestic life of England has no parallel in any part of Europe, save, perhaps, in some of the French provinces, where the old "*vie du château*" presents something similar; but, even there, it rather lingers like the spirit of a departed time, the relic of bygone associations, than in the full reign of a strong national taste. In Germany, notwithstanding the general impression to the contrary there is still less of it: the passion for household duties by the woman, the irresistible charms of beer and tobacco to the men, suggest different paths; and while she indulges her native fondness for cookery and counting napkins at home, he, in some wine-garden, dreams away life in smoke-inspired visions of German regeneration and German unity. In Italy, however, the points of contact between the members of a family are still fewer again: the mealtimes, that summon around the board the various individuals of a house, are here unknown; each rises when he pleases, and takes his cup of coffee or chocolate in solitary independence—unseen, unknown, and, worse still, unwashed!

The drawing-room, that paradise of English home-existence, has no place in the life of Italy. The lady of the house is never seen of a morning; not that the cares of family, the duties of a household, engross her—not that she is busied with advancing the education of her children, or improving her own. No: she is simply *en déshabille*. That is, to be sure, a courteous expression for a toilet that has cost scarce five minutes to accomplish, and would require more than the indulgence one concedes to the enervation of climate to forgive.

The master of the family repairs to the *café*: his whole existence revolves around certain little tables, with lemonade, sorbets, and dominoes; his physical wants are, indeed, few, but his intellectual ones even fewer; he cares little for politics—less for literature; his thoughts have but one theme—intrigue; and his whole conversation is a sort of *chronique scandaleuse* on the city he lives in.

There is a tone of seeming good-nature—an easy mock charity, in the way he treats his neighbours' backslidings —that have often suggested to strangers favourable impressions as to the kindliness of the people; but this is as great an error as can be: the real explanation of the fact is the levity of national feeling, and the little impression that breaches of morality make upon a society dead to all the higher and better dictates of virtue—such offences being not capital crimes, but mere misdemeanours.

The dinner-hour occasionally, but not always, assembles

the family to a meal that in no respect resembles that in more civilized communities. The periodical return of a certain set of forms—those *convénances* which inspire, at the same time, regard for others and self-respect—the admixture of courtesy with cordial enjoyment—have no representatives around a board where the party assemble, some dusty and heated, others wrapped up in dressing-gowns—all negligent, inattentive to each other, and weary of themselves—tired of the long unbroken morning, which no occupation lightens, no care beguiles, no duty elevates. The Siesta follows, evening draws near, and at last the life of Italy dawns—dawns when the sun is setting! It is the hour of the theatre—the Theatre, the sole great passion of the nation, the one rallying point for every grade and class. Thither, now, all repair; and for a brief interval the silent streets of the city bustle with the life and movement of the inhabitants, as, on foot or in carriages, they hasten past.

The "business of the *scène*" is the very least among the attractions of a theatre in Italy. The opera-box is the drawing-room, the only one of an Italian lady; it is the club-room of the men. Whist and faro, ombre and piquet, dispute the interest with the prima donna or the danseuse in one box; while in another the fair occupant turns from the ardent devotion of stage-passion to listen to the not less impassioned, but as unreal, protestation of her admirer beside her.

That the drama, as such, is not the attraction, it is sufficient to say that the same piece is often played forty, fifty, sometimes seventy nights in succession, and yet the boxes lose few, if any, of their occupants. Night after night the same faces re-appear, as regularly as the actors; the same groupings are formed, the selfsame smiles go round; and were it not that no trait of *ennui* is discernible, you would say that levity had met its own punishment in the dreariness of monotony. These boxes seldom pass out of the same family; from generation to generation they descend with the family mansion, and are as much a part of the domestic property of a house as the rooms of the residence. Furnished and lighted up according to the

taste and at the discretion of the owner, they present to
eyes only habituated to our theatres the strangest variety,
and even discordance, of aspect: some, brilliant in wax-
light and gorgeous in decoration, glitter with the jewelled
dresses of the gay company; others, mysteriously sombre,
show the shadowy outlines of an almost shrouded group,
dimly visible in the distance.

The theatre is the very spirit and essence of life in Italy.
To the merchant it is the Bourse; it is the club to the
gambler, the *café* to the lounger, the drawing-room and
the boudoir to the lady.   But where is the domestic life?

CHAPTER III.

ANOTHER note from Favancourt, asking me to dine and meet Alfred de Vigny, whose "Cinque Mars" I praised so highly. Be it so; I am curious to see a Frenchman who has preferred the high esteem of the best critics of his country to the noisy popularity such men as Sue and Dumas write for.

De Vigny is a French Washington Irving, with more genius, higher taste, but not that heartfelt appreciation of tranquil, peaceful life that the American possesses. As episode, his little tale, the " Canne de Jonc," is one of the most affecting I ever read. From the outset you feel that the catastrophe must be sad, yet there is nothing harassing or wearying in the suspense. The cloud of evil, not bigger than a man's hand at first, spreads gradually till it spans the heavens from east to west, and night falls solemn and dark, but without storm or hurricane.

I scarcely anticipate that such a writer can be a brilliant converser. The best gauge I have ever found of an author's agreeability is in the amount of dialogue he throws into his books. Wherever narrative, pure narrative, predominates, and the reflective tone prevails, the author will be, perhaps necessarily, more disposed to silence. But he who writes dialogue well, must be himself a talker. Take Scott, for instance; the very character of his dialogue scenes was the type of his own social powers: a strong and nervous common sense; a high chivalry that brooked nothing low or mean; a profound veneration for antiquity; an innate sense of the humorous ran through his manner in the world, as they display themselves in his works.

See Sheridan, too; he talked the " School for Scandal"

all his life; whereas Goldsmith was a dull man in company. Taking this criterion, Alfred de Vigny will be quiet, reserved, and thoughtful; pointed, perhaps, but not brilliant. Apropos of this talking talent, what has become of it? French *causerie*, of which one hears so much, was no more to be compared to the racy flow of English table-talk some forty years back, than a group of artificial flowers is fit to compete with a bouquet of richly-scented dew-spangled buds, freshly plucked from the garden. Lord Brougham is our best man now, the readiest—a great quality—and, strange as it may sound to those who know him not, the best-natured, with anecdote enough to point a moral, but no story-teller; using his wit as a skilful cook does lemon-juice—to flavour, but not to sour the *plat*.

Painters and anglers, I have remarked, are always silent, thoughtful men. Of course I would not include under this judgment such as portrait and miniature painters, who are about, as a class, the most tiresome and loquacious twaddlers that our unhappy globe suffers under. Wilkie must have been a real blessing to any man sentenced to sit for his picture : he never asked questions, seldom, indeed, did he answer them; he had nothing of that vulgar trick of calling up an expression in his sitter; provided the man stayed awake, he was able always to catch the traits of feature, and, when he needed it, evoke the *prevailing* character of the individual's expression by a chance word or two. Lawrence was really agreeable—so, at least, I have always heard, for he was before my day ; but I suspect it was that officious agreeability of the artist, the smartness that lies in wait for a smile or the sparkle of the eye, that he may transmit it to the panel.

The great miniature painter of our day is really a specimen of a miniature intelligence—the most incessant little driveller of worse than nothings : the small gossip that is swept down the back-stairs of a palace, the flat commonplaces of great people, are his stock-in-trade; the only value of such contributions to history is, that they must be true. None but kings could be so tiresome! I remember once sitting to this gentleman, when only just recovering

from an illness, and when possibly I endured his forced
and forty-horse power of small talk with less than ordinary
patience. He had painted nearly every crowned head in
Europe—kings, kaisers, archdukes, and grand-duchesses in
every principality, from the boundless tracts of the Czar's
possessions to those states which emulate the small green
turf deposited in a bird's cage. Dear me! how wearisome
it was to hear him recount the ordinary traits that marked
the life of great people, as if the greatest Tory of us all
ever thought kings and queens were anything but men
and women!

I listened, as though in a long distressing dream, to
narratives of how the Prince de Joinville, so terribly eager
to burn our dockyards and destroy our marine, could be
playful as a lamb in his nursery with the children. How
Louis Philippe held the little Count de Paris fast in his
chair till his portrait was taken. (Will he be able to seat
him so securely on the throne of France?) How the Emperor of Austria, with the simplicity of a great mind and a
very large head, always thought he could sit behind the
artist and watch the progress of his own picture! I listened, I say, till my ears tingled and my head swam, and
in that moment there was not a "bounty man" from Ken-
tucky or Ohio that held royalty more cheaply than myself.
Just at this very nick, my servant came to whisper me,
that an agent from Messrs. Lorch, Rath et Co., the wine
merchants of Frankfort, had called, by my desire, to take
an order for some hock. Delighted at the interruption, I
ordered he should be admitted, and the next moment a
very tall, pretentious-looking German, with a tremendously
frogged and Brandenburged coat, and the most extensive
beard and moustaches, entered, and with all the ceremonial of his native land saluted us both, three times
over.

I received him with the most impressive and respectable
politeness, and seemed, at least, only to resume my seat
after his expressed permission. The artist, who understood nothing of German, watched all our proceedings
with a "miniature eye," and at last whispered gently,
"Who is he?"

"Heavens!" said I, in a low tone, "don't you know?
—he is the Crown Prince of Hanover!"

The words were not uttered when my little friend let fall
his palette and sprang off his chair, shocked at the very
thought of his being seated in such presence. The
German turned towards him one of those profoundly
austere glances that only a foreign bagman or an American
tragedian can compass, and took no further notice of
him.

The interview over, I accompanied him to the ante-
chamber, and then took my leave, to the horror of Sir
C——, who asked me at least twenty times "why I did
not go down to the door."

"Oh, we are old friends," said I; "I knew him at
Göttingen a dozen years ago, and we never stand on any
ceremony together." My fiction, miserable as it was,
saved me from further anecdotes of royalty, since what
private history of kings could astonish the man on such
terms of familiarity with the Crown Prince of Hanover?

Talking of Hanover, and à *propos* of "humbugs," reminds me of a circumstance that amused me at the time
it occurred. Soon after the present king of Hanover
ascended the throne, the Orangemen of Ireland, who had
long been vain of their princely Grand Master, had sufficient influence on the old corporation of Dublin to carry a
motion that a deputation should be despatched to Hanover,
to convey to the foot of the throne the sincere and respectful gratulations of the mayor, aldermen, and livery of
Dublin on the auspicious advent of his Majesty to the crown
of that kingdom. The debate was a warm one, but the
majority which carried the measure large, and now
nothing remained but to name the happy individuals who
should form the deputation, and then ascertain in what
part of the globe Hanover lay, and how it should be
come at.

Nothing but the cares of state and the important consi-
derations of duty, could prevent the mayor himself accepting this proud task: the sheriffs, however, were free. Their
office was a sinecure, and they accordingly were appointed,
with a sufficient suite, fully capable of representing to ad-

vantage abroad the wealth, splendour, and intelligence of the "ancient and loyal corporation."

One of the sheriffs, and the chief member of the mission, was, if I remember aright, a Mr. Timothy Brien ; the name of the "lesser bear" I have forgotten. Tim was, however, the spokesman, whenever speaking was available; and when it was not, it was he that made the most significant signs.

I was at the period a very young *attaché* of the mission at Hanover; our secretary, Melmond, being *chargé d'affaires* in the absence of our chief. Melmond was confined to bed by a feverish attack, and the duties of the mission, limited to signing a passport or two once a month, or some such form, were performed by me. Despatches were never sent. The Foreign Office told us, if we had anything to say, to wait for the Russian courier passing through, but not to worry them about nothing. I therefore had an easy post, and enjoyed all the dignities of office without its cares. If I had only had the pay, I could have asked nothing better.

It was, then, of a fine morning in May that Count Beulwitz, the Minister for Foreign Affairs, was announced, and the same moment entered my apartment. I was, I own it, not a little fluttered and flattered by this mark of recognition on the part of a minister, and resolved to play my part as deputy-assistant *chargé d'affaires* to my very utmost.

" I come, Mr. Templeton," said the minister, in a voice not quite free from agitation, " to ask your counsel on a question of considerable nicety ; and as Mr. Melmond is still unable to attend to duty, you must excuse me if I ask you to bestow the very gravest attention upon the point."

I assumed the most Talleyrand of looks, and he went on.

" This morning there has arrived here in four carriages, with great pomp and state, a special mission, sent from Ireland to convey the congratulations of the Government on his Majesty's accession to the throne. Now we have always believed and understood that Ireland was a part of the British empire, living under the same monarchy and

the same laws. If so, how can this mission be accredited?
It would be a very serious thing for us to recognise the
partition of the British empire, or the separation of an
integral portion, without due thought and consideration.
It would be also a very bold step to refuse the advances of
a State that deputes such a mission as this appears to be.
Do your despatches from England give any clue by which
we may guide our steps in this difficulty? have you heard
latterly what are the exact relations existing between
England and Ireland? You are aware that his Majesty is
at Berlin, and Barring and Von der Decken, who know
England so well, are both with him?"

I nodded assent, and, after a second's silence, a strong
temptation to quiz the Minister crossed my mind; and
without even a guess at what this mysterious deputation
might mean, I gravely hinted that our last accounts from
Ireland were of the most serious nature. It was certainly
true that kingdom had been conquered by the English and
subjected to the crown of England, but there were the
most well-founded reasons to fear that the arrangement
had not the element of a permanence. The descendant
of the ancient sovereigns of the land was a man of bold
and energetic and adventurous character ; he was a
prince of the house of O'Connell, of which, doubtless,
his Excellency had heard. There was no saying what
events might have occurred to favour his ambitious views,
and whether England might not have found the advantage
of restoring a troublesome land to its ancient dynasty.

"How does the present mission present itself—how
accredited?"

"From the court of Dublin, with the great seal, so far
as I can understand the representation, for none of the
embassy speak French."

"That sounds very formal and regular," said I with
deep gravity.

"So I think it, too," said his Excellency, who really
was impressed by the state-coach of Sheriff Timothy and
three footmen in bag-wigs. "At any rate," said he,
"we must decide at once, and there can be no hesitation
about the matter. I suppose we must give them an

audience of the Crown Prince, and then let all rest till his Majesty returns, which he will do on Friday next."

Without compromising myself by any assent, I looked as if he had spoken very wisely, and his Excellency departed.

That same afternoon two state-carriages of the court, with servants in dress livery, drew up at the Hof von London, the hôtel where the deputation had taken up their quarters, and a *maréchal de cour* alighted to inform the " Irish ambassador " that his Royal Highness the Crown Prince would receive their homage in the absence of the King. The intimation, more conveyed by pantomime than oral intelligence, was replied to by an equivalent telegraph ; but the sheriffs, in all their gala, soon took their places in the carriage and set out for the palace.

Their reception was most flattering ; enough to say, they had the honour to address and be replied to by one of the most courteous princes of Europe. An invitation to dinner, the usual civility to a newly arrived mission, ensued, and the Irish embassy, overwhelmed with the brilliant success of their journey, returned to the hôtel in a state of exaltation that bordered on ecstasy.

Their corporation address, formidable by its portentous parchment and official seal, had puzzled the Foreign Office in no ordinary way, and was actually under their weighty consideration the following day, when the King most unexpectedly made his *entrée* into the capital. King Ernest heard with some amazement, not unmingled by disbelief, that an Irish diplomatic body had actually arrived at his court, and immediately demanded to see their credentials. There is no need to recount the terrible outbreak of temper which his Majesty displayed on discovering the mistake of his ministers. The chances are, indeed, that, had he called himself Pacha instead of King, he would have sentenced the Irish ambassador and his whole following to be hanged like onions on the one string. As it was, he could scarcely control his passion ; and whatever the triumphant pleasures of the day before, when a dinner-card for the palace was conveyed by an aide-de-camp to the hôtel, the "second Epistle to Timothy" was a very awful contrast to its predecessor. The hapless deputation, however, got leave to return unmolested, and betook themselves to their homeward journey, the chief of the mission by no means so well satisfied of his success in the part of the "Irish Ambassador."

Now to dress for dinner. I wish I had said "No" to this same invitation.

Nothing is pleasanter when one is in health and spirits than a *petit diner;* nothing is more distressing when one is weak, low, and dejected. At a large party there is always a means of lying *perdu*, and neither taking any share in the cookery or the conversation. At a small table one must eat, drink, and be merry, though the *plat* be your doom and the talk be your destruction. There is no help for it; there is no playing "supernumerary" in farce with four characters.

Is it yet too late to send an apology?—it still wants a quarter of six, and six is the hour. I really cannot endure the fatigue and the exhaustion. Holland, besides, told me that any excitement would be prejudicial. Here goes, then, for my excuse. . . . So! I'm glad I've done it. I feel myself once more free to lie at ease on this ottoman and dream away the hours undisturbed.

"Holloa! what's this, Legrelle?"

"De la part de Madame la Comtesse, sir."

How provoking!—how monstrously provoking! She writes me, "You really must come. I will not order dinner till I see you.—Yours, &c., B. de F——." What a bore! and what an absurd way to incur an attack of illness! There's nothing for it, however, but submission; and to-morrow, if I'm able, I'll leave Paris.

"Legrelle, don't forget to order horses for to-morrow at twelve."

"What route does monsieur take?"

"Avignon—no, Strasbourg—Couilly, I think, is the first post. I should like to see Munich once more, or, at least, its gallery. The city is a poor thing, worthy of its people, and, I was going to say—no matter what! Germany, in any case, for the summer, as I am sentenced to die in Italy. I feel I am taking what the Irish call ' a long day ' in not crossing the Alps till late in autumn ! "

How many places there are which one has been near enough to have visited, and somehow always neglected to see ! and what a longing, craving wish to behold them comes over the heart at such a time as this ! What, then, is " this time," that I speak it thus?

*　　*　　*　　*　　*　　*

How late it is ! De Vigny was very agreeable, combining in his manner a great deal of the refinement of a highly cultivated mind, with the shrewd perception of a keen observer of the world. He is a *Légitimiste*, I take it, without any hope of his party. This, after all, is the sad political creed of all who adhere to the " elder branch." Their devotion is indeed great, for it wars against conviction. But where can an honest man find footing in France nowadays? Has not Louis Philippe violated in succession every pledge by which he had bound himself? Can such an example of falsehood so highly placed be without its influence on the nation? Can men cry " Shame ! " on the Minister, when they witness the turpitude of the Monarch?

But what hope does any other party offer ?—None. Henri Cinq, a Bourbon of the *vieille roche*, gentle, soft-hearted, sensual, and selfish, who, if he returned to France to-morrow, would never believe that the long interval since the Three Days had been anything but an accident; and would not bring himself to credit the possibility that the succession had been ever endangered.

I believe, after all, one should be as lenient in their judgment of men's change of fealty in France as they are indulgent to the capricious fancies of a spoiled beauty. The nation, like a coquette, had everything its own way. The cold austerities of principle had yielded to the changeful fortunes of success for so many years, that men very naturally began to feel that instability and uncertainty were the normal state of things, and that to hold fast one set of opinions was like casting anchor in a stream when we desired to be carried along by the current. Who are they who have risen in France since the time of the Great Revolution? Are they the consistent politicians, the men of one unvarying, unaltered faith? or are they the expediency makers, the men of emergencies and crises, yielding, as they would phrase it, to "the enlightened temper of the times"—the Talleyrands, the Soults, the Guizots of the day—not to speak of one higher than them all, but not more conspicuous for his elevation than for the subserviency that has placed him there?

Poor Chateaubriand! the man who never varied, the man that was humblest before his rightful sovereign, and prouder than the proudest Marshal in presence of the Emperor, how completely forgotten is he—standing like some ruined sign-post to point the way over a road no longer travelled! A more complete revolution was never worked in the social condition of a great kingdom than has taken place in France since the time of the Emperor. The glorious career of conquering armies had invested the soldier's life with a species of chivalry that brought back the old days of feudalism again. Now, it is the *bourgeoisie* are uppermost. Trade and money-getting, railroads and mines, have seized hold of the nation's heart; and where the *bâton* of a Maréchal was once the most coveted of all earthly distinctions, a good bargain on the Bourse, or a successful transaction in scrip, are now the highest triumphs. The very telegraph, whose giant limbs only swayed to speak of victories, now beckons to an expectant crowd the rates of exchange from London to Livorno, and with a far greater certainty of stirring the spirits it addresses.

I fell into all this moody reflection from thinking of an incident—I might almost call it story—I remembered hearing from an old cuirassier officer some years ago. I was passing through the north of France, and stopped to dine at Sédan, where a French cavalry regiment, three thousand strong, were quartered. Some repairs that were necessary to my carriage detained me till the next day ; and as I strolled along the shady boulevards in the evening I met an old soldier-like person, beside whom I dined at the table-d'hôte. He was the very type of a *chef-d'escadron* of the Empire, and such he really proved to be.

After a short preamble of the ordinary common-places, we began to talk of the service in which he lived, and I confess it was with a feeling of surprise I heard him say that the old soldiers of the Empire had met but little favour from the new dynasty ; and I could not help observing that this was not the impression made upon us in England, but that we inclined to think it was the especial policy of the present reign to conciliate the affections of the nation by a graceful acknowledgment of those so instrumental to its glory.

"Is not Soult as high, or rather, is he not far higher, in the favour of his sovereign, Louis Philippe, than ever he was in that of the Emperor? Is not Moncey a man nobly pensioned as Captain of the Invalides?"

"All true ! But where are the hundreds—I had almost said thousands, but that death has been so busy in these tranquil times with those it had spared in more eventful days—where are they, the old soldiers, who served in inferior grades, the men whose promotions for the hard fighting at Montereau and Chalons needed but a few days more of prosperity to have confirmed, but who saw their best hopes decline as the sun of the Emperor's glory descended? What rewards were given even to many of the more distinguished, but whose principles were known to be little in accordance with the new order of things ? What of Pajol, who captured a Dutch fleet with his cavalry squadrons ;—ay ! charged the three-deckers as they lay ice-locked in the Scheldt, dismounted half of his force and boarded them, as in a sea-fight ? Poor Pajol ! he died the other day, at eighty-three or four, followed to the grave by the comrades he had fought and marched beside, but with no honours to his memory from the King or his government. No, sir, believe me, the present people never liked the Buonapartists ; the sad contrasts presented by all their attempts at military renown with those glorious spectacles of the Empire were little flattering to them."

"Then you evidently think Soult and some others owe their present favour less to the eminence of their services than to the plasticity of their principles?"

"Who ever thought Soult a great general?" said he, abruptly answering my question by this transition. "A great military organizer, certainly—the best head for the administration of an army, or the Emperor's staff—but nothing more. His capacity as a tactician was always third rate."

I could not help acknowledging that such was the opinion of our own great captain, who has avowed that he regarded Massena as the most accomplished and scientific general to whom he was ever opposed.

"And Massena's daughter," cried the veteran, indignantly, "lives now in the humblest poverty—the wife of a very poor man, who cultivates a little garden near Brussels, where *femmes de chambre* are sent to buy bouquets for their mistresses! The daughter of a *Maréchal de France*, a title once that kings loved to add to their royalty, as men love to ennoble station by evidences of high personal desert!"

"How little fidelity, however, did these men show to him who had made them thus great! How numerous were the desertions!—how rapid too!"

"Yes, there was an epidemic of treason at that time in France, just as you have seen at different epochs here, other epidemics prevail: in the Revolution the passion was for the guillotine; then came the lust of military glory—that suited us best, and lasted longest; we indulged in it for twenty years: then succeeded that terrible revulsion, and men hastened to prove how false-hearted they could be. Then came the Restoration—and the passion was to be Catholic; and now we have another order of things, whose worst feature is, that there is no prevailing creed. Men live for the day and the hour. The King's health—the state of Spain—a bad harvest— an awkward dispute between the commander of our squadron in the Pacific with some of your admirals,—anything may overturn the balance, and our whole political and social condition may have to be built up once more."

"The great remedy against this uncertainty is out of your power," said I: "you abolished the claims of Sovereignty on the permanent affection of the people, and now you begin to feel the want of 'Loyalty.'"

"Our kings had ceased to merit the respect of the nation when they lost it."

"Say, rather, you revenged upon them the faults and vices of their more depraved, but bolder, ancestors. You made the timid Louis XVI. pay for the hardy Louis XIV. Had that unhappy monarch but been like the Emperor, his Court might have displayed all the excesses of the regency twice told, and you had never declared against them."

"That may be true; but you evidently do not—I doubt, indeed, if any but a Frenchman and a soldier can—feel the nature of our attachment to the Emperor. It was something in which personal interest partook a large part, and the hope of future advancement, *through him*, bore its share. The army regarded him thus, and never forgave him perfectly, for preferring to be an Emperor rather than a General. Now, the very desertions you have lately alluded to would probably never have occurred if the leader had not merged into the monarch."

"There was a fascination, a spirit of infatuating ecstasy, in serving one whose steps had so often led to glory, that filled a man's entire heart. One learned to feel that the rays of his own splendid achievements shed a lustre on all around him, and each had his portion of undying fame. This feeling, as it became general, grew into a kind of superstition, and even to a man's own conscience it served to excuse many grave errors, and some direct breaches of true faith."

"Then, probably, you regard Ney's conduct in this light?" said I.

"I know it was of this nature," replied he, vehemently. "Ney, like many others, meant to be faithful to the Bourbons when he took the command. He had no thought of treachery in his mind; he believed he was marching against an enemy until he actually saw the Emperor, and then——"

"I find this somewhat difficult to understand," said I, dubiously. "Ney's new allegiance was no hasty step, but one maturely and well considered. He had weighed in his mind various eventualities, and doubtless among the number the possibility of the Emperor's return. That the mere sight of that low cocked-hat and the *redingote gris* could have at once served to overturn a sworn fealty and a plighted word——"

"Have you time to listen to a short story?" interrupted the old dragoon, with a degree of emotion in his manner that bespoke a deeper interest than I suspected in the subject of our conversation.

"Willingly," said I. "Will you come and sup with me at my hotel, and we can continue a theme in which I feel much interest?"

"Nay; with your permission, we will sit down here —on the ramparts. I never sup: like an old campaigner, I only make one meal a day, and mention the circumstance to excuse my performance at the table d'hôte: and here, if you do not dislike it, we will take our places under this lime-tree."

I at once acceded to this proposal, and he began thus:—

CHAPTER IV.

You are, perhaps, aware, that in no part of France was the cause of the exiled family sustained with more perseverance and courage than Auvergne. The nobles, who, from generation to generation, had lived as seigneurs on their estates, equally remote from the attractions and advantages of a court, still preserved their devotion to the Bourbons as a part of religious faith; nor ever did the evening mass of a château conclude without its heartfelt prayer for the repose of that "saint roi," Louis XVI., and for the blessing of heaven on him, his rightful successor, now a wanderer and an exile.

In one of these antique châteaux, whose dilapidated battlements and shattered walls showed that other enemies than mere time had been employed against it, lived an old Count de Vitry: so old was he, that he could remember the time he had been a page at the court of Louis XV., and could tell many strange tales of the Regency, and the characters who flourished at that time.

His family consisted of two grandchildren, both of them orphans of his two sons. One had fallen in La Vendée; the other, sentenced to banishment by the Directory, had died on the passage out to Guadaloupe. The children were nearly of the same age—the boy a few months older than the girl—and regarded each other as brother and sister.

It is little to be wondered at if these children imbibed from the very cradle a horror of that system and of those men which had left them fatherless and almost friendless, destitute of rank, station, and fortune, and a proportionate attachment to those who, if they had been suffered to reign, would have preserved them in the enjoyment of all their time-honoured privileges and possessions.

If the members of the executive government were then remembered among the catalogue of persons accursed and to be hated, the names of the royal family were repeated among those saintly personages to whom honour and praise were rendered. The venerable Père Duclos, to whom their education was confided, certainly neglected no available means of instilling these two opposite principles of belief; and if Alfred de Vitry and Blanche were not impressed with this truth, it could not be laid to the charge of this single-hearted teacher; every trait and feature that could deform and disgrace humanity being attributed to one, and all the graces and ennobling virtues of the race associated with the name of the other. The more striking and impressive to make the lesson, the Père was accustomed to read a comment on the various events then occurring at Paris, and on the campaigns of the Republican army in Italy; dwelling, with pardonable condemnation, on the insults offered to the Church and all who adhered to its holy cause.

These appeals were made with peculiar force to Alfred, who was destined for an ecclesiastic, that being the only career which the old Count and his chaplain could satisfy themselves as offering any hope of safety; and now that the family possessions were all confiscated, and a mere remnant of the estate remaining, there was no use in hoping to perpetuate a name which must sink into poverty and obscurity. Blanche was also to become a member of a religious order in Italy, if, happily, even in that sacred land, the privileges of the Church were destined to escape.

The good Père, whose intentions were unalloyed by one thought unworthy of an angel, made the mistake that great zeal not unfrequently commits—he proved too much; he painted the Revolutionary party in colours so terrible that no possible reality could sustain the truth of the portraiture. It is true the early days of the Revolution warranted all he did or could say; but the party had changed greatly since that, or, rather, a new and a very differently minded class had succeeded. Marat, Danton, and Robespierre had no resemblance with Sièyes, Carnot, and Buona-parte. The simple-minded priest, however, recognised no distinction : he thought that, as the stream issued from a tainted source, the current could never become purer by flowing ; and he delighted, with all the enthusiasm of a *dévot*, to exaggerate the evil traits of those whose exploits of heroism might have dazzled and fascinated unthinking understandings.

Alfred was about sixteen, when one evening, nigh sun-set, a peasant approached the château in eager haste to say that a party of soldiers were coming up the little road which led toward the house, instead of turning off, as they usually did, to the village of Puy de Dôme, half a league further down the valley.

Père Duclos, who assumed absolute authority over the household since the old Count had fallen into a state of childlike dotage, hastened to provide himself with the writ of exemption from billet the Directory had conferred on the château—an *amende* for the terrible misfortunes of the ruined family—and advanced to meet the party, the leading files of which were already in sight.

Nothing could less have suggested the lawless depre-dators of the Republic than the little column that now drew near. Four chasseurs-à-pied led the van, their clothes ragged and torn, their shoes actually in ribbons ; one had his arm in a sling, and another carried his shako on his back, as his head was bound up in a handkerchief, whose blood-stained folds showed the marks of a severe sabre-cut. Behind them came a litter, or, rather, a cart with a canvas awning, in which lay the wounded body of their officer ; the rear consisting of about fourteen others, under the command of a sergeant.

They halted and formed as the old Père approached them, and the sergeant, stepping to the front, carried his hand to his cap in military salute ; and then, without waiting for the priest to speak, he began a very civil, almost an humble, apology for the liberty of their intrusion.

" We are," said he, " an invalid party, *en route* for Paris, with an officer who was severely wounded at the bridge of Lodi." And here he lowered his voice to a whisper: " The poor lieutenant's case being hopeless, and his constant wish—his prayer—being to see his mother before he dies, we are pushing on for her château, which is near St. Jean de Luc, I hear."

Perhaps the mention of the word château—the claim of one whose rank was even thus vaguely hinted at—had nearly an equal influence on the Père with the duties of humanity. Certain is it he laid less stress than he might have done on the writ of exemption, and blandly said that the out-offices of the château should be at their disposal for the night; apologising if late events had not left its inhabitants in better circumstances to succour the unfortunate.

"We ask very little, Père," said the sergeant, respectfully—"some straw to sleep on, some rye-bread and a little water for supper; and to-morrow, ere sunrise, you shall see the last of us."

The humility of the request, rendered even more humble by the manner in which it was conveyed, did not fail to strike the Père Duclos, who began to wonder what reverses had overtaken the "Blues" (the name the Republicans were called), that they were become thus civil and respectful; nor could he be brought to believe the account the sergeant gave of a glorious victory at the Ada, nor credit a syllable of the bulletin which, in letters half-a-foot long, proclaimed the splendid achievement.

A little pavilion in the garden was devoted to the reception of the wounded lieutenant, and the soldiers bivouacked in the farm-buildings, and some even in the open air, for it was the vintage time and the weather delightful. There was nothing of outrage or disturbance committed by the men; not even any unusual noise disturbed the peaceful quiet of the old château; and, except that a lamp burned all night in the garden-pavilion, nothing denoted the presence of strangers.

Before day broke the men were mustered in the court of the château; and the sergeant, having seen that his party were all regularly equipped for the march, demanded to speak a few words to the Père Duclos. The Père, who was from his window watching these signs of approaching departure with some anxiety, hastily descended on hearing the request.

"We are about to march, reverend father," said the sergeant, saluting, "all of us, save one—our poor lieutenant; his next billet will be for another, and, we hope, a better place."

"Is he dead?" asked the Père, eagerly.

"Not yet, father; but the event cannot now be far off. He raved all through the night, and this morning the fever has left him, but without strength, and evidently going fast. To take him along with us would be inhuman, were it even possible—to delay would be against my orders; so that nothing else is to be done than leave him among those who would be kind to his last hours, and minister to the wants of a death-bed."

The Père, albeit very far from gratified by his charge, promised to do all in his power; and the sergeant, having commanded a "present arms" to the château, wheeled right-about and departed.

For some days the prediction of the sergeant seemed to threaten its accomplishment at every hour. The sick man, reduced to the very lowest stage of debility, appeared at moments as if struggling for a last breath; but by degrees these paroxysms grew less frequent and less violent: he slept, too, at intervals, and awoke seemingly refreshed; and thus between the benefits derived from tranquillity and rest, a mild and genial air and his own youth, his recovery became at length assured, accompanied, however, by a degree of feebleness that made the least effort impossible, and even the utterance of a few words a matter of great pain and difficulty.

If, during the most sad and distressing periods of the sick bed, the Père indirectly endeavoured to inspire Alfred's mind with a horror of a soldier's life—depicting, by the force of the terrible example before him, the wretchedness of one who fell a victim to its ambition—so did he take especial care, as convalescence began to dawn, to forbid the youth from ever approaching the pavilion, or holding any intercourse with its occupant. That part of the garden was strictly interdicted to him, and the very mention of the lieutenant at last forbidden, or only alluded to when invoking a Christian blessing upon enemies.

In this way matters continued till the end of autumn, when the Père, who had long been anxiously awaiting the hour when the sick man should take his leave, had one morning set off for the town to make arrangements for his departure, and order post-horses to be ready on the following day.

It was a calm and mellow day of autumn, and Alfred, who had at first determined to set out on a fishing excursion, without any reason changed his mind, and sauntered into the garden. Loitering listlessly for some time, from walk to walk, he was at length returning to the château, when he beheld, seated under the shade of a walnut tree, a young man, whose pale and languid look at once bespoke the invalid, even had not the fact been proclaimed by his dress, the uniform of a *lancier rouge.*

Mindful of the Father's precept, and fully impressed with an obedience never violated, the youth was turning hastily away, when the wounded man slowly arose from his seat, and removing his cap, made a salute of deep and most respectful meaning.

Alfred returned it, and stood irresolute. The eyes of the sick man, full of an expression of mild and thankful beaming, were on him. What should he do? to retire without speaking would be a rudeness, even a cruelty: besides, what possible harm could there be in a few words of friendly greeting with one so long their guest? Ere he could resolve the point, the wounded officer was slowly advancing towards him, still uncovered, and in an attitude betokening a most respectful gratitude.

" I pray you will permit me, Mons. le Comte," said he, " to express my heartfelt thanks for the hospitality and kindness of your treatment. I feared that I should leave this without the occasion of saying how grateful I feel for the remnant of life your care has been the means of preserving."

Alfred tried to answer: but a dread of his disobedience and its consequences, and a strange sense of admiration for the stranger, whose manner and appearance had deeply impressed him, made him silent.

" I see," said the lieutenant, smiling, " that you are indisposed to receive an acknowledgment for what you set such small store by—a kindness to a mere 'soldier of the Republic;' but when you wear a sword yourself, Mons. le Comte, as you will doubtless one of these days——"

" No," said Alfred, hastily interrupting him, " never! I shall never wear one."

" How, never! What can you mean?"

" That I shall never be a soldier," said Alfred. " I am to be a priest."

" A priest! You, Mons. le Comte de Vitry, of the best blood of Auvergne—you, a monk!"

" I did not say a monk," said Alfred, proudly; " there are other ranks among churchmen. I have heard tell of Prince-bishops and Cardinals."

" And if one were to begin life at the age they usually take leave of it, such a career might not be held so cheaply; but for a young man of good birth and blood, with a heart to feel proudly, and a hand to wield a weapon—no, no, that were a shame not to be thought of."

Stung alike by the severity of the sarcasm, and animated by the old spirit of the père's teaching, Alfred hastily answered,—

" And if men of rank and station no longer carry arms as their forefathers did, with whom lies the blame? Why do they now bend to adopt a path that in former days was only trodden by the weak-hearted and the timid? Because they would not draw the sword in a cause they abhor, and for a faction they despise; neither would they shed their blood to assure the triumph of a rabble."

" Nor would I," interposed the lieutenant, while a slight flush coloured his cheek. " The cause in which I perilled life was that of France, my country. You may safely trust that the nation capable of such conquests will neither be disgraced by bad rulers nor dishonoured by cowardly ones."

" I have no faith in Republicans," said Alfred, scornfully.

"Because they were not born to a title, perhaps! But do you know how many of those who now carry victory into foreign lands belong to this same class that includes all your sympathy?—prouder, far prouder, that they sustain the honour of France against her enemies, than that they carry the blazon of a marquis or the coronet of a duke on their escutcheon? You look incredulous! Nay, I speak no more than what I well know: for instance, the humble lieutenant who now addresses you can claim rank as high and ancient as your own. You have heard of the Liancourts?"

"Le Duc de Liancourt?"

"Yes; I am, or rather I was, the Duc de Liancourt," said the lieutenant, with an almost imperceptible struggle: "my present rank is Sous-Lieutenant of the Third Lancers. Now listen to me calmly for a few moments, and I hope to show you that in a country where a dreadful social earthquake has uprooted every foundation of rank, and strewed the ground with the ruins of everything like prescription, it is nobler and better to show that nobility could enter the lists, unaided by its prestige, and win the palm, among those who vainly boasted themselves better and braver. This we have done, not by assuming the monk's cowl and the friar's cord, but by carrying the knapsack and the musket; not by shirking the struggle, but by confronting it. Where is the taunt now against the nobility of France? Whose names figure oftenest in the lists of killed and wounded? Whose lot is it most frequently to mount first to the assault or the breach? No, no, take to the alb and the surplice if your vocation prompt it, but do not assume to say that no other road is open to a Frenchman because his heart is warmed by noble blood."

If Alfred was at first shocked by hearing assertions so opposed to all the precepts of his venerated tutor, he was soon ashamed of offering opposition to one so far more capable than himself of forming a just judgment on the question; while he felt, inwardly, the inequality of the cause for which he would do battle against—that glorious and triumphant one of which the young officer assumed the championship.

Besides, De Liancourt's history was his own; he had been bred up with convictions precisely like his, and might, had he followed out the path intended for him, been a priest at the very hour that he led a charge at Lodi.

"I was saved by an accident," said he. "In the march of Berthault's division through Chalons, a little drummer-boy fell off a waggon when asleep, and was wounded by a wheel passing over him : they brought him to our château, where we nursed and tended him till he grew well. The curé, wishing to snatch him as a brand saved from the burning, adopted him, and made him an acolyte; and so he remained till one Sunday morning when the 'Chasseurs gris' marched through the town during mass. Pierre stole out to see the soldiers; he heard a march he had often listened to before; he saw the little drummers stepping out gaily in front; worse too, *they* saw him, and one called out to his comrades, ' Regarde donc le Prêtre; ce petit drôle là—c'est un Prêtre.'

" ' Du tout,' cried he, tearing off his white robe, and throwing it behind him, ' Je suis tambour comme toi,' and snatching the drum, he beat his ' Ran tap-plan ' so vigorously and so well, that the drum-major patted him on the head and cheek, and away marched Pierre at the head of the troop, leaving Chalons, and curé, and all behind him, without a thought or a pang.

"I saw it all from the window of the church; and suddenly, as my eyes turned from the grand spectacle of the moving column, with its banners flying and bayonets glistening, to the dim, half-lighted aisles of the old church, with smoky tapers burning faintly, amid which an old decrepit priest was moving slowly, a voice within me cried,—' Better a tambour than this!' I stole out, and reached the street just as the last files were passing. I mingled with the crowd that followed, my heart beating time to the quick march. I tracked them out of the town, further and further, till we reached the wide open country.

" ' Will you not come back, Pierre ?' said I, pulling him by the sleeve, as, at last, I reached the leading files, where the little fellow marched, proud as a tambour-major.

"'*I* go back, and the regiment marching against the enemy!' exclaimed he, indignantly; and a roar of laughter and applause from the soldiers greeted his words.

"'Nor I either!' cried I. And thus I became a soldier, never to regret the day I belted on the knapsack. But here comes the Père Duclos: I hope he may not be displeased at your having kept me company. I know well he loves not such companionship for his pupil—perhaps he has reason."

Alfred did not wait for the priest's arrival, but darted from the spot and hastened to his room, where, bolting the door, he threw himself upon his bed and wept bitterly. Who knows if these tears decided not all his path in life?

That same evening the lieutenant left the château; and in about two months after came a letter, expressing his gratitude for all the kindness of his host, and withal a present of a gun and a chasseur's accoutrement for Alfred. They were very handsome and costly, and he was never weary of trying them on his shoulder and looking how they became him; when, in examining one of the pockets for the twentieth time, he discovered a folded paper. He opened it, and found it was an appointment for a cadet in the military school of St. Cyr. Alfred de Vitry was written in pencil where the name should be inscribed, but very faintly, and so that it required sharp looking to detect the letters. It was enough, however, for him to read the words. He packed up a little parcel of clothes, and, with a few francs in his pocket, he set out that night for Chalons, where he took the *malle*. The third day, when he was tracked by the père, he was already enrolled a cadet, and not all the interest in France could have removed him against his consent.

I will not dwell on a career which was in no respect different from that of hundreds of others. Alfred joined the army in the second Italian campaign—was part of Dessaix's division at Marengo—was wounded at Aspern, and finally accompanied the Emperor in his terrible march to Moscow. He saw more service than his promotion seemed to imply, however; for, after Leipsig, Dresden, Bautzen, he was carried on a litter, with some other dying comrades, into a little village of Alsace—a lieutenant of hussars, nothing more.

An hospital, hastily constructed of planks, had been fitted up outside the village—there were many such on the road between Strasbourg and Nancy—and here poor Alfred lay, with many more, their sad fate rendered still sadder by the daily tidings, which told them that the cause for which they had shed their blood was hourly becoming more hopeless.

The army that never knew defeat now counted nothing but disasters. Before Alfred had recovered from his wound, the allies bivouacked in the Place du Carrousel, and Napoleon was at Elba !

When little dreaming that he could take any part in that general joy by which France, in one of her least-thinking moments, welcomed back the Bourbons, Alfred was loitering listlessly along one of the quays of Paris, wondering within himself by what process of arithmetic he could multiply seven sous—they were all he had—into the price of a supper and bed ; and while his eyes often dwelt with lingering fondness on the windows of the restaurants, they turned, too, with a dreadful instinct towards the Seine, whose eddies had closed over many a sorrow and crime.

As he wandered thus, a cry arose for help : an unfortunate creature—one whose woes were greater, or whose courage to bear them less, than his own—had thrown herself from the Pont-Neuf into the river, and her body was seen to rise and sink several times in the current of the rapid stream. It was from no prompting of humanity —it was something like a mere instinct, and no more— mayhap, too, his recklessness of life had some share in the act—whatever the reason, he sprang into the river, and after a long and vigorous struggle, he brought her out alive ; and then, forcing through the crowd that welcomed him, he drew his miserable and dripping hat over his eyes. He continued his road—Heaven knows he had little purpose or object to warrant the persistence !

He had not gone far when a number of voices were heard behind him, calling out,—

"That is he!—there he is!" and at the same instant an officer rode up beside him, and, saluting him politely, said that her royal highness the Duchess of Berri desired to speak to him ;—her carriage was just by.

Alfred was in that humour when, so indifferent is every object in life, that he would have turned at the bidding of the humblest *gamin* of the streets ; and, wet and weary, he stood beside the door of the splendid equipage.

"It was *thou* that saved the woman?" said the Duchess, addressing him, and using the conventional "Tu," as suitable to his mean appearance.

"Madame," said Alfred, removing his tattered hat, "I am a gentleman! These rags were once—the uniform of the Guard."

"My God!—my cousin!" cried a voice beside the Duchess ; and, at the same instant, a young girl held out her hands towards him, and exclaimed,—

"Knowest thou not me, Alfred? I am Alice—Alice de Vitry—thy cousin and thy sister!"

It would little interest you to dwell on the steps that followed, and which, in a few weeks, made of a wretched outcast—without a home or a meal—an officer of the *Guard du Corps*, with the order of St. Louis at his breast.

Time sped on, and his promotion with it ; and at length his Majesty, graciously desiring to see the old nobility resume their place and grade, consented to the union of Alfred with his cousin. There was no violent love on either side, but there was sincere esteem and devoted friendship ; and if they neither of them felt that degree of attachment which becomes a passion, they regarded each other with true affection.

Alice was a devoted Royalist ; all that she had suffered for the cause had endeared it to her ; and she could forgive, but not forget, that her future husband had shed his blood for the Usurper.

Alfred was what every one, and with reason, called a most fortunate fellow ; a colonel at twenty-eight—a promotion that, under the Empire, nothing but the most distinguished services could have gained—and yet he was far from happy. He remembered with higher enthusiasm his first grade of "corporal," won at Aspern, and his epaulettes that he gained at Wilna. His soldiering had been learned in another school than in the parade-ground at Versailles, or the avenue of the Champs Elysées.

"Come, *mon ami!*" said Alice, gaily, to him one morning, about ten days before the time appointed for their marriage ; "thou art about to have some occasion for thy long-rusting sword : the Usurper has landed at Cannes."

"The Emperor at Cannes!"

"The Emperor, if thou wilt—but without an Empire."

"No matter. Is he without an army ? " said Alfred.

"Alone—with some half-dozen followers, at most. Ney has received orders to march against him, and thou art to command a brigade."

"This is good news!" said Alfred; for the very name of war had set his heart a-throbbing ; and as he issued forth into the streets, the stirring sounds of excitement and rapid motion of troops increased his ardour.

Wondering groups were gathered in every street, some, discussing the intelligence, others, reading the great placards, which, in letters of portentous size, announced that "the Monster" had once more polluted by his presence the soil of France.

Whatever the enthusiasm of the old Royalists to the Bourbon cause, there seemed an activity and determination on the part of the Buonapartists who had taken service with the King to exhibit their loyalty to the new sovereign ; and Ney rode from one quarter of Paris to the other, with a cockade of most conspicuous size, followed by a staff equally remarkable.

That same day Alfred left Paris for Lyons, where his regiment lay, with orders to move to the south, by forced marches, and arrest the advance of the small party which formed the band of the invader. It was Alice herself fastened the knot of white ribbon in his shako, and bade him adieu with a fondness of affection he had never witnessed before.

From Paris to Lyons, and to Grenoble, Alfred hastened with promptitude. At Lesseim, at last, he halted for orders.

His position was a small village, three leagues in advance of Lesseim, called Dulaure, where, at nightfall on the 18th of March, Alfred arrived with two companies of his regiment, his orders being to reconnoitre the valley towards Lesseim, and report if the enemy should present himself in that quarter.

After an anxious night on the alert, Alfred lay down to sleep towards morning, when he was awoke by the sharp report of a musket, followed immediately after by the roll of the drum and the call for the guard to "turn out." He rushed out, and hastened towards the advanced picket. All was in confusion; some were in retreat; others stood at a distance from their post, looking intently towards it; and at the picket itself were others, again, with piled arms, standing in a close group. What could this mean? Alfred called out, but no answer was returned. The men stared in stupid amazement, and each seemed waiting for the other to reply.

"Where is your officer?" cried De Vitry, in an angry voice.

"He is here!" said a pale, calm-featured man, who, buttoned up in a great surtout, and with a low *chapeau* on his head, advanced towards him.

"You the officer!" replied Alfred, angrily; "you are not of our regiment, sir."

"Pardon me, Colonel," rejoined the other; "I led the twenty-second at Rovigo, and they were with me at Wagram."

"*Grand Dieu!*" said Alfred, trembling; "who are you, then?"

"Your Emperor, Colonel de Vitry!"

Alfred stepped back at the words. The order to arrest and make him prisoner was almost on his lips. He turned towards his men, who instinctively had resumed their formation; his head was maddened by the conflict within it; his eyes turned again towards Napoleon—the struggle was over—he knelt and presented his sword.

"Take mine in exchange, *General* de Vitry," said the Emperor; "I know you will wear it with honour."

And thus, in a moment, was all forgotten—plighted love and sworn faith—for who could resist the Emperor?

The story is now soon told. Waterloo came, and once more the day of defeat descended, never to dawn upon another victory. Alfred, rejected and scorned, lived years in poverty and obscurity. When the fortunes of the Revolution brought up once more the old soldiers of the Empire, he fought at the Quai Voltaire and was wounded severely. The Three Days over, he was appointed to a sous-lieutenancy in the dragoons. He is now *chef-d'-esca-dron*, the last of his race, weary of a world whose vicissitudes have crushed his hopes and made him broken-hearted.

The relator of this tale was Alfred de Vitry himself, who, under the name of his maternal grandfather, St. Amand, served in the second regiment of Carabiniers.

CHAPTER V.

12 o'clock, Tuesday night,
May 31st, 184—.

" Que bella cosa " to be a king! Here am I now, returned from Neuilly, whither I dreaded so much to venture,
actually enchanted with the admirable manner of his
Majesty Louis Philippe, adding one more to the long list
of those who, beginning with Madame de Genlis and Johnson, have delighted to extol the qualities whose pleasing
properties have been expended on themselves.

There is, however, something wonderfully interesting in
the picture of a royal family living *en bourgeois*—a King
sitting with his spectacles on his forehead and his newspaper on his knee, playfully alluding to observations whose
fallacy he alone can demonstrate; a Queen busily engaged
amid the toils of the work-table, around which Princesses
of every European royalty are seated, gaily chatting over
their embroidery, or listening while an amusing book is
read out by a husband or a brother: even an American
would be struck by such a view of monarchy.

The Duc de Nemours is the least prepossessing of the
princes; his deafness, too, assists the impression of his
coldness and austerity; while the too-studied courtesy of
the Prince de Joinville towards Englishmen is the reverse
of an amicable demonstration.

I could not help feeling surprised at the freedom with
which his Majesty canvassed our leading political characters; for his intimate acquaintance with them all, I was
well prepared. One remark he made worth remembering,
—" The Duke of Wellington should always be your Minister of Foreign Affairs, no matter what the changes of
party. It is not that his great opportunities of knowing

the Continent, assisted by his unquestionable ability, alone distinguish him, but that his name and the weight of his opinion on any disputed question exert a greater influence than any other man's over the various sovereignties of Europe. After the Emperor himself, he was the greatest actor in the grand drama of the early part of the century; he made himself conspicuous in every council, even less by the accuracy of his views than by their unerring, unswerving rectitude. The desperate struggle in which he had taken part had left no traces of ungenerous feeling or animosity behind, and the pride of conquest had never disturbed the equanimity of the negotiator."

What other statesman in England had dared to ratify the Belgian revolution, and, by his simple acknowledgment, place the fact beyond appeal? It is with statesmen as with soldiers; the men who have been conversant with great events maintain the prestige of their ascendency over all who "never smelt powder;" and Metternich wields much of his great influence on such a tenure.

Apropos of Metternich; the King told a trait of him which I have not heard before. In one of those many stormy interviews which took place between him and the Emperor, Napoleon, irritated at the tone of freedom assumed by the Austrian envoy, endeavoured by an artifice to recall him to what he deemed a recollection of their relative stations, and then, as it were, inadvertently let fall his hat for the Prince to take it up; instead of which Metternich moved back and bowed, leaving the Emperor to lift it from the ground himself.

Napoleon, it would seem, was ever on the watch to detect and punish the slightest infraction of that respect which "doth hedge a king," even in cases when the offender had nothing further from his mind than the intention to transgress: a rather absurd illustration was mentioned by the King. The Emperor was one day seeking for a book in the library at Malmaison, and at last discovered it on a shelf somewhat above his reach. Marshal Moncey, one of the tallest men in the army, who was present, immediately stepped forward, saying, " Permettez, Sire. Je suis plus grand que votre Majesté!" " Vous voulez dire plus long, Maréchal," said the Emperor, with a frown that made the reproof actually a severity.

From the tone of his Majesty's observations on our nobility, and the security such an order necessarily creates, I thought I could mark a degree of regret at the extinction of the class in France. How natural such a feeling! For how, after all, can a monarchy long subsist with such a long interval between the crown and the people? The gradations of rank are the best guarantees against any assault on its privileges; a House of Lords is the best floating breakwater against the storms of a people in revolt.

With a marked condescension, his Majesty inquired after my health and the object of my journey; and when I mentioned Naples, hastily remarked, "Ah, well! I can promise you a very agreeable house to pass your evenings in: we are going to send Favancourt there as envoy, and Madame la Comtesse is your countrywoman. This, however, is a secret which even Favancourt himself is ignorant of."

I am not casuist enough to say if this intimation of the King is binding on me as to secrecy; but, possibly, I need not risk the point, as I shall not be likely to see Favancourt or Madame de Favancourt before I start to-morrow.

I am already impatient for the hour to go; I want to be away—afar from the gorgeous glitter of this splendid capital. Something nigh to misanthropy creeps over me at the sight of pleasures in which I am no more to take a part, and I would not that a feeling thus ungenerous should be my travelling companion. I do not experience the inordinate love of life which, we are told, ever accompanies my malady. If I have a wish to live, it is to frame a different kind of existence from what I have hitherto followed, and I believe most sick people's love of life is the desire of dwelling longer amid the pursuits they have followed. And now for the map, to see how I may trace a route, and see—shame that I must say so!—fewest of my countrymen. Well, then, from Strasbourg to Fribourg, and through the Höhlen-Thal. So far, so good! This is all new to me. Thence to Munich, or direct to Innspruck, as I may decide later on. This, at least, avoids

Switzerland, and all its radicalism and roguery, not to speak of the "Perkinses," who are "out" by this time, touring it to Lausanne and Chamouni.

What a tremendous noise a carriage makes coming through these *portes-cochères!* Truly, the luxury is heavily paid for by all the inhabitants of a house. Is that a tap at my door?

* * * * *

A few lines before I lie down to sleep! It is already daybreak. What would poor Dr. S—— say if he knew I had been sitting up to this hour, and at a *petit souper* too, with some half-dozen of the wealthiest people in Paris, not to speak of the prettiest? Madame de F—— would take no refusal, however, and averred she had made the party expressly for me; that V—— H—— had declined another engagement to come; and, in fact—no matter what little flatteries—I went; and here I am, with my cheek flushed and my head on fire, my brain whirling with mad excitement, laughter still ringing in my ears, and all the exaltation he feels who, drinking water while others sip champagne, is yet the only one whose faculties are intoxicated.

What a brilliant scene in a comedy would that little supper have been, just as it really was; scenery, decorations, people all unchanged! the dimly lighted boudoir, where all the luxury of modern requirement was seen through a chiaroscuro, that made it seem half unreal; and then, the splendid brilliancy of the supper-room beyond, where, amid the gorgeous display of *vaisselle* and flowers, shone still more brightly the blaze of beauty and the fire of genius.

How often have I remarked in these little "jousts of the table," where each man puts forth his sharpest weapons of wit and pleasantry, that the conqueror, like an Ivanhoe, is an unknown knight, and with a blank shield.

So was it, I remember once, where we had a sprinkling of every class of celebrity, from the Chamber of Deputies to the Théâtre Français; and yet the heart of all was taken by a young Spaniard, whom nobody seemed to know whence or how he came,—a handsome, dark-eyed fellow, with a short upper lip that seemed alive with energy, combining in his nature the stern dignity of the Castilian and the hot blood of Andalusia. It was the Marquis de Brabançon brought him, presenting him to the lady of the house in a half whisper.

There are men it would be utter ruin to place in positions of staid and tranquil respectability, and yet who make good names. They are born to be adventurers. I remained the last, on purpose to hear who he was, feeling no common curiosity, even though—as so often happens —the name, when heard, conveys nothing to the ear, and leaves as little for the memory.

I could not avoid remarking that he bore, in the mild and thoughtful character of his brow, a strong resemblance to the portraits of Claverhouse.

"Alike in more than looks," said the hostess: "they have many traits in common, and show that the proud Dundee was no exceptional instance of humanity uniting the softness of a girl with a courage even verging upon ferocity."

The stranger was the Spanish General Cabrera!

"And now that you have seen him, let me tell you a short anecdote of him, only worth remembering as so admirably in colouring with his appearance on entering.

"Last year, at the head of a division of the army, the Bishop of Grenada, accompanied by all his clergy, received him in a grand procession, and safely escorted him to the episcopal palace, where a splendid collation was prepared. The soldierlike air and manly beauty of the young General were even less the theme of admiration than his respectful reception of the Bishop, to whom he knelt in devout reverence, and kissed the hand with deep humility, walking at his side with an air of almost bashful deference.

"At table, too, his manner was even more marked by respect. As the meal proceeded, the Bishop could not fail remarking that his guest seemed deeply possessed by some secret care, which made him frequently sigh, in a manner betokening heavy affliction. After some pressing, it came out; the source of the grief was, the inability of the General to pay his troops, for the military chest was quite empty, and daily desertions were occurring. The sum required was a large one, 20,000 contos, and the venerable Bishop hastened to assure him, with unfeigned sorrow, that the poor and suffering city could not command one-fourth of the amount. Cabrera rose, and paced the room in great excitement, ever throwing, as he passed, a glance into the courtyard, where a party of grenadiers stood under arms, and then, resuming his place at the table, he seemed endeavouring, but vainly, to join in the festivity around him.

"'It is evident to me, my son,' said the Bishop, 'that some heavier sorrow is lying at your heart; tell it, and let me, if it may be, give you comfort and support.' Cabrera hesitated; and at last avowed that such was the case. Considerable entreaty, however, was necessary to wring the mystery from him: when at last he said, in a voice broken and agitated, 'You know me, Holy Father, for a good and faithful son of the Church—for one who reveres its ordinances, and those who dispense them. Think, then, of my deep misery when——but I cannot—I am utterly unable to proceed.' After much pressing he resumed, with sudden energy, 'Yes—I know I shall never feel peace and happiness more, for although I have done many a hard and cruel deed, I never, till now, had the dreadful duty to order a Bishop to be shot! This is what is breaking my heart—this is my secret misery.'

"It is scarcely necessary to say, that he was speedily recovered from so dreadful an embarrassment, for the Bishop was too good a Christian to see a devout soldier reduced to such extremity. The money was paid, and the Bishop ransomed."

Our celebrity of to-night was of less mark—indeed, nominally, of none—but he has but to escape "rope and gun," and he will make a name for himself.

He is a young Frenchman, one who, beginning at the lowest rung of the ladder, may still climb high. Strange paths are open to eminence nowadays, and there is no

reason why a man may not begin life as a "Vaudevillist,"
and end it " Pair de France."

Jules de Russigny—whence the "de" came from we
must not inquire—like most of the smart men of the day,
is a Provençal; he was educated at a *Séminaire*, and
destined for the priesthood. Some slight irregularity
caused his dismissal, and he came to Paris on foot to seek
his fortune. When toiling up a steep ascent of the road
at St. Maurice, he saw before him on the way a heavily
laden travelling carriage, which, with the aid of the
struggling post-horses, was also labouring up the hill; an
elderly gentleman had descended to walk, and was
plodding wearily after his lumbering equipage. As Jules
reached the crest of the ridge, all were gone, and nothing
but a deep column of dust announced the course of the
departed carriage: at his feet, however, he discovered a
paper, which, closely written, and, by its numerous
corrections, appeared as closely studied, must have fallen
from the pocket of the traveller.

Jules sat down to inspect it, and found to his surprise
it was a species of memorandum on the subject of the
educationary establishments of France, with much statistic detail, and a great amount of information, evidently
the result of considerable labour and research. There
were many points, of course, perfectly new to him, but
there were others with which he was well acquainted, and
some on which he was so well informed as to be able to
detect mistakes and fallacies in the memorandum. Conning the theme over, he reached a little wayside inn, and
inquiring who the traveller was that passed, he heard,
to his surprise, it was the Minister of Public Instruction.

When Jules reached Paris, it was about a fortnight
before the opening of the Chambers, and the newspapers
were all in full cry discussing the various systems of
education, and with every variety of opinion pronouncing
for and against the supposed views of the Government.
Most men, in his situation, would have sought out the
Minister's residence, and, restoring to him the lost paper,
retired well satisfied with a very modest recompense for a
service that cost so little.

Not so Jules; he established himself in a cheap corner
of the Pays Latin, and spent his days conning over the
various journals of Paris, until, by dint of acute study and
penetration, he had possessed himself of every shade and
hue of political opinion professed by each. At last he
discovered that the *Siècle* was the most decidedly ob-
noxious to the Government, and the *Moniteur* most
favourable to the newly projected system. To each he
sent an article: in one, setting forth a dim, but sugges-
tive idea, of what the Minister might possibly attempt,
with a terrific denunciation annexed to it; in the other, a
half defence of the plan, supported by statistic detail, and
based on the information of the manuscript.

These two papers both appeared, as assertion and re-
joinder: and so did the polemic continue for above a week,
increasing each day in interest, and gradually swelling in
the number of the facts adduced, and the reasons for which
the opinion was entertained, Considerable interest was
created to know the writer, but although he was then
dining each day, and that his only meal, for four sous in
the " Ile St. Louis," he preserved his incognito unbroken,
and never divulged to any one his secret. At last came
an announcement in the *Siècle*, at the close of one of
the articles, that on the next day would appear a full dis-
closure of the whole Government measure, with the
mechanism by which its views were to be strengthened,
and the whole plan of conception on which it was based.
That same evening a young man, pale and sickly-looking,
stood at the *porte-cochère* of a splendid mansion in the
Rue St. George, and asked to see the owner. The rude
repulse of the porter did not abash him, nor did the insolent glance bestowed on his ragged shoes and threadbare
coat cost him a pang of displeasure : he felt that he could
bide his time, for it would come at last.

"His Excellency is at the Council!" at last said the
porter, somewhat moved by a pertinacity that had nothing
of rudeness in it.

With a calm resolve he sat down on a stone bench,
and fell a-thinking to himself. It was full three hours
later when the Minister's carriage rolled in, and the

Minister, hastily descending, proceeded to mount the stairs.

" One word, your Excellency," cried Jules, in a voice collected and firm, but still of an almost imploring sound.

" Not now—at another time," said the Minister, as he took some papers from his secretary.

" But one word, sir—I crave no more," repeated Jules.

" See to that man, Delpierre," said the Minister to his secretary; but Jules, passing hastily forward, came close to the Minister, and whispered in his ear, " M. le Ministre, je suis Octave," the name under which the *Siècle* articles appeared. A few words followed, and Jules was ordered to follow the Minister to his cabinet. The article of the *Siècle* did appear the next day, but miserably inefficient in point of ability; and so false in fact, that the refutation was overwhelming. The *Moniteur* had a complete triumph, only to be exceeded by that of the Minister's own in the Chamber. The Council of Ministers was in ecstasy, and Jules de Russigny, who arrived in Paris by the mail from Orleans—for thither he was despatched, to make a more suitable entry into the great world—was installed as a clerk in the office of the Finance Minister, with very reasonable hopes of future advancement. Such was the fortune of him who was one, and, I repeat it, the pleasantest of our convives.

This is the age of smart men—not of high intelligences. The race is not for the thoroughbred, but the clever hackney, always " ready for his work," and if seldom pre-eminent, never a dead failure.

Of my own brief experience, all the first-rate men, without exception, have broke down. All the moderates —the " clever fellows "—have carried the day. Now I could pick out from my contemporaries, at school and university, some half-dozen brilliant, really great capacities, quite lost—some, shipwrecked on the first venture in life—some, disheartened and disgusted, have retired early from the contest, to live unheard of and die broken-hearted. But the smart men ! What crowds of them come before my mind in high employ—some at home, some abroad, some waxing rich by tens of thousands, some running high up the ambitious road of honours and titles! There is something in inordinate self-esteem that buoys up this kind of man. It is the only enthusiasm he is capable of feeling—but it serves as well as the " real article."

For the mere adventurer, the man of ready wit and a fearless temperament, politics offer the best road to fortune. The abilities that would have secured a mere mediocrity of position in some profession will here win their way upwards. The desultory character of reading and acquirements, so fatal to men chained to a single pursuit, is eminently favourable to him who must talk about everything, with, at least, the appearance of knowledge ; while the very scantiness of his store suggests a recklessness that has great success in the world.

In England we have but one high road to eminence— Parliament. Literature, whose rewards are so great in France, with us only leads to intimacy with the " Trade " and a name in " the Row." It is true, Parliamentary reputation is of slow growth, and dependent on many circumstances totally remote from the capacity and attainments of him who seeks it. Are you the son of a great name in the Lords, the representative of an immense estate, or of great commercial wealth? are you high in the esteem of Corn men or Cotton men? are you a magnate of Railroads, or is your word law in the City ? then your way is open and your path easy. Without these, or some one of them, you must be a segment of some leading man's party.

My own little experience of Parliament—about the very briefest any man can recall—presents little pleasurable in the retrospect. Lord Collyton was one of my Christchurch acquaintances, and at his invitation I spent the autumn of 18— at his father, the Duke of Wrexington's.

The house was full of company, and, like an English house in such circumstances, the most delightful *séjour* imaginable. Every second day or so brought a relay of new arrivals, either from town or some other country house, full of the small-talk of the last visit—all that strange but most amusing farrago which we designate by the humble title of "gossip," but which, so far as I can judge, is worth ten thousand times more than the boasted *causerie* of France, and the perpetual effort at smartness so much aimed at by our polite neighbours.

The guests were numerous, and presented specimens of almost every peculiarity observable in Englishmen of a certain class. We had great lords and high court functionaries, deep in the mysteries of Buckingham House and Windsor; a sprinkling of distinguished foreigners; ministers, and secretaries of embassy; some parliamentary leaders, men great on the Treasury benches or strong on the Opposition. Beauties there were too, past, present, and some, coming; a fair share of the notorieties of fashion, and the last winner of the Derby, with—let me not forget him—a Quarterly Reviewer. This last gentleman came with the Marquis of Deepdene, and was, with the exception of a certain pertinacity of manner, a very agreeable person.

Although previously unknown to the host, he had come down "special" under the protection of his friend Lord Deepdene, hoping to secure his Grace's interest in the borough of Collyton, at that time vacant. He was a man of very high attainments, had been an *optime* at Cambridge, was a distinguished essayist, and his party had conceived the very greatest expectations of his success in Parliament. Of the world, or at least that portion of it that moves upon Tournay carpets, amid Vandykes and Velasquez, with sideboards of gold and lamps of silver, he had not seen much, and learned still less; and it was plain to see that, in the confidence of his own strong head, he was proof against either the seductions of fashion or the sneers of those who might attempt to criticize his breeding.

Before he was twenty-four hours in the house he had corrected his Grace in an historical statement, caught up the B—— of D—— in a blunder of prosody, detected a sapphire in Lady Dollington's suite of yellow diamonds, and exposed an error of Lord Sloperton's in his pedigree of Brown Menelaus. It is needless to say he was almost universally detested, for of those he had suffered to pass free, none knew how soon his own time might arrive. His patron was miserable; he saw nothing but failure where he looked for triumph. The very acquirements he had built upon for success were become a terror to every one, and " the odious Mr. Kitely " became a proverb. His political opponents chuckled over the " bad tone " of such men in general; the stupid ones gloried over the fall of a clever man ; and the malignant part of the household threw out broad hints that he was a mere adventurer, and they should not wonder if actually—— an Irishman! Indeed, he had been heard to say " entirely " twice upon the same evening in conversation, and suspicion had almost become a certainty.

It was towards the end of my first week, as I was one day dressing for dinner, Lord Collyton came hastily into my room, exclaiming, " By Jove, Templeton! Mr. Kitely has done the thing at last, as he would say himself, entirely."

" How do you mean? what has he done ? "

" You know my father is excessively vain of his land-scape-gardening, and the prodigious improvements which he has made in this same demesne around us. Well, com-passionating some one whom Kitely was mangling, *more suo*, in an argument, he took that gentleman out for a walk, and, with a conscious pride in his own achievements, led him towards the Swiss cottage beside the waterfall. Kitely was pleased with everything ; the timber is really well grown, and he praised it; the view is fine, and he said so. Even of the *châlet* he condescended a few words of approval, as a feature in the scene. The waterfall, how-ever, he would not praise; it might foam, and splash, and whirl as it would ; in vain it threw its tiny spray aloft, and hissed beneath the rocks below ; he never wasted even a word upon it.

" ' You'd scarce fancy, Mr. Kitely,' said my father, whose patience was sorely tried ; ' you'd scarce fancy that river you see there was only a mill-stream.'

" ' I'd scarcely think of calling that mill-stream a river, my lord,' was the reply.

" Hence the borough of Collyton is still open, and I

have come, by his Grace's request, to say that if you desire to enter Parliament it is very much at your service."

This was my introduction to the House.

My parliamentary life was, as I have said, a brief one, but not without its triumphs. I was long enough a member to have excited the ardent hopes of my friends, and make my name a thing quoted in the lists of party.

Had I remained, I was to have spoken second to the Address on the opening of the new session. There was, I own, a most intoxicating sense of pleasure in the first success. The moment in which, fatigued and almost overpowered, I sank into a chair at Bellamy's, with some twenty around me, congratulating, praising, flattering, and foretelling, was worth living for; and yet, perhaps, in that same instant of triumph were sown the seeds of my malady. I was greatly heated; I had excited myself beyond my strength, and spoken for two hours—to myself it seemed scarce twenty minutes; and then, with open cravat and vest, I sat in the current of air between a door and window, drinking in delicious draughts of iced water and flattery. I went home with a slight cough, and something strange, like an obstruction to full breathing, in my chest. Brodie, who saw me next day, I suppose guessed the whole mischief; for these men look far ahead, and, like sailors, they see storm and hurricane in the cloud not bigger than a man's hand.

I often regret—I shall continue to do, perhaps, still oftener—that I did not die in the harness. To quit the field for the sake of life, and not secure it after all, was a paltry policy. But what could I do? a severe and contested election would have killed me, and for Collyton it was impossible I could continue to sit.

Irish politics would seem the rock ahead of every man in the House. On these unhappy questions all are shipwrecked: the Premier loses Party—Party loses confidence —members displease constituents, and *protégés* offend their patrons. Such was my own case. The Duke who owned the borough of Collyton, resolved on making a great stand and show of his influence in both Houses. All his followers, myself among the number, were summoned to a conference, when the tactic of attack should be adopted, and each assigned his fitting part. To me was allotted the office of replying to the first speaker of the Treasury Bench—a post of honour and of danger, and only distasteful because impossible : the fact was, that my own opinions were completely with the Government on the subject in dispute, and consequently at open variance with those of my own friends. This I declared at once, endeavouring to show why my judgment had so inclined, and what arguments I believed to be unanswerable.

Instead of replying to my reasons, or convincing me of their inefficiency, my colleagues only appealed to the "necessity of union"—the imperative call of party— and "the impossibility," as they termed it, "of betraying the Duke."

I immediately resolved to resign my seat, and accept the Chiltern Hundreds. To this there was a unanimous cry of dissent, one and all pronouncing that such a step would damage them more even than my fiercest opposition. The Duke sat still and said nothing. Somewhat offended at this, I made a personal appeal to him, resolving by the tone of his reply to guide my future conduct. He was too old a politician to give me any clue to his sentiments, shrouding his meaning in vague phrases of compliment to my talents, and his perfect confidence that, however my judgment inclined, I should be able to show sufficient reasons for my opinion. I went home baffled, worried, and ill. I sent for Brodie. " You cannot speak on the coming question," said he; " there is a great threat of hæmorrhage from the lungs—you must have rest and quiet. Keep beyond the reach of excitement for a few weeks—don't even read the newspapers. Go over to Spa—there you can be quite alone."

I took the advice, and without one word of adieu to any one—without even leaving any clue to my hiding-place—I left London. Spa was as quiet and retired as Brodie described it. A little valley shut in among the hills, that a Cockney would have called mountains ; a clear little trout stream, and some shady alleys to stroll among, being all I wanted. Would that I could have brought there the tranquil spirit to enjoy them! But my mind was far from at ease. The conflict between a sense of duty and a direct obligation, raged continually within me. What I owed to my own conscience, and what I owed to my patron, were at variance, and never did the sturdiest Radical detest the system of nomination boroughs as I did at this moment. Each day, too, I regretted that I had not done this or that—taken some line different from what I adopted, and at least openly braved the criticism that I felt I had fled from.

To deny me all access to newspapers was a measure but ill calculated to allay the fever of my mind. Expectation and imagination were at work, speculating on every possible turn of events, and every likely and unlikely version of my own conduct. The first two days over, all my impatience returned, and I would have given life itself to be once again back "in my place," to assert my opinions, and stand or fall by my own defence of my motives.

About a week after my arrival I was sitting under the shade of some trees, at the end of the long avenue that forms the approach to the town, when I became suddenly aware that, at a short distance off, an Englishman was reading aloud to his friend the report of the last debate on the "Irish Question." My attention was fettered at once; spell bound, I sat listening to the words of one of the speakers on the Ministerial side, using the very arguments I had myself discovered, and calling down the cheers of the House as he proceeded. A sarcastic allusion to my own absence, and a hackneyed quotation from Horace as to my desertion, were interrupted by loud laughter, and the reader laying down the newspaper, said,—

"Can this be the Duke of Wrexington's Templeton that is here alluded to?"

"Yes. He wrote a paper on this subject in the last *Quarterly*, but the Duke would not permit of his taking the same side in the House, and so he affected illness, they say, and came abroad."

"The usual fortune of your *protégé* members—they have

the pleasant alternative of inconsistency or ingratitude. Why didn't he resign his seat ? "

"It is mere coquetry with Peel. They told me at Brookes's that he wanted a mission abroad, and would ' throw over' the Duke at the first opportunity. Now Peel gives nothing for nothing. For open apostasy he will pay, and pay liberally ; but for mere defalcation he'll give nothing."

" Templeton has outwitted himself, then ; besides that, he has no standing in the House to play the game alone."

" A smart fellow, too, but no guidance. If he had been deep, he must have seen that old Wrexington only gave him the borough till Collyton was of age to come in. It was meant for Kitely, but he refused the conditions. ' I cannot be a tenant-at-will, my lord,' said he ; and so they took Templeton."

I could bear no more. How I reached my inn I cannot remember. A severe fit of coughing overtook me as I ascended the stairs, and a small vessel gave way—a bad symptom, I believed ; but the doctor of the place, whom my servant soon brought to my bedside, applied leeches, and I was better a few hours after.

The first use I made of strength was to write a brief note to the Duke, resigning the borough. The next post brought me his reply, full of compliment and assurance of esteem, accepting my resignation, and acknowledging his full concurrence in the reasons I had given for my step. The division was against him ; and he half-jestingly remarked, it might have been otherwise if I had fought on his side.

The letter was civil throughout, but in that style that shows a tone of careless ease had been adopted to simulate frankness. I had had enough of his Grace, and of politics too !

CHAPTER VI.

So, all is settled!—I leave Paris to-morrow. I hate leave-takings, even where common acquaintanceship only is concerned. I shall just write a few lines to the Favancourts, with the volume of Balzac—happily I know no one else here—and then for the road!

Why this haste to set out, I cannot even tell to myself. I know, I feel, I shall never pass this way again; I have that sense of regret a last look at even indifferent objects suggests, and yet I would be *en route*. There are places and scenes I wish to see before I go hence, and I feel that my hours are numbered.

And now for a moonlight stroll through Paris! Already the din and tumult is subsiding—the many-voiced multitude that throngs the streets long after the roll of equipage and the clattering hoofs of horses have ceased. How peacefully the long shadows are sleeping in the garden of the Tuileries! and how clearly sounds the measured tread of the sentinel beneath the deep arch of the palace!

Not a light twinkles along that vast *façade*, save in that distant pavilion, where a single star seems glistening—it is the apartment of the King. "The cares of Agamemnon never sleep;" and royalty is scarce more fortunate now than in the days of Homer.

Louis Philippe has a task not less arduous than had Napoleon to found a dynasty. There is little prestige any longer in the name of Bourbon; and the members of his family, brave and high-spirited though they be, are scarcely of the stuff to stand the storm that is brewing for them.

As for the Emperor, the incapacity of his brothers was

a weight upon his shoulders all through life. His family contributed more to his fall than is generally believed: it was a never-ending struggle he had to maintain against the childish vanity and extravagance of Josephine, the wrongheadedness of Joseph, the simple credulity of Louis, and the fatuous insufficiency of Jerome and Lucien. All, more good than otherwise, were manifestly unsuited to the places they occupied in life, and were continually mingling up the associations and habits of their small identities with the great requirements of newly-acquired station.

Napoleon created the Empire—the vast drama was his own. However he might please to represent royalty, however he might like to ally the slendours of a throne with the glories of a great captain, it was all his own doing. But how miserably deficient were the others in that faculty of adaptation that made him *de pair* with every dynasty of Europe!

Into these thoughts I was led by finding myself standing in the Rue Taibout, opposite the house which was once celebrated as the "Café du Roi"—a name which it bore for many years under the Empire, and, in consequence, was held in high esteem by certain worthy *Légitimistes*, who little knew that the "King" was only a pretender, and, so far from being his sainted majesty Louis Dix-huit, was merely Jerome Buonaparte, King of Westphalia.

The name originated thus:—One warm evening in autumn, a young man, somewhat overdressed in the then *mode*, with a very considerable border of pinkish silk stocking seen above the margin of his low boots, *à revers*, and a most inordinate amount of coat-collar, lounged along the Boulevard des Italiens, occasionally ogling the passers-by, but oftener still throwing an admiring glance at himself, as the splendid windows of plate-glass reflected back his figure. His whole air and mien exhibited the careless *insouciance* of one with whom the world went easily, asking little from him of exertion, less still of forethought.

He had just reached the angle of the Rue Vivienne, and

was about to turn, when two persons advanced towards him, whose very different style of dress and appearance bespoke very different treatment at the hands of Fortune. They were both young, and, although palpably men of a certain rank and condition, were equally what is called out-at-elbows ; hats that exhibited long intimacy with rain and wind, shoes of very questionable colour, coats suspiciously buttoned about the throat, being all signs of circumstances that were far from flourishing.

"Ah, Chopard, is't thou?" said the fashionably dressed man, advancing with open hand to each, and speaking in the "*tu*" of intimate friendship. "And thou, too, Brissole, how goes it? What an age since we have met! Art long in Paris?"

"About two hours," said the first. "Just as I stepped out of the Place des Victoires I met our old friend here; and, strange enough, now we have come upon *you:* three old schoolfellows thus assembled at hazard!"

"A minute later, and we should have missed each other," said Brissole. "I was about to take my place in the *malle* for Nancy."

"To leave Paris?" exclaimed both the others.

"Even so—to leave Paris! I've had enough of it."

"Come, what do you mean by this?" said Chopard ; "it sounds very like discouragement to me, who have come up here with all manner of notions of fortune, wealth and honours."

"So much the worse for you," said Brissole, gaily ; "I've tried it for five years, and will try it no longer. I was vaudevillist, journalist, novelist, feuilletonist—I was the glory of the Odéon, the prop of the *Moniteur*, the hope of the *Siècle*—and look at me——"

"And thou?" said the fashionable, addressing him called Chopard.

"I have just had a little opera damned at Lyons, and have come up to try what can be done here."

"Poor devil!" exclaimed Brissole, shrugging his shoulders ; then, turning abruptly towards the other, he said, "And what is thy luck? for, so far as externals go, thou seemest to have done better."

"Ay, Jerome," chimed in Chopard, "tell us, how hast thou fared?—thou wert ever a fortunate fellow."

"Pretty well," said he, laughing. "I've just come from St. Cloud — they've made me King of Westphalia!"

"The devil they have!" exclaimed Chopard; "and dost know, *par hazard*, where thy kingdom lies on the map?"

"Why should he torment himself about that?" said Brissole. "It's enough to know they have capital hams there."

"What if we sup together," said Jerome, "and taste one? I am most anxious to baptize my new royalty in a glass of wine. Here we are in the Rue Taibout—this is Villaret's. Come in, gentlemen—I'm the host. Make your minds easy about the future: you, Brissole, I appoint to the office of my private secretary. Chopard, you shall be *maitre de chapelle*."

"Agreed," cried the others gaily; and with a hearty shake of hands was the contract ratified.

Supper was quickly prepared, and, in its splendour and profusion, pronounced, by both the guests, worthy of a king. Villaret could do these things handsomely, and as he was told expense was of no consequence, the entertainment was really magnificent. Nor was the spirit of the guests inferior to the feast. They were brilliant in wit, and overflowing in candour; concealing nothing of their past lives that would amuse or interest, each vied with the other in good stories and ludicrous adventures—all their bygone vicissitudes so pleasantly contrasting with the brilliant future they now saw opening before them. They drank long life and reign to the King of Westphalia in bumpers of foaming champagne.

The pleasant hours flew rapidly past—bright visions of the time to come lending their charm to the happiness, and making their enjoyment seem but the forerunner of many days and nights of festive delight. At last came day break, and, even by the flickering of reason left, they saw it was time to separate.

"Bring the bill," said Jerome to the exhausted-looking

waiter, who speedily appeared with a small slip of paper ominously marked "eight hundred francs."

"*Diable!*" exclaimed Jerome; "that is smart, and I have no money about me. Come, Brissole, this falls among your duties—pay the fellow."

"*Parbleu!* then—it comes somewhat too soon. I am not yet installed, and have not got the key of our treasury."

"No matter—pay it out of thine own funds."

"But I have none—save this;" and he produced two francs, and some sous in copper.

"Well, then, Chopard must do it."

"I have not as much as himself," said Chopard.

"Send the landlord here," said Jerome; but indeed the command was unnecessary, as that functionary had been an anxious listener at the door to the very singular debate.

"We have forgotten our purses, Villaret," said Jerome, in the easy tone his last ten hours of royalty suggested; "but we will send your money when we reach home."

"I have no doubt of it, gentlemen," said the host, obsequiously; "but it would please me still better to receive it now—particularly as I have not the honour of knowing the distinguished company."

"The distinguished company is perfectly satisfied to know you: the *cuisine* was excellent," hiccupped Brissole.

"And the wine unexceptionable."

"The champagne might have been a little more *frappé*," said Brissole; "the only improvement I could suggest."

"Perhaps there was a *nuance*, only a *nuance*, too much citron in the *rognons à la broche*, but the *filets de sole* were perfect."

"If I had the happiness of knowing messieurs," said Villaret, "I should hope, that at another time I might be more fortunate in pleasing them."

"Nothing easier," said Chopard. "I am *maître de chapelle* to the King of Westphalia."

Villaret bowed low.

"And I am the Private Secretary and Privy Purse of his Majesty."

Villaret bowed again—a slight smile of very peculiar
omen flitting across his cunning features, while, turning
hastily, he whispered a word in the ear of the waiter.
"And this gentleman here?" said he, looking at Jerome,
who, with his legs resting on a chair, was coolly awaiting
the termination of the explanation. "And this gentleman, if I might make so bold, what office does he hold in
his Majesty's service?"

"I am the King of Westphalia!" said Jerôme.

"Just as I suspected. François," said the landlord
insolently, "go fetch the gendarmes."

"No, no, *parbleu!*" said Jerome, springing up in alarm;
"no gendarmes, no police. Here, take my watch—that is
surely worth more than your bill? When I reach home
I'll send the money."

The landlord, more than ever convinced that his suspicions were well grounded, took the watch, which was a
very handsome one, and suffered them to depart in peace.

They had not been gone many minutes when, on
examining the watch, the landlord perceived that it bore
the emblematic " N " of the Emperor within the case, and
at once suspecting that it had been stolen from some
member of the imperial household, he hurried off in terror
to communicate his fears to the commissary of police.
This functionary no sooner saw it that he hastened to
Fouché, the minister, who, making himself acquainted
with the whole details, immediately hurried off to the
Tuileries and laid it all before the Emperor. The watch
had been a present from Napoleon to Jerome; but this
was but a small part of the cause of indignation. The
derogation from dignity, the sacrifice of the regard due
to his station, were crimes of a very different order; and,
summoned to the imperial presence, the new-made king
was made to hear, in terms of reproachful sarcasm, a
lesson in his craft that few could impart with such cutting
severity.

As for the *maître de chapelle* and the Secretary, an
agent of the police waited on each before they were well
awake, with strict injunctions to them to maintain a
perfect secrecy on the whole affair; and while guarantee-

ing them an annual pension in their new offices, assuring them that the slightest indiscretion as to the mystery would involve their ruin and their exile from France for ever.

It was years before the landlord learned the real secret of the adventure, and, in commemoration of it, called his house " Le Café du Roi," a circumstance which the Government never noticed, for the campaign of Russia and the events of 1812–13 left little time to attend to matters of this calibre.

The " Café du Roi " is now a shop where artificial flowers are sold ; as nearly like nature perhaps, or more so, than poor Jerome's royalty resembled the real article.

CHAPTER VII.

IT is like a dream to me now to think of that long, dusty road from Paris, with its rattling pavement, its noisy postilions, shouting ostlers, bowing landlords, dirty waiters, garlic diet, and hard beds ; and here I sit by my open window, with a bright river beneath my feet, the song of birds on every side, a richly wooded mountain in front, and at the foot a winding road, which ever and anon gives glimpses of some passing equipage, bright in all the butterfly glitter of female dress, or, mayhap, resounding with merry laughter and sweet-voiced mirth. How brilliant is everything !—the cloudless sky, the sparkling water, the emerald grass, the foliage in every tint of beauty, the orange-trees and the cactus along the terraces, where lounging parties come and go ; and then the measured step of princely equipages, in all the panoply of tasteful wealth ! Truly, Vice wears its holiday suit in Baden, and the fairness of this lovely valley seems to throw a softened light over a scene where, as in a sea, the stormy waves of every bad passion are warring.

When, in all the buoyant glow of youth and health, I remembered feeling shocked as I strolled through the promenade at Carlsbad, at the sight of so many painful objects of sickness and suffering ; the eager, almost agonising, expressions of hoping convalescence ; the lustreless stare of those past hope; the changeful looks of accompanying friends, who seemed to read the fate of some dear one in the compassionate pity of those who passed, were all sights that threw a chill, like death, over the warm current of my blood. Yet never did this feeling convey the same intense horror and disgust that I felt last night as I walked through the Cursaal.

To pass from the mellow moonlight, dappling the pathway among the trees and kissing the rippling stream, from the calm, mild air of a summer's night, when every leaf lay sleeping and none save the nightingale kept watch, into the glare and glitter of a gilded saloon, is somewhat trying to the jarred nerves of sickness. But what was it to the sight of that dense crowd around the play-tables, where avarice, greed of gain, recklessness, and despair are mingled, giving, even to faces of manly vigour and openness, expressions of low cunning and vulgar meaning? There is a terrible sameness in the gambler's look, a blending of slavish terror with a resolution to brave the worst, almost demoniacal in its fierceness. I knew most of the persons present; I need not say, not personally, but from having seen them before at various other similar places. Many were professed gamblers, men who starved and suffered for the enjoyment of that one passion, living on the smallest gain, and never venturing a stake beyond what daily life demanded ; haggard, sad, wretched-looking creatures they were, the abject poverty of their dress and appearance vouching that this *métier* was not a prosperous one. Others farmed out their talents, and played for those who were novices. These men have a singular existence ; they exact a mere percentage on the winning, and are in great request among elderly ladies, whose passion for play is modified by the fears of its vicissitudes. Then there were the usual sprinkling of young men, not habitually gamblers, but always glad to have the opportunity of tempting Fortune, with here and there some old votary of the "table" satisfied to witness the changeful temper of the game without risking a stake.

Into many vices men are led by observing the apparent happiness and pleasure of others who indulge in them. Not so with regard to play. No man ever became a gambler from this delusion, there being no such terrible warning against the passion as the very looks of its votaries.

But it is not in such a low *tripot* of vice I care to linger. Is was a ball-night, and I turned with a sense of relief from the aspect of sordid, vulgar iniquity to gaze on its more polished brother (*quære*, sister ?) in the *salle de danse*.

Here there was a large—I might almost call it a brilliant—company assembled: a less exclusive assemblage cannot be conceived; five francs and clean gloves being the only qualification needed. The guests were as varied, too, in nation as in rank. About equal numbers of German and French, several Russians, and a large proportion of English, with here and there a bilious-looking American, or a very dubious marquis from beyond the Alps. Many of the men I knew to be swindlers and blacklegs of the very lowest stamp; some others I recognised as persons of the highest station in my own country. Of the lady part of the company the disparities were even greater.

There was, it is true, a species of sifting process discernible, by which the various individuals fell among those of their own order; but though this was practicable enough where conversation and grouping were concerned, it was scarcely attainable in other circumstances, and thus, the mazurka and the polka assembled ingredients that should never have been placed in close propinquity.

The demoralising influence of such *réunions* upon the daughters of our own land need not be insisted upon. Purity of mind and simplicity of character are no safeguard against the scenes which, in all the propriety of decorum, are ever occurring. And how terribly rapid are the downward steps when the first bloom and blush of modesty have faded! It demands but a very indifferent power of observation to distinguish the English girl for the first time abroad from her who has made repeated visits to foreign watering-places; while even among those who have been habituated to the great world at home, and passed the ordeal of London seasons, there is yet much to learn in the way of cool and self-possessed effrontery from the habits of Baden and its brethren.

I was dreadfully shocked last night by meeting one I had not seen for many years before. How changed from what I knew her once!—what a terrible change! When first I saw her, it was during a visit I made to her mother's house in Wales; her brother was an Oxford friend, and brought me down with him for the shooting season to Merionethshire. Poor fellow! he died of consumption at two-and-twenty, and left all he possessed—a handsome estate—to his only sister. Hence all her misery! Had she remained comparatively portionless, rich only in her beauty and the graces of a manner that was fascination itself, she might now have been the happy wife of some worthy Englishman—one, whose station is a trust held on the tenure of his rectitude and honour; for such is public feeling in our country, and such is it never elsewhere.

She was then about eighteen or nineteen, and the very ideal of what an English girl at that age should be. On a mind highly stored and amply cultivated, no unworthy or depreciating influence had yet descended; freedom of thought, freshness almost childish, had given her an animation and buoyancy only subdued by the chastening modesty of coming womanhood. Enthusiastic in all her pursuits, for they were graceful and elevating, her mind had all the simplicity of the child with the refinement of the highest culture; and, like those who are brought up in narrow circles, her affections for a few spread themselves out in the varied forms that are often scattered and diffused over the wider surface of the world. Thus her brother was not merely the great object of her affection and pride, but he was the companion of her rides and walks, the confidant of all her secret feelings, the store in which she laid up her newly acquired knowledge, or drew, at will, for more. With him she read and studied; delighted by the same pursuits, their natures blended into one harmonious *chorde*, which no variance or dissonance ever troubled.

His death, although long and gradually anticipated, nearly brought her to the grave. The terrible nature of the malady, so often inherent in the same family, gave cause for the most anxious fears on her account, and her mother, herself almost broken-hearted, took her abroad, hoping by the mildness of a southern climate and change of scene to arrest the progress of the fell disease.

In this she was successful; bodily health was indeed secured. But might it not have been better that she had wasted slowly away, to sleep at last beneath the yews of her own ancient churchyard, than live and become what she has done?

Some years after this event I was, although at the time only an *attaché* of the mission, acting as *chargé d'affaires* at Naples, during the absence of the minister and the secretary. I was sitting one morning reading in my garden, when my servant announced the visit of an Italian gentleman, il Signor Salvatori. The name was familiar to me, as belonging to a man who had long been employed as a spy of the Austrian government, and, indeed, was formerly entrusted in a secret capacity by Lord W. Bentinck in Sicily—a clever, designing, daring rascal, who obtained his information no one knew how; and although we had always our suspicions that he might be " selling " us, as well as the French, we never actually traced any distinct act of treachery to his door. He possessed a considerable skill in languages, was very highly informed on many popular topics, and, I have been told, was a musician of no mean powers of performance. These and similar social qualities were, however, never displayed by him in any part of his intercourse with us, although we have often heard of their existence.

As I never felt any peculiar pleasure in the relations which office compels with men of his stamp, I received him somewhat coldly, and asked, without much circumlocution, the reason of his visit.

He replied, with his habitual smile of self-possession, that his present duty at " the Mission " was not a business-call, but concerned a matter purely personal;—in fact, " with his Excellency's permission, he desired to get married."

Not stopping him on the score of his investing me with a title to which, no one knew better than himself I had no pretensions, I quietly assured him that his relation with " the Mission " did not, in any way, necessitate his asking for such a permission—that, however secret and mysterious the nature of his communications, they were still beyond the pale of affairs personally private.

He suffered me to continue my explanation, somewhat scornful as it was, to the end, and then calmly said,—

" Your Excellency will pardon my intrusion, when I inform you that the marriage should take place here, at ' the Mission,' as the lady is an Englishwoman."

Whether it was the fact itself, or his manner of delivering it, that outraged me, I cannot now remember; but I do recollect giving expression to a sentiment of surprise and anger not exactly suitable.

He merely smiled, and said nothing.

" Very well, M. Salvatori," said I, corrected by the quietude of his manner; " what is your day?"

" Wednesday, if your Excellency pleases."

" Wednesday be it, and at eight o'clock."

" As your Excellency desires," said he, bowing and retiring.

It had never occurred to me to ask for any information about the happy fair one; indeed, if I had given a thought at all to the matter, it would have been that she was of the rank of a *femme de chambre*, or, at least, some unhappy children's governess, glad to exchange one mode of tyranny for another. As he was leaving the room, however, some sense of remorse, perhaps, at the *brusquerie* I had shown towards him, suggested the question, " Who might the lady be?"

" Mademoiselle Graham."

" Ah! a very good name indeed," said I; and so, with a word or two of common-place, I bade him goodbye.

The Wednesday morning arrived, and two carriages drove into the court of " the Mission:" out of one sprang Signor Salvatori and a very bearded gentleman, who accompanied him as his friend; from the other alighted, first, an elderly lady, whose dress was a mixture of wedding finery and widow's mourning; then came a very elegant-looking girl, veiled from head to foot, followed by her maid; and, lastly, the chaplain to " the Mission."

They were some minutes too early, and I equally behind my time; but I dressed hastily, and descended to the *salon*, where M. Salvatori received me with a very gracious expression of his self-satisfaction. Passing him by, I advanced to address a few words to the old lady, who had risen from her seat; when, stepping back, I exclaimed,—

"Mrs. Graham—my old friend, Mrs. Graham! Is this possible?"

"Oh, Caroline, it is Mr. Templeton!" said she; while her daughter, drawing her veil still closer over her face, trembled dreadfully. Meanwhile Mrs. Graham had seized my hand with cordial warmth, and pressed it in all the earnestness of friendship. Her joy—and it was very evident it was such—was little participated in by her son-in-law elect, who stood, pale and conscience-stricken, in a distant part of the room.

"I must entreat these gentlemen's permission to speak a few words here alone, as these ladies are very old friends I have not seen for some years."

"I would humbly suggest to your Excellency that, as the ceremony still waits——"

"I wish it, marquis," said Mrs. Graham, in a tone half-command, half-entreaty; and, with a deep bow of submission, Salvatori and his friend withdrew, accompanied by the chaplain.

"The title by which you have just addressed that person, Mrs. Graham," said I, in a voice trembling from agitation, "shows me how you have been duped and deceived by him, and in what total ignorance you are as to his real character."

"Oh, Mr. Templeton!" broke in her daughter, now speaking for the first time, and in accents I shall never forget, such was their heart-thrilling earnestness,—"Oh, sir, this does indeed exceed the licence of even old friendship! We are well aware how the Marquis of Salvatori has suffered from persecution; but we little expected to have found *you* among the number of his enemies."

"You do me great wrong, Miss Graham," said I eagerly; "in nothing greater than supposing me capable of being the enemy of such a man as this. Unworthy as the sentiment is, it at least implies a sense of equality. Now, are you certain of what this person is? are you aware in what capacity he has been employed by our government, and by that of other countries?"

"We know that the marquis has been engaged in secret missions," said Miss Graham, proudly.

"Your reply, brief as it is, conveys two errors, Miss Graham. He is not a marquis; little as the title often implies in Italy, he has no right to it. He asked Lord William Bentinck to let him call himself marquis, and so to address him, as a means of frequenting circles where important information was accessible. Lord William said, 'Call yourself what you please—grand duke, if you like it —I am no dispenser of such designations.' The gentleman was modest—he stopped at marquis. As to his diplomatic functions, we have a short and expressive word for them—he was and is, a spy!"

Not heeding the scornful reception of the daughter, I turned towards Mrs. Graham, and, with all the power I possessed, urged her, at least, to defer this fatal step—that she was about to bestow her child upon a man of notoriously degraded character, and one whose assumption of rank and position was disregarded and despised in the very humblest circles. The mother wept bitterly; at one moment turning to dissuade her daughter from her rashness, at the next appealing to me against what she called my unjust prejudices against the marquis. Miss Graham scornfully refused to vouchsafe me even a word.

I confess more than once my temper prompted me to abandon the enterprise, and suffer wilfulness to reap its own bitter harvest; but then, my better feelings prevailed, and old memories of my poor friend Graham again enlisted me in defence of his sister.

Of no avail was it that I followed these worthier promptings. It seemed as if the man had thrown a spell over these two unhappy women, one being perfectly enthralled, the other, nearly so, by the artful fascinations of his manner; and yet he was neither young, handsome, rich, nor of high lineage. On the contrary, the man was at least fifty-three or four, a perfect monster of ugliness, with an expression of sardonic sycophancy actually demoniac.

If I were not relating "a fact"—one of which I can answer, that many now living can entirely corroborate—

I would hesitate about dwelling on a case where improbabilities are so strong, and where I have nothing to offer like an explanation of them.

Wilkes has long since convinced the world how little good looks are concerned in winning a woman's heart, and how, indeed, a very considerable share of ugliness can be counterbalanced by captivations of manner and personal agreeability. But, judging from the portraits—even Hogarth's fearful sketch—Wilkes was handsome compared to Salvatori; and in point of reputation, low as it was, the libeller and the satirist was still better than the spy.

To go back again: I argued, I entreated, begged, threatened, and denounced. I went further—I actually transgressed the limits of official authority, and refused to sanction the ceremony—a threat which, I soon remembered, I dare not sustain. But, do what, say what, I would, they were equally resolute and determined; and nothing was left for me but to recall M. Salvatori and his friend, and suffer the affair to proceed.

I do not remember, among the varied incidents of my life, one whose effect weighed more heavily upon me. Although acquitted by my conscience, I felt at moments horror-struck at even my share in this infamy, and would have given anything that it had never occurred. It may be believed I was happy to hear that they all left Naples the same day.

Years rolled over, and I never even heard of them, till one morning, when waiting along with a diplomatic friend for an interview with the French Minister for Foreign Affairs, a person hastily passed through the room, saluting us as he went.

"I have seen that face before," said I to my friend; "do you know him?"

"To be sure!" said he, smiling; "one must be young in diplomacy not to know the Mephistophiles of the craft; and I guess why he is here, too. That fellow is in the pay of the Prince de Capua, but has sold him to Louis Philippe. The reconciliation with Naples would have been long since effected but for the King of the French."

"And his name—this man's name—what is it?"

"Salvatori."

"What! the same who married an English girl at Naples?"

"And sold her to the Marquis Brandini for ten thousand sequini. The very man. But here comes the messenger to say his Excellency will receive us."

My friend quitted Paris the moment his interview ended, and I heard no more.

Last night I saw her in the Cursaal—beautiful, perhaps more beautiful than ever! At least there was a lofty elegance and a splendour about her that I never remember in her girlish days; nor was it till she smiled that I could now believe that the queen-like beauty before me was the timid, delicate girl I first saw tripping along the narrow path of a Welsh mountain.

Even from the gossip of Baden I could learn no more about her than that she was a Sicilian countess of great wealth, and a widow; that she was intimately received into the very highest circles—even of royalty—and constantly was seen driving in the carriage of the Archduchess. It was, then, possible that I might be mistaken, after all! Great people are not accessible so easily.

I tried in various quarters to get presented to her—for she showed not the slightest sign of having ever met me —but failed everywhere: they who knew her did not do so intimately enough to introduce me.

The reminiscences I have just jotted down have made me miserably feverish and ill; for, although I now begin to doubt that I ever saw this countess before, the sad story of Caroline Graham is ever present to my mind—a terrible type of the fortune of many a fair English girl left to the merciless caprice of a foreign husband!

I am not bigot enough to fancy that happy, eminently happy, marriages do not exist abroad as well as with us; but I am fully minded to say that the individuals should be of the same nation, reared in the midst of the same traditions, imbued with feelings that a common country, language, and religion bestow.

I know of nothing that presents so pitiable a picture of

unhappy destiny, as a fair and delicately-minded English girl the wife of a foreigner! How I wish to resolve my doubts in this case! for although I began this memorandum fully persuaded it was Caroline Graham that I had seen, every line I write increases my uncertainty.

CHAPTER VIII.

It was with a rare audacity that the devil pitched his tent in Baden! Perhaps on the whole continent another spot could not be found so fully combining, in a small circuit, as many charms of picturesque scenery; and it was a bold conception to set down vice, in all its varieties, in the very midst of—in open contrast, as it were, to—a scene of peaceful loveliness and beauty.

I do confess myself one of those who like living figures in a landscape. I like not only those groupings which artists seem to stereotype, so nearly alike they all are, of seated foreground figures, dark-shadowed observers of a setting sun, or coolly watering cattle beneath a gushing fountain. I like not merely the red-kirtled peasant knee-deep in the river, or the patient fisherman upon his rock; but I have a strong regard—I mean here, where the scene is Nature's own, and not on canvas—a strong regard for those flitting glimpses of the gayer world which in the brightest tints that fashion sanctions, are caught, now in some deep dell of the Tyrol, now on some snow-peaked eminence of a Swiss glacier, beside the fast-rolling Danube or the sluggish Nile.

I have no sympathy for those who exclaim against the incongruity of pink parasols and blue reticules in scenes of mild and impressive grandeur. Methinks it speaks but scanty store of self resources in those who thus complain, not knowing anything of the feelings that have prompted their presence there. No one holds cheaper than I do the traveller who, under the guidance of his John Murray, sees what is set down for him through the eyes of the " Handbook "—mingling up in his addled brain crude notions of history and antiquarianism, with the names of inns and post-houses—counsels against damp sheets—cheating landlords—scraps of geology, and a verse of "Childe Harold." This is detestable: but far otherwise is the meeting with those whose dress and demeanour tell of the world of fashion—the intertwined life of dissipation and excess in solitary unfrequented places. Far from being struck by their inaptitude and unfitness for such scenes, I willingly fall back upon the thought of how such people must be impressed by objects so far beyond the range of daily experience, of objects whose wondrous meaning speaks to hearts the most cloyed and jaded, "as never man spoke." I can luxuriate in fancying how long-forgotten feelings, old memories of the past, long buried beneath the load of daily cares, come back fresh and bright under the influence of associations that recall purer, happier hours. I can dwell in imagination on the sudden spring made from the stern ordinances of a world of forms and conventionalities, to that more beautiful and grander world, whose incense is the odour of wild flowers and whose music is the falling cataract.

I love to speculate how the statesman, the wily man of forecasting thought and deep devices, must feel in presence of agencies which make those of mere man's contrivance seem poor and contemptible; and how the fine lady, whose foot knows no harder surface than a velvet carpet, and whose artificial existence palls by its own voluptuousness, contemplates a picture of grand and stern sublimity. Disguise it how they will, feign indifference how they may, such scenes always are felt, and deeply felt! The most accomplished lounger of St. James's Street does not puff his cigar so coolly as he affects to do, nor is that heart all unmoved that throbs beneath the graceful folds of a rich Cashmere. Now and then some Brummagem spirit intrudes, who sees in the falling torrent but a wasted "water-power:" but even he has his own far-reaching thoughts imbued with a poetry of their own. He sees in these solitudes new cities arise, the busy haunts of acting heads and hands; he hears in imagination the heavy bang of the iron hammer, the roar of the furnace, the rush of steam, the many-voiced multitude called by active labour to new activity of mind; and perhaps he soars away, in thought, to those far-off wilds of the new world, whose people, clothed by these looms, are brought thus into brotherhood with their kindred men.

I myself have few sympathies in common with these; but I respect the feelings that I do not fathom. "*Nihil humani a me alienum puto.*"

What has suggested these thoughts? A little excursion that I made this evening from the village of Lichtenthal towards the Waterfall, a winding glen narrowing as you advance; wilder too, but not less peopled; every sheltered spot having its own dwelling-place—the picturesque *chalet*, with its far-stretching eave, and its quaint galleries of carved wood, its brightly shining windows sparkling between the clustering vine leaves, and its frieze of Indian corn hung up beneath the roof to dry. Leaving the carriage, I followed the bank of the stream—just such a river as in my boyish days I loved to linger by, and fancy I was fishing. It was no more than fancy: for although my rod and landing-net were in most fitting perfection, my hackles and orange bodies, my green drakes and may-flies, all that could be wished, I was too dreamy and *distrait* for "the gentle craft;" and liked Walton better in his rambling discursions than in his more practical teaching. What a glorious day for scenery, too! Not one of those scorching, blue-sky, cloudless days, when a general hardness prevails, but a mingled light of sun and cloud shadow, with misty distances, and dark, deep foregrounds on the still water, where ever and anon a heavy plash, breaking in widening circles, told of the speckled trout: save that, no other sound was heard. All was calm and noiseless, as in some far-off valley of the Mississippi, a little surging of the water on the rocky shore—a faint melancholy plash—scarce heard even in the stillness.

I sat thinking, not sadly, but seriously, of the past, and of that present time that was so soon to add itself to the past; for the future I felt, by sensations that never deceive, it must be brief! My malady gained rapidly on me; symptoms, I was told to guard against, had already shown themselves, and I knew that the battle was fought and lost.

"It is sad to die at thirty," saith Balzac somewhere; and to the Frenchman of Paris, who feels that death is the cessation of a round of pleasures and dissipations, whose hold is hourly stronger; who thinks that life and self-indulgence are synonymous; whose ideal is the ceaseless round of exciting sensations that spring from every form of human passion nurtured to excess;—to him, the sleep of the grave is the solitude and not the repose of the tomb.

To me, almost alone in the world, to die suggests few sorrows or regrets; without family, without friends, save those the world's complaisance calls such; with no direct object for exertion, nothing for hope or fear to cling to; no ambition that I could nourish, no dream of greatness or distinction to elevate me above the thought of daily suffering; life is a mere monotony—and the monotony of *waiting*.

While watching the progress of my malady, seeing day by day the advancing steps of the disease that never sleeps, I recognise in myself a strange adaptation in my mind and feelings to the more developed condition of my illness. At first, my cough irritated and fevered me. It awoke me if I slept—it worried me as I read; my fast and hurried breathing, too, exciting the heart's action, rendered me impatient and discontented. Now, both these symptoms are in excess, and yet, by habit and some acquired power of conforming to them, I am scarcely aware of their existence. I have learned to look on them as my normal, natural condition. My cough on awaking in the morning—my hectic as night falls—only tell of the day's dawn and decline. I fancy that this dreamy calm, this spirit of submissive waiting that I feel, is dependent on my infirmity; for how otherwise could I, if strong in mind and body, endure the thraldom of my present life? The watchful egotism of sickness demands the mind of sickness.

In the whole phenomena of malady, nothing is more striking than the accommodation of the mind to the condition of suffering. I remember once—I was then in all

the strength and confidence of youth and health—discussing this point with a friend, a physician of skill and eminence, now no more, and was greatly struck by a theory
which was new, at least to me. He regarded every species of disease, from the most simple to the most compli-
cated, as a sanatory process, an effort—not always successful, of course—on the part of Nature to restore the
system to its condition of health. He instanced maladies
the most formidable, some of them attended by symptoms
of terrible suffering; but in every case he assumed to
show that they were efforts to oppose the march of some
other species of disorganization. So far from there being
any taint of Materialism in these views, he deduced from
them a most devout and conscientious belief in a Supreme
Power; and instead of resting upon Contrivance and
Design as the great attributes of the Deity, he went further, and made the Forethought, the Providence of God
for His creatures, the great object of his wonderment and
praise. His argument, if I dare trust my memory, was
briefly this: the presence of a superintending guardian
spirit, ever watchful to avert evil from its charge, is the
essential difference which separates every object of God's
creation from the mere work of man's hand. The ingenuity that contrived the mechanism of a steam-engine or
a clock was yet unable to endow the machinery with latent
powers of reparation; secret resources against accident
or decay, treasured up for the hour of necessity, and not
even detectable, if existent, before the emergency that
evoked them. Not so with the objects of creation. *They*
are each and all, according to various laws, provided with
such powers; their operations, whether from deficient
energy or misdirection, constituting what we call disease.
What is dropsy, for instance, save the resolution of an
inflammatory action that would almost inevitably prove
fatal? Formidable as the malady is, it yet affords time for
treatment; its march is comparatively slow and uniform,
whereas the disease that originated it would have caused
death, if effusion of fluid had not arrested the violence
of the inflammation.

Take the most simple case—a wounded blood-vessel, a

cut finger: by all the laws of hydraulics, the blood must escape from this small vessel, and the individual bleed to death as certainly, though not so speedily, as from the largest artery. But what ensues? after a slight loss of blood, the vessel contracts—a coagulum forms—the bleeding is arrested—the coagulum solidifies and forms a cicatrix; and the whole of these varied processes—a series of strange and wonderful results—will follow, without any interference of the will, far less any aid from the individual himself, being powers inherent in the organization, and providentally stored up for emergency.

The blood poured out upon the brain from an apoplectic stroke must, and does, prove fatal, save when the *vis medicatrix* is able to interpose in time, by encircling the fluid, enclosing it with a *sac*, and subsequently by absorption removing the extraneous pressure. All these are vital processes, over which the sufferer has no control—of which he is not even conscious.

The approach of an abscess to the surface of the body, by a law similar to that which determines the approach of a plant to the surface of the earth—the reparation of a fractured bone, by the creation and disposition of elements not then existing in the body—and many similar cases, warranted him in assuming that all these processes were exactly analogous to what we call disease, being disturbances of the animal economy accompanied by pain; and that disease of every kind was only a curative effort, occasionally failing from insufficient energy—occasionally from the presence of antagonistic agency,—and occasionally from our ignorance of its tendency and object.

I feel I have been a lame expositor of my friend's theory. I have omitted many of his proofs—some of them the best and strongest. I have, besides, not adverted to objections which he foresaw and refuted. Indeed, I fell into the digression without even knowing it, and I leave it here in the same fashion. I fancy a kind of comfort in the notion that my malady is, at least, an attempt at restoration. The idea of decay—of declining slowly away, leaf by leaf, branch by branch—is very sad; and even this conceit is not without its consolation.

And now to wander homewards. How houseless the man is who calls his inn his home! It was all very well for Sir John to say, "I like to take mine ease in mine inn;" and in his day the thing was practicable. The little parlour, with its wainscot of walnut-wood and its bright tiles, all shining in the tempered light through the diamond-paned window; the neatly-spread table, where smoked the pasty of high-seasoned venison, beside the tall cup of sack or canary; and the buxom landlady herself, redolent of health, good spirits, and broad jest;—these were all accessories to that abandonment to repose and quiet so delightful to the weary-minded. But think of some "Cour de Russie," some "Angelo d'Oro," or some "Schwarzen Adler," all alive with dusty arrivals and frogged couriers—the very hall a fair, with fifty bells, all ringing; postboys blowing—whips cracking—champagne corks flying—and a babel of every tongue in Europe, making a thorough-bass din that would sour a saint's temper! . . . . .

I'll leave at once—I'll find some quiet little gasthaus in the Tyrol for a few weeks, till the weather moderates, and it becomes cool enough to cross the Alps—and die!

CHAPTER IX.

THESE watering-place doctors have less tact than their *confrères* elsewhere : their theory is, "THE WELLS AND AMUSEMENT;" they never strain their faculties to comprehend any class but that of hard-worked, exhausted men of the world, to whom the regularity of a Bad-ort, and the simple pleasures it affords, are quite sufficient to relieve the load of over-taxed minds and bodies. The "distractions" of these places suit such people well ; the freedom of intercourse, which even among our straight-laced countrymen prevails, is pleasant. My Lord refreshes in the society of a clever barrister, or an amusing essayist of the *Quarterly*. The latter puts forth all his agreeability for the delectation of a grander audience than he ever had at home. But to one who has seen all these ranks and conditions of men—who finds nothing new in the *morgue* of the Marquis, or the last *mot* of the Bench—it is somewhat too bad to be told that such intercourse is a part of your treatment.

My worthy friend Dr. Guckhardt has mistaken me ; he fancies my weariness is the result of solitude, and that my exhaustion is but *ennui ;* and, in consequence, has he gone about on the high roads and public places inquiring if any one knows Horace Templeton, who is "sick and ill." And here is the fruit ; a table covered with visiting cards and scented notes of inquiry. My Lord Tollington—a Lord of the Bedchamber, a dissolute old fop—very amusing to very young men, but intolerable to all who have seen anything themselves. Sir Harvey Clifford, a Yorkshire Jesuit, who travels with a *socius* from Oscot and a whole library of tracts controversial. Reginald St. John, a "levanter" from the Oaks. Colonel Morgan O'Shea, absent without

leave for having shot his father-in-law. Such are among
the first I find. But whose writing is this? . . . . I know
the hand well . . . . Frank Burton, that I knew so well
at Oxford! Poor devil! he joined the 9th Lancers when
he came of age, and ran through everything he had in the
world in three years. He married a Lady Mary somebody, and lives now on her family. What is his note
about?

"DEAR TEMPY,

"I have just heard of your being here, and would have
gone over to see you, but have sprained my ancle in a
hopping-match with Kubetskoi—walked into him for two
hundred, nevertheless. Come and dine with us to-day at
the France, and we'll show you some of the folk here.
That old bore, Lady Bellingham Blakely, is with us, and
gives a pic-nic on Saturday at the Waterfall—rare fun for
you, who like a field-day of regular quizzes! Don't fail—
sharp seven—and believe me,

"Yours,

"F. B."

This requires but brief deliberation; and so, my dear
Frank, you must excuse my company, both at dinner and
picnic. What an ass he must be to suppose that a man
of thirty has got no farther insight into the world, and
knows no more of its inhabitants, than a boy of eighteen!
Those "quizzes," doubtless, had been very amusing to me
once—just as I used to laugh at the "School for Scandal"
the first fifty times I saw it; but now that I have *épuisé
les ridicules*—have seen every manner of absurdity the
law of Chancery leaves at large—why hammer out the
impression by repetition?

What is here by way of postcript?

"Lady B. has made the acquaintance of a certain
Sicilian Countess, the handsomest woman here, and has
engaged her for Saturday. If you be the man you used
to be, you'll not fail to come."

"DEAR F——

"I cannot dine out. I can neither eat, drink, nor talk

nor can I support the heat or 'confuz' of a dinner; but, if permitted, will join your party on Saturday for half an hour.

"Yours truly,

"H. TEMPLETON."

Now has curiosity—I have no worthier name to bestow on it—got the better of all my scruples and dislikes to such an agglomeration as a picnic? Socially I know nothing so bad; the liberty is license, and the license is an intolerable freedom, where only the underbred are at ease. *N'importe*—I'll go; for while I now suspect that I was wrong in believing the Countess to have been my old acquaintance Caroline Graham, I have a strange interest, at least, in seeing how one so like her, externally, may resemble her in traits of mind and manner. And then I'll leave Baden.

I am really impatient to get away. I feel—I suppose there is nothing unusual in the feeling—that, as I meet acquaintances, I can read in their looks those expressions of compassion and pity by which the sick are admonished of their hopeless state; and for the very reason that I can dare to look it steadily in the face myself, I have a strong repugnance to its being forcibly placed before me. My greatest wish to live—if it ever deserved the name of wish—is to see the upshot of certain changes that time inevitably will bring out. I have watched the game in some cases so closely, I should like to know who rises the winner.

What will become of France under a regency? How will the new government turn the attention of the *mauvaises têtes*, and where will they carry their arms? What will Austria do, when the Pope shall have given the taste for free institutions, and the Italians fancy that they are strong enough for self-government? What America, when the government of her newly acquired territory must be a military dictation, with a standing army of great strength? What Ireland, when the landlords, depressed by an increasing poor-rate, have brought down the gentry to a condition of mere subsistence, with Romanism hourly assuming a bolder, higher tone, dictating its terms with the Minister, and treating the Government *de pair?*

What Prussia, when democracy grows quicker, when Constitutional Liberty and Freedom of the Press get a-head of the Censor?

For Belgium and Switzerland I have little interest. Priest-ridden and mob-ridden, they may indulge their taste for domestic quarrel so long as a general war is remote; let *that* come, and their small voices will be lost in the louder din of far different elements.

As for the Peninsula, Spain and Portugal are in as miserable a plight as free institutions combined with Popery can make them. If Romanism is to be the religion of the State, let it be allied with Absolutism. The right to think, read, and speak are incompatible with the dictates of a Church that forbids all three. Rome is the type. It is a grand and a stupendous tyranny. *Gare!* to those who try to make it a popular rule!

So . . . I find that all Baden is full of our great picnic! Ours, I say, for here lies Lady B—— B——'s respectful compliments, &c., and my own replication is already delivered. It seems that we have taken the true way to create popular interest, by trespassing on popular enjoyment. We have engaged M. Gougon, the *chef* of the Cursaal; engaged the band who usually perform before the promenade; engaged all the saddle-horses, and most of the carriages—in fact, we have enlisted everything save the *genius loci*, the hump-backed croupier of the roulette-table.

Why we should travel twelve miles or so, out of our way, to bring Baden with us I cannot so clearly see. Why we cannot be satisfied with vice without a change of *venue* I do not understand. But with this I have nothing to do. Like the Irishman, "I am but a lodger." Indeed, I believe my own poor presence was less desired at this *fête* than that of my London phaeton and my two black ponies, which, I am told, are very much admired here—a certain sign that they are not in the most correct taste. However, I have my revenge. As Hussars, when invited to dine out at questionable places, always appear in plain clothes, so shall I come to the rendezvous in a *fiacre;* though, I own, it is very like obtaining a dinner under false pretences.

Already the little town is astir; servants are hastening to and fro; ominous-looking baskets and hampers are seen to pass and repass; strange quadrupeds are led by as saddle-horses, their gay head-stalls and splendid saddle-cloths scarce diverting the eye from "groggy" fore-legs and drawn-up quarters; curiously dressed young gentlemen, queer combinations of Jockeyism with an Arcadian simplicity, stand in groups about; and, now and then, a carriage rolls by, and disappears up some steep street in search of its company.

Ah! there go the Tollingtons! and in a "conveniency," too, they'd scarcely like to be seen with in Hyde Park. What a droll old rattle-trap! and what a pair of wretched hacks to draw it! After all, one cannot help avowing that these people, seated there in that most miserable equipage, where poverty exhibits its most ludicrous of aspects, even there they preserve as decisive an air of class and rank as—as—yes, I have found the exact equivalent—as almost every foreigner seated in a handsome carriage does of the opposite. Prejudice, bigotry, narrow-mindedness, or anything else of the same kind it may be; but, after a great part of a life spent abroad, my testimony is, that for one person of either sex, whose appearance unmistakably pronounces condition, met, abroad—I care not where—at least one hundred are to be seen in England. So much for the nation of shopkeepers!

Ah! a tandem, by Jove! and rather well got up. Of course it could be no other than Burton—"the ruling passion strong in 'debt!'" Well, he may have forgotten his creditors, but he has not forgotten how to hold the ribbons.

What's this heavy old coach with a cabriolet over the rumble?—the Russian minister, Kataffsky! Lord bless us! from all the strong braces and bars of wood and iron, one would say that it was built to stand a journey to Siberia. Who knows but it may travel that road yet! . . . . Pretty woman the Princess, but with all the characteristic knavery of her race in the eyes. Paul was right when he refused to license Jews in Russia, because he knew his subjects would cheat *them!*

"*Bon jour, marquis.*" Monsieur de Tavanne, a very absurd but a chivalrous Frenchman of the old school. They say that, meeting the late Duc d'Orléans at Lady Grenville's, he took a very abrupt leave, expressing as his reason that he did not know her ladyship received *des gens comme cela.*"

A Vienna *coupé*, with a Vienna coachman, and a Vienna countess inside, are very distinctive in their way. The Grafin von Löwenhaufen, one of those pretty *intriguantes* of modern political warfare who frequent watering-places and act as the tirailleurs for Metternich and Guizot. Talleyrand avowed the great advantage of such assistance, which he said was impossible for an English minister, for "les Anglaises" always fell in love and blabbed!

Here comes a showy affair!—a real landau with four horses, as fine as bouquets and worsted tassels can make them! No mistaking it—*Erin go bragh!* Sir Roger M'Causland and my lady and the four Misses and Master M'Causland. They are the invincibles of modern travel; they have stormed every court in Europe, and are the terror of Grand Maréchals from Naples to the Pole. Heaven help the English Minister in whose city they squat for a winter! He would have less trouble with a new tariff or a new boundary than in arranging their squabbles with court functionaries and the police. Sir Roger *must* know the King and his Ministers, and expound to them his own notions of the government, with divers hints about free trade and other like matters. My lady *must* be invited to all court balls and concerts, and a fair proportion of dinners; and this, *de droit*, because "the M'Causland" was a King of Ballyshandera in the year 4, and my lady herself being an O'Dowde, also of blood royal. People may laugh at these absurd, shameless pretensions, but "*il rit le mieux qui rit le dernier,*" says the proverb; and if the sentiment be one the M'Causlands' dignity permit, they have the right to laugh heartily. Boredom, actual boredom—a perseverance that is dead to all shame—a persistence that no modesty rebukes—a steady resolve to push forward, wins its way socially as well as strategically; and even the folding-doors of court saloons fly open before its magic sesame.

And who are these gay equestrians with prancing hackneys, flowing plumes, and flaunting habits?—The Fothergills, four handsome, dashing, *effrontés* girls, who, under the mock protection of a small schoolboy brother, are really escorted by a group of moustachioed heroes, more than one of whom I already recognize as scarcely fit company for the daughters of an English church dignitary. *Mais que voulez-vous?* They would not visit the curate's wife and sister in Durham, but they will ride out at Baden with blacklegs and swindlers! The Count yonder, Monsieur de Mallenville, is a noted character in Paris, and is always attended, when there, by an emissary of the police, who, with what Alphouse Karr calls an *empressement de bonne compagnie,* never leaves him for a moment.

And here we have the " dons " of the entertainment, la Princesse de Rubetzki, as pretty a piece of devilry as ever Poland manufactured to sow treason and disaffection, accompanied by her devoted admirer the Austrian general, Count Cohary. Poor fellow! all his efforts to appear young and *volage* are as nothing to the difficulties he endures in steering between the fair Princess's politics and her affection. An Austrian of the *vieille roche,* he is shocked by the Liberalism of his lady-love; and yet, with Spielberg before him, he cannot tear himself away.

They who are not acquainted with the world of the Continent may think it strange that society, even in a watering-place, should assemble individuals so different in rank and social position; but a very little experience will always show that intercourse is really as much denied between such parties as though they were in different hemispheres. As the Rhone rolls its muddy current through the blue waters of the Lake of Geneva, and never mingles its turbid stream with the clear waves beside it, so these people are seen pouring their flood through every assemblage, and never disturbing the placid surface in their course. To effect this, two requisites are indispensable to the company—a very rigid good-breeding and a very lax morality. No one can deny that both are abundant.

And here, if I mistake not, comes my own *char-à-banc*. Truly, my excellent valet has followed my directions to the letter. I said, "Something of the commonest," and he has brought me a *fiacre* that seems as moribund and creaky as myself. No matter, I am ready. And now to be off!

CHAPTER X.

Now has there happened to me one of the strangest
adventures of my strange life, and before I sleep I have
determined to note it down, for no other reason than this:
that my waking thoughts to-morrow will refuse to credit
mere memory, without some such corroboration. Nay,
I have another witness—this glove!

Were it not for this, I should have chronicled our *fête*,
which really was far more successful than such things
usually are. Not only was there no *contretemps*, but all
went off well and pleasantly. The men were witty and
good-tempered; the women—albeit many of them handsome—were *aimable*, and disposed to be pleased; the
weather and the champagne were perfect. They who
could eat—which I couldn't—say that Gougon was
admirable; and the band played some of Donizetti's
pieces with great precision and effect. *Ainsi*, the elements
were all favourable; each instrument filled its part; and
the *ensemble* was good—rather a rare event where people
come out expressly bent on enjoyment, and determined to
take pleasure by storm. Premeditated happiness, like
marriage for love, is often too much premeditated. Here,
however, " the gods were propitious." Unlike most
picnics, there neither was rain nor rancour; and con-
sidering that we had specimens of at least half-a-dozen
different nationalities, and frequently as many different
languages going at once, there was much amusing
conversation, and a great deal of pleasant gossipping
anecdote: not that regular story-telling which depends
upon its stage-effect of voice and manner, but that far
more agreeable kind of narrative that claims interest from
being about people and places that we know beforehand,

conveying traits of character and mind of well-known persons, always amusing and interesting.

There was a French secretary of legation for Berne, a most pleasant *convive;* and the Austrian general was equally amusing. Some of his anecdotes of the campaign of 1805 were admirable: by the way, he felt dreadfully shocked at his own confession that he remembered Wagram. The Countess Giordani came late. We were returning from our ramble among rocks and cliffs when she appeared. I did not wish to be presented; I preferred rather the part of observing her, which acquaintance would have prevented. But old Lady B—— did not give me the choice: she took my arm, and, after a little tour through the company, came directly in front of the Countess, saying, with a bluntness all her own,—

"Madame la Comtesse, let me present a friend whose long residence in your country gives him almost the claim of a countryman:—M. Templeton."

If I was not unmoved by the suddenness of this introduction—appealing as it did, to me at least, to old memories—the Countess was composure itself: a faint smile in acknowledgment of the speech, a gentle expression of easy satisfaction on meeting one who had visited her country, were all that even my prying curiosity could detect.

"What part of Sicily have you seen?" said she to me.

"My friend Lady B——," said I, "has made me a greater traveller than I can pretend to be: I have been no further south than Naples."

"Oh! I am not Neapolitan," said she, hastily, and with an air like disappointment.

I watched her closely as she spoke, and at once said to myself, "No! this is not, this cannot be, Caroline Graham."

We conversed but little during dinner. She evidently did not speak French willingly, and my Italian had been too long in rust for fluency. Of English she showed not the least knowledge. There were stories told in her hearing, at some of which to avoid laughter would have been scarcely possible, and still she never smiled once. If I wanted any additional evidence that she was not of English origin, chance presented one, as she was referred to by the Russian for the name of a certain Sicilian family where a "vendetta" had been preserved for two entire centuries ; and the Countess replied, with a slight blush, "The Marquis of Bianconetti—my uncle."

I own that, while it was with a sense of relief I learned to believe that the Countess was not the sister of my poor friend, I still could not help feeling something akin to disappointment at the discovery. I felt as though I had been heaping up a store of care and anxiety around me for one I had never seen before, and for whom I could really take no deep interest. One husbands their affections as they grow older. The spendthrift habit of caring for people without even knowing why, or asking wherefore, which is one of the pastimes—and sometimes a right pleasant one, too—of youth, becomes rarer as we go further on in life, till at last we grow to be as grudging of our esteem as of our gold, and lend neither, save on good interest and the best security. Bad health has done for me the work of time, and I am already oppressed and weary of the evils of age.

Something, perhaps, of this kind—some chagrin, too, that the Countess was not my old acquaintance, though, Heaven knows, it had grieved me far more to know she had been—some discontent with myself for being discontented—or " any other reason why,"—but so was it, I felt what in fashionable slang is called "put out," and, in consequence, resolved to leave the party and make my way homeward at the first favourable opportunity. Before setting out I had determined, as the night would be moonlit, to make a slight *détour* and thus avoid all the fracas and tumult of driving home in a mob; and, with this intention, had ordered my phaeton to meet me in the Mourg-Thal, at a small inn, whither I should repair on foot, and then make my tour back by the Castle of Eberstein.

A move of the company to take coffee on a rock beside the waterfall gave me the opportunity I desired, and I sauntered along a little path which in a few moments led me into the Pine Forest, and which, from the directions I had received, I well knew conducted over the mountain, and descended by a series of steep zigzags into the valley of the Mourg.

Although I had quitted the party long before sunset, the moon was high and bright ere I reached the spot where my carriage awaited me. Exhilarated by the unwonted exertion—half-gratified, too, by the consciousness of supporting a degree of fatigue I had been pronounced incapable of,—I took my seat in good spirits, to drive back to Baden. As I ascended the steep road towards Eberstein, I observed that lights were gleaming from the windows of the large *salon* of the castle, that looks towards the glen. I knew that the Grand Ducal family were at Carlsruhe, and was therefore somewhat surprised to see these signs of habitation in one of the state apartments of the château.

Alternately catching glimpses of and again losing these bright lights, I slowly toiled up the steep acclivity, which, to relieve my ponies, I ascended on foot. We were near the top, the carriage had preceded me some fifty yards or so, and I, alone, had reached a deeply-shaded spot, over which an ancient outwork of the castle threw a broad shadow, when suddenly I was startled by the sound of voices, so close beside me that I actually turned to see if the speakers were not following me; nor was it till they again spoke that I could believe that they were standing on the terrace above me. If mere surprise at the unexpected sound of voices was my first sensation, what was it to that which followed, as I heard a man's voice say,—

" But how comes this M. Templeton to be of any consequence in the matter? It is true he was a witness, but he has no interest in troubling himself with the affair. He is an invalid besides—some say, dying."

" Would he were dead!" interrupted a lower voice; but although the accents were uttered with an unusual force, I knew them—at once I recognised them. It was the Countess spoke.

" Why so, if he never recognised you? "

" How am I certain of this? " said she again. " How

shall I satisfy my own fears, that at every instant are ready to betray me? I dread his reserve more than all."

"If he be so very inconvenient," interposed the man, in a half-careless tone, "there may surely be found means to induce him to leave this. Invalids are often superstitious. Might not a civil intimation that his health was suffering from his *séjour* incline him to depart?"

The Countess made no reply; possibly the bantering tone assumed by her companion displeased her. After a brief silence, he resumed,—

"Does the man play? does he frequent the Saal? There surely are a hundred ways to force a quarrel on him."

"Easier than terminate it with advantage," said she, bitterly.

I heard no more; for, although they still continued to speak, they had descended from the terrace and entered the garden. I was alone. Before me, at the turn of the road, stood my servant, waiting with the horses. All was still as the grave. Was this I had heard real? were the words truly spoken, or were they merely some trick of an overwrought, sickly imagination? I moved into the middle of the road, so as to have a better view of the old "Schloss;" but, except a single light in a remote tower, all was shrouded in darkness : the *salon* I believed to have been lit up lay in deepest shadow. There was nothing I had not given, at that instant, to be able to resolve my doubts.

I walked hurriedly on, eager to question my servant both as to the voices and the lights; and as I went my eye fell upon an object before me in the road. I took it up—it was a glove—a lady's glove! How came it there, if it had not fallen from the terrace?

With increased speed I moved forward, my convictions now strengthened by this new testimony. My servant had neither seen nor heard anything; indeed, his replies to me were conveyed in a tone that showed in what light he regarded my questioning. It was scarcely possible that he could not have been struck with the bright glare that illuminated a portion of the castle, yet he had not seen it : and as to voices, he stoutly averred that, although he could distinctly note the clatter of the mill in the valley below us, he had heard no human sound since we left the little inn.

It was to no purpose that I questioned and cross-questioned. I soon saw that my eagerness was mistaken by him for evidence of wandering faculties; and I perceived, in his anxiety that I should return, a fear that my malady had taken some new turn. So far, too, was he right. My head was, indeed, troubled—strange fancies and shadowy fears crossing my excited mind as I went; so that, ere I reached my inn, I really was unable to collect my faculties, and separate the dream-land from the actual territory of fact. And now it is with painful effort I write these lines, each moment doubting whether I should not erase this, or insert that. Were it not for this glove, that lies on my paper before me, I should believe all to be mere illusion. What a painful struggle this is, and how impossible to allay the fears of self-deception ! At one moment I am half resolved to order saddle-horse and return to Eberstein—for what ?—with what hope of unravelling the mystery ? At the next I am determined to repair to the Countess's villa near the town, and ask if she has returned : but how shall I venture on such a liberty ? If my ears had not deceived me, she is and must be Caroline Graham ; and yet would I not rather believe that my weary brain had wandered, than that this were so ?

But what are these sounds of voices in the antechamber? I hear Guckhardt's voice!

Yes : my servant had thought it prudent to fetch the doctor, and he has been here and felt my pulse, and ordered cold to my temples, and a calming draught. It is clear, then, that I have been ill, and I must write no more !

CHAPTER XI.

GASTHAUS, ZUM BÄR, DALLAS, TYROL.

IT is exactly seven weeks this day since I last opened my
journal. I promised Guckhardt not to look into it for a
month, and so I have well kept my word! It would
seem, indeed, a small privation in most circumstances to
abstain from chronicling the ebbing hours of a life; but
Egotism is next of kin to Sickness, and I can vent mine
more harmlessly here than if spent in exhausting the
patience of my friends. Some listener must be found to
the dreamy querulousness of the invalid, and why not his
own heart?

Even to those nearest and dearest to our affections,
there is always a sense of shame attendant on the
confessions of our weakness, more so than of our actual
vices. But what a merciful judge is Self! how gentle to
rebuke! how reluctant to punish! how sanguine to hope
for reformation! Hence is it that I find a comfort in
jotting down these " mems " of the past; but from a
friend, what shaking of the head, what regretful sorrow-
ings, should I meet with! How should I hear of faculties
and fortune—life itself—wasted without one object, even
a wish, compassed! When I reflect upon the position in
life attainable by one who starts with moderate abilities, a
large fortune, reasonable habits of industry, and a fair
share of well-wishers, and then think of what I now am,
I might easily be discontented and dispirited; but if I
had really reached the goal, can I say that I should be
happy? can I say that all the success within my reach
could have stilled within me the tone of peaceful solitude
I have ever cherished as the greatest of blessings? But
why speculate on this? I never could have been highly

successful. I have not the temper, had I the talent, that climbs high. I must always have done my best *at once ;* put forth my whole strength on each occasion—husbanded nothing, and consequently gained nothing.

Here I am at Dallas, in the Tryol, a wild and lonely glen, with a deep and rushing river foaming through it. The mountain in front of me is speckled with wooden *chalets,* some of them perched on lofty cliffs, not distinct from realms of never-melting snow.

All is poverty on every side ; even in the little church, where Piety would deck its shrine at any sacrifice, the altar is bare of ornament. The curé's house, too, is humble enough for him who is working yonder in his garden, an old and white-haired man, too feeble and frail for such labour ; and already the sun has set, and now he ceases from his toil ; for the " Angelus " is ringing, and soon the village will be kneeling in prayer. Already the bell has ceased, and through the stilly air rises the murmur of many voices.

There was somewhat of compassionate pity in the look of the old man who has just passed the window ; he stopped a moment to gaze at me—at the only one whose unbended knee and closed lips had no brotherhood in the devotion. He seemed very poor, and old, and feeble, and yet he could look with a sense of pity upon me, as an outcast from the faith. So did I feel his steady stare at least ; for, at that instant, the wish was nearest to my heart that I, too, could have knelt and prayed with the rest. And why could I not? was it that my spirit was too stubborn, too proud, to mingle with the humble throng? did I feel myself better, or nobler, or greater than the meanest, there, when uttering the same words of thankfulness or hope? No, far from it ; a very different, but not less powerful barrier interposed. Education, habits of thought, prejudices, convictions, even party spirit, had all combined to represent Romanism to my mind in all the glaring colours of its superstitions, its cruelties, and its deceptions. Then arose before me a kind of vision of its tyranny over mankind,—its inquisitions, its persecutions, its mock miracles, and its real bloodshed ;

and I could not turn from the horrible picture, even to the sight of those humble worshippers who knelt in all the sincerity of belief.

I actually dreaded the sway of the devotional influence lest, when my heart had yielded to it, some chance interruption of ceremonial, some of those fantastic forms of the Church, should turn my feelings of trust and worship to one of infidelity and scorn.

There, all is over now, and the villagers are returning homeward—some to the little hamlet—others are wending their way upwards, to homes high amid the mountains—and here I sit alone, in my little whitewashed room, watching the shadows as they deepen over the glen, and gazing on that mountain peak that glows like a carbuncle in the setting sun.

It is like a dream to me how I have come to sojourn in this peaceful valley. The last entry I made was in Baden, the night of that party at the Waterfall. The next day I awoke ill—fevered from a restless night. Guckhardt came early, and thinking I was asleep, retired without speaking to me. He laid his hand on my temples, and seemed to feel that I required rest and quiet, for he cautioned my servant not to suffer the least disturbance near me.

I conclude I must have been sleeping, for the sudden noise of voices and the tramp of many feet aroused me. There was evidently something strange and unexpected going forward in the town. What could it mean? My servant seemed most unwilling to tell me, and only yielded to my positive commands to speak. Even now I tremble to recall the tidings—a murder had been committed! One of the guests at our late *fête*, a young Englishman named Lockwood, had been discovered dead on the side of the road about two miles from the Waterfall; his watch, and purse with several gold pieces, were found on his person, so that no robbery had been the reason of the crime. I remember his having come on foot, and hearing that I should not require my *char-à-banc* to return, he engaged it. The driver's story is, that the stranger always got out to walk at the hills, usually lingering slowly in his ascent of them ; and that at last, at the top of the highest, he had waited for a considerable time without his appearing, and growing weary of expectancy he returned, and at the foot of the hill discovered something dark, lying motionless beside the pathway; he came closer, and saw it was the stranger quite dead. Three wounds, which from their depth and direction seemed to have been given by a dagger, were found in the chest ; one entered from the back between the shoulders; the fingers of the right hand were also cut nearly through, as though he had grasped a sharp weapon in his struggle. Death must have been immediate, as the heart was twice wounded ; probably he expired almost at once. The direction and the position of the wounds refuted every idea of a suicide—and yet how account for the crime of murder ? The stranger was scarcely a week in Baden, not known to any one before his arrival here, and since had merely formed those chance acquaintance-ships of watering-places. There was not, so far as one could see, the slightest ground to suspect any malice or hatred towards him. The few particulars I have here set down were all that my servant could tell me. But what from the terrible nature of the tidings themselves, my own excitable state when hearing them, but, more than either, the remembrance of the dialogue I had overheard the night before—all combined and increased my fever to that degree that ere noon I became half wild with delirium. What I said, or how my wandering faculties turned, I cannot—nor would I willingly—remember. There was enough of illness in my ravings, and of method in them too, to bring Guckhardt again to my bedside, accompanied by a high agent of the police. The attempt to examine a man in such a state relative to the circumstances of a dreadful crime could only have entered the head of a *préfet de police* or a *juge d'instruction*. What my revelations were I know not ; but it is clear they assumed a character of independent fancy that balked the scrutiny of the official, for he left me to the unmixed cares of my doctor.

By his counsel I was speedily removed from Baden,

under the impression that the scene would be prejudicial to my recovery. I was indifferent where, or in what way, they disposed of me; and when I was told I was to try the air of the Lake of Constance, I heard it with the apathy of one sunk in a trance. Nor do I yet know by what means the police, so indefatigable in tormenting the innocent, abandoned their persecution of me. They must have had their own sufficient reasons for it; so much is certain.

And now, once more, I ask myself, is all that I have here set down the mere wanderings of a broken and dis-jointed brain? have these incidents no other foundation than a morbid fancy? I would most willingly accept even this sad alternative, and have it so; but here is evidence too strong to disbelieve. Here before me lies an English newspaper, with a paragraph alluding to the mysterious murder of an English gentleman at Baden. The dates, circumstances, all tally in the minutest particulars. Shall I discredit these proofs?

The Countess is married to the Marquis de Courcelles; a distant relative of the Archduchess, it is said. Let me dismiss the theme for ever—that is, if I can. And now for one whose interest to me is scarcely less sad, but of a very different shade of sadness.

This is my birthday, the 31st August. "Why had the month more than thirty days?" is a question I have been tempted to hazard more than once. Nor is it from in-gratitude that I say this. I have long enjoyed the easy path in life; I have tasted far more of the bright, and seen less of the shady side of this world's high road than falls to the share of most men. With fortune more than sufficient to supply all that I could care for, I have had, without any pretension to high talent, that kind of readi-ness that is often mistaken for ability; and, what is pro-bably even more successful with the world, I have had a keen appreciation of talent in other men—a thorough value for their superior attainments; and this—no great gift, to be sure—has always procured me acceptance in circles where my own pretensions would have proved feeble supporters. And then, this delicacy of health—

what many would have called my heaviest calamity—has often carried me triumphantly through difficulties where I must have succumbed. Even in "the House" have I heard the prognostications of what I might have been, "if my health permitted;" so that my weak point ministered to me what strength had denied me.

Then, I have the most intense relish for the life of idleness I have been leading; the lounging "do-nothingism" that would kill most men with *ennui* is to me inexpressibly delightful. All those castle-buildings which, in the real world, are failures, succeed admirably in imagination. I overcome competitors, I convince opponents, I conciliate enemies at will, so long as they are all of my own making; and so far from falling back disappointed from the vision to the fact, I revel in the conviction that I can go to work again at new fancies; and that, in such struggles, there is neither weariness nor defeat. A small world for ambition to range in! but I value it as Touchstone did his mistress—"a poor thing, but it was mine own."

It would be a strange record if a man were to chronicle his birthdays, keeping faithful note of his changed and changing nature as years stole on. For myself I have always regarded them somewhat like post-stations in a journey, ever expecting to find better horses and smoother roads next stage, and constantly promising myself to be more equable in temperament and more disposed to enjoy my tour. But the journey of life, like all other journeys, puts to flight the most matured philosophy, and the accidents of the way are always ready to divert the mind from its firmest resolves.

Tuesday morning.

When I had written so far last night, the arrival of a travelling carriage and four, with a courier preceding, caused such a commotion in the little inn that, notwithstanding all my assumed indifference, I could not entirely escape the contagion, and, at last, was fain to open my window and stare at the new arrival with all the hardihood that becomes him already in possession of an apartment. "I took little by my motion." All I saw was a

portly travelling carriage, heavily laden with its appurte-
nances and imperials, well-corded springs, rope-lashed
pole, and double drag-chains—evidences of caution and
signs of long-projected travel.

I might have readily forgotten the new comer—indeed,
I had almost done so ere I closed the window—had not
his memory been preserved for me by a process peculiar to
small and unfrequented inns—a species of absorption by
which the traveller of higher pretensions invariably draws
in all the stray articles of comfort scattered through the
establishment. First my table took flight, and in its place
a small and ricketty thing of white deal had arrived; next
followed a dressing-glass; then waddled forth a fat, un-
wieldy old arm-chair, that seemed by its difficulty of
removal to have strong objections to locomotion; and
lastly, a chest of drawers set out on its travels, but so
stoutly did it resist, that it was not captured without the
loss of two legs, while every drawer was thrown out upon
the floor, to the manifest detriment of the waiter's shins
and ankles. These "distraints" I bore well and equably,
and it was only a summary demand to surrender a little
sofa on which I lay that at length roused me from my
apathy, and I positively demurred, asking, I suppose,
querulously enough, who it was that required the whole
accommodation of the inn, and could spare nothing for
another traveller? An "English Prince" was the
answer; at which I could not help laughing, well knowing
that the title is tolerably indiscriminate in its application.
Indeed, I once heard Colonel Sibthorp called such.

It is all very well to affect indifference and apathy, to
pretend that you care nothing who or what your neighbour in an inn may be. This is very practicable where his
identity takes no more corporeal shape than No. 42 or 53
in some great overgrown hotel. But imagine yourself in
some small secluded spot, some little nook, of which you
had half fancied you were the first discoverer—conceiving
yourself a kind of new Pérouse; fancy, then, when in the
very ecstasy of your adventure, the arrival of a travelling
carriage and four, with a belted courier and a bearded
valet; not only are your visions routed, but your own

identity begins to dissolve away with them. You are
neither a hero to yourself nor to "mine host." His best
smiles, his deepest reverence, are now for the last comer,
for whose accommodation a general tribute is levied. Do
what you will, say what you will, there is no remaining
deaf to the incessant turmoil that bespeaks the great man's
wants. There is a perpetual hurry-scurry to seek this
and fetch that; soda-water—tea—champagne—a fire—hot
water—are continually echoing along the corridor, and
"the Prince" seems like some vast "maelstiöm" that all
the larder and the cellar contain can never satiate. Such,
certainly, the least exacting of men appear when under
the auspices of a courier and the host of a small inn.

The poverty of the establishment makes the commonest
requirements seem the demand of a Sybarite indulgence,
and every-day wants are luxuries where cleanliness is the
highest of virtues.

I was—I own it—worried and vexed by the clamour
and movement, that not even coming night calmed down.
The repose and quiet I had been so fully enjoying were
gone, and, in their place, the vulgar noises and tumult of
a little inn. All these interruptions, intimately associated
in my mind with the traveller, invested him, to me, with
a character perfectly detestable, so that there was
somewhat of open defiance in my refusal to yield up my
sofa.

A pause followed. What was to come next? I listened
and waited in half anxiety, wondering what new aggres-
sion might ensue; but all was still: nay, there was a
clattering of knives and forks, and then went the pop of a
cork—"the Prince" was eating. "Well," thought I,
"there is some vengeance here, for the *cuisine* is detestable." "His Highness" thought so too, for more than
one *plat* was dismissed, accompanied by a running com-
mentary of abuse on the part of the courier.

At last came a really tranquil moment. The cheese
had been sent away as uneatable, and the courier had
followed it, cursing manfully, if I might pronounce from
the odour wafted to my own chamber, not unreasonably.
"Mi Lor le Prince" was probably composing himself to a

siesta; there was a stealthy quietude in the step of his servant along the corridor that said so much. I had scarcely made the reflection when a tap came to my door. "The prince" wished for an English newspaper, and the host had seen two on my table. The *Post* and the *Chronicle* were both before me, and I sent them, half wondering which best might suit his Highness's politics.

Another tap at the door! Really this is intolerable. Has he not had my table, my arm-chair, my newspapers— what will he ask for next? Come in," said I, now trying English, after in vain shouting "*Entrez*" and "*Herein*" three times over.

An English servant entered, and in that peculiarly low, demure tone so distinctive of his caste, said—

"Sir Robert Chawuth presents his compliments, and begs to know if he may pay his respects to Mr. Templeton?"

"Is Sir Robert here? is that his carriage?" said I, hastily.

"Yes, sir; he came about an hour ago."

"Oh, very well. Say I shall feel great pleasure in seeing him. Is he disengaged at present?"

"Yes, sir, he is quite alone."

"Show me his apartment, then."

"So," thought I, as I arose to seek the chamber, "this time they were nearer right than usual; for, if not an 'English prince,' he has wielded more substantial power, and exerted a much wider sway over the destinies of the world than ever a 'foreign Prince' from the Baltic to the Bosphorus."

Strange enough, our last meeting was at Downing Street; he was then Minister. I waited upon him by appointment, as I was leaving England for the Prussian mission, and *he* desired to give me his own instructions before I sailed; and now, I visit him in a little Tyrol "Gasthaus," he destitute of power, and myself——

*   *   *   *   *

It would be presumptuous in one so humbly placed to hazard an opinion on the subject; but if I were to dare it, I should say that the statesmen of England possess a range of knowledge and a wider intimacy with the actual condition of the world as it is than any other class, in any country. I was greatly struck with this last evening. The topics wandered far a-field, varying from the Poor Laws to Hong-Kong, from the Health of Towns to the state of the Peninsula : Austria, Ireland, Switzerland, the Navigation Laws, the policy of Louis Philippe, and the rot in the potatoes ; and on each of these themes he not only spoke well, but he spoke with a degree of knowledge that smacked of a special study. "How comes it," I asked myself, " that this man, with the weighty cares of a mighty empire on his brain, has time to hear and memory to retain little traits of various people in remote quarters of the world ? How, for instance, did he hear, or why remember, these anecdotes of the present Landamman of Switzerland, Ochsenbein ? " And yet there were good reasons, perhaps, to remember them. The man who has personally shown the white feather will scarcely be courageous as the head of a government, though there is great reason to suspect that he may exhibit all the rashness of cowardice—its worst, because its most dangerous, quality.

I had often suspected, but I never knew before, how completely this Minister had usurped every department of the Cabinet, and concentrated in himself the Home, the Foreign, and the Colonial Governments. The very patronage, too, he had assumed ; so that, in fact, his colleagues were comparatively without influence or occupation. I confess that, on hearing him talk so unconcernedly of mighty events and portentous changes, of great interests and powerful states, my heart beat strongly with an ambitious ardour, and a feverish throbbing of my temples suggested to me that the longing for rank, and station, and power had not yet died away within me. Was it with serious intention that he spoke to me of again entering Parliament and taking office in some future arrangement, or was it merely from a sense of compassion that he ministered this meed of encouragement to the hopes of a sick man ? Whatever the motive, the result has been an increased buoyancy, more of vitality about me, than I have known for some time—a secret wishing for life and strength to "do something" ere I die.

He rather appeared pleased with a suggestion I threw out for augmenting the elective franchise in Ireland, by making the qualification "an intellectual one," and extending the right of voting to all who should take a certain degree or diploma in either the University of Dublin or any of the provincial colleges, all admitted as members of learned bodies, and all licentiates of law and physic. This would particularly suit the condition of Ireland, where property is a most inadequate and limited test, and at the same time, by an infusion of educated and thinking men into the mass, serve to counterbalance and even guide the opinions of those less capable of forming judgments. We are becoming more democratic every day. Let our trust be in well-informed, clear-sighted democracy, and let the transition be from the aristocracy to the cultivated middle classes, and not to the rule of Feargus O'Connor and his Chartists.

And now to wander down this lonely glen, and forget, if I may, these jarring questions, where men's passions and ambitions have more at stake than human happiness. Do what I will, think of what I will, the image of—Caroline Graham—yes, I must call her so—rises before me at every step. It is a sad condition of the nervous system when slight impressions cut deep. Like the diseased state of the mucuous membrane, when tastes and odours cling and adhere to it for days long, I suppose that the prevalence of such images in the brain would at last lead to insanity, or, at least, that form of it called monomania. Let no man suppose that this is so very rare a malady. Let us rather ask, "Who is quite free from some feature of the affection?" The mild cases are the passionate ardour we see exhibited by men in the various and peculiar pursuits in life ; the bad ones, only greater in degree, are shut up in asylums.

The most singular instance that ever occurred within my own knowledge was one I met several years back in

Germany; and as "thereby hangs a tale," I will set it
down in the words of the relator. This is his own recital
—in his own handwriting too!

There are moments in the life of almost every man
which seem like years. The mind, suddenly calling up
the memory of bygone days, lives over the early hours of
childhood—the bright visions of youth, when all was
promise and anticipation—and traverses with a bound the
ripe years of manhood, with all their struggles, and cares,
and disappointments; and even throws a glance into the
dark vista of the future, computing the "to come" from
the past; and, at such times as these, one feels that he is
already old, and that years have gone over him.

Such were to me the few brief moments in which I stood
upon the Meissner hill that overhangs my native city. Dresden, the home of my childhood, of my earliest and my dearest
friends, lay bathed in the soft moonlight of a summer's eve.
There rose the ample dome of the cathedral in all the
majesty of its splendid arch, the golden tracery glittering
with the night dew; here wound the placid Elbe, its
thousand eddies through purple and blushing vineyards,
its fair surface flashing into momentary brilliancy, as the
ripples broke upon the buttresses of that graceful bridge,
long accounted the most beautiful in Europe; while from
the boat that lay sleeping upon its shadow came the rich
tones of some manly voices, bearing to my ear the evening
hymn of my fatherland! Oh, how strong within the heart
of the wanderer in distant lands is the love of country!—
how deeply rooted amid all the feelings which the cares
and trials of after life scatter to the wind! It lives on,
bringing to our old age the only touch and trace of the
bright and verdant feelings of our youth. And oh, how
doubly strong this love, when it comes teeming with a flood
of long-forgotten scenes—the memory of our first, best
friends—the haunts of our boyhood—the feats of youthful
daring—and, far more than all, the recollection of that
happy home around whose hearth we met with but looks
of kindness and affection, where our sorrows were soothed,
our joys shared in! For me, 'tis true, there remained

nought of this. The parents who loved me had gone to their dark homes—the friends of my childhood had doubtless forgotten me. Years of absence had left me but the scenes of past happiness—the actors were gone. And thus it was as I looked down upon the city of my native land. The hour which in solitude and lowness of heart I had longed and prayed for had at length arrived—that hour which I believed in my heart would repay me for all the struggles, the cares, the miseries of fourteen years of exile; and now I stood upon that self-same spot where I had turned to take a farewell look of my native city, which I was leaving poor, unfriended, and unknown, to seek in Italy those opportunities my forlorn condition had denied to me at home. Years of toil and anxiety had followed; the evils of poverty had fallen on me; one by one the cheerful thoughts and bright fancies of youth deserted me; yet still I struggled on, unshaken in courage. The thought of one day returning to my loved Saxon land, rich in reputation, crowned with success, had sustained and upheld me. And now that hour was come—my earliest hopes more than realized—my fondest aspirations accomplished. Triumphant over all the difficulties of my hard lot, I returned, bearing with me the well-won spoils of labour and exertion. But, alas! where were they who should rejoice with me, and share my happiness? The very home of my infancy was tenanted by strangers; they knew me not in my poverty, they could not sympathize in my elevation. My heart sickened within me as I thought of my lone and desolate condition; and as the tears coursed faster and faster down my cheeks, how gladly would I have given all the proud triumph of success for one short and sunny hour of boyhood's bright anticipation, shared in by those who loved me!

Oh! how well were it for us if the bright visions of happiness our imaginations picture forth should ever recede as we advance, and, mirage-like, evade us as we follow! and that we might go down to the grave, still thinking that the "morrow" would accomplish the hopes of to-day—as the Indian follows the phantom-bark, ever pursuing, never reaching. The misery of hope deferred never equalled the anguish of expectation gratified, only to ascertain how vain was our prospect of happiness from the long-cherished desire, and how far short reality ever falls of the bright colouring hope lends to our imaginings. In such a frame of deep despondency I re-entered my native city—no friend to greet, no voice to welcome me.

Happily, however, I was not long left to the indulgence of such regrets; for no sooner was my arrival made known in the city than my brother artists waited on me with congratulations; and I learned, for the first time, that the reputation of my successes had reached Saxony, and that my very best picture was at that moment being exhibited in the Dresden Gallery. I was now invited to the houses of the great, and even distinguished by marks of my sovereign's favour. If I walked the streets, I heard my name whispered as I passed; if I appeared in public, some burst of approbation greeted me. In a word, and that ere many days had elapsed, I became the reigning favourite of a city in which the love of "art" is an inheritance: for, possessed of a gallery second to none in Europe, the Dresdeners have long enjoyed and profited by the opportunity of contemplating all that is excellent in painting; and, in their enthusiastic admiration of the fine arts, thought no praise too exalted to bestow on one who had asserted the claim of a Saxon painter among the schools of Italy.

To the full and unmeasured intoxication of the flattery that beset me on every side, I now abandoned myself. At first, indeed, I did so as a relief from the sorrowful and depressing feelings my unfriended solitude suggested; and at last, as the passion crept in upon and grasped my very heart-strings, the love of praise took entire possession of my being, and in a short time the desire for admiration had so completely supplanted every other emotion, that I only lived with enjoyment when surrounded by flattery; and those praises which before I heard with diffidence and distrust, I now looked for as my desert, and claimed as my right. The "spoiled child of fortune," my life was one round of gaiety and excitement. For *me* and for my amusement *fêtes* were given, parties contrived, and entertainments planned, and the charmed circle of royalty was

even deserted to frequent the places at which I was expected.

From these circumstances it may readily be believed
how completely I was beset by the temptations of flattery,
and how recklessly I hurried along that career of good
fortune which, in my mad infatuation, I deemed would last
for ever. I saw my name enrolled among the great ones
of my art—myself the friend of the exalted in rank and
great in wealth—my very praise, patronage. Little know
I that such sudden popularity is often as fleeting as it is
captivating, that the mass of those who admire and are
ever loudest in their praises are alike indifferent to and
ignorant of art. Led along by fashion alone, they seemed
delighted, because it was the rage to appear so. They
visited, because my society was courted by others; and if
their knowledge was less their plaudits were louder than
those of the discriminating few, whose caution and reserve seemed to me the offspring of jealousy and envy.

It is well known to almost all, how, in the society of
large cities, some new source of interest or excitement is
eagerly sought after to enliven the dull routine of nightly
dissipation, and awaken the palled and jaded appetite of
pleasure to some new thrill of amusement!—how one suc-
ceeds another, and how short-lived are all! The idol of
to-day is forgotten to-morrow; and whether the object of
momentary attraction be a benefactor of mankind, or some
monster of moral deformity, it matters but little, so that
for the hour he furnish· an article for the fashionable
journalist, and a subject of conversation to the *coterie;*
the end and aim of his being seems to be perfectly accomplished, and all interest for him as readily transferred
to his successor, who or whatever he may be, as though
his existence had been as unreal as the spectre of a magic
lantern.

Little did I suppose when, in the full blaze of my popularity, that to such an ordinance of fashion alone I was in-
debted for the proud eminence I occupied. I was not long
destined to enjoy the deception.

It chanced that about three months after my arrival in
Dresden, circumstances required my absence from the city for

a few days. The occasion which called me detained me
beyond the time I had calculated on, and it was not till
after a fortnight I reached my home.   I had travelled that
day from sunrise till late in the evening, being anxious, if
possible, to redeem a promise I had made to my friend
and patron, Count Lowenstein, to be present at a *fête* in
honour of his sister's birthday.   The weather had been
unusually hot and sultry, even for the season ; and although
I felt much fatigued and jaded, I lost not a moment on my
arrival to dress for the *fête*, over which, calculating on my
late career, I deemed my absence would throw a gloom.
Besides that, I longed once more to drink of that Circean
cup of flattery, for which my short absence from the city
had given me new zest; and it was with a high-beating
heart and fevered brain I hung upon my breast the many
crosses and decorations I had been gifted with in my hours
of brilliant success.

Lights gleamed brightly from the ample windows of the
Lowenstein palace.   Numerous equipages stood at the portico.   I followed the chasseur up the spacious marble
steps which led to the ante-chamber.   I stopped one moment before a large mirror, and almost startled at the
brilliancy of my dress, which, a present from my sovereign,
I now wore for the first time.   With a high-swelling heart
and bounding step—for all fatigue was long since forgotten—I approached the door ; and oh ! the throb with
which I heard my name now, for the first time, announced
with the title of " Baron," which his Majesty had conferred
upon me the day of my departure ! That name, which
alone had, talisman like, opened for me the doors of all
who were illustrious and exalted in rank—that name, which
heard, silenced the hum of voices, to break forth the
moment after in accents of praise and welcome ! Again
it rang through the crowded *salon*, and I stood within the
door.   Formerly, when appearing in society, the moment
I made my *entrée* I found myself the centre of a group of
friends and admirers, all eagerly pressing forward to pay
their homage to the star of fashion.   Now, what was my
amazement to mark no thrill of pleasure, as of old, ani-
mate that vast assembly !—not even surprise ! group after

group passed by me, as though I were unknown, and had no claim to their attention. It is true, I heard some friendly voices and kind inquiries; but I could neither distinguish the words nor the speaker. My brain was in a whirl; for, alas! long since had I learned to care less for the language of affection than the voice of the flatterer. I stood thunderstruck and amazed; and it was some minutes before I could, with any appearance of composure, reply to the salutations I met with. Something must have occurred in my absence to weaken the interest my appearance ever excited;—but what could that be? And the assembly, too! had my own baffled hopes lent their gloomy colouring to all around? I certainly thought it far less brilliant than usual; a sad and depressing influence seemed to pervade all the guests, which they appeared vainly to struggle against. Tortured with doubt and disappointment, I hastened through the crowd to where the Count was standing, surrounded by his suite. His quick eye instantly perceived me, and, familiarly kissing his hand to me, he continued to converse with those about him. Up to this moment I had borne all the chilling indifference of manner I met with, from the secret satisfaction that told me in my heart that he, my protector, my friend, would soon vindicate my claim to notice and distinction, and that, in the sunshine of his favour, I should soon receive the attention my heart thirsted for. But now that hope deserted me, the cold distance of his manner chilled me to the very heart's core. Not one word of kind inquiry, no friendly chiding for protracted absence, no warm welcome for my coming! I looked around on every side for some clue to this strange mystery; I felt as if all eyes were upon me, and thought for a moment I could perceive the sneer of gratified malice at my downfall. But no: I was unnoticed and unobserved; and even this hurt me still more. Alas! alas! the few moments of heart-cutting humbling misery I then endured, too dearly paid for all the selfish gratification I reaped from being the idol of fashion. While I remained thus the Count approached me, and, with something like his usual tone of familiarity, said,—

"Ah, Carl!—you here? You have, of course, heard of our sad disappointment?"

"No, my lord," I replied, with some bitterness of tone, "I have scarcely had time, for I have not been yet an hour in Dresden."

Without noticing either the manner of my answer or the allusion to my absence, the Count continued,—

"This evening we were to have had the happiness to have amongst us one who seems to be gifted with some magic power of diffusing delight and ecstasy on every side where she appears. Those whose hearts were cold to beauty in all others, have yielded to the fascination of hers; and the soul that never before was touched by melody has thrilled with transport at her heavenly voice. Divine La Mercia! the paragon of beauty and the soul of song! There, there stands her harp, and here you see her music; but she is absent. Alas! we have only the wand of the magician—the spell is not there."

In an instant the veil was lifted from my eyes; the whole truth burst on me like a lightning flash—the course of my popularity was run, the sun of my favour had set for ever.

The fatigue of my journey, the heat of the *salon*, the confusion of my mind, and the bitter conflict of my feelings, all conspired to unman me, and I sank upon a sofa. As I sat thus unnoticed (for the tone of the Count's manner had divested the few who were previously attentive of all interest to me), I overheard the conversation of those around me. But one name was mentioned, but one person seemed to engross every tongue or heart—that was La Mercia. From what I could collect it appeared that she, a most beautiful and interesting girl, had appeared at the opera a few evenings since, and by the charms of her surpassing beauty, as well as the surprising richness and clearness of her voice, had captivated the whole city, from the palace to the cottage. The enthusiastic repetition of her praises gradually led to regrets for her absence, and surmises as to the cause, while a young nobleman, who had just joined the circle said,—

"Trust me, La Mercia would have come if *she* alone

were consulted; but I fear that ill-tempered looking old fellow, whom she calls her 'Dottore,' has had much to say to this refusal."

"Yes," said another; "so late as yesterday evening, at the palace, when she was surrounded by several members of the royal family, eagerly pressing her to repeat a song she had just sung—just as she consented, a look from the 'Dottore' shot across the room and met her eyes; she immediately hesitated, begged to be permitted not to sing, and immediately afterwards withdrew."

"How strange!" said the nobleman who spoke before, "how very strange! It was but a few nights since, at the opera, I witnessed the deference and submission with which she addressed him, and the cold indifference with which he met looks and heard tones that would have made another's heart beat beyond his bosom. It must, indeed, be a strange mystery that unites two beings so every way unlike; one all beauty and loveliness, and the other the most sarcastic, treacherous-looking wretch, ever my eyes beheld."

The deep interest with which I listened to those particulars of my rival—for such I now felt her to be—gradually yielded to a sense of my own sunken and degraded condition; and envy, the most baleful and pernicious passion that can agitate the bosom, took entire possession of me: envy of one whose very existence one hour before I was ignorant of. I felt that *she—she* had injured me—robbed me of all for which life and existence was dear. But for *her*, I should still be the centre of this gay and brilliant assembly, by whom I am already forgotten and neglected: and, with a fiendish malignity, I thought how soon this new idol of a fickle and ungrateful people would fall from the pinnacle from which she had displaced me, and suffer in her own heart the cruel pangs I was then enduring.

I arose from where I had been sitting, my brain maddened with my sudden reverse of fortune, and fled from the *salon* to my home. In an agony of grief I threw myself upon my bed, and that night was to me like years of sorrowing and affliction. When morning broke, my

first resolve was to leave Dresden for ever; my next to
remain, until, by applying all my energies to the task, I
had accomplished something beyond all my former efforts;
and then, spurning the praise and flattery my success would
inspire, take a proud farewell of my fickle and ungrateful
countrymen. The longer I thought upon, the more was I
pleased with, this latter resolution, and panted with
eagerness for the moment of contemptuous disdain, in
which, flinging off the caresses of false friends, I should
carry to other lands those talents which my own was
unworthy to possess. It was but a few days before this
the Prior of the Augustine monastery had called upon
me to beg I would paint an altar-piece for their chapel:
they wished to have a kneeling figure of Mary, to whom
the shrine was dedicated; but the subject, being a favourite
one of Titian's, had at that time deterred me. Its difficulty was now its charm; and as I pondered over in my
mind the features I wished to transfer to my canvas, I
suddenly remembered a painting which I had had for
some years in my possession, and which, from the surpassing loveliness of the countenance it represented, as well
as the beauty of its execution, had long fascinated me. I
now reverted to it at once, and opening a secret drawer
in my cabinet, took out the picture and placed it before
me. It was a small and most beautifully painted enamel,
representing two figures—one that of an old and stern-
visaged man, upon whose harsh and severe features there
played a scowl of deadly hate and scorn: he stood, drawn
up to his full height, his hands and arms widely extended
before him, as if in the act of performing some mystic or
sacred rite over the lovely being who knelt at his feet in
an attitude of the deepest and most reverential supplica-
tion. This was a lovely girl, her age scarcely eighteen
years; her forehead, fair as alabaster, was shaded by two
braids of dark brown hair, which hung back in heavy
locks upon her neck and shoulders. Her eyes, of the
deepest blue, were upraised and tearful, and the parted
lips seemed almost to utter a murmured prayer, as her
heaving bosom told some inward anguish; her hands were
firmly clasped, but the arms hung powerless before her,

and the whole figure conveyed the most perfect abandonment to grief it was possible to conceive. Here were the
features, here the very attitude, I desired. Could I only
succeed in imparting to my Madonna the lovely and
sorrow-struck countenance before me, my triumph were
certain. I had walked every gallery of Europe from one
end to the other; I had visited every private collection
where a good picture was to be found, yet never had I
beheld the same magic power of conveying, in one single
scene, so much of storied interest as this small picture
displayed. The features of that beautiful girl, too, had
the semblance of being copied from the life. There are
certain slight and indescribable traits by which a painter
will, in almost every case, distinguish when nature, and
when only fancy, have lent the subject; and here, everything tended to make me believe it to be a portrait. The
manner in which I became possessed of it also contributed to invest it with a more than common interest in
my eyes. The circumstances were these:—When a very
young man, and only a short time settled at Rome,
whither I had gone to prosecute my studies as a painter,
the slender state of my purse had compelled me to take
up my residence in one of the less known suburbs of the
city. In the same humble dwelling in which I took
up my abode there lived an old and paralytic man,
whom age and infirmity had rendered bed-ridden for
years.

At first, my occupation being entirely without doors,
left me but little opportunity to see or know much of
him; but when winter closed in, and confined me whole
days to the house, my acquaintance with him gradually
increased, and, to my great surprise, I discovered in this
poverty-struck and decrepit old man one who possessed
the most intimate and critical knowledge of art; every
gallery was familiar to him—he knew the history of each
celebrated picture, and distinguished originals from their
copies by such traits of discernment as evinced the most
consummate intimacy with the deepest secrets of colouring, and, in a word, showed himself to be, what I afterwards learned he was, a most accomplished artist: but

the circumstances which threw him into his present mean
and wretched condition ever remained a mystery. Various
little acts of kindness and attention, which I had in my
power to bestow, seemed to make a great impression on
him, while my own friendless and solitary situation drew
me into closer intimacy with one who seemed to have
fewer of this world's comforts than myself. To him,
therefore, I confided all the circumstances which led me
to Rome—my ardent desire for distinction—my longing
for eminence in art: while he, by his advice and counsel,
which he was well qualified to afford, directed my studies
and encouraged my efforts.

Our acquaintance thus formed, rapidly ripened into
friendship, and it was with pleasure I hurried from my
gayer and more volatile companions to the poor and
humble abode, where my old and feeble friend awaited
me with impatience.

As the winter advanced, the infirmities of the old painter
rapidly gained ground; he became daily weaker, and, by
degrees, the calm serenity of his mind, which was his
most remarkable trait, yielded to fits of impatience, in
which, sometimes, his very reason seemed to struggle for
empire: and at such times as these he would drop hints,
and give vent to thoughts, that were awful and appalling
to listen to. It appeared to me that he regarded his present afflicted state as the dreadful retribution of some real
or imaginary crime; for, in addition to the unceasing
depression which seized him, his fears of death were incessant, and great beyond measure. Sometimes, the thought
that there was no future state would shoot across his
mind, and a species of reckless gaiety would follow; but
in a moment after, the strong and full conviction of his
self-deception would visit him—and then his agony was
frightful to witness. In the sad alternation of these states
of hope and fear, in which the former was, if possible,
more affecting to witness, weeks rolled on. One night,
when recovering from a nervous attack, which, by its
duration and severity seemed to threaten more fatally
than usual, he called me to him, and desired me to
bring, from a concealed drawer in his trunk, a small

ebony box clasped with silver. I did so. He took it with trembling hands, and placed it beside him on the pillow, while, with a voice scarcely audible from agitation, he whispered,—

"Leave me, Carl—leave me to myself! There is in this box what may meet no other eye than mine. And, oh! would to Heaven that its bright lightnings had struck and blighted me, rather than I should ever have looked upon it."

The energy with which these words were spoken seemed to weary and overcome him, and he was barely able to say,—

"Leave me now, my friend. But stay: ere you go, promise me—swear to me, as you hope—ay, as you hope your deathbed may be not like mine—swear, when all is at rest within this torn and afflicted heart, that you will, with your own hands, place this box within my coffin— swear to place it there unopened: better far you had not enjoyed the blessed gift of sight, than look upon what it contains. I grow weaker—promise me this."

"I do," I replied hurriedly. "I promise."

"Swear it," he said; while the large drops of sweat stood upon his brow, and his bloodshot eyes glared upon me like a maniac.

"I swear," said I, anxious to relieve the terrific convulsion which his eagerness brought on; "I swear." And as he lay back slowly upon the bed, I left the room.

When again, after a considerable time, I entered the chamber, he had turned his face towards the wall—his head buried between both his hands; while sobs, which he appeared struggling to control, burst from him at intervals. The casket lay locked beside him. I took it up, and placed it within my portmanteau; and, not daring to interfere with the course of that sorrow, the cause of which he had not confided to me, I stole noiselessly from the room.

When next I saw him he appeared to be somewhat better; but the feeble powers of life had received a severe shock, and his haggard and broken look showed how much a few hours had hastened the approach of death. That

evening he never once alluded to the subject which had
agitated him, and bade me " Good night" earlier than
usual, wishing to relieve his fatigue by sleep.—I never
saw him after.

I had scarcely composed myself to sleep, my mind full
of the events of the day, when an express arrived from an
English nobleman, who had been my most influential and
steadiest friend, requiring me immediately to set out for
Naples, to make a picture of his only daughter ere her
body was committed to the earth. She had died of the
malaria, and her funeral could not be long delayed. I
immediately set out, taking with me the portmanteau that
contained the casket, and such requisites for painting as I
could hurriedly collect. With all my anxiety to return to
my old companion, I was unable to leave Naples before
the tenth day; I then turned my face homewards, with a
heart beating with anxiety, lest his death should have
taken place in my absence. The diligence in which I
travelled was attacked near Calvi by banditti. Several of
the passengers, being well armed, made resistance, and a
dreadful conflict took place. Severely wounded in the
side with a stiletto, I remained for dead upon the ground,
and lost all remembrance of everything till the moment
I discovered myself a patient in the public hospital of
Naples.

Several weeks of fever and delirium had passed over
me, and I lay now weak and powerless. By degrees my
strength was restored, and as I lay, one day, meditating a
speedy departure from the hospital, the intendant of the
police came to inform me that several articles of value,
contained in a portmanteau bearing my initials, had been
discovered near the scene of the late encounter, where they
had probably been dropped by the robbers in their flight,
and that, on my identifying and claiming them as mine
they should be restored to me. Among other things he
mentioned the ebony casket. I dared not ask if it were
opened, lest my agitation might occasion surprise or suspicion, and promised to inspect them the following morning
and identify such as were my property.

The next day I appeared at the bureau of the police,

The portmanteau was produced and unlocked, and the very first thing I set my eyes upon was the picture. The case had been rudely torn open, and it lay there exposed to all. My promise—my solemnly pledged oath, came instantly to my mind, and all the awful denunciations the old man had spoken of, as in store for him who should look upon that picture! I was horror-struck and speechless, and only remembered where I was, as the *Commissaire*, who stood behind me and looked at it, asked if I were the painter? I replied not.

"The likeness is, indeed, wonderful," said he.

I started ; but immediately recovering myself, said,—

"You must be under some mistake. You could scarcely have seen the person for whom this was intended?" I said this because, from the attentive consideration I had given it, as well as the initials in the corner of the drapery, I perceived it to be one of the most beautifully executed enamels of Julio Romano, and must, at least, have been nearly two centuries old.

"Impossible I can be mistaken!" said he ; "that is not only the Comtesse d'Alvini herself, but there, and even more like, stands her uncle, 'Il Dottore Albretto,' as he was called. Why, I remember as well as though it were but yesterday, though I was only a boy at the time, her marriage—with one of your own profession, too. How can I forget his name!—ah, I have it—Antonio Gioventa! By the bye, they said, too, the union was none of the happiest, and that they separated soon after. But of that I know nothing myself, for they never appeared in Naples after the morning they were married."

How I longed to make one or two inquiries! but fear prevented me ;—fear lest my own ignorance concerning the history of the picture might be discovered, and I confess, too, something like dread ; for the evident age of the picture tallied but ill with the account the *Commissaire* gave of the characters represented ; and I longed for the moment I should put into execution, at least, so much of my promise as was yet in my power: putting it up, therefore, with such of my effects as I recognized, I returned to my hotel.

The entire evening I could think of nothing but the story of the *Commissaire*. The artist could have been none other than my old friend Nichola Calertio—for by this name I had known him,—and that lovely creature must have been his wife! And what was her fate? and what could have been the awful mystery that wrapt their history? These thoughts dwelt in my mind, and, framing ten thousand solutions of the secret, I at last sunk into sleep.

The following day I took my departure for Rome. On my arrival, what was my horror to discover that Nichola had died the day after my departure from Naples, and that he had been buried in the strangers' burial-ground; but in what spot, no one knew—nor had he one left who could point out his grave. Again my oath came to my mind, and I could not divest myself of the thought, that in the series of events which prevented its accomplishment chance had nothing to do; and that the hand of a guiding Providence had worked these apparent accidents for His own wise ends.

From that hour I guarded, how closely I cannot say, this picture from all human eye; but if I did so, the very impulse which drove me to conceal it from all others led me to look upon it myself. Like the miser who possesses a hidden treasure, ten thousand times dearer that it is known to him alone, I have sat, hour by hour, in the silent contemplation of it in my chamber; I have studied the features one by one, till I almost thought the figure lived and breathed before me; and often have I left the crowded and brilliant *salon* to seek, in the stillness of my own home, the delicious calm and dreamy tranquillity that painting ever inspired me with.

And so it had been my custom, when first I returned to Dresden, to sit for days long with that picture open before me. As a work of art, it possessed undoubted excellence; but I could not help feeling that its mysterious history had invested it with an interest altogether deeper and more powerful than the beauty of the execution could alone account for. This habit had been first broken in upon by the numerous and varied occupations my newly-arisen popularity brought upon me; and amid the labours of the painting-room, and the gay hours of fashionable dissipation, I had been now some weeks without once having seen it, when the events I have just detailed, and my determination to copy from it, brought it again fully to my mind.

The day which followed that long night of misery passed I know not how. When I awoke from the deep musing my thoughts had fallen into, it was already evening: the sun had set, and a soft twilight was sleeping on all around. I opened my window, and let the cool breeze of the evening blow upon my heated and fevered brain; and as I sat thus, lost in reverie, the last traces of daylight gradually faded away, and a thin, crescent-like moon showed itself over the hill of the Meissner. The city lay in deep shadow, and almost in silence; the mournful plashing of the river being plainly heard above all other sounds. There is something sad, and almost awful, in the sight of a large and populous city bathed in the silence and sleep of night; its busy voice hushed, its streets untrodden, or echoing to the tread of a solitary passer-by. To me this was now most welcome. The dreamy melancholy of my mind felt pleasure in the death-like stillness about me, and I wandered forth to enjoy the free air and balmy breeze upon the bank of the Elbe. After some time I crossed the bridge, and continued my walk through the suburb, intending to return by a beautiful garden which lies on that side of the river. As I approached the Elbe I was struck by the bright glare of light which, proceeding from some building near, illuminated the river nearly the whole way across, displaying upon its glassy surface several boats, in which the people sat resting on their oars, and scarcely moving in the gentle tide of the stream. I remembered for a moment, and then it occurred to me that the brilliant glare of light proceeded from the villa of Count Lowenstein, which stood upon a small promontory of land, about two miles from Dresden, this being the night of a private *soirée*, to which only his nearest and most intimate friends were ever invited. Report had spoken loudly of the singular beauty of the villa itself, the splendour of its decorations, the richness and taste of its furniture; and, indeed, around the whole character of the place, and the nature of the entertainments held there, the difficulty of *entrée*, and the secrecy observed by the initiated, had thrown an air of the most romantic interest. To these *soirées*, although honoured by marks of the greatest distinction, and even admitted to the closest intimacy, the Count never invited me, and in the days of my prosperity it had ever been with a sense of pique I called to mind the circumstance. Thither I now inadvertently bent my steps, and it was only when the narrowness of the path which lay between the hedge of the garden and the river required my caution in walking, that I remembered I must have entered the grounds, and was then actually within a few paces of the villa. While I stood for a moment, uncertain whether to retreat or advance, I was struck by observing that the boats had gradually and noiselessly approached the bank, a short way from where I was, and, by the attitudes of the figures I could perceive that they were listening most eagerly and attentively. I approached a few steps, till, at the sudden turning of the walk, I found myself beneath the terrace of a splendid *salon*, brilliantly lighted, and crowded by numerous and full-dressed guests. The rarest plants and most beautiful exotics stood in jars along the balustrade, diffusing their perfume around, and the cheerful hum of voices was heard in the still night air as parties walked to and fro upon the balcony. Suddenly the din of voices was hushed, those that were walking stood still, as if spell-bound,—a few seconds of the most perfect silence followed—then two or three chords of a harp, lightly but tastefully struck,—and then flowed forth a burst of melody, so full, so rich, so swelling, in the recitative of Rossini, " Oh, Patria!—oh, dolce ingrata Patria!"—that it filled my heart with transport, and my eyes with tears; and to my wounded and broken spirit there came a holy and delicious calm, as if by some magic spell another had divined my inward sorrow, and, in giving it expression, had given it relief.

The recitative over, oh with what triumphant gladness

came the brilliant *aria*, diffusing joy and happiness through every fibre of my frame! and, as one delicious cadence succeeded another, I felt my heart beat stronger and stronger against my side. My sorrow—my deep, depressing sorrow—was forgotten; a very heaven of brilliant hopes was opened before me, and peace flowed in upon my soul once more. The singer paused; then came a melting cadence, followed by a thrilling shake—so low, so plaintive, and so clear, I felt as if the last emotion of happiness fled with it. A silence of a moment followed, and then a thunder of applause flowed in on every side; and the words, "Divine La Mercia!" burst from every voice around.

I stood amazed and thunderstruck. The quick transition of my feelings had completely overpowered me, and I was only aroused by hearing a voice so near me as to startle me. It was the Count who spoke: he stood directly above me, leaning against a pillar of the portico, and supported upon his arm a lady, but, from her position, I could not catch her features. From his soft, low, and earnest tone of voice, it was plain the nature of his suit was one of heartfelt interest; while the few words she spoke in answer, from their soft tones and foreign accent, left me no doubt they came from La Mercia. I crept nearer the balcony, and, concealed behind the balustrades, waited anxiously to catch a glance at her as she passed. The light fell strongly from an open window upon this part of the terrace; and I could perceive, as she came forward, that, disengaging herself from the Count's arm, she assumed a more gay and lively manner. She was now within a few feet of where I stood eagerly waiting for the moment she would turn to enter the *salon*. She curtsied deeply to some persons in the crowd; and ere I could recover from the effect of the graceful and beautiful attitude she assumed, she turned. Merciful Heaven! could it be true? I almost screamed aloud, and, but for the hold I took of the balcony, should have fallen. The picture was La Mercia: the same calm brow, the same melting look, that beautiful outline of neck and throat, and, above all, that lovely contour of head, to see which once was never to forget. She was gone ! the guests disappeared one by one from the terrace, the *salon* became again crowded, and the windows were closed against the now chilling night air ; and yet so suddenly all seemed to happen, I could scarcely believe but that still that lovely voice and beauteous form were before me ; and I could not help thinking, as I left the spot, that to an excited brain and fevered imagination the likeness of the picture to La Mercia must have been owing, as with slow steps I retraced my way homeward.

The next morning early I left Dresden for the Augustine monastery at Tetchen, and ardently commenced the intended altar-piece ; but, fearing lest the likeness to La Mercia might have been real, I did not copy from the painting as I had resolved. For three months I laboured unceasingly ; and, whether from the perfect occupation of my time, or that the peaceful and tranquil life of the holy men with whom I lived had its influence, I know not, but my mind once more regained its calmness and serenity, and I felt almost happy again.

In this frame of mind I was when, one morning, one of the fathers, entering my apartment, informed me that my old friend and patron, Count Lowenstein, was about to be married. I started, and hurriedly asked to whom, while the deep blush which suffused my cheek told too plainly the interest I took in the answer.

"I know not," said the monk ; "but report speaks of her as eminently beautiful."

"Would you recognize the name if you heard it ?" I asked.

"I have heard it but once, but think I might remember it again," said he.

"Then it is La Mercia," I replied.

"The same—La Mercia was the name ; and they say a more splendid wedding Dresden has never witnessed than this will be."

I cannot explain why, but never did I feel, at any period of my life, so completely overcome as when I listened to this report. Never before had I confessed to myself how I had felt towards La Mercia, nor even now could I tell :

it was not love; I had never seen her but for a few brief seconds, and yet in my heart she lived, the guiding-star of all my thoughts and aspirations; and though my most sanguine dreams never anticipated my calling her mine, yet I could not bear the thought that she was to belong to another. I resolved at once to set out for Dresden, and, if possible, see her once before the wedding would take place. I thought it would be a balm to my feelings should I look upon her, before she was lost to me for ever, and I longed ardently to trace, with what calmness I was able, how far the likeness with the picture was real or imaginary. With these intentions I left the monastery that evening, and returned to Dresden.

When I reached home I learned that the Count had been married, and found upon my table a most pressing invitation from him to his *soirée* at the villa that evening. At first I resolved not to accept it. The full measure of my loneliness had never so pressed on me before; for although, in reality, La Mercia was not, nor could ever have been, aught to me, yet I felt as if my fate and happiness were, by some inexplicable ties, wound up with hers; and now that tie was to be broken. I had begun to believe that the extraordinary impression she had made upon my mind had entirely suggested the resemblance with the picture, which some chance trait of likeness might have contributed to, and I longed ardently to see her;—but then, to see her the bride of another! These conflicting thoughts agitated me during the entire day, and I knew not what to decide on.

When evening came I embarked upon the Elbe, and, after a half-hour's rowing, reached the villa of the Count. Lights gleamed from every window, and delicious music was borne on the night wind, that blew gently along the river. Numerous servants, in gorgeous liveries, passed and repassed along the spacious veranda, which ran the entire length of the building, carrying fruit, wine, and ices to those who preferred the balmy air and starry sky without, to the heat and glitter of the crowded *salon* within.

With difficulty I made my way through the dense

mass that filled the antechamber, and at length reached one of the reception-rooms, scarcely less crowded. On every side I beheld some of the highest persons of the city : groups of officers in splendid uniforms, ambassadors glittering in orders and crosses, distinguished foreigners, artists, authors, were all mingled together in thick profusion, enjoying the magnificence and splendour which unbounded wealth, guided and directed by the most cultivated taste, could create. Standing in mute admiration of a beautiful figure of Psyche, which seemed fresh from the chisel of Canova, I was roused by a voice addressing me, while at the same moment my shoulder was gently tapped. I turned;—it was the Count himself.

"Ah, Monsieur le Baron," said he, "'*Enfin après un an!*' as Racine has it. Where have you buried yourself and all your agreeability these ages past? But come, I shall not tax your invention for excuses and apologies; follow me—the Countess has heard me frequently speak of you, and longs to make your acquaintance. This way —after me as well as you can."

The friendly tone of the Count, as well as its being almost the first time of my being addressed by my new title, brought a deep blush to my cheek, which fortunately was unobserved as I followed him in the crowd. He passed through this room to one still larger, filled with parties playing at several small tables, and thence into an oval *salon*, where waltzing was going on. With great difficulty we got through this, and arrived at a curtain of white cloth, fringed at the bottom with deep and massive silver lace; this he drew gently aside, and we entered the boudoir. Upon a small ottoman, over which was thrown a rich Persian shawl, sat the Countess.

"Isadora," said the Count, as he approached—"Isadora, *carissima mia*, this is my friend, Carl Stelling."

She lifted her head from the picture she was showing to a lady beside her, and as her eye beamed fully upon me and her lips parted to address me, I fell fainting to the ground.

"It is!—it is!" I muttered, as the last ray of consciousness was leaving my whirling brain.

"' It is !—it is !' I muttered, as the last ray of consciousness was leaving my whirling brain."

When I recovered, the Count was standing over me bathing my temples. I looked wildly around. I saw we were still in the boudoir, although all but one or two had departed; and from the window, now opened, there came a cool and refreshing breeze. I looked anxiously around for the Countess: she stood at a table, her cheek deadly pale, and I thought her appearance evinced great agitation. I heard her, in a low whisper, ask,—

" What can this mean ? "

I immediately recovered myself sufficiently to say, that, overcome by the heat of the *salon*, in my then weak state, that I felt completely overpowered. But I saw my explanation seemed incomplete, and that some words must have fallen from me which I did not remember.

The Count, at the same instant, putting his lips to my ear, said,—

" Carl, this must be explained at another and more fitting moment."

This increased my agitation, for I now perceived that my merely being suddenly taken ill could never have given rise to such a feeling as all around seemed to labour under. Before, then, I could at all determine how to act, the Countess approached me, and in her softest and kindest manner, asked if I were better.

In a moment all my agitation was forgotten; and, indeed, every one of the party seemed to participate, as if by magic, in the balmy influence her few words shed around. Conversation soon resumed its course. For some time the Count's manner was constrained and uncertain, but that soon wore away as the joyous tone and sparkling gaiety of his lovely bride seemed to have their effect upon every one about her; and even I—torn, as I was, by feelings I could neither trace nor divine—felt under the mystic spell that so much beauty and grace diffused on every side. With a wonderful tact she alluded at once to such subjects that compelled me, as an artist, to speak, and speak warmly; and, seemingly, catching the enthusiasm from me that she herself had created, she spoke of Venice —its thousand recollections—its treasures of art—its rich historical associations—its ancient glory; and then, taking up her guitar, played with such tenderness and feeling one of the well-known gondolier *canzonette*, as made the very tears stand in my eyes.

The victory was complete: I forgot the past—I knew no longer where I was. A bright Elysium of bliss had opened before me; and even now, after years of such misery as few have known, I could say that one hour of such intoxicating happiness would be almost cheaply bought by even such affliction.

I started from my trance of pleasure on observing that the guests were taking leave. I at once arose, and as she extended her hand to me, I felt the blood rush to my face and forehead. I barely dared to touch it with my lips, and retired. I hurried from the villa, and springing into my boat, was soon landed at the bridge of Dresden.

From that time my visits at the villa were frequent; seldom a week elapsed without my receiving one or two invitations from the Count; and, at last, to such an extent did my intimacy proceed, and so superior in attraction was the society there, that for it I deserted all other, and only felt happy when with my kind patrons. During this, by far the most delightful period of my life, I was not entirely free from unhappiness. Sometimes the likeness of the Countess to the picture would appear to me so striking as not to be mistaken: one day particularly, when some sudden intelligence was brought to her that caused momentary alarm for the Count's safety, her pale cheek and quivering lip brought the portrait so perfectly before me, that I was unable to speak or offer her advice when she asked my opinion; and then, vague and horrid doubts, and a dread of some unknown and unforeseen calamity, would flash upon my mind; and those who have experienced how deeply they can be impressed by a presentiment of evil, can tell how little it is in their power to rally their spirits against terrors which take every or any shape. And while I reasoned with myself against what might be mere groundless fear, yet I never could look upon the picture and call to mind the deathbed sorrow of the old artist, without feeling that some dreadful fate was connected with its history, in which, as its mere possessor,

I might be involved. Sometimes to such a degree did this anxiety prevail upon me, that I had fully determined to show it to the Countess, and either endeavour to trace its history from her, or at once rid myself of all apprehension concerning it, if she disclaimed all knowledge of it; but then, if she really were connected with its story—if, as it was possible, a mother's fate (for the resemblance could warrant such a relationship) were wound up with the story,—what right had I, or how could I answer to myself, for the mere satisfaction of my own doubts, to renew the sorrows, and, perhaps, even be the means of publishing to the world the sad detail of forgotten crime or misfortune? Perhaps, however, the picture was not, as I supposed, an antique; it might be an admirable copy. But this idea was relinquished at once : the more I examined, the more fully did it corroborate my opinion of its being the work of a master. Such thoughts as these—and they grew upon me daily more and more—embittered the happiest moments of my intercourse with my friends; and often, when the merry laugh and the joyous glee which pervaded our parties at the villa were at the highest, I thought of that picture, and my heart sank at the recollection, and I would hasten to my home to conceal from every eye the terror and anguish these thoughts ever inspired me with.

One evening, when dressing for the Count's villa, I received a *billet*, written in pencil and evidently in haste; it came from himself, and informed me that the Countess, who had that morning made a short excursion upon the river, had returned home so ill that the entertainment was deferred. I was, however, requested to call the following morning, to take some sketches of Pirna from the villa, which I had long since promised to make for them. So completely had I withdrawn myself from all other society during my great intimacy with Count Lowenstein, that I now felt the *billet* I received left me unable to say where or how I should pass my evening.

In this uncertainty I wandered forth, and without thinking whither my steps led me, it was only on hearing the boatman ask if I were ready that I perceived that I had strolled to the steps beside the bridge, where I usually took my departure for the villa. Lost in reverie and led captive by habit, I had walked to this spot unconsciously to myself.

I was about to dismiss the boatmen for the night, when a whim seized me to drop on board and visit those small and wooded islands that lie about a league up the river. It was a calm and beautiful night; and in the wild and untrodden solitude of these romantic islands I remained till near midnight.

As we passed the grounds of the Count, I ordered the boatmen to land me at a spot remote from the house, whence I could proceed on foot, wishing to make some inquiry for the Countess before I returned home. They accordingly put me on shore at a small flight of steps which descended to the water's edge from a terraced path that ran a considerable distance through the park, and was concealed in its entire length by tall hedges of beech, completely overgrown with flowering creeping shrubs, and so impenetrable that, even in noonday, it was impossible for those without to see persons walking within, while the closely-shaven sod effectually prevented footsteps being heard. The moon was up, and nearly at the full, and all beneath me in the richly-ornamented flower-garden was bathed in a sea of mellow light. The marble statues that adorned the walks threw their lengthened shadows at their bases, while their own whiteness seemed purer and fairer than ever. The villa itself, half obscured by trees, seemed, in its tranquil beauty, the very emblem of peace; and as the pillars of the portico threw a deeper shadow, gave a broadness to the effect which struck me as wonderfully beautiful. I gazed around me with momentarily increasing admiration. The gentle murmuring of the leaves agitated by the breeze, and the plash of the river, made the silence around me even more striking. I stood lost in the enjoyment of the delicious repose of the whole scene, when a slight noise upon the gravel walk attracted my attention; I listened, and now distinctly heard footsteps approaching, and also the voices of persons whispering in a low and much-suppressed tone. They came nearer, and were now only concealed from my view by the tall hedge, beneath which they walked; and soon the shadow of two figures were cast along the broad walk in the bright moonlight. For a moment they stopped speaking, and then I heard a laugh in a low and under-tone—but such a laugh! My very blood ran chilled back upon my heart as I heard it. Oh, if the fiend himself had given that dreadful and heart-appalling laugh, it could not be more awful! It scarcely died away in the faint echo, ere I heard the sobs, deep and low, of another and far different voice. At this instant the figures emerged from the darkness, and stood in the bright moonlight. They stood beside an old and broken pillar, which had once supported a sun-dial, and around whose shaft the clustering ivy had wound itself. They were entirely concealed by large cloaks, which enveloped their entire figures, but still I could perceive that one was much larger and more robust than the other. This latter taking a small lamp, which was concealed beneath the folds of his cloak, placed it upon the pillar, while at the same instant the other figure, throwing off the cloak, knelt at his feet. Oh, that reason had left me, or that life itself had parted from me, ere I should look upon that scene! She—she who knelt and held her suppliant hands was La Mercia; and he who, now divested of his mantle, stood over her, was the dark and awful-looking man of the picture! There they stood. The dresses of both were copied to the life; their looks—oh, Heaven! their very looks were pictured as they stood. She spoke: and as she did so her arms fell powerless before her; he scowled the same horrid scowl of hate and scorn. My brain was turning; I tried to scream out, my voice failed me—I was mute and powerless; my knees rocked and smote each other; convulsive tremor shook me to the centre, and with a groan of agony I sank fainting to the earth.

The day was breaking ere I came to myself; I arose, all was quiet around me. I walked to the boat—the boatmen were sleeping; I·awoke them, and we returned to Dresden. I threw myself upon my bed—my brain seemed stupefied and exhausted—I fell into a profound sleep, and woke not till late the following evening. A messenger had brought a note from the Count—"The Countess is worse." The note detailed briefly that she had passed a feverish and disturbed night, and that the medical attendants had never left the villa. Was it then but a dream, my dreadful vision of the past night? and had my mind, sorrowing for the affliction of my best friend, conjured up the awful scenes I believed to have witnessed? How could it be otherwise? The *lillet* I received told most distinctly that she was confined to her bed, severely, dangerously ill; and of course watched with all the care and attention the most sedulous anxiety could confer. I opened the picture, and then conviction flashed with lightning's rapidity upon me, that it was not delusion—that no dream had brought these images before my mind. "Ah," I cried, "my friend, my patron, how have I betrayed thee? Why did I not earlier communicate the dreadful story of the picture, and thus guard you against the machinations by which the fiend himself has surrounded you? But then, what had I to tell? how embody the vague and shadowy doubts that took, even in my own mind, no palpable shape or form?"

That entire day was passed in alternate resolution and abandonment; now, determined to hasten to the villa, and disclose to the Count every circumstance I had seen, and then thinking how little such mere suspicion would gain credence, and how unfit the present moment to obtrude upon his breaking and distracted heart the horrid dread that haunted mine. Towards evening a messenger arrived, breathless with haste. He brought no note, but merely bade me hasten to the villa, as the Count wished to see me with all possible despatch. I mounted the servant's horse, and in a few minutes reached the place. Servants were running hither and thither distractedly. I asked, eagerly, How was the Countess? No one could tell, but all seemed to imply that there was no hope of recovery. I entered the large and spacious hall, and threw myself upon a sofa; and as I looked around upon the splendid hangings, the gilded cornices, and marbled pillars, and thought upon that sorrow such splendour surrounded, my heart sickened. A shadow fell upon the brightly polished floor. I looked up—a figure stood at the window of the hall, and stared me steadily in the face. The eyes glared wildly, and the dark, malignant features were lit up with a scornful scowl of more than human hate and triumph. It was the incarnation of the Evil One exulting over a fallen and lost spirit. A loud shriek rent the air behind me. I dared not turn my eyes from the horrid sight before me. "Oh, Heavens! it is true!—he is, he is the Tutore!" I cried, as the features, convulsed for an instant with fiendish triumph, resumed their cold and even more appalling aspect. A threatening gesture from his hand arrested me, as I was about to call aloud. My voice came not, though my lips moved. I could not rise from the seat—a dreadful scream rang through the building— another, and another followed—the figure was gone. At the same moment the Count rushed forward—his dress disordered, his hair falling loosely upon his shoulders— madness, wild insanity, in his look. He turned and saw me; and bursting into a torrent of hysterical laughter, cried out,—

"Ha, ha, Carl!—welcome to our abode of pleasure; here, all is gaiety and happiness. What sorrow ever crosses this threshold?" and then, with a sudden revulsion, he stared me fixedly, and said in a low sepulchral voice, "She is dead—dead! But the time is passing—a few minutes more, and 'twill be too late. This, Carl, will explain all. Take this, and this—these papers must be your care—promise me to observe them to the letter; they were her—her last wishes, and you knew her. Oh, is this a dream? it is too, too horrible to be real. Ah!" said he, after a moment's pause; "I am ready!" and springing from me wildly, rushed through the door towards the inner apartments.

I started up and followed him—I knew not which way he took in the corridor; and as I stood uncertain, a loud report of firearms crashed on my ear. I flew to the sick chamber—servants stood gasping and trembling without. I tore open the door; there, lay the Count upon the floor, his head rent asunder by the bullets from the pistol his hand still grasped. He had endeavoured to reach the bed, and fell half upon a chair. In the bed lay the still warm corpse of the Countess, beautiful as in life. I looked from one to the other; my scared and stony heart, turned to apathy by the horrors I had witnessed, gave no relief to its feeling in tears, and I spoke not as I slowly left the room.

For two days I spoke not to any one. A dreamy unconsciousness seemed to wrap my faculties, and I felt not the time passing. On the third day I rallied sufficiently to open the papers the Count had entrusted to me. One contained an affectionate farewell to myself, from the Count, with a dying bequest; the other, was in a lady's hand—it bore the Countess's signature; and here I discovered with surprise and horror, that to the performance of the rash act, by which the Count had terminated his existence, he was bound by a solemn oath. I read, and re-read, to assure myself of the fact. It was true! Such was the terrible promise she extorted from the wretched lover, under the delusive hope of their meeting in another and happier life. Then followed the directions for the funeral, which were minute to a degree. The bodies of both, when coffined, were to be placed in a small temple in the garden, near the river; the key of which was to be sent to a Dominican monk, who lived in an obscure part of the city. By him were the coffins to be closed, which it was strictly enjoined should be done by him, alone and unaccompanied, the night before the burial.

All was done as the wish of the deceased enjoined, and the key despatched by a trusty servant of my own to the friar, who appeared to be in expectation of it, and knew its import.

I sat in a lonely and desolate room, which had formerly been mine, in the villa of the Count: that long and dreary night the wind poured its mournful wailing through the pine-trees in dirgeful memory of him who was no more. From the window of the temple a bright light gleamed till near morning, when it gradually faded away. Thither I repaired at daybreak, with the household. All was still —the door lay open—the coffins were closed and screwed down. The friar was gone. We afterwards found that he had not returned to his lodgings in the city, nor was he ever after seen in Dresden. The bodies were committed to the earth, and I returned to my home alone in the world.

It was several years after this—the awful death of my earliest, best friend—that I arrived in Paris to exhibit, in the gallery of the Luxembourg, an historical picture, upon which I had laboured for years. I must be brief—my picture was exhibited, and my most sanguine expectations surpassed by its success; and in a few short days the whole scene of my early triumph was re-enacted. Praise and flattery poured in upon me; and as in Dresden before, so now in Paris, I became the fashion and the rage. But how changed was I! No longer exulting in my success and buoyant with hopes, I received all the adulation I met with, with cold indifference and apathy.

Among the many attentions which my popularity had conferred upon me, was an invitation to the Hôtel de Rohan. The duke, a most distinguished connoisseur in painting, having seen and applauded my picture, waited on me. Thus bound in duty, I went; and fatigued by the round of soulless gaiety, in what I could no longer feel happy, or even forgetful, I was retiring early, when the duke met me, and said—

"Ah, monsieur, I have been looking for you. The Comtesse de Julliart has desired me to present you to her; and when I tell you that she is the most beautiful woman in Paris, I need not say how much you must prize the honour among all the distinctions your talents have earned. Come this way."

I followed mechanically—my heart took no interest in the scene—and I only longed to be once more alone and unobserved. As I walked after the duke, he gave me a short account of the beautiful countess, whom he mentioned as the last descendant of an old and honoured family, supposed to have been long since extinct, when she, a few months before, appeared in Paris, and laid claim to the title. As she possessed unbounded wealth, and had no great favours to ask anywhere, the Court were charmed with her beauty, and readily admitted her claims, which some were ill-natured enough to say were, perhaps, merely assumed without foundation.

I took little interest in the story. My thoughts were far away, as they ever were for many years, from everything of the present; and 'twas only as I heard the duke announce my name, among a group who stood near a sofa, that I remembered why I was there.

The countess sat with her back to us, but rose immediately on hearing my name. I bowed deeply as she stood up; and recovering myself from my obeisance, looked up. Oh, merciful Heaven, with what horror I looked!—It was no other than La Mercia! With one loud cry of " 'Tis she! 'tis she!" I fell fainting to the floor.

Weeks of wild raving and delirium followed. I left Paris—I returned to Dresden. There, all reminded me of the past. I fled from my home; and now, after years of wandering in solitary and distant lands, I feel deep in my heart the heavy curse that has followed upon my broken oath, and which has made me an outcast and a broken-hearted wanderer in the world for ever.

THE PASS OF THE ARLBERG.

Before leaving the Vorarlberg, and while now on its very frontier, I would wish to keep some record of two very different but yet very characteristic actions, of which this place was the scene. As you begin the ascent of the Arl-berg from the westward, the road makes two very abrupt zigzags, being carred along the edge of a deep precipice. On looking down over the low battlements that guard the side of the way, you discover, immediately under you, the spire and roofs of a small village several hundred feet below. The churchyard, the little gardens, the narrow streets, and the open " Platz," where stands a fountain, are all mapped out distinctly. This is the village of Steuben. A strange spot you would deem it for any to have chosen as a dwelling-place, hemmed in between lofty mountains, on whose bleak sides the snow is seen in the very midsummer; surrounded by wild crags and yawning clefts, without even pasturage for anything save a goat: but your surprise will increase on learning that twice within the last century has this village been swept away by falling avalanches. The first time, the snow meeting in its descent from the mountains on either side, actually formed a bridge over a portion of the village; and the houses thus saved were long regarded as under the special favour of the Virgin, with whose image they were most bounteously decorated. The next calamity, however, destroyed the prestige, for they were mingled in the common destruction.

It would be difficult for " gentlemen of England, who live at home in ease," to fancy any reason for this unaccountable selection of a residence which adds the highest amount of peril to all the woes of poverty. But every traveller has seen many such instances. In every mountain land they are to be met with, and in each of the Alpine passes little groups of houses—they can scarcely be called villages—can be detected in spots where access is most difficult, where no feature around indicates any means of supporting life, and where the precautions—simple and ineffectual enough—against avalanches, show that danger to be among their calculations. How explain this? By what associations have these dreary spots become hallowed into homes? Possibly the isolated lives of these little families of men give them the same distaste to mixing with their brethren of the great world, that is felt by a solitary recluse to entering into society. Mayhap, too, the sense of peril itself has its share in the attraction. There is no saying how far this feeling may go, so strange and wayward are the caprices of human nature.

If you enter any of these villages, the narratives of snow storms, of falling precipices, and " Lavines," as avalanches are called, meet you at every step. They are the great topics of these communities, as the movements of politics or the vacillations of the Bourse are elsewhere. Scarcely one who has reached the middle term of life has not been, at least once, in the most imminent peril; and these things are talked of as the common accidents of existence, the natural risks of humanity! Very strange does it sound to us who discuss so eagerly the perils of a wooden pavement in our thoroughfares!

It is curious, too, to hear, as one may, most authentic-
ally, the length of time life can be preserved beneath the
snow. Individuals have been buried so long as three
entire days, and yet taken out alive. The cold, of
which it would be supposed they had suffered dreadfully,
seems scarcely very great; and the porous nature of the
snow, and possibly the chinks and crevices left between
falling masses, have usually left air sufficient for respiration. That individuals in such circumstances of peril
are not, always at least, devoid of their exercise of the
faculties, I remember one instance which is sufficiently
convincing. It was in the Via Mala, about five miles
from the village of Splügen, where, in the year 1829, the
little cabriolet that conveyed the mail was swept away by
an avalanche. The calamity was not known for full seven
or eight hours afterwards, when some travellers from
Andeer reaching the spot, found the road blocked up by
snow, and perceived a portion of the wooden rail of the
road, and a fragment of a horse-harness adhering to it,
half-way down the precipice. The guides of the party,
well accustomed to reason from such sad premises, at
once saw what had happened. Conceiving, however, that
the driver had been carried down over the cliff, and consequently to certain death, they directed their sole care to
clearing a passage for the travellers. In so doing, they
proceeded with long poles to sound the snow, and ascertain to what depth it lay unhardened. It was in one of
these "explorations," and when the pole had sunk above
ten feet deep into a mass of soft unfrozen snow, that the
man who held it found himself unable to withdraw the
staff, and called his comrades to aid him.

They soon perceived, however, that the resistance gradually yielded, and from the instinct peculiar to the "hand"
—another illustration for Sir Charles Bell—they recognized that it must be the grip of human fingers which
held the other end of the pole. They immediately began
to excavate on the spot, and in half an hour liberated the
poor postilion of the mail car, who, although hearing the
shouts and cries of the party for nearly an hour over his
head, could not succeed in making his own voice heard,

and but for the fortunate accident of the pole must have perished.

Many curious escapes were told to me, but this appeared most singular of all ; and now I come back to Steuben, or rather to the wild mountain above it, over which, by a succession of windings, the road leads which joins the Vorarlberg to the Tyrol. About one-third of the ascent accomplished, you come upon an abrupt turning of the way, in rounding which a wide carriage can scarcely escape grating on the rock on one side, while from the window on the opposite, the traveller looks down upon a gorge actually yawning at his feet; the low barrier of wall, which does not rise above the nave of the wheel, is a very frail and insignificant protection on such a spot, but when hid from view, as it is to those seated in a carriage, the effect of the gulf is really enough to shake common nerves. A little inscription upon a stone in this wall records the name of the engineer—Donegani, if I remember aright—who, deeming this spot the triumph of his skill, has selected it whereon to inscribe his achievement. There is another meaning connected with the place, but unrecorded ; it could not, indeed, have been transmitted like that of the engineer, for when the event of which it treats occurred, there was neither wall nor railing, and the road passed some twelve feet higher up, over a ledge of rock, and actually seemed to jut out above the precipice. There is, indeed, a memorial of the transaction to which I allude, but it stands about twelve hundred feet down in the gorge below—a small wooden cross of rudest workmanship, with the equally rudely inscribed words, " Der Vorspann's Grab."

Now for the story, which happily is short.

It was late on a severe evening of winter, as a *calèche* drawn by two horses drew up to the door of the post-house at Steuben ; for then, as now, Steuben was the last post-station before commencing the ascent of the Arlberg. The travellers, two in number, wore military cloaks and foraging caps ; but what the precise rank, or to what arm of the service they belonged, not even the prying observations of the host could fathom. Their orders were for fresh horses immediately to cross the mountain, and although the snow-drift was falling fast, and the night dark as pitch, they peremptorily insisted on proceeding. The post regulations of those days were not very stringent and arbitrary; as a post-master may seem nowadays, he was nothing to the autocrat that once ruled the comings and goings of unhappy travellers.

When he averred that his horses had done enough— that it was a saint's-day—that the weather was too bad or his postilions too weary, the case was hopeless, and the traveller was consigned, without appeal, to the consolations of his own philosophy.

It chanced that on this occasion the whole disposable cavalry of the post consisted of two blind mares, which were both too old and weak to tempt the cravings of the commissary, who a few days before had seized on all the draught-cattle to convey stores to Feldkirch, at that time menaced by a French force under Massena.

The officers, however, were urgent in their demand—it was of the last importance that they should reach Innspruck by the following evening. At last, half by menace, half by entreaty, it was arranged that the two old mares should be harnessed to the carriage, the host remonstrating all the while on the inability of the expedient, and averring that, without a Vorspann, a relay of horses, to lead at the steepest parts of the mountain, the attempt would be fruitless. "Nay," added he, "if you doubt me, ask the boy who is sleeping yonder, and has been driving the Vorspann for years over the Arlberg." The travellers turned and beheld on a heap of straw, in the corner of the kitchen, a poor little boy, whose ragged uniform of postilion had evidently reached him at third or fourth hand, so large and loosely did it hang around his slender figure. He was sleeping soundly, as well he might, for he had twice crossed the mountain to St. Cristoph on that same day.

"And this book," said one of the travellers, taking a very tattered and well-thumbed volume which had dropped from the sleeper's fingers, "has this poor little fellow time to read?"

"He contrives to do it somehow," said the host, laughing; "nay, more, as you may see there, he has begun to teach himself French. Since he heard that the French army was about to invade us, he has never ceased his studies, sitting up half the night working at that old grammar there, for which he gave all his month's earnings."

"And what may be his reason for this?" said the elder traveller, evidently interested in the recital.

"He has got the notion that if the French succeed in forcing the pass of Feldkirch and enter the Tyrol, that, as he will be constantly engaged as Vorspann on the mountain, his knowledge of French would enable him to discover many secrets of the enemy, as no one would ever suspect a poor creature like him of having learned a foreign language."

"And his motive was then purely a patriotic one?"

"Purely; he is poor as you see, and an orphan, but his Tyrol blood runs warm and thick in his veins."

"And what progress has he made?"

"That I cannot answer you, *mein herr;* for no one hereabout knows anything of French—nor, I suppose, had he ever the opportunity of testing the acquirement himself. They are driven back, I am told."

"For the present," said the elder stranger, gravely; "but we shall need all the reserves at Innspruck to hold our ground whenever they renew the attack."

The sleeper was now aroused to take the saddle; for in the absence of the regular postilion the Vorspann was obliged to take his place.

Still but half awake, the little fellow stood up, and mechanically buttoning up his worn jacket, he took down his whip and prepared for the road. The travellers were soon ready, and ere many minutes elapsed the *calèche* had left the village, and, with the best pace the old mares could accomplish, was breasting the snow-drift and the first rise of the mountain. After about an hour's driving, during which Joseph had exhibited his utmost skill in taking advantage of every available bit of trotting ground, they came at length to the commencement of the steep ascent; and there, hanging his whip on the saddle-peak, the little fellow got down, to relieve his cattle as they toiled up the precipitous ascent. He had not gone far, when, happening to drop behind beside the *calèche*, what did he hear but the sounds of that very language upon which all his day and night dreams were set? All that he had remarked of the two travellers was, that they wore cloaks of military cut and foraging caps, and now he heard them conversing in French. The whole train of events on which his mind so long had been dwelling came now forcibly before him. "Feldkirch had been forced, the French were already masters of the pass ; in a few days they would be over the Arlberg and in possession of all Tyrol!" Such was the terrible series of events a few words of French revealed to his excited imagination. With this conviction he drew nearer and nearer the door, till he could hear the very words they spoke. Now the truth was that the travellers, by way of amusing themselves with the poor boy's eccentric devotion, had no sooner seen him within ear-shot of the carriage than they began speaking French together. And when they perceived that they had gained his attention, the younger one, in a tone of assumed warmth, exclaimed, "If we do but reach Innspruck in time, the whole country is our own."

Then suddenly changing to German, he cried out,—

"Holloa, Vorspann, we are pressed for time. Spring into the saddle, my lad, and use your spurs well, and ye shall have a Baierisch ducat for your stage."

As if obedient to the command, Joseph mounted at once ; and steep as the road was, by dint of spurs, whip, and voice, he struck out into a half-shuffling canter, the very utmost speed his beasts could accomplish. With many a shock and bound the *calèche* sprang from side to side of the narrow road, while the same who last spoke called out—

"So much for patriotism! The promise of a ducat would open the Tyrol from Bregenz to Trent."

The words were not well uttered when a loud cry rent the air; the horses sprang abruptly to one side, and the *calèche*, with a tremendous jerk, upset, and had not the wheel become entangled in a stunted oak-tree, must have

"The horses hung as if suspended, and then, as the strained tackle gave way, fell with a thundering crash into the dark abyss."

fallen over the cliff, where, for a second or two, the
horses hung as if suspended, and then, as the strained
tackle gave way, fell with a thundering crash into the
dark abyss—the last cry of the boy being the war-cry of
his Vaterland, " *Frey tis Tyrol!* "

Such was the devotion of this poor child—he was
scarcely more—that he dashed the blind horses over the
steepest precipice of the Arlberg, ready to meet death in
its most terrible form, if he could involve in his fate his
country's enemies. His mangled body was found the
following day beside the stream in the glen. The
travellers escaped with slight injury, to brood over their
own unhappy trifling with a peasant's faith and a Tyroler's
devotion.

There is another memory associated with this mountain
pass, and it is of a heroism nobler and more exalted than
that of the poor Vorspann: I mean the "Hospice" for forlorn
travellers built and endowed by the exertions of an orphan
child, who, being impressed in his earlier years with the
sad fate of many a wayfarer, devoted a whole life to seeking aid to build this house of refuge. In this glorious
pilgrimage he wandered over nearly the whole of Europe
and a great part of America, and returned to accomplish
the great purpose he had planned.

This " Zuflucht-Haus," or Hospice of Heinrich " Findel-
kind "—for he was named the " Foundling," having none
to claim or acknowledge him—has been superseded by a
more commodious and better endowed edifice under the
auspices of the Imperial Government, who have gracefully
preserved the memory of the first founder : thus showing
themselves not ashamed to be reminded of their own
devoirs by a poor orphan.

And now from the heights of St. Christopher I look
down upon the winding glens and bold mountains of
Tyrol! The great cross yonder on the rock marks the
boundary. And now, adieu! the square fur caps of the
Bregenzer Walderin; the huge silver filigree leaves,
which look like peacock's tails of frosted silver, fastened
to the back of the head; the short-waisted dresses, gaily

embroidered with the wearers' initials upon the stomacher; and the stockings, so piously adorned with saintly emblems; and last, but not least, the peaceful quietude of a primitive people—to have lived among whom is to carry away for life-long a pleasant memory of a simple-minded, kindly peasantry.

On descending the Arlberg by the eastward, or the Tyrol side, there is a little low ruin not far from the road. It stands nestled in a small nook between the hills, and shows the stunted and cattle-cropped remains of a few fruit-trees around. This was an ancient shrine where four monks formerly lived, devoting their lives to aiding the travellers of the pass ; and some say that its foundation dates from that of the establishment of St. Gallen in Switzerland, and that both owe their origin to the same pious hand—an Irish monk. So is it incontestably true that the great monastery of St. Gall, and the spacious convents of Mehrer-Au and Loch Au on the borders of the Lake of Constance, were founded by an Irishman. What a destiny, that the nation whose mission should have been the spread of Christianity in the earliest centuries, should present such a spectacle of crime and God-forgetfulness in our own !

CHAPTER XII.

I WISH my travelling countrymen—and what land turns out such myriads of wanderers?—would betake themselves, in their summer rambles, to the Tyrol, rather than Switzerland. If the use of German be not as frequent with us as French, still very little suffices for the every-day necessities of the road; and while, in point of picturesque beauty the tour is little, if anything, inferior to Switzerland in all that regards the people, the superiority of the Tyrolese is without a question.

Switzerland—save in some few remote spots of the German cantons, and these not generally worth the visiting—is a land of extortion and knavery. The whole country is laid out pretty much as St. Paul's in London used to be, some years back—so much for the aisle, so much for the whispering gallery, so much for the ball, &c. Each mountain, each glen, every glacier and snow-peak, has its corps of guides, farming out by a tariff the wild regions of the roe and the chamois, and vulgarizing the features of nature to the level of the Colosseum in London, and its pasteboard avalanches.

This may be all very delightful for those junketing parties who steam up the Rhine on a three weeks' excursion, and want to "do Switzerland" before they reach home—jogging to Chamouni in an omnibus, and riding up the Rigi in an ass-pannier. But to enjoy mountains—to taste really of the exquisite sense of impressive solemnity a wild mountain-scene can suggest—give me the Tyrol—give me the land where the crashing cataract is heard in the midst of unbroken stillness—where, in the deep valleys, the tinkling bell of the herd sounds for miles afar—where, better than all, the peasant is not degraded from his self-respect to become a hanger-on of each stranger that he sees, but is still a peasant, stout of heart and limb, ready to do the honours of his humble *chalet* if you cross his threshold, but not bartering his native hospitality for gold! What a fine national character is made up of that sturdy independence—that almost American pride of equality—with the devoted loyalty to their sovereign! How admirably does the sense of personal freedom blend with obedience to the Kaiser! How intimately is love of country bound up with fealty to the country's king! O Austria! if all thy subjects were like these, how little need you fear revolutionary Poles or reforming Popes! The sounds of the national sign, *Gott erhalte unser Kaiser!* would drown the wildest cry that ever Anarchy shouted.

The gifted advocates of Progress and Enlightenment, who write in Penny Magazines and People's Journals, may sneer at the simple faith of a people who recognize a father in their monarch—who are grateful for a system of government that secures to them the peaceful enjoyment of their homes and properties, with scarcely the slightest burden of taxation.

Such travellers as Inglis may record conversations with individuals disposed to grumble at the few opportunities for social convulsion and change; but, taking the mass of the people, judging from what is palpable to every sojourner in the land, where does one see less of poverty—where so much contentment, so much of enjoyment of life, such a general feeling of brotherhood in every rank and class? —where are the graceful virtues of charity and kindliness more conspicuous?—and, above all, where is there so little of actual crime?

It may be said, the temptations are not so great to breaches of law where a general well-being prevails, where each has enough for his daily wants, and life displays no inordinate ambitions. I am willing to acknowledge all this; I cavil not for the cause—I only ask acceptance for the fact. If one would wish to see the boldest spirit of personal freedom united to implicit obedience to a ruler, the most stubborn independence of character with a courteous submission to the will of him recognized as superior, a manly self-reliance with a faithful trust that there are others better, wiser, and more far-seeing than himself—then let him come to the Tyrol !

The Tyrol is, perhaps, the only part of Europe where any portion of romance still dwells—where the little incidents of daily life are tinctured with customs that derive from long ago—where facts of bygone days, traditions of their fathers' time, are interwoven with the passing hour—and where primitive habits and tastes are believed to carry with them a blessing, as to those who honour their fathers' memories. National gratitude is far more closely allied with individual gratitude than is usually believed. Under the shade of the great tree the little plant is often nurtured. It is easy to imagine well of the individual, where the masses are moved by noble aspirations.

Scarcely a valley, not a single defile here, is without its historic glories—many of them as of yesterday, and yet, in their simple heroism, recalling a time when personal valour was of greater worth than strategic skill and science. I always regret that Scott, who understood mountains and those who dwell thereon so thoroughly, should never have made the Tyrol the scene of a romance.

Even among the " simple annals of the poor " here are little incidents eminently romantic in their character, while so distinctly national that they tell, in every detail, the mind of the people who enacted them.

How I should like once more to be young of heart and limb, and able to travel these winding glens and climb these mountain steeps as once I could have done ! Even now, as I sit here in this little " Wirth's-Haus," how the old spirit of wandering comes back again as I watch the peasant, with his long staff in hand, braving the mountain side, or standing for a second on some rocky peak, to gaze down into the steep depth below—that narrow valley filled by road and river.

HANZ JÖRGLE.

" Gott hat sein plan
Für Jedenmann."

WHAT a road is that from Landeck to Meran!—at once the most beautiful and the grandest of all the Tyrol passes. The gorge is so narrow, that it seems rather like a deep channel cut by the river itself; where, on either side, hundreds of feet in height, rise the rocks—not straight, but actually impending above the head, leaving, in some places, the ravine narrower above than beneath.

Escarped in this rock, the road winds on, protected by a little parapet along the edge of the precipice. Beneath, at a depth to make the head dizzy to gaze at, is seen the river, whose waters are of a pale sky-blue, the most delicate and beautiful colour I ever beheld. As the necessities of the road require, you have to cross the river, more than once, on wooden bridges, which in themselves are curious for their ingenuity of construction, if one could think of aught save the grandeur of the scene around them.

At the second of these bridges, called the Pontlatzer Brücke, the ravine grows wider, and opens a distant prospect of the " Kaunser-Thal," backed by the tremendous glacier of Gebatsch. A glorious valley is it, with its grouped cottages and village spires studded along the plain, through which the Inn winds its rapid stream, its surface still ruffled and eddying from the deep descent of the Fünstermünze.

Above the Pontlatzer Brücke, high upon a little tableland of the mountain, stands a small village—if even that humble name be not too dignified for the little group of peasant-houses here assembled. This, called the " Kletscher," derives its title from a mountain torrent which, leaping from cliff to cliff, actually divides the village into two portions, over each of which, with pretty fair equality, it distributes its spray and foam and then plunges madly down till, by a succession of bounds and springs, it reaches the r'ver Inn beneath. The Kletscher, it must be owned, deserves its name : it is at once the most boisterous and foam-covered torrent of the whole region ; and as frequently in its course it pierces the soft rock of the mountain the roaring stream echoes more loudly still beneath these natural bridges. These, however, are not the only sounds which greet the ear on nearing the spot. The whole air is tremulous with the thumping and crashing noise of saw-mills, every second cottage having one of these ingenious contrivances at work ; and thus, between the roaring torrent itself and its forced labour, such a tremendous uproar is created, that the uninitiated are completely stunned.

It is indeed a curious transition from the deathlike stillness of the pine forest, the unbroken silence of the steep path by which you wend your way upward, to emerge at once into this land of active life and turmoil, to see here, high amidst the Alps, where the roe and chamois are wild and free—to see here a little colony busied in all the arts of life, and carrying their industry into the regions of cataract and glacier.

What animation and movement on every side does that bright-flowing torrent carry with it ! The axe of the woodcutter—the rustling branches sweeping, as twenty or thirty peasants tug some mighty pine-tree along—the hacking clink of the bark adzes—the voices of the children gathering and peeling the bark, and above and through all the heavy throbbing of the mill-timbers shaking the frail sheds and even the very cottages with their giant strokes ! There is a character of enterprise in the selection of such a wild spot irresistibly captivating. One cannot look upon those hardy peasants without a sense of respect and admiration for those who have braved climate and danger—and such there is—to seek a livelihood and a home rather than toil in indigence and dependence in the valley beneath.

The Kletscher is not picturesque for situation only. Its houses built of the pine-wood are covered over with a kind of varnish which while it preserves the colour protects the timber from the effects of weather. Each story is flanked externally by a little gallery, whose ornamental balustrades display their native skill in carpentry, and are often distinguished by grotesque carvings, executed with an ability that none but a Tyroler could pretend to. The door and window-frames too are finished in the same taste, while instead of other designation each cottage is known by some animal of the owner's selection which stands proudly above the door-porch : and thus some old white-headed Bauer of eighty winters is called the Chamois ; a tart-looking, bitter-faced Frau, his neighbour, being known as the Lamb ; a merry little cheerful-eyed peasant being a Buffalo ; and the schoolmaster—I blush to write it—diffusing "Useful Knowledge" under the sign of a braying Donkey.

Animated and cheerful as the scene is by day, alive with all the instincts and sounds of happy labour, I like better to look upon it by night, when all is calm and still and nothing but the plash of the waterfall stirs the air—to see these quaint old houses with their sculptured pinnacles and deep-shadowing eaves sleeping in the mellow moonlight—mill and miller sunk in slumber—not a footstep nor a voice to be heard save one, the village watchman, going his nightly round, chanting his little verse of assuring comfort to the waking ear, and making the sleeper's dream a peaceful one.

See how he moves along, followed by his little dog, sleepy-looking and drowsy as its master! He stands in front of that cottage—it belongs to the Vorsteher, or ruler of the Dorf. Power has its privileges even here, and the great man should know how the weather fares, and what the hour is, if, perchance, the cares of state have kept him waking, as Homer tells us that they can. Now he has ended his little song, and he wends his way over the bridge of a single plank that spans the torrent ; he slowly descends the flight of stone steps, slippery with falling spray, and, guided by the wooden railing, he treads the narrow path along the edge of the cliff, which, nearly perpendicular, stands over the valley of the Inn. There is a little hut here—a very poor and humble one, the very poorest of the whole village—and yet it is before the door of this lowly dwelling that the "Nachtwachter" stands at midnight each night throughout the year, and then, as he calls the hour, he cries, "Hans Jörgle, good night!—rest soundly, Hans Jörgle!"

Who can be this Hans Jörgle, for whose peaceful slumber authority is watchful? If you care for the answer of the question, you must listen to a story—if I dare to call by so imposing a name the following little narrative—which, for want of better, I shall call

"THE LAME SOLDIER."

Something short of forty years ago, there came to dwell at the Kletscher a poor widow with one child, a boy of about nine years old. She never told much of her history to the neighbours, and merely accounted for her choice of this secluded spot from the circumstance that she had known it when a child, her grandfather having been many years an inhabitant of the "Dorf;" and that, from dwelling on the pleasant days she had known there once, and talking over them so often with her little Hans, she at last determined to gratify him and herself by revisiting the cherished spot, hoping to end her days there in peace.

The grandfather of whom she spoke—long since dead— had been well known and respected in the village; so that, at first on his account, and subsequently on her own, the widow was welcomed kindly amongst them. Her subsistence was derived principally from a small pension she received from the Government, for her husband had been a grenadier of the Austrian Imperial Guard, and fell on the field of Austerlitz. This little pittance would not have sufficed for wants even humble as hers, without the aid of her own industry; but she was clever at her needle, and could accomplish many a triumph in millinery above village skill; and by the exertion of this art she contrived to eke out a subsistence—in poverty, it is true, but in con· tentment also.

If little Hans Jörgle could not contribute to the common

stock by any efforts of his labour, his gentle, quiet nature,
his guileless innocence, won for him the love of all the
village.   Old and young were pleased to see him and to
talk to him ; for, child as he was, Hans had read a great
many books, and could tell the most wonderful stories
about the Swedes in the Thirty Years' War, and also what
happened in the long wars between Frederic of Prussia
and the Austrians—stories that, if Hans were fond of telling, his audience were far more delighted to listen to.
This amusing gift, joined to the claims of infirmity—for
he was lame, the effect of a fall in his infancy—made him
a favourite with every one ; for even they—and the
number was a small one—who could not relish his stores
of narrative could feel compassion for the little fatherless
boy, bereft of the means of earning a livelihood, and wholly
dependent on one whose frail health gave little promise of
long life.

Hans was tall and slight, and, but for his lameness,
would have been as remarkable for the symmetry of his
form, as, even with it, he was for agility.   His countenance was eminently handsome ; the brow lofty, and the
eyes, which were of the darkest blue, were set deeply ;
their habitual expression was one of great melancholy—
not the sorrow of infirm health, or the depression of a
heart in conflict with itself, but the sadness of a spirit too
finely attuned for its daily associations—above, immeasurably above, all around in its ambitions, and yet an object
of actual pity and compassion !   The prevailing tone of
his mind, though sorrowful, did not prevent his joining
the village children at their play ; nor was he, perhaps,
the less welcome amongst them for those strange fits of
absence which, seizing him in the midst of some rural
sport, would make him forget all around, and burst out
with some exciting anecdote of heroic daring, some bold
achievement of the Austrians in their memorable battles
with the Turks.   Then, would the play cease ; gradually
gathering around him, the children would form a circle,
soon to be strengthened by their elders, who took the most
lively pleasure in these recitals—tales which many a setting sun and rising moon shone upon.

It may have been remarked by the reader that Hans' literary stores were all military. Such was the case. Battles and sieges, campaigns and marches, were a passion so exclusive, that he had no interest left for any other form of reading. This may seem strange in one so young, and in one, too, whose nature was gentleness itself; his very infirmity, besides, might have turned his thoughts away from themes in which he never could be a participator; but how little have material influences power over the flight of a highly imaginative nature! His father's stories as he sat at the fireside, his earliest lessons in reading, implanted the impulse, which the very events of the time served to strengthen and mature.

It was just the period when the Tyrol, crushed by the oppression of Bavaria, insulted and outraged in every feeling, had begun to think of vengeance. The transient success of the Austrians on the Danube animated the brave mountaineers, and cheered them with the hope of freedom. Already the low muttering of the distant storm was heard. Wherever a group of peasants gathered, their low whisperings, their resolute looks, their clenched hands, denoted some stern purpose. Secret masses were said in the chapels for the " rescue of the Vaterland ;" the ancient legends of the land were all remembered; sights and sounds of ominous meaning were reported to have been observed; all indicative of a speedy convulsion, all suggesting hope and courage. Rumour had told of conferences between the Archduke John of Austria and the Tyrol leaders; not failing to exaggerate the aid proffered by the Imperial Government in the event of a struggle. The ancient spirit of the land was up, and only waited the signal for the fight.

Remote and secluded as the little village of my story lay, the news of the coming conflict did not fail to reach it. Little Hans formed the link which bound them to the world of the valley beneath; and daily did he, in despite of lameness, descend the steep path that led to the Pontlatzer Brücke, bringing back with him towards nightfall the last rumours of the day. Vague and uncertain as they were, they were listened to with breathless eagerness.

Sometimes. the intelligence merely announced a gathering of the peasants in a mountain glen ; sometimes, the arrival of a messenger with secret dispatches from Vienna.   Now, Hofer had passed through Maltz the night before ; now, it was a Bavarian reinforcement was seen arriving at Landeck.

These simple tidings had seemed of little meaning to their ears if Hans were not there to give them significance, filling up all the blanks by wise surmises, and suggesting reasons and causes for everything.   He had his own theory of the war—where the enemy should be met, and how ; in what manner certain defiles should be defended, and how, in case of defeat, the scattered forces might re-unite ; little views of strategy and tactics, that seemed like inspiration to the simple ears who heard him.

Hans' tidings grew daily more important ; and one evening he returned to the Kletscher with a sealed note for the Curate—a circumstance which excited the most intense curiosity in the Dorf.   It was not long ungrati-fied, for the old priest speedily appeared in the little square before the Vorsteher's house, and announced that each evening, at sunset, a Mass would be said in the chapel, and a prayer invoked on all who loved ",Gott, der Kaiser, und das Vaterland."   Hans was pressed on every side ; some asking what was going on in the valley, others eager to hear if the Austrians had not been defeated, and that the Mass was for the slain.   Hans knew less than usual ; he could only tell that large bodies of the peasan-try were seen ascending the mountain towards Landeck, armed with saws and hatchets, while kegs of blasting powder were borne along between others.   "We shall know more soon," added Hans ; " but come ! the chapel is lighted already ; the Mass has begun."

How picturesque was the effect the chapel presented ! The sun was setting, and its long golden rays, mingled with the red light of the tapers, tipping the rich draperies of the altar and its glittering vessels with a parti-coloured light ; the kneeling figures of the peasantry, clad in all the varied colours of Tyrol taste ; the men bronzed by sun and season, dark-bearded, stern, and handsome ; the women fairer, but not less earnest in expression; the white-haired priest, dressed in a simple robe of white, with a blue scarf over it—the Bavarians had stripped the chapels even of the vestments of the clergy—the banners of the little volunteer battalion of the mountain waving overhead,—all, made up a picture simple and unpretending, but still solemn and impressive.

The Mass ended, the priest addressed a few words on the eventful position of the Vaterland—at first, in terms of vague, uncertain meaning; but growing warmer as he procceded, more clearly and more earnestly, he told them that the "Wolves"—none needed to be told that Frenchmen were meant—that the "Wolves" were about to ravage the flocks and overrun the villages, as they had already done twice before; that the Bavarians, who should be their friends, were about to join their bitterest enemies; that although the "Gute Franzerl"—for so familiarly did they ever name the Emperor—wished them well, he could help them but little. "The Tyroler's hand alone must save Tyrol," he exclaimed. "If that cannot be, then God pity us; for there is no mercy to be looked for from our enemies!"

If many a bold and patriotic heart sorrowed over these things, not one felt them with a more intense sense of anguish than little Hans Jörgle. The French, who had crushed his country, had killed his father; and now they were coming to bring fire and sword among those lonely glens, where his widowed mother had hoped to live her last years peacefully. Oh! if he had been a man to stand beside his father in the day of battle, or if even now he could hope to see the time when he should be strong of limb as he was of heart .... a burst of tears was the ever-present interruption to utterings which, in the eagerness of his devotion, he could not resist from making aloud.

These thoughts now took entire possession of his mind. If the clatter of horses' hoofs was heard unusually loud over the wooden bridge in the valley, Hans would start up and cry, "Here they are!—the cavalry picquets are upon us!" If a Bauer-house in the plain caught, it was the French were approaching and burning the villages. The rumbling of heavily-laden sledges over the hard snow was surely "the drums of the advanced guard;" and never could the ring of jäger's rifle be heard, that he did not exclaim, "Here come the skirmishers!" If the worthy villagers were indifferent to these various false alarms, the epithets and terms of war employed by Hans realized no small portions of its terror; and while they could afford to smile at his foolish fears, they exchanged very grave looks when he spoke of cavalry squadrons, and looked far from happy at the picture of a brigade of artillery in position on the bridge, while the tirailleurs ascended the face of the mountain in scattered parties.

While the winter continued, and the snow lay deep upon the roads, and many of the bridges were removed for safety from the drifting ice, the difficulties to a marching force were almost insurmountable; but as the spring came, and the highways cleared, the rumour again grew rife that the enemy was preparing his blow: the great doubt was, by which of the Alpine passes he would advance.

Staff-officers and engineers had been despatched from Vienna to visit the various defiles, and suggest the most efficient modes of defence. Unhappily, however, all their counsels were given with a total ignorance of the means of those by whom they were to be executed. To speak of fortifying Landeck, and entrenching here and stockading there, sounded like an unknown tongue to these poor chamois-hunters, whose sole idea of defence lay in the cover of a crag and the certainty of a rifle bullet.

Disappointed, then, in their hope of aid, they betook themselves to their own devices, and hit upon a plan the most perfectly adapted to the crisis, as well as the most suitable to their own means of accomplishment. Is it necessary that I should speak of what is so familiar to every reader? the rude preparations of the Tyrolers to defend their native defiles, by trunks of trees and fragments of rocks, so disposed that at a word they could be hurled from the mountains down into the valleys beneath. The pass I here speak of was eminently suited for this,

not only from its narrowness and the precipitate nature
of its sides, but that the timber was large and massive,
and the rocks, in many cases, so detached by the action
of the torrents, that little force was required to move
them.   Once free, they swept down the steep sides,
crushing all before them ; loosening others as they went,
and with a thunder louder than any artillery, plunging
into the depths below.   Simple as these means of defence
may seem—it is but necessary to have once seen the
country to acknowledge how irresistible they must have
been—there was positively no chance of escape left.   The
road, exposed in its entire length, lay open to view ;
beneath it, roared a foaming torrent, above, stood cliffs
and crags the hardiest hunter could not clamber ; and if,
perchance, some little path led upwards to a mountain
chalet or a Dorf, a handful of Tyrol riflemen could have
defended it against an army.

All was arranged early in the year, and it was determined that the revolt should break forth a week or ten
days before the time when the Bavarians were to march
the reliefs to the various garrisons—a movement which,
it was known, would take place in the spring.   By signal-
fires in the mountain-tops, intimation was to be given to
those who inhabited the Alpine regions ; while for those
in the plains, and particularly in the valley of the Inn—
the great line of operations—the signal was to be given
by sawdust thrown on the surface of the stream.   A
month, or even more, was to elapse from the time I have
just spoken of ere the preparations would be fully made.
What an interval of intense anxiety was that to poor Hans !

A small detachment of Bavarian infantry, now stationed
at the Pontlatzer Brücke, made it unsafe to venture often,
as before, into the valley.   Such frequent coming and
going would have excited suspicion ; and the interval
between suspicion and a drum-head tribunal was a short
one, and generally had a bloody ending.   Hans could do
little more, then, than sit the livelong day on the brow of
the cliff, watching the valley, straining his eyes along the
narrow glen towards Landeck, or gazing over the wide
expanse to the Kaunser-Thal.   How often did his

imagination people the space beneath with an armed host! and how did he build up before his mind's eye the glitter of steel, the tramp and dust of mounted squadrons, the long train of ammunition waggons, the gorgeous staff—all the "circumstance of glorious war!" And how strangely did it seem, as he rubbed his eyes and looked again, to see that silent valley and that untrodden road, the monotonous tramp of the Bavarian sentry the only sound to be heard! On the chapel door the previous Sunday some one had written in chalk, *Ist' zeit?*—Is it time?" to which another had written for answer "*Bald zeit*—It will soon be!" "Oh," thought Hans, "that it were come at last!" And a feverish eagerness had so gained possession of him, that he scarcely could eat or sleep, starting from his bed at night to peep out of the window and see if the signal fire was not blazing.

The devotional feeling is, as I have remarked, the most active and powerful in a Tyroler's heart; and deeply intent as each was now on the eventful time that drew nigh, the festival of Easter, which intervened, at once expelled all thoughts save those pertaining to the solemn season. Not a word, not a syllable, fell from any lip evincing an interest in their more worldly anxieties. The village chapel was crowded from before daybreak to late in the evening; the hum of prayer sounded from every cottage; and scarcely was there time for the salutations of friends, as they met, in the eagerness to continue the works of some pious ritual.

I know not if Hans Jörgle was as deeply impressed as his neighbours by these devout feelings; I only can tell that he refrained as rigidly as the others from any allusion to the coming struggle, and never by a chance word showed that his thoughts were wandering from the holy theme. A very prying observer, had there been such in the Dorf, might perhaps have detected that the boy's eyes, when raised in prayer, rested longer on the spot where the striped banners of Tyroler chivalry waved overhead, or that an expression of wild excitement rested on his features as the different groups, before entering the church, deposited their broadswords and rifles in the porch,—every

clank of the weapons seemed to thrill through Hans'
heart.

The devotional observances over, Easter Monday came
with all the joyous celebrations with which the villagers
were wont to *fête* that happy day. It was a time for
families to assemble their scattered members, for old and
attached friends to renew the pledges of their friendship,
for those at variance with each other to become reconciled;
little children paid visits to their grandfathers and grand-
mothers, with bouquets of spring flowers, repeating the
simple verses of some village hymn to welcome in the
morning; garlands and wreaths hung from every door-
porch; lovers scaled up the galleries to leave a rose, or an
Alp daisy, plucked some thousand feet high among the
snow-peaks, at their sweethearts' window. Pious souls
made little presents to the Curé in the chapel itself. The
cattle were led through the village in a great procession,
with garlands on their heads and fresh flowers fastened to
their horns; the villagers accompanying them with a
Tyrol song, descriptive of the approaching delights of
summer, when they could quit their dark dwellings and
rove free and wild over their native hills. It was joy
everywhere: in the glad faces and the glancing eyes,
the heartfelt embraces of those who met and saluted with
the well-known " *Gott grüse dich*—God greet thee! " in
the little dwellings pranked with holly-boughs and wild
flowers; in the chapel glittering with tapers on every
altar, pious offerings of simple hearts; in the tremulous
accents of age, in the boisterous glee of childhood, it was
joy.

It was the season of gifts, too. And what scenes of
pleasure and delight were there, as some new arrival from
the valley displayed before the admiring eyes of a household some little toy, the last discovery of inventive genius;
bauer-houses that took to pieces and exhibited all their
interior economy at will; saw-mills, that actually seemed
to work, so vigorously did they perform the incessant time
that mark their labour; dolls of every variety of attraction,
but all in Tyrol taste; nutcrackers that looked like old
men, but smashed nuts with the activity of the youngest;

soldiers of lead, stout-looking fellows, that never quitted the posts committed to them, if the wire was not too powerful—all were there ; appearing, besides, with a magic in true keeping with their wonderful properties. Some emerged from unknown pockets in the cuff of a jacket ; others, from the deep waistband of parti-coloured leather ; some, from the recesses of a hat ; but all in some wonderful guise that well became them.

In one cottage only this little festive scene was not enacted. Hanserl's mother, who for some time back had been in declining health, was unable to contribute, as she was wont, to their support. Too proud to confess her poverty in the village, she contrived to keep up all the externals of their condition as before. She and her son were seen on Sunday as well dressed as ever ; perhaps, if anything, a more than ordinary attention in this respect could be detected. Her offering to the curate rather exceeded than fell short of its customary amount. These were, however, costly little sacrifices to pride ; for these, their meal was made scantier and poorer ; for these, the hours of the wintry night were made longer and drearier, as, to save the cost of candle-light, they sat in darkness beside the stove ; a hundred little privations, such as only poverty knows or can sympathize with, fell to their lot ; all, borne with fortitude and patience, but in their slow process chilling and freezing up the hope from which these virtues spring.

"Hanserl, my love," said the poor widow, and her eyes swam and her tongue faltered as she spoke, "thou hast had none of the pleasures of this joyous day. Take these twelve kreutzers and buy thyself something in the Dorf. There be many pretty things cost not more than twelve kreutzers."

Hanserl made no answer ; his thoughts were wandering far away. Heaven knows whether they had strayed back to the bold days of Wallenstein, or the siege of Prague, or were now, with the stormy cataract of the Danube—at the iron gate, as it is called, the desperate scene of many a bloody meeting between Turks and Austrians.

"Hans, love, dost hear me? I say, thou canst buy a

bow with arrows; thou hast long been wishing for one. But bring no more books of battles, child," added she, more feelingly; "strife and war have cost us both dearly. If thy father had not served the Kaiser, he would not have fallen at Elchingen."

"I know it well," said the boy, his features flashing as he spoke. "He would not have stood beside the ammunition-waggons when the French dragoons bore down, and with a loud voice called out, 'Halt! these tumbrels are powder; another step and I'll explode the train!' How they reined up and fled! My father saved the train; didn't he mother?"

"He did," sobbed the widow; "and fell under the wall of the citadel as the last waggon entered the gate."

"God preserve Franz the Emperor!" said the boy, with a wild enthusiasm; "he has given many a brave soldier a glorious grave. But for this," here he struck his shrunken limb violently with his hand, "I, too, had been able to serve him. But for this——" a passion of sorrow, that found vent in tears, checked his words, and he buried his head in his hands and sobbed hysterically.

The poor mother did everything she could think of to console her son. She appealed to his piety for submission under a visitation of God's own making; she appealed to his affection for her, since, had it not been for his helplessness, he might one day have left her to be a soldier.

"The conscription is so severe now, Hanserl, that they take only sons away, like the rest—ay, and when they are but thirteen years of age! Take them away, and leave the mothers childless! But they cannot take thee, Hans!"

"No, that they cannot," cried the boy, in a burst of grief. "The cripple and the maimed have not alone to weep over their infirmity, but to feel themselves dishonoured before others."

The widow saw the unhappy turn her consolations had taken, and tried in different ways to recall her error. At last, yielding to her entreaties, Hans left the cottage, taking the twelve kreutzers in his hand to buy his Easter gift.

It was from no want of affection to his mother he acted, nor was it from any deficiency of gratitude that when he left the hut he forgot all about the toy, and the twelve kreutzers, and the *fête* itself. It was that a deeper sentiment had swallowed up every other, and left no place in his heart for aught else. Hans then sauntered along, and at last found himself on the little projecting point of rock from which he usually surveyed the valley of the Kaunser-Thal. There, he sat down and watched till the darkness thickened around and hid out every thing.

When he arose to turn homeward the lights were glittering in every window of the village, and the merry sounds of rustic music filled the air. Hans suddenly remembered it was Easter-night, the glad season of home rejoicings, and he thought of his poor mother, who sat alone, unfriended and suffering, in her little cabin. A feeling of self-reproach at once struck him, and he turned speedily towards the cottage. His shortest way was through the village, and thither he bent his steps. The night was starlit but dark, and none of the villagers were in the street; indeed, all were too happy within doors to wander forth. In the Vorsteher's house the village band was assembled, and there the merry notes of a *höpsa* waltz were accompanied by the tramp of feet and the sound of mirthful voices. A little farther on was a rich peasant's house. Hans stopped to peep through the half-closed shutters, and there sat the family at their supper. It was a well-filled board, and many a wine-flask stood around, while the savoury steam rose up and hung like a faint cloud above the dishes—not sufficiently, however, to obscure a little larch-tree, which, set in a small bucket, occupied the centre of the table. On this all the candles were fastened, glittering like stars through the sprayey branches, and glancing in bright sparkles over a myriad of pretty toys that hung suspended around. For this was the Easter-tree, to which every friend of the house attaches some little present. Many a more gorgeous epergne has not yielded one hundredth part of the delight. Every eye was fixed upon it; some in pure astonishment and wonder, others speculating what might fall to their share; and while the old grandfather tried to curb impatience among the elder children, the young baby, with the destructive privilege that belongs to infancy was permitted to pull and tear from time to time at the glittering fruit—little feats which excited as much laughter from the grown people as anxiety from the younger.

Hans moved on, with a sigh, at these new signs of home happiness in which he had no share. The next was the Curate's cabin, and there sat a pleasant party round the stove, while the old priest read something from an amusing volume; the lecture never proceeding far without some interruption to comment upon it, to indulge a laugh, or mayhap clink their glasses together as in token of friendship. they pledged each other health and long life. Beyond this again was a new cabin, just taken possession of; and here Hans, peeping in, beheld a young Tyroler exhibiting to his wife—they had been married but a few weeks—his new rifle. It was strange to see how she admired the weapon, gazing at it with all the delight most of her sex reserve for some article of dress or decoration. She balanced it, too, in her hand, and held it to her shoulder, with the ease of one accustomed to its use.

In every cabin some group, some home picture, met his eye; peaceful age, happy manhood, delighted childhood, beamed around each hearth and board. The song, the dance, the merry story, the joyous meal, succeeded each other, as he went along. He alone, of all, was poor and sad: in his mother's hut all was darkness and gloom; the half-suppressed sigh of pain the only sound. The last cabin of the village, and the poorest too, belonged to an old peasant, who had been a soldier under the Emperor Joseph; he was a very old man, and being burdened with a large family of grandchildren, whose parents were both dead, all he could do by hard labour was to maintain his household. "Here," thought Hans, as he stopped to look in, "here are some poor as ourselves,—I hope they are happier." So they seemed to be. They were all seated on the floor of the cabin, with the grandfather among them on a low stool, while he performed for them the evolutions of the Grand Army at Presburg—the great review which Maria Theresa held of all the Imperial troops. The old man was sorely puzzled to convey a sufficiently formidable notion of the force, for he had only some twenty little wooden soldiers to fill up the different arms of the service, and was obliged to plant individuals to represent entire corps, while walnut-shells answered for field-pieces and mortars; the citadel of Presburg being performed by the bowl of his Meerschaum pipe.

There were many more brilliant displays met Hans' eyes that evening than this humble spectacle, and yet not one had the same attraction for him. What would he not have given to be among that group—to have watched all the evolutions, many of which were now hidden from his view—perchance to be permitted to move some of the regiments, and suggest his own ideas of tactics. Ah, that would have been happiness indeed! How long he might have watched there is no saying, when a slight incident occurred which interrupted him—slight and trivial enough was it, and yet in all its seeming insignificance to be the turning point of his destiny!

It chanced that one of the little soldiers, from some accident or other would not stand upright, and a little boy, whose black eyes and sunburnt cheeks bespoke a hasty temper, in endeavouring to set him on his legs, broke one of them off. "Ah, thou worthless thing!" cried he passionately, "thou art no use now to King or Kaiser, for thou art as lame as Hans Jörgle;" and as he spoke he opened the little pane of the window, and flung the little figure into the street.

"Shame on thee, Carl!" said the old man reprovingly; "he would have done for many a thing yet. The best scout we ever had on the Turkish frontier was so lame, you couldn't think him able to walk. Besides, don't you remember the Tyrol proverb?—

> ' Gott hat sein plan
> Fur Jedenmann:'
>
> God has his plan
> For every man,

So never despise those who are unfit for thine own duties ; mayhap, what thou deemest imperfectiou, may fit them for something far above thee."

Oh, how Hans drank in these words! the grief that filled him, on the insulting comparison of the child was now changed to gratitude, and seizing the little soldier, his own sad emblem, he kissed it a hundred times, and then placed it in his bosom.

Hanserl's mother was asleep when he reached home, so, creeping silently to his bed, he lay down in his clothes, dreading lest he might awaken ker ; and with what a happy heart did he lie down that night ! How full of gratitnde and of love as he thought over the blessed words ! How he wished to remain awake all night long and think over them, fancying, as he could do, the various destinies which, even to such as him, might still fall ! But sleep, that will not come when wooed, stole over him as he lay, and in a deep, heavy slumber, he clasped the little wooden figure in his hands.

The first effects of weariness over, Hans dreamed of all he had seen ; vague and confused images of the different objects passed and repassed before his mind, in that disorder and incoherency that belong to dreams. The scene of the Vorsteher's house become mingled with the remembrance of the Pontlatzer bridge, where, until night-fall, he had been watching the Bavarian sentinel ; and the curate's parlour beside its listening group, had, now, a merry mob of children dancing around the Easter-tree, under whose spreading branches a cavalry picquet were lying—the horses grazing—while the men lay stretched before the watch-fires, smoking and chattering.

The memory of the soldiers once touched upon, every other fled ; and now he could ouly think of the evolutions around Presburg : and he fancied he saw the whole army defiling over the bridge across the Danube, and disappearing within the ancient gates of the city. The white-cloaked cuirassiers of Austria, gigantic forms, seeming even greater from the massive folds of their white drapery ; the dark Bohemians on their coal-black horses ; the Uhlans with their banners floating from their tall lances; the prancing Hungarians mounted on their springing white steeds of Arab blood; the gay scarlet of their chakos, the clink of their dolmans, all glittering with gold, eclipsing all around them. Then came the Jägers of the Tyrol, a countless host, marching 'like one man, their dark plumes waving like a vast forest for miles in distance. These followed again by the long train of guns and ammunition carts.

Fitful glances of distant lands, of which he had once read, passed before him: the wide-spreading plains of the Lower Danube—the narrow passes of the Styrian Alps—the bleak vast tracts of sterile country on the Turkish frontier, with here and there a low mud-walled village, surmounted by a minaretted tower; all, however, were peopled with soldiers, marching or bivouacking, striking their tents at daybreak, or sitting around their campfires by night. The hoarse challenge of the sentries, the mellow call of the bugle, the quivering tramp of a mounted patrol, were all vividly presented to his sleeping senses. From these thoughts of far-away scenes, he was suddenly recalled to home, and his own Tyrol land. He thought he stood upon the rocky cliff, and looked down into the valley which he had left so tranquil at nightfall, but which now presented an aspect of commotion and trouble. The inhabitants of the little village at the head of the Kaunser-Thal were all preparing to quit their homes and fly up the valley; carts covered with their furniture and effects crowded the little street; packhorses and mules laden with everything portable; while in the eager and affrighted gestures of the peasants it was easy to see that some calamity impended. Now and then some horseman would ride in amongst them, and by his manner it was plain the tidings he brought were full of disaster. Hans looked towards the bridge: and there, to his astonishment, he saw the very same soldiers the old man had manœuvred with. They had, seemingly, come off a long march, and with their knapsacks unstrung, and their arms piled, were regaling themselves with wine from the guard-house.

Hans' first thought was to hasten back and tell his

mother what he saw; and now he stood up and leaned over her bed, but her sleep was so tranquil and so happy he could not bear to awaken her. "What can it mean?" thought he. "Are these the movements of our own people? or are the French wolves coming down upon us?" As he ruminated thus, he thought there came a gentle tap at the door of the hut: he opened it cautiously, and there, who should be standing before him but the lame soldier, his own poor little fellow, the castaway?

"Come along, Hans," said he in a friendly voice; "there is little time to lose. The Wolves are near." He pressed his finger to his lips, in token of caution, and led Hans without the door. No sooner were they outside than he resumed,—

"Thou art maimed and crippled like myself, Hans Jörgle. We should be but indifferent front-rank men before the enemy: but remember the Tyrol proverb,—

> ' Gott hat sein plan
> Fur Jedenmann.'

Who knows if even we cannot serve the Vaterland? We must away, Hanserl—away to the top of the Kaiser-fells, where the fagots lie ready for the signal fire. The Bavarians have found out where it lies, and have sent a scout party to destroy it, while their battalions are advancing by forced marches up the Inn Thal. Thou knowest all these paths well, Hans; so lead the way, my brave boy, and I'll do my best to follow."

Hans waited for no further bidding, but hastily crossing the little wooden bridge commenced the ascent of the mountain with an activity that bore no trace of his infirmity.

"We must light the beacon, Hans," said the lame soldier. "When it is seen blazing, the signal will be repeated up the Kaunser-Thal; Fünstermünze will have it; and then Nauders. Maltz will shew it next, and then all Tyrol will be up. The war *jodeln* will resound in every valley and glen, and then let the Wolves beware!"

Oh, how Hans strained each nerve and sinew to push forward! The path led across several torrents, many of them by places which, in day, demanded the greatest circumspection, but Hans cleared them now at a spring. The deep marshy ground, plashy with rivulets and melted snow, he waded through ankle deep, climbing the briery rocks and steep banks without a moment's halt.

He thought that the lame soldier continued to exhort him, and encourage his zeal, while gradually his own pace slackened, and at last he cried out, "I can do no more, Hans. Thou must go forward alone, my boy—to thee all the glory—I am old and worn out! Hasten, then, my child, and save the Vaterland. Thou wilt see the tinder-box and the rags in the hollow pine-tree beside the fagot. It is wrapped in tow, and will light at once. Farewell, and Gott guide thee!"

I cannot tell a thousandth part of the dangers and difficulties of that night's walk: in one place the path, for several yards is on the brink of a ravine, eleven hundred feet deep, and so abrupt is the turn at the end, that an iron hook is inserted in the rock, by which the traveller must grip; a steep glacier is to be crossed farther on; and lastly, the torrent of the Kletscher must be traversed on a tree, whose bark, wet and slippery from the falling spray, would be impossible to all but the feet of a mountaineer. Each of these did Hans now surmount with all the precision and care of waking senses; with greater courage, by far, than in his waking moments he could have confronted them.

Gorges he never gazed on before without a shudder, he passed now in utter disregard; paths he trembled to tread, he stepped along now in nimble speed, and at last caught sight of a large dark object that stood out against the sky—the great heap of fire-wood for the beacon.

As he came nearer, his eagerness grew greater; each minute now seemed an hour—every false step he made appeared to him as though it might prove fatal to his mission; and when, by any turn of the way, the beacon pile disappeared for a moment from his eyes, his heart

throbbed so powerfully as almost to impede his breath.
At last he gained the top—the wild mountain-peak of the
Kaiser-fells. The snow lay deep, and a cold, cutting wind
swept the drift along, and made the sensation far more
intense. Hans cared not for this: his whole soul was on
one object; suffering, torture, death itself, he would have
braved and welcomed, could he only accomplish it. The
mist lay heavily on the side by which he had ascended,
but towards Landeck the air was clear, and Hans gazed
down in that direction as well as the darkness would permit; but all seemed tranquil—nothing stirred, nor showed
the threatened approach. "What if he should be mistaken?" thought Hans. "What if the lame soldier should
have only fancied this? or could he be a traitor, that would
endeavour by a false alarm to excite the revolt before its
time?"

These were torturing doubts, and while he yet revolved
them he stood unconsciously peering into the depth below,
when suddenly, close beneath him—so close that he
thought it almost beside him, though still about eighty
yards off—he saw two figures emerge from the shadow of
a pine copse, and commence the steep ascent of the peak.
They were followed by two others, and now a long compact line issued forth, and began to clamber up the pass.
Their weapons clinked as they came: there could be no
doubt of it—they were the enemy.

With one spring he seized the tinder-box and struck
the light: the wood, smeared with tar, ignited when
touched, and before a minute elapsed a bright pillar of
flame sprung up into the dark sky. Hans, not content
with leaving anything to chance, seized a brand and
touched the fagots here and there, till the whole reeking
mass blazed out—a perfect column of fire.

No sooner had the leading files turned the cliff, than
with a cry of horror and vengeance they sprung forward.
It was too late: the signal was already answered from the
Kaiser-fells, and a glittering star on the Gebatsch told
where another fire was about to blaze forth. Hans had
but time to turn and fly down the mountain as the soldiers
drew up. A particle of burning wood had touched his

jacket, however, and, guided by the sparks, four bullets followed him.   It was at the moment when he had turned for a last look at the blazing pile.   He fell, but speedily regaining his feet, continued his flight.   His mission was but half accomplished if the village were not apprised of their danger.   All the dangers of his upward course were now to be encountered in his waking state; and with the agony of a terrible wound—for the bullet had pierced him beneath the left breast—half frantic with pain and excitement, he bounded from cliff to cliff, clearing the torrents by leaps despair alone could have made, and at length staggered rather than ran along the village street, and fell at the door of the Vorsteher's house.

Already the whole village was a-foot: the signal blazing on the mountain had called them to arm, but none could tell by whom it was lighted, or by which path the enemy might be expected.   They now gathered around the poor boy, who, in accents broken and faltering, could scarce reply.

"What! thou hast done it?" cried the Vorsteher, angrily.   "So, then, thou silly fool, it is to thy mad ravings we owe all this terror—a terror that may cost our country bitter tears!   Who prompted thee to this?"

"The lame soldier told me they were coming," said Hans, with eyes swimming in tears.

"The lame soldier!—he is mad!" cried an old peasant: "there is none such in all the Dorf."

"Yes, yes," reiterated Hans; "they flung him away last night, because he was lame—lame, and a cripple like me: but he told me they were coming: and I had only time to reach the Kaiser-fells when they gained the top too."

"Wretched fool!" said the Vorsteher, sternly; "thy mad reading and wild fancies have ruined the Vaterland.   See, there is the signal from Pfunds, and the whole Tyrol will be up!   If thy life were worth anything, thou shouldst die for this!"

"So shall I!" said Hans, sobbing; "the bullet is yet here."   And he opened his jacket, and displayed to their horrified gaze the whole chest bathed in blood, and the round, blue mark of a gun-shot wound.

This terrible evidence dispelled every doubt of Hans' story: and all its strange incoherency vanished before that pool of blood, which, welling forth at every respiration, ran in currents over him. Dreadful, too, as the tidings, were, the better nature of the poor villagers prevailed over their fears, and in the sorrow the child's fate excited all other thoughts were lost.

In a sad procession they bore him home to his mother's cottage, the Vorsteher walking at his side; while Hans, with rapid utterance, detailed the events which have been told. Broken and unconnected as parts of his recital were—incomprehensible as the whole history of the lame soldier appeared—the wounded figure—the blazing fires that already twinkled on every peak—were facts too palpable for denial; and the hearers stared at each other in amazement, not knowing how to interpret the strange story.

The agonizing grief of the bereaved mother, as she beheld the shattered and bleeding form of her child, broke in upon these doubtings; and while they endeavoured to offer her their consolation, none thought of the impending danger.

For a while after he was laid in bed, Hans seemed sunk in a swoon; but, suddenly awaking, he made an effort to rise. Too weak for this, he called the chief people of the village around, and said,——

"They are coming from the Kaiser-fells; they will be down soon, and burn the village, if you do not cut away the bridges over the Kletscher, and close the pass on the Weissen Spitze. Throw out skirmishers along the mountain side, and guard the footpath from the Pontlatzer Brücke."

Had the words been the dying orders of a general commanding an army, they could not have been heard with more implicit reverence, nor more strictly obeyed. From the spot the Vorsteher issued commands for these instructions to be followed. Hans' revelations were, to the superstitious imaginations of the peasants, of divine inspiration: and many already stoutly affirmed that the lame soldier was St. Martin himself, their patron saint, at whose shrine a crowd of devout worshippers were soon after seen kneeling.

The village doctor soon pronounced the case above his skill, but did not abandon hope. Hans only smiled faintly, and whispered,——

"Be it so! The proverb is always right,—

> ' Gott hat sein plan
> Fur Jedenmann.'

"What do you see there, Herr Vorsteher?" cried he, as the old man stared with astonished eyes from the little window that commanded the valley. "What is it you see?"

"The Dorf in the Kaunser-Thal seems all in commotion," answered the Vorsteher. "The people are packing everything in their waggons, and preparing to fly."

"I know that," said Hans, quietly; "I saw it already."

"Thou hast seen it already?" muttered the old man, in trembling awe.

"Yes, I saw it all. Look sharply along the river side, and tell me if a child is not holding two mules, who are striving to get down into the stream to drink."

"God be around and about us!" murmured the Vorsteher; "his power is great!" He crossed himself three times, and the whole company followed the pious motion; and a low murmuring prayer, was heard to fill the chamber.

"There is a waggon with eight bullocks, too, but they cannot stir the load," continued Hans, as, with closed eyes, he spoke with the faint accents of one half-sleeping.

"Who are these coming along the valley, Hans?" asked the Vorsteher; "they seem like our own Jägers, as well as my eyes can make out."

"He is asleep!" whispered his mother, with a cautious gesture to enforce silence.

It was true. Wearied, and faint, and dying, he had fallen into slumber.

While poor Hans slept, the tidings of which he was the singular messenger had received certain confirmation. The village scouts had already exchanged shots with the Bavarian troops upon the mountains, and driven them back. The guard at the Pontlatzer Brücke was seen to withdraw up the valley towards Landeck, escorting three field-pieces which had only arrived the preceding day. Every moment accounts came of garrisons withdrawn from distant outposts stations, and troops falling back to concentrate in the open country. It was seen, from various circumstances, that a forward movement had been intended, and was only thwarted by the inexplicable intervention of Hans Jörgle.

The Tyrolers could not fail to perceive that their own hour was now come, and the blow must be struck at once or never! So felt the leaders; and scarcely had the Bavarians withdrawn their advanced posts, than emissaries flew from village to village, with little scraps of paper, bearing the simple words, "*Es ist zeit!*—It is time!" while, as the day broke, a little plank was seen floating down the current, with a small flag-staff, from which a pennon fluttered—a signal that was welcomed by the wildest shouts of enthusiasm as it floated along:—the Tyrol was up! "*Für Gott, der Kaiser, und das Vaterland!*" rung from every glen and every mountain.

I dare not suffer myself to be withdrawn, even for a moment, to that glorious struggle—one of the noblest that ever a nation carried on to victory. My task is rather within that darkened room in the little hut, where, with fast-ebbing life, Hans Jörgle lay.

The wild cheers and echoing songs of the marching peasants awoke him from his sleep, which, if troubled by pangs of pain, had still lasted for some hours. He smiled, and made a gesture as if for silence, that he might hear the glorious sounds more plainly, and then lay in a calm peaceful reverie, for a considerable time.

The Vorsteher had, with considerable difficulty, persuaded the poor widow to leave the bedside for a moment, while he asked Hans a question.

The wretched mother was borne, almost fainting, away; and the old man sat in her place, but, subdued by the anguish of the scene, unable to speak. At last, while the tears ran down his aged cheeks, he kissed the child's hand, and said,—

"Thou wilt leave us soon, Hans!"

Hans gave a smile of sad, but beautiful, meaning, while his upturned eyes seemed to intimate his hope and his faith.

"True, Hans—thy reward is ready for thee!"

He paused a second, and then went on:—

"But even here, my child, in our own poor village, let thy devotion be a treasure, to be handed down in memory to our children, that they may know how one like themselves—more helpless, too—could serve his Vaterland. Say, Hans Jörgle, will it make thy last moments happier to think that our gratitude will raise a monument to thee in the Dorf, with thy father's name who fell at Elchingen, above thine own? The villagers have bid me ask thee this."

"My mother—my poor mother!" murmured Hans.

"She shall never want, Hans Jörgle. The best house in the Dorf shall not have a better fireside than hers. But my question, Hans—time presses."

Hans was silent, and lay with closed eyes for several minutes; then, laying his hand on the old man, he spoke with an utterance clear at first, but which gradually grew fainter as he proceeded—

"Let them build no monument to one poor and humble as I am; mine were not actions glorious enough for trophies in the noon-day; but let the *Nachtwachter* come here at midnight—at the same hour of my blessed dream —and let him wish me a good night. They who are sleeping will dream happier; and the waking will think, as they hear the cry, of Hans Jörgle!"

CHAPTER XIII.

THE Ortl'er is the Mont Blanc of the Tyrol, and seen from Nauders, a village on a green, grassy table land, more than four thousand feet above the sea, can well bear comparison with the boldest of the Swiss Alps. Nauders itself, a type of a Tyroler village, is situated in a wild and lonely region ; it has all the picturesque elegance and neat detail of which Tyrolers are so lavish in their houses, and, like every other Dorf in this country, has its proud castle standing sentry over it. The Barons of the Naudersberg were men of station in olden times, and exacted a tribute over a tract extending deep into the Engadine ; and now, in this great hall, whose chimney would contain the heaviest diligence that ever waddled over the Arlberg, a few Nauders notabilities are squabbling over some mysterious passage in a despatch from Vienna, for it is the high court of the district, while I wait patiently without for some formality of my passport. To judge from their grave expressions and their anxious glances towards me, one would say that I was some dangerous or suspected personage—some one whose dark designs the government had already fathomed, and were bent on thwarting If they did but know how few are, in all likelihood, the days I have yet to linger on, they would not rob me of one hour of them in this wild mountain.

And yet I have learned something while I wait. This little dorf, Nauders, is the birthplace of a very remarkable man, although one whose humble name, Bartholomew Kleinhaus, is little known beyond Tyrol. Left an orphan at five years old, he lost his sight in the small-pox, and was taken into the house of a carpenter who compassionated his sad condition. Here he endeavoured to learn something of his protector's trade; but soon relinquishing the effort, he set to work, forming little images in wood, at first from models, and then self-designed, till, at the age of thirteen, he completed a crucifix of singular beauty and elegance.

Following up the inspiration, he now laboured assiduously at his new craft, and made figures of various saints and holy personages, for his mind was entirely imbued with a feeling of religious fervour; and to such an extent that, in order to speak his devotion by another sense, he actually learned to play the organ, and with such a proficiency, that he performed the duties of organist for nearly a year in the village church of Kaltenbrunnen. As sculptor, his repute is widely spread and great in Tyrol. A St. Francis by his hand is at present in the Ambras collection at Vienna; many of his statues adorn the episcopal palaces of Chur and Brixen, and the various churches throughout the province.

Leaving the sculptor and his birthplace, which already a mountain mist is shrouding, I hasten on, for my passport is at last discovered to be in order, and I am free to pursue my road to Meran.

Of all spots in the Tyrol, none can compare with Meran, the wildest character of mountain uniting with a profusion of all that vegetation can bring. The snow peak, the glacier, the oak forest, the waving fields of yellow corn, the valley, one vast vineyard—where have such elements of grandeur and simple beauty in scenery been so gloriously commingled? And then the little town itself—what a strange reminiscence of long-buried years! The street—there is properly but one—with its deep arched passages, within which the quaint old shops, without windows, display their wares; and the courtyards, galleried around, story above story, and covered at top by a great awning to keep off the sun; for already Italy is near, and the odour of the magnolia and oleander is felt from afar.

I wandered into one of these courts last night; the twilight was closing, and there was a strange, mysterious effect in the dim distances upwards, where figures came and went along the high-perched galleries. Beyond the court lay a garden, covered over with a vine-roofed trellis, under whose shade various tables were placed. A single light, here and there, showed where one or two guests were seated; but all so still and silently, that one would have thought the place deserted. It seemed as if the great charm was that mellow air softened by silence, for none spoke.

I walked for some time through the alleys, and at last sat down to rest myself at a little table, over which a wide-leaved fig-tree spread its dark canopy.

At first I did not remark that another person was seated near the table; but as my eyes became more accustomed to the shade, I descried a figure opposite to me, and immediately rising, I offered my apology in German for intruding. He replied in French, by politely requesting I would be seated; and the tone and manner of his words induced me to comply.

We soon fell into conversation; and although I could barely distinguish his shadow as the night fell thicker, I recognized that he was an old man; his accent proclaimed him to be French. We chatted away, the topics ranging, with that wilfulness conversation always inclines to, from the " Wein-cur "—the " Grape cure "—for which Meran is celebrated, to the present condition and the past grandeur of the ancient town. With its bygone history my companion seemed well acquainted, and narrated with considerable skill some of its illustrious passages, concluding one by saying, " Here, in this very garden, on a summer morning of 1342, the Emperor and the Margrave of Brandenburg sat at breakfast, when a herald came to announce the advance of the procession with the future bride of the Duke, Margaretta, while the Bishops of Augsburg and Regensberg, and all the chivalry of the Tyrol, rode beside and around her. In yonder little chapel, where a light now glitters over a shrine, was the betrothal performed. From that day forth Tyrol was Austrian. Of all this gorgeous festivity, nothing remains but an iron horse-shoe nailed to the chapel door. The priest who performed the betrothal somewhat indiscreetly suggested that, with such a dowry as the bridegroom received, he might well be generous towards the Church; on which the Duke, a man of immense personal strength, at once stooped down and wrenched a fore-shoe from the bride's white palfrey, saying, with sarcastic bitterness, ' Here, I give thee iron for stone!' in allusion to the rocks and precipices of the Tyrol land.

"Ungratefully spoken at the time," continued the stranger, "and equally false as a prophecy.　These wild fastnesses have proved the best and last defences of that same Austrian Empire.　Indeed, so well aware was Napoleon of the united strength and resources of the Tyrol, that one of his first measures was to partition the country between Bavaria, Austria, and Illyria.　And yet this Tyrol loyalty is inexplicable.　They are attached to the house of Hapsburgh, but they are not Austrian in feeling.　The friends of free trade need not go far in Meran to find disciples to their doctrine.　Every one remembers the time that an aume of Meraner wine was worth seventy-five gulden, which now is to be had for five; but then they were Bavarian, and might barter the grape-juice for the yellow produce of the Baierisch corn-fields.　At the present day they are isolated, shut up, and imprisoned by custom-houses and toll; and they are growing daily poorer, and neglecting the only source they possessed of wealth."

We talked of Hofer, and I perceived that my companion was strongly imbued with an opinion, now very general in the Tyrol, that his merits were much less than foreigners usually ascribe to him.　Sprung from the people, the host of a little wayside inn, a man with little education, and of the very roughest manner, it is somewhat singular that his claims are most disputed among the very class he came from.　Had he been an aristocrat, in all likelihood they had never ventured to canvass the merits they now so mercilessly arraign.　They judge of his efforts by the most unfair of tests in such matters—the result.　They say, " To what end has Tyrol fought and bled ?　Are we better, or richer, or freer than before ? "　They even go further, and accuse him of exciting the revolt as a means of escaping the payment of his debts, which assuredly were considerable. What a terrible price is paid for mob popularity, when the hour of its effervescence is past.

We fell to chat over the character of revolutions generally, and the almost invariable tendency to reaction that ensues in all popular commotions. The character of the three days and the present condition of France, more despotically governed than ever Napoleon dared, was too palpable an example to escape mention. I had the less hesitation in speaking my opinion on this subject, that I saw my companion's leanings were evidently of the legitimist stamp.

From the revolution we diverged to the struggle itself of the three days; and being tolerably familiar, from various personal narratives, with the event, I ventured on expressing my concurrence with the opinion that a mere mob, unprepared, unarmed, and undisciplined, could never have held for an hour against the troops had there not been foul play.

"Where do you suspect this treachery to have existed?" asked my companion.

The tone of the question, even more than its substance, confused me, for I felt myself driven to a vague reply in explanation of a direct charge. I answered, however, that the magnitude of the danger could scarcely have been unknown to many men highly placed in the service of Charles X.; and yet it was clear the King never rightly understood that any real peril impended. The whole outbreak was treated as an "*échauffourée*."

"I can assure you of your error, so far," replied my companion. "The greatest difficulty we encountered——" There was a slight pause here, as if by use of the word "we" an unwitting betrayal had escaped him. He speedily, however, resumed: "The greatest difficulty was to persuade his Majesty that the entire affair was anything but a street brawl. He treated the accounts with an indifference bordering on contempt; and at every fresh narrative of the repulse of the troops, he seemed to feel that the lesson to be inflicted subsequently would be the

most efficacious check to popular excess in future. To give
an instance—a very slight one, but not without its moral,
of the state of feeling of the court,—at four o'clock of the
afternoon of the third day, when the troops had fallen
back from the Place du Carrousel, and with great loss been
compelled to retreat towards the Champs Elysées, Captain
Langlet, of the 4th Lancers, volunteered to carry a verbal
message to Versailles, in doing which he should traverse
a great part of Paris in the occupation of the insurgents.
The attempt was a bold and daring one, but it succeeded.
After innumerable hairbreadth dangers and escapes, he
reached Versailles at half-past seven. His horse had twice
fallen, and his uniform was torn by balls ; and he entered
the courtyard of the Palace just as his Majesty learned
that his dinner was served. Langlet hastened up the great
staircase, and, by the most pressing entreaties to the officer
in waiting, obtained permission to wait there till the King
should pass.   He stood there for nearly a quarter of an
hour ; it seemed an age to him, for though faint, wounded,
and weary, his thoughts were fixed on the scene of struggle
he had quitted, and the diminishing chances of success
each moment told.   At last the door of a *salon* was flung
wide, and the Grand Maréchal, accompanied by the officers
in waiting, were seen retiring in measured steps before
the king.   His Majesty had not advanced half-way along
the corridor when he perceived the splashed and travel-
stained figure of the officer.   'Who is that ? ' demanded
he, in a tone of almost asperity.   The officer on guard
stepped forward, and told who he was and the object of
his coming.   The king spoke a few words hastily and
passed on.   Langlet awaited in breathless eagerness to
hear when he should have his audience—he only craved
time for a single sentence.   What was the reply he received ?—an order to present himself, ' suitably dressed,'
in the morning.   Before that morning broke there was no
king in France !

     "Take this—the story is true—as a specimen of the
fatuity of the Court.   *Quem Deus vult perdere :*—so it is
we speak of events, but we forget ourselves."

     "But still," said I, " the army scarcely performed their

devoir—not, at least, as French troops understand *devoir*—where their hearts are engaged."

"You are mistaken again," said he. "Save in a few companies of the line, never did troops behave better: four entire squadrons of one regiment were cut to pieces at the end of the Rue Royale; two infantry regiments were actually annihilated at the Hôtel de Ville. For eight hours, at the Place du Carrousel, we had no ammunition, while the insurgents poured in a most murderous fire; so was it along the Quai Voltaire."

"I have heard," said I, "that the Duc de Raguse lost his head completely."

"I can assure you, sir, they who say so calumniate him," was the calm reply. "Never before that day was a Marshal of France called upon to fight an armed host, without soldiers and without ammunition."

"His fate would induce us to be superstitious, and believe in good luck. Never was there a man more persecuted by ill fortune!"

"I perceive they are shutting the gates," said my companion, rising; "these worthy Meraners are of the very earliest to retire for the night." And so saying, and with a "Good-night," so hastily uttered as to forbid further converse, my companion withdrew, while I wandered slowly back to my inn, curious to learn who he might be, and if I should ever chance upon him again.

*   *   *   *   *

I heard a voice this morning on the bridge, so exactly like that of my companion of last night, that I could not help starting. The speaker was a very large and singularly handsome man, who, though far advanced in life, walked with a stature as erect, and an air as assured, as he could have worn in youth. Large bushy eye-brows. black as jet, although his hair was perfectly white, shaded eyes of undimmed brilliancy—he was evidently "some-one," the least observant could not pass him without this conviction. I asked a stranger who he was, and received for answer, "Marshal Marmont—he comes here almost every autumn."

CHAPTER XIV.

THE TYROL.

EVERY traveller in the Tyrol must have remarked, that, wherever the way is difficult of access, or dangerous to traverse, some little shrine or statue is always to be seen, reminding him that a higher Power than his own watches over his safety, and suggesting the fitness of an appeal to Him who is "A very present help in time of trouble."

Sometimes a rude painting upon a little board, nailed on a tree, communicates the escape and gratitude of a traveller ; sometimes a still ruder fresco, on the very rock, tells where a wintry torrent had swept away a whole family, and calling on all pious Christians who pass that way to offer a prayer for the departed. There is an endless variety in these little "Votive Tablets," which are never more touching than when their very rude poverty attests the simplest faith of a simple people. The Tyrolers are indeed such. Perhaps alone, of all the accessible parts of Europe, the Tyrol has preserved its primitive habits and tastes for centuries unchanged. Here and there, throughout the continent, to be sure, you will find some little "Dorf," or village, whose old-world customs stand out in contrast to its neighbours : and where in their houses, dress, and bearing, the inhabitants seem unlike all else around them. Look more closely, however, and you will see that, although the grandmother is clothed in homespun, and wears her leathern pocket at her girdle, all studded with copper nails, that her granddaughter affects a printed cotton or a Swiss calico ; and instead of the broad-brimmed and looped felt of the old "Bauer," the new generation sport broad-cloth and beaver.

Such hamlets are, therefore, only like the passengers left behind by their own coach, and waiting for the next conveyance that passes to carry them on their journey.

In the Tyrol, however, such evidences of progress—as it is the fashion to call it—are rare. The peasantry seem content to live as their fathers have done, and truly he must be sanguine who could hope to better a condition, which, with so few privations, comprises so many of life's best and dearest blessings. If the mountain peaks be snow-clad, even in midsummer, the valleys (at least all in South Tyrol) are rich in vineyards and olive groves; and although wheat is seldom seen, the maize grows everywhere; the rivers swarm with trout; and he must be a poor marksman who cannot have venison for his dinner. The villages are large and well built; the great wooden houses, with their wide projecting roofs and endless galleries, are the very types of comfort. Vast piles of fire-wood, for winter use, large granaries of forage for the cattle—the cattle themselves with great silver bells hanging to their necks—all bespeak an ease, if not an actual affluence, among the peasantry. The Tyrolers are, in a word, all that poets and tourists say the Swiss are, and of which they are exactly the reverse.

It would be difficult to find two nations so precisely alike in all external circumstances, and so perfectly dissimilar in every feature of character. Even in their religious feelings, Romanism, generally so levelling, has not been able to make them of the same measure here, The Swiss Catholic—bigotted, overbearing, and plotting—has nothing in common with the simple-minded Tyroler, whose faith enters into all the little incidents of his daily life, cheering, exalting, and sustaining, but never suggesting a thought, save of charity and good will to all.

That they have interwoven, so to say, their religious belief into all their little worldly concerns, if not making their faith the rule, at least establishing it as the companion of their conduct, is easily seen. You never overtake a group, returning from fair or market, that all are not engaged in prayer, repeating together some litany of the Church; and as each new arrival joins the party, his voice chimes in, and swells the solemn hum as naturally as if pre-arranged or practised.

If you pass a village, or a solitary farmhouse, at sunset, the same accents meet your ears, or else you hear them singing some hymn in concert. Few " Bauer " houses, of any pretension, are without the effigy of a patron saint above the door, and even the humblest will have a verse of a psalm, or a pious sentence, carved in the oaken beam. Their names are taken from the saintly calendar, and everything, to the minutest particular, shows that their faith is an active working principle, fashioning all their actions, and mingling with all their thoughts. Their superstitions, like all simple-minded and secluded people's, are many ; their ignorance is not to be denied ; mayhap the Church has fostered the one, and done little to enlighten the other: still, if Romanism had no heavier sin to account for, no darker score to clear up, than her dealings in these mountains, there would be much to forgive in a creed that has conferred so many good gifts, and sowed the seeds of so few bad ones.

These pious emblems find their way, too, into places where one would scarce look for them—over the doors of village inns, and as signs to little wine and beer-houses: and frequently the Holy personages are associated with secular usages, strangely at variance with the saintly character. This I have seen, in the village beside me, a venerable St. Martin engaged in the extraordinary operation of shoeing a horse ; though what veterinary tastes the saint ever evinced, or why he is so represented, I can find no one to inform me. On the summit of steep passes, where it is usual, by a police regulation, to prescribe the use of a drag to all wheel carriages, the board which sets forth the direction is commonly ornamented by a St. Michael, very busily applying the drag to a heavy waggon, while the driver thereof is on his knees hard by, worshipping the saint, in evident delight at his dexterity. In the same way many venerable and holy men are to be seen presiding over savoury hams and goblets of foaming beer, and beaming with angelic beatitude at a party of hard-drinking villagers in the distance. Our present business is, however, less with the practice in general, than a particular instance, which is to be met with in the Bavarian Tyrol, mid-way between the villages of Murnou and Steingaden, where over the door of a solitary little way-side inn hangs a representation of the Virgin, with a starling perched upon her wrist. One has only to remark the expression of unnatural intelligence in the bird's look, to be certain that it was not a mere fancy of the artist to have placed her thus, but that some event of village tradition, or history, is interwoven with her presence.

The motto contributes nothing to the explanation. It is merely a line from the Church Litany, "Maria, Mutter Gottes, hülf uns—Mary, Mother of God, help us!"

There is then a story connected with the painting, and we shall, with your leave, tell it; calling our tale by the name of the little inn,

"MARIA HÜLF!"

Has our reader ever heard, or read, of those strange gatherings, which take place at the early spring in the greater number of southern German cities and are called, "Year Markets?" The object is simply to assemble the youth of the mountain districts in Tyrol and Vorarlberg, that they may be hired, by the farmers of the rich pasture countries, as herds. Thither they go—many a mile—some children of ten or eleven years old, and seeming even still younger, away from home and friends, little adventurers on the bleak wide ocean of life, to sojourn among strangers in far-off lands; to pass days long in lonely valleys or deep glens, without a sight or sound of human life around them; watching the bright sun and counting the weary minutes over, that night and rest may come, perchance with dreams of that far-off home, which, in all its poverty, is still cheered by the fond familiar faces! Some, ruddy and stout-looking, seem to relish the enterprise, and actually enjoy the career so promising in its vicissitudes; others, sad and care-worn, bear with them the sorrows of their last leave-taking, and are only comforted by the thought that autumn will come at last, and then the cattle must be housed for the winter: and then they shall be free to wend their way over mountain and plain, far, far away beyond Maltz—high in the wild peaks of the Stelvio, or deep in the lovely glens below Meran.

It was one of these "Markets" at Innspruck that a little boy was seen, not standing with the groups which usually gather together under a single leader, but alone and apart, seemingly without one that knew him. His appearance bespoke great poverty; his clothes, originally poor, were now in rags; his little cap, of squirrel skin, hung in fragments on either side of his pallid cheeks; his feet—a rare circumstance—were bare, and bloodstained from travel; want and privation were stamped in every feature: and his eyes, which at that moment were raised with eager anxiety as some Bauer drew nigh, grew wan, and filling at each new disappointment to his hopes, for this was his third day to stand in the market, and not one had even asked his name. And yet he heard that name; ever and anon it met his ears in sounds which stirred his feeble heart, and made it throb faster. "Fritzerl! ah, Fritzerl, good fellow!" were the words; and poor Fitzerl would stoop down when he heard them, and peep into a little cage where a starling was perched—a poor emaciated little thing it was, as wayworn and poverty struck, to all seeming, as himself: but he did not think so: he deemed it the very paragon of the feathered tribe, for it had a little toppin of brown feathers on its head, and a little ring of white around its neck, and would come when he called it; and, better than all, could sing, "Good Fritzerl—nice Fritzerl!" when it was pleased, and "Potztausend!" when angry. This was all its education; his master, poor little fellow, had not much more. How could he? Fritzerl's mother died when he was a baby; his father was killed by a fall from a cliff in the Tyrol Alps, for he was by trade a birdcatcher, and came from the Engadine, where every one loves birds, and in the pursuit of this passion met his fate.

Fritzerl was left an orphan at eleven years old, and all

his worldly wealth was this little starling ; for although
his father had left a little cabin in the high alps, and a
rifle, and some two or three articles of house-gear, they all
were sold to pay the expenses of his funeral, and feast
the neighbours who were kind enough to follow him to
the grave : so that poor Fritz kept open house for two
days ; and when he walked out the third after the coffin,
he never turned his steps back again, but wandered away
far, far away—to seek in the year-market of Innspruck
some kind peasant who would take him home to herd his
cattle, and be a father to him now.

Fritzerl knew not that the children who desire to be
hired out assemble together in little groups or gangs,
electing some one to bargain for them with the Bauers,
setting forth in vehement language their various excellen-
cies and good gifts, and telling where they have served
before, and what zeal and fidelity they have shown to their
trust. Fritz, I say, knew not this ; perhaps if he had it
would have availed him but little ; for he was so poorly
clad and so weak-looking, and so ignorant of all about
tending cattle besides, that he would soon have been driven
from the fraternity with disgrace. It was, then, as fortunate for him that he did not know the custom of the craft,
and that he took his stand alone and apart beside the
fountain in the main street of Innspruck.

And a lovely object is the same fountain, and a beautiful street it stands in, with its stately houses, all rich in
stuccoed arabesques, and gorgeously carved doors and
gates! And bright and cheerful, too, it looks, with its
Tyroler people clad in their gay colours and their gold-
banded hats !

Fritz saw little of these things, or, if he saw, he marked
them not. Cold, hunger, and desolation, had blunted the
very faculties of his mind ; and he gazed at the moving
crowd with a dreamy unconsciousness that what he saw
was real.

The third day of his painful watching was drawing to
a close. Fritz had, several hours before, shared his last
morsel of black bread with his companion ; and the bird,
as if sympathizing with his sorrow, sat moody and silent

on his perch, nor even by a note or sound broke the stillness.

"Poor Jacob!"* said Fritz, with tears in his eyes, "my hard luck should not fall on thee! If no one comes to hire me before the shadow closes across the street, I'll open the cage and let thee go!"

The very thought seemed an agony, for scarcely had he uttered it when his heart felt as if it would break, and he burst into a torrent of tears.

"Potztausend!" screamed Jacob, alarmed at the unusual cries—"Potztausend!" And as Fritz sobbed louder, so were the starling's cries of "Potztausend!" more shrill and piercing.

There were few people passing at the moment, but such as were, stopped; some to gaze with interest on the poor little boy—more, far more, to wonder at the bird; when suddenly a venerable old man, with a wide-leaved hat, and a silken robe reaching down to his feet, crossed over towards the fountain. It was the curate of Lenz, a pious and good man, universally respected in Innspruck.

"What art thou weeping for, my child?" said he, mildly.

Fritz raised his eyes, and the benevolent look of the old man streamed through his heart like a flood of hope. It was not, however, till the question had been repeated, that Fritz could summon presence of mind to tell his sorrow and disappointment.

"Thou should'st not have been here alone, my child," said the curate; "thou should'st have been in the great market with the others. And now the time is well-nigh over: most of the Bauers have quitted the town."

"Potztausend!" cried the bird, passionately.

"It will be better for thee to return home again to thy parents," said the old man, as he drew his little leathern purse from between the folds of his robe—"to thy father and mother."

"I have neither!" sobbed Fritz.

"Potztausend!" screamed the starling—"Potztausend!"

* Every Starling in Germany is called Jacob.

"Poor little fellow! I would help thee more," said the kind old priest, as he put six kreutzers into the child's hand, "but I am not rich either."

"Potztausend!" shrieked the bird, with a shrillness excited by Fritz's emotion; and as he continued to sob, so did the starling yell out his exclamation till the very street rang with it.

"Farewell, child!" said the priest, as Fritz kissed his hand for the twentieth time; "farewell, but let me not leave thee without a word of counsel: thou should'st never have taught thy bird that idle word. He that was to be thy companion and thy friend, as it seems to me he is, should have learned something that would lead thee to better thoughts. This would bring thee better fortune, Fritz. Adieu! adieu!"

"Potztausend!" said the starling, but in a very low, faint voice, as if he felt the rebuke; and well he might, for Fritz opened his little handkerchief and spread it over the cage—a sign of displeasure, which the bird understood well.

While Fritz was talking to the curate, an old Bauer, poorly, but cleanly clad, had drawn nigh to listen. Mayhap he was not overmuch enlightened by the curate's words, for he certainly took a deep interest in the starling; and every time the creature screamed out its one expletive he would laugh to himself, and mutter,—

"Thou art a droll beastie, sure enough."

He watched the bird till Fritz covered it up with his handkerchief, and then was about to move away, when, for the first time, a thought of the little boy crossed his mind. He turned abruptly round, and said,—

"And thou, little fellow!—what art doing here?"

"Waiting," sighed Fritz, heavily—"waiting!"

"Ah, to sell thy bird?" said the old man;—"come, I'll buy him from thee. He might easily meet a richer, but he'll not find a kinder, master. What wilt have?—twelve kreutzers, isn't it?"

"I cannot sell him," sobbed Fritz; "I have promised him never to do that."

"Silly child!" said the Bauer, laughing; "thy bird

cares little for all thy promises : besides, he'll have a better life with me than thee."

"That might he easily!" said Fritz: "but I'll not break my word."

"And what is this wonderful promise thou'st made, my little man?—come, tell it!"

"I told him," said Fritz, in a voice broken with agitation, "that if the shadow closed over the street down there before any one had hired me, that I would open his cage and let him free; and look! it is nearly across now—there's only one little glimpse of sunlight remaining!"

Poor child! how many in this world live upon one single gleam of hope—ay, and even cling to it when a mere twilight, fast fading before them!

The Bauer was silent for some minutes; his look wandered from the child to the cage, and back again from the cage to the child. At last he stooped down and peeped in at the bird, which, with a sense of being in disgrace, sat with his head beneath his wing.

"Come, my little man," said he, laying a hand on Fritz's shoulder, "I'll take thee home with me! 'Tis true I have no cattle—nothing save a few goats—but thou shalt herd these. Pack up thy bird, and let us away, for we have a long journey before us, and must do part of it before we sleep."

Fritz's heart bounded with joy and gratitude. It would have been, in good truth, no very splendid prospect for any other to be a goatherd to a poor Bauer—so poor that he had not even one cow; but little Fritz was an orphan, without a home, a friend, or one to give him shelter for a single night. It may be believed, then, that he felt overjoyed; and it was with a light heart he trotted along beside the old Bauer, who never could hear enough about the starling—where he came from? how he was caught? who taught him to speak? what he liked best to feed upon? and a hundred other questions, which, after all, should have been far more numerous ere Fritz found it any fatigue to answer them. Not only did it give him pleasure to speak of Jacob, but now he felt actually grateful to him, since, had the old Bauer not taken a fancy to the bird, it was more than likely he had never hired its master.

The Bauer told Fritz that the journey was a long one, and true enough. It lay across the Zillar-thal, where the garnets are found, and over the great mountains that separate the Austrian from the Bavarian Tyrol—many a long, weary mile—many, I say, because the Bauer had come up to Innspruck to buy hemp for spinning when the evenings of winter are long and dark, and poor people must do something to earn their bread. This load of hemp was carried on a little wheeled cart, to which the old man himself was harnessed, and in front of him his dog—a queer-looking team would it appear to English eyes, but one meets them often enough here; and as the fatigue is not great, and the peasants lighten the way by many a merry song — as the Tyrol *jodeln* — it never suggests the painful idea of over-hard or distressing labour. Fritzerl soon took his place as a leader beside the dog, and helped to pull the load; while the starling's cage was fastened on the sheltered side of the little cart, and there he travelled quite safe and happy.

I never heard that Fritz was struck—as he might possibly, with reason, have been—that, as he came into Bavaria, where the wide-stretching plains teem with yellow corn and golden wheat, the peasants seemed far poorer than among the wild mountains of his own Tyrol; neither have I any recollection that he experienced that peculiar freedom of respiration, that greater expansion of the chest, travellers so frequently enumerate as among the sensations whenever they have passed over the Austrian frontier, and breathed the air of liberty, so bounteously diffused through the atmosphere of other lands. Fritz, I fear, for the sake of his perceptive quickness, neither was alive to the fact nor the fiction above quoted; nor did he take much more notice of the features of the landscape, than to mark that the mountains were further off and not so high as those among which he lived—two circumstances which weighed heavily on his heart, for a Dutchman loves not water as well as a Tyroler loves a mountain.

The impression he first received did not improve as he drew near the Dorf where the old Bauer lived. The country was open and cultivated; but there were few trees: and while one could not exactly call it flat, the surface was merely a waving tract that never rose to the dignity of mountain. The Bauer houses, too, unlike the great wooden edifices of the Southern Tyrol—where three, ay, sometimes four, generations may be found dwelling under one roof—were small, misshapen things, half stone, half wood. No deep shadowing eave along them to relieve the heat of a summer sun; no trellised vines over the windows and the doorway; no huge yellow gourds drying on the long galleries, where bright geraniums and prickly aloes stood in a row; no Jäger either, in his green jacket and gold-tasselled hat, was there, sharing his breakfast with his dog; the rich spoils of his day's sport strewed around his feet—the smooth-skinned chamois, or the stag with the gnarled horns, or the gorgeously-feathered wild turkey, all so plentiful in the mountain regions. No; here was a land of husband-men, with ploughs, and harrows, and deep-wheeled carts, driven along by poor-looking ill-clad peasants, who never sung as they went along, scarce greeted each other as they passed.

It was true the great plains were covered with cattle, but to Fritz's eyes the prospect had something mournful and sad. It was so still and silent. The cows had no bells beneath their necks like those in the Alpine regions; nor did the herds *jodeln* to each other, as the Tyrolers do, from cliff to cliff, making the valleys ring to the merry sound. No, it was as still as midnight; not even a bird was there to cheer the solitude with his song.

If the aspect without had little to enliven Fritz's spirits, within doors it had even less. The Bauer was very poor; his hut stood on a little knoll outside the village, and on the edge of a long tract of unreclaimed land, which once had borne forest trees, but now was covered by a low scrub, with here and there some huge trunk, too hard to split, or too rotten for firewood. The hut had two rooms, but even that was enough, for there was nobody to dwell in it but the Bauer, his wife, and a little daughter, Gretchen, or, as they called her in the Dorf, " Grettl'a." She was a year younger than Fritz, and a good-tempered little " Mädle ; " and who, but for over-hard work for one so young, might have been even handsome. Her eyes were large and full, and her hair bright-coloured, and her skin clear ; yet scanty food and continual exposure to the air, herding the goats, had given her a look of being much older than she really was, and imparted to her features that expression of premature cunning which poverty so invariably stamps upon childhood.

It was a happy day for Grettl'a that brought Fritz to the cottage ; not only because she gained a companion and a playfellow, but that she needed no longer to herd the goats on the wild bleak plain, rising often ere day broke, and never returning till late in the evening. Fritz would do all this now ; and more, he would bring in the firewood from the little dark wood-house, where she feared to venture after nightfall ; and he would draw water from the great deep well, so deep that it seemed to penetrate to the very centre of the earth. He would run errands, too, into the Dorf ; and beetle the flax betimes ; in fact, there was no saying what he would not do. Fritz did not disappoint any of these sanguine expectations of his usefulness ; nay, he exceeded them all, showing himself daily more devoted to the interests of his humble protectors. It was never too early for him to rise from his bed—never too late to sit up when any work was to be done ; always willing to oblige—ever ready to render any service in his power. Even the Bauer's wife, a hard-natured, ill-thinking creature, in whom poverty had heightened all the faults, nor taught one single lesson of kindliness to others who were poor—even she felt herself constrained to moderate the rancour of her harshness, and would even at times vouchsafe a word or a look of good humour to the little orphan boy. The Bauer himself, without any great faults of character, had no sense of the fidelity of his little follower. He thought that there was a compact between them, which, as each fulfilled in his own way, there was no more to be said of it.

Gretchen more than made up for the coldness of her parents. The little maiden, who knew by hard experience the severe lot to which Fritz was bound, she felt her whole heart filled with gratitude and wonder towards him. Wonder, indeed! for not alone did his services appear so well performed, but they were so various and so numerous. He was everywhere and at everything; and it was like a proverb in the house—"Fritz will do it." He found time for all; he neglected—stay, I am wrong—poor little fellow, he did neglect something—something that was more than all, but it was not his fault. Fritz never entered the village church—he never said a prayer; he knew nothing of the Power that had created him, and all that he saw around him. If he thought on these things, it was with the vague indecision of a mind without guidance or direction. Why, or how, and to what end, he and others like him, lived or died, he could not, by any effort, conceive. Fritz was a bond-man—as much a slave as many who are carried away in chains across the seas, and sold to strange masters. There was no bodily cruelty in his servitude; he endured no greater hardships than poverty entails on millions; his little sphere of duties was not too much for his strength; his humble wants were met, but the darkest element of slavery was there! The daily round of service over, no thought was taken of that purer part which in the peasant claims as high a destiny as in the prince. The Sunday saw him go forth with his flock to the mountain, like any other day; and though from some distant hill he could hear the tolling bell that called the villagers to prayer, he knew not what it meant. The better dresses and holiday attire suggested some notion of a fête-day; but as he knew there were no fête-days for him, he turned his thoughts away, lest he should grow unhappy.

If Fritz's companion, when within doors, was Grettl'a, when he was away on the plain, or among the furze hills, the Starling was ever with him. Indeed he could easier have forgotten his little cap of squirrel skin, as he went forth in the morning, than the cage, which hung by a string on his back. This he unfastened when he had led his goats into a favourable spot for pasturage, and sitting down beside it, would talk to the bird for hours. It was a long time before he could succeed in obeying the Curate's counsel, even in part, and teach the bird not to cry "Potztausend." Starlings do not unlearn their bad habits much easier than men; and, despite all Fritz's teaching, his pupil would burst out with the forbidden expression on any sudden emergency of surprise; or sometimes, as it happened, when he had remained in a sulky fit for several days together without uttering a note, he would reply to Fritz's caresses and entreaties to eat by a sharp, angry "Potztausend!" that any one less deeply interested than poor Fritz would have laughed at outright. They were no laughing matters to him. He felt that the work of civilization was all to be done over again. But his patience was inexhaustible; and a circumstance, perhaps, not less fortunate—he had abundant time at his command. With these good aids he laboured on, now punishing, now rewarding, ever inventing some new plan of correction, and at last—as does every one who has that noble quality, perseverance—at last succeeding, not, indeed, all at once perfectly; for Star's principles had been laid down to last, and he struggled hard not to abandon them, and he persisted to cry "Potz——" for three months after he had surrendered the concluding two syllables; finally, however, he gave up even this; and no temptation of sudden noise, no riotous conduct of the villagers after nightfall, no boiling over of the great metal pot that held the household supper, nor any more alarming ebullition of ill temper of the good Frau herself, would elicit from him the least approach to the forbidden phrase.

While the Starling was thus accomplishing one part of his education by unlearning, little Fritz himself, under Grettl'a's guidance, was learning to read. The labour was not all to be encountered, for he already had made some little progress in the art under his father's tuition. But the evening hours of winter, wherein he received his lessons, were precisely those in which the poor bird catcher, weary and tired from a day spent in the mountains, would fall fast asleep, only waking up at intervals to assist Fritz over a difficulty, or say, "Go on," when his blunders had made him perfectly unintelligible even to himself. It may be well imagined, then, that his proficiency was not very great. Indeed, when first called upon by Grettl'a to display his knowledge, his mistakes were so many, and his miscallings of words so irresistibly droll, that the little girl laughed outright; and, to do Fritz justice, he joined in the mirth himself.

The same persistence of purpose that aided him while teaching his bird, befriended him here. He laboured late and early, sometimes repeating to himself by heart little portions of what he had read, to familiarize himself with new words; sometimes wending his way along the plain, book in hand; and then, having mastered some fierce difficulty, he would turn to his Starling to tell him of his victory, and promise, that when once he knew how to read well, he would teach him something out of his book— "Something good;" for, as the Curate said, "that would bring luck."

So long as the winter lasted, and the deep snow lay on the hills, Fritz always herded his goats near the village, seeking out some sheltered spot where the herbage was still green, or where the thin drift was easily scraped away. In summer, however, the best pasturages lay further away among the hills near Steingaden, a still and lonely tract, but inexpressibly dear to poor Fritz, since there the wild flowers grew in such abundance, and from thence he could see the high mountains above Reute and Paterkirchen, lofty and snow-clad like the "Jochs" in his own Tyrol land. There was another reason why he loved this spot. It was here that, in a narrow glen where two paths crossed, a little shrine stood, with a painting of the Virgin enclosed within it—a very rude performance, it is true; but how little connection is there between the excellence of art and the feelings excited in the humble breast of a poor peasant child! The features, to his thinking were beautiful; never had eyes a look so full of compassion and of love. They seem to greet him as he came and follow him as he lingered on his way homeward. Many an hour did Fritz sit upon the little bench before the shrine, in unconscious worship of that picture. Heaven knows what fancies he may have had of its origin, it never occured to him to think that human skill could have achieved anything so lovely.

He had often remarked that the villagers, as they passed, would kneel down before it, and with bowed heads and crossed arms seemed to do it reverence; and he himself, when they were gone, would try to imitate their gestures, some vague sentiment of worship struggling for utterance in his heart.

There was a little inscription in gilt letters beneath the picture; but these he could not read, and would gaze at their cabalistic forms for hours long, thinking how, if he could but decipher them, that the mystery might be revealed.

How he longed for the winter to be over and the spring to come, that he might lead the goats to the hills, and to the little glen of the shrine! He could read now. The letters would be no longer a secret; they would speak to him, and to his heart, like the voice of that beauteous image. How ardently did he wish to be there! and how, when the first faint sun of April sent its pale rays over the plain, and glittered with a sickly delicacy on the lake, how joyous was his spirit and how light his step upon the heather!

Many a little store of childish knowledge had Grettl'a opened to his mind in their winter evenings' study; but somehow, he felt as if they were all as nothing compared to what the golden letters would reveal. The portrait, the lonely glen, the solemn reverence of the kneeling worshippers, had all conspired to create for him a mass of emotions indescribably pleasurable and thrilling. Who can say the secret of such imaginings, or bound their sway?

The wished-for hour came, and it was alone and unseen that he stood before the shrine and read the words, "Maria, Mutter Gottes, hülf uns." If this mystery were unrevealed to his senses, a feeling of dependent helplessness was too familiar to his heart not to give the words a strong significance. He was poor, unfriended, and an

orphan : who could need succour more than he did ?
Other children had fathers and mothers, who loved them
and watched over them ; their little wants were cared for,
their wishes often gratified. His was an uncheered existence : who was there to " *help him ?* "

Against the daily load of his duties he was not conscious of needing aid ; his burden he was both able and
willing to bear. It was against his thoughts in the long
hours of solitude—against the gloomy visions of his own
free-thinking spirit, he sought assistance ; against the sad
influence of memory, that brought up his childhood before
him, when he had a father who loved him—against the
dreary vista of an unloved future, he needed help. " And
could *she* befriend him ? " was the question he asked his
heart.

" He must ask Grettl'a this ; she would know it all ! "
Such were the reflections with which he bent his way
homeward, as eagerly as in the morning he had sought the
glen. Grettl'a did know it all, and more too, for she had a
prayer-book, and a catechism, and a hymn-book, though
hitherto these treasures had been unknown to Fritz,
whose instructions were always given in a well-thumbed
little volume of fairy tales, where " Hans Daümling " and
" The Nutzcracker " figured as heroes. ·

I am not able to say that Grettl'a's religious instruction
was of the most enlightened nature—not any more than it
was commemsurate with the wishes and requirements of
him who sought it ; it went, indeed, little further than an
explanation of the " golden letters." Still, slight and
vague as it was, it comforted the poor heart it reached, as
the most straggling gleam of sunlight will cheer the
dweller in some dark dungeon, whose thoughts soar out
upon its rays to the gorgeous luminary it flows from.
Whatever the substance of his knowledge, its immediate
effect upon his mind was to diffuse a hopeful trust and
happiness through him he had never known till now.
His loneliness in the world was no longer the solitary
isolation of one bereft of friends. Not only with his own
heart could he commune now. He felt there was One above
who read these thoughts, and could turn them to his will.

And in this trust his daily labour was lightened, and his lot more happy.

"Now," thought he, one day, as he wandered onward among the hills, "now, I can teach thee something good—something that will bring us luck. Thou shalt learn the lesson of the golden letters, Starling—ay, truly, it will be hard enough at first. It cost me many a weary hour to learn to read, and thou hast only one little line to get off by heart—and such a pretty line, too! Come, Jacob, let's begin at once." And, as he spoke, he opened the cage and took out the bird, and patted his head kindly and smoothed down his feathers. Little flatteries, that Starling well understood were preparatory to some educational requirement; and he puffed out his chest proudly, and advanced one leg with an air of importance: and drawing up his head, seemed as though he could say, "Well, what now, Master Fritz?—what new scheme is this in thy wise head?"

Fritz understood him well, or thought he did so, which in such cases comes pretty much to the same thing; and so, without more ado, he opened his explanation, which perhaps, after all, was meant equally for himself as the Starling—at least I hope so, for I suspect he comprehended it better.

He told him that for a long time his education had been grossly neglected; that having originally been begun upon a wrong principle, the great function of his teacher had been to eradicate the evil, and, so to say, to clear the soil for the new and profitable seed. The ground, to carry out the illustration, had now lain long enough in fallow—the time had arrived to attend to its better culture.

It is more than probable Fritz had never heard of the great controversy in France upon the system of what is called the "Secondary Instruction," nor troubled his head on the no less active schism in our own country between the enemies and advocates of National Education. So that he has all the merit, if it be one, of solving a very difficult problem for himself without aid or guidance; for he resolved that a religious education should precede all other.

" Now for it," said he, at the close of a longer exposi-
tion of his intentions than was perhaps strictly necessary,
" now for it, Starling ! repeat after me—' Maria, Mutter
Gottes, hülf uns ! ' "

The bird looked up in his face with an arch drollery
that almost disconcerted the teacher. If a look could
speak, that look said, as plainly as ever words could,—

" Why don't you ask me to say the whole Litany,
Fritz ?"

" Ay, ay," replied Fritz, for it was a reply, " I know
that's a great deal to learn all at once, and some of the
words are hard enough, too; but with time, Star, time
and patience—I had to use both one and the other before
I learned to read; and many a thing that looks difficult
and impossible even at first, seems quite easy afterwards.
Come, then, just try it: begin with the first word—
' Maria.'

It was in vain Fritz spoke in his most coaxing accents,
in vain did he modulate the syllables in twenty different
ways; all his entreaties and pettings, all his blandishments
and caresses, were of no avail, Star remained deaf to them
all. He even turned his back at last, and seemed as if no
power on earth should make a Christian of him. Fritz
had had too much experience of the efficacy of perseverance
in his own case to abandon the game here; so he went to
work again, and with the aid of a little lump of sugar
returned to the lecture.

Had Star been a Chancery lawyer he could not have
received the fee more naturally, though, for the honour of
the equity bar, I would hope the similitude ends there, for
he paid not the slightest heed to the "instructions."

It would, perhaps, be rash in us "featherless bipeds" to
condemn Star all at once; there is no saying on what
grounds he may have resisted this educational attempt.
How do we know that his reasoning ran not somewhat in
this strain ?—

" What better off shall I be when I have learned all
your hard words ?—or how is it that you, my teacher,
knowing them so well, should be the poor, half-fed, half-
naked thing I see there before me ?"

These very conjectures would seem to have crossed Fritz's mind, for he said,—

" It is not for a mere whim that I would have thee learn this; these words will bring us luck, Star! Ay, what I say is true, though thou mayst shake thy head and think otherwise. I tell thee, ' Good words bring luck.' "

Whether it was that Star assumed an air of more than ordinary conceit and indifference, or that Fritz had come to the end of patience, I cannot affirm; but he hastily added, and in a voice much louder and more excited than was his wont,—" It is so; and thou shalt learn the words whether thou wilt or no—that I tell thee ! "

" Potztausend ! " cried the bird, frightened by his excitement, and at once recurring to his long unused exclamation : " Potztausend ! "

" Hush, shameless thing ! " said Fritz, angrily ; " there is nothing for it but punishment ! " And so he replaced him in the cage, covered him close on every side with his handkerchief, and trudged sorrowfully towards home.

For several days Fritz never spoke to Starling, even one word. He brought him his food in silence ; and instead of taking him, as of old, along with him into the fields, he hung his cage in a gloomy corner of the hut, whence he could see little or nothing of what went on in the house—no small privation for a bird so alive to inquisitiveness. At length, when he believed punishment had gone far enough, he took him down and hung him on his back as usual, and brought him a long long way into the hills. The day was fine, a fresh but balmy spring breathed over the young flowers, and the little stream danced and rippled pleasantly ; and the clouds moved along overhead in large soft masses, bordered with a silvery edge. Star never noticed these things ; he was indignant at the neglect, as he deemed it, which had been shown him of late. His pride and spirit—and Starlings are not deficient in either—had sustained grievous injury ; and he felt that, without due reparation made to him, he could not, consistently with honour, sign a treaty of reconciliation.

Fritz mistook these indications altogether—and who

can blame him? What the world calls dignity is not unfrequently mere sulk. How should poor Fritz make distinctions great ministers and princes are sometimes incapable of?

The end of all this was a struggle, a long and violent struggle on each side for the ascendancy. Fritz, however, had the advantage, for he could starve out the enemy— a harsh measure no doubt; but greater folks have adopted even more severe ones to enforce their principles. Fritz, besides, had all the stern enthusiasm of a fanatic in the cause. The dark zeal of the Holy Office itself never enforced its decrees with more inflexible purpose than did he his. "Accept this creed or die in your sins," was, if not exactly his dictum, certainly his full meaning. Star stood out long, so long that Fritz began at last to fear that the creature meditated martyrdom, and in this dread he relaxed somewhat of his prison discipline.

It would scarcely be instructive—not any more than amusing—to recount the painful progress of this long contest, a contest after all in which there is nothing new to any reader of history; for when force is on one side and weakness on the other, the result may be deferred but is never doubtful. It is enough that we say Star made submission. True, it was the submission of coercion—no matter for that, it was submission, for after three weeks of various successes on either side, the creature greeted Fritz one morning as he arose with a faint cry of "Maria, Maria!"

This was enough, more than enough, and Fritzerl could have hugged him to his heart.

His authority recognized, his will acknowledged, he was but too happy to take his rebellious subject into full favour again. Whether Star felt the benefits of his changed conduct so very satisfactory to his comfort, or that he was really disposed to please his master, I cannot say; but from that hour out he laboured strenuously to learn his new profession of faith, and screamed "Maria!" from day-dawn to dusk. The two following words were, however, downright puzzles: "Mutter-Gottes" was a combination that no starling, even a German one, bred up among strong gutturals and flat labials, could master. He worked hard, however, and so did Fritz. If life depended upon it, neither of them could have exerted themselves more zealously; but it was no use. In any other language, perhaps, Star might have been able to invoke the Virgin, but here it was out of the question. The nearest approach the poor fellow could make was something like a cry of " Mörder—Mörder " (Murder—murder); so unfortunate a change that Fritz abandoned the lesson with the best grace he could, betaking himself to the concluding words which happily presented no such unseemly similitudes.

His success here was such as to obliterate all memory of his former defeat. Starling made the most astonishing progress and learned the words so perfectly, with such accuracy of enunciation, that to hear him at a little distance any one would say it was some pious Catholic invoking the Virgin with all his might. The " Hülf uns " was not a mere exclamation but a cry for actual aid so natural as to be perfectly startling.

So long as the bird's education was incomplete, Fritzerl carefully screened him from public observation. He had all the susceptibility of a great artist who would not let his canvas be looked upon before the last finishing touch was laid on the picture. No sooner, however, had full success crowned his teaching than he proudly displayed him in a new cage made for the occasion at the door of the Bauer's hut.

It was Sunday and the villagers were on their way to mass ; and what was their astonishment to hear themselves exhorted as they passed by the fervent cry of " Maria, hülf uns ! Hülf uns, Maria ! " Group after group stood in mute amazement gazing at the wonderful bird, some blessing themselves with a pious fervour, others disposed to regard the sounds as miraculous, and more than either stood in dumb astonishment at this new specimen of ghostly counsel.

All this while Fritzerl lay hid beneath the window, enjoying his triumph with a heart full almost to bursting. Never did singing-master listen to the syren notes of his pupil, while as the *prima donna* of a great opera she elec-

trified or entranced a crowded audience with more enthusiastic rapture than did Fritz at his starling's performance.
Poor little fellow! it was not merely vanity gratified by
public applause—it was a higher feeling was engaged here.
A sense of religious exaltation worked within him that he
had laboured in a great cause ; a thrill of ecstasy trembled
at his heart that another voice than his own was asking aid
for him, and incessantly invoking the Virgin's protection
on his own head.   Happy had it been for him that no other
sentiment had intervened, and that he had not also indulged
a vain pride in the accomplishment of his pupil!

It so chanced that among those who passed the hut and
stood to wonder at this astonishing creature, was a tall,
ragged-looking, swarthy fellow, whose dress of untanned
leather, and cap ornamented with the tail of many a wood
squirrel, told that he was an " Engadiner," one from the
same land Fritz came himself. A strange wild land it is!
where in dress, language, custom, and mode of life, there
is no resemblance to anything to be seen throughout
Europe. A more striking representative of his strange
country need not have been wished for. His jacket was
hung round with various tufts of plumage and fur for
making artificial birds, with whistles and bird-calls to
imitate every note that ever thrilled through a leafy
grove ; his leathern breeches only reached to the knee,
which was entirely bare, as well as the leg, to below the
calf, where a rude sandal was fastened ; his arms, also,
copper-coloured as those of an Indian, were quite naked,
two leathern bracelets enclosing each wrist, in which
some metal hooks were inserted : by these he could hang
on the branch of a tree, or the edge of a rock, leaving his
hands at liberty. He wore his coal-black hair far down
on his back and shoulders, and his long moustache
drooped deep beneath his lank jaw. If there was something wild almost to ferocity in his black and flashing
eyes, the mouth, with its white and beautifully regular
teeth, had a look of almost womanly delicacy and softness—a character that was well suited to the musical
sounds of his native language—one not less pleasant to
the ear than Italian itself. Such was he who stopped to

listen to the bird, and who, stealing round to the end of the hut, lay down beneath some scattered branches of firewood to delight his ear to the uttermost.

It may be doubted whether a connoisseur ever listened to Grisi or Jenny Lind with more heartfelt rapture than did the Engadiner to the starling; for while the bird, from time to time, would break forth with its newly acquired invocation, the general tenor of its song was a self-taught melody—one of those wild and delicious voluntaries in which conscious power displayed itself; now, astounding the ear by efforts the wildest and most capricious, now subduing the sense by notes plaintive almost to bring tears. In these latter it was that he mingled his cry of " Maria, hülf—hülf—hülf uns, Maria ! "—words so touching and so truthful in their accents that at every time the Engadiner heard them he crossed himself twice on the forehead and the breast; which devout exercise, I am constrained to say, had in his case more of habit than true piety, as the sequel proved.

I forget whether it is not Madame de Scuderi has built a little theory upon the supposition that every mind has within it the tendency to yield to some one peculiar temptation. The majority, I fancy, have not limited their weakness to units. Poverty has so many wants to be supplied, wealth so many seductions to offer, that it may be affirmed he is not worse than his fellows whose heart has only one undefended bastion. I am not anxious to claim for my Engadiner any more than ordinary powers of resistance : neither his race nor his country, the habits of his life, nor his principles—if it be permitted to use the word—had taught him such self-control; but, if they had—if they had steeled his nature against every common seduction, they could not have stifled within him the native passion for bird-catching, or, what is very much akin to it, bird-stealing He would as soon have thought it needful to restrict his lungs in their requisite quantity of atmospheric air, as to curb what he regarded as a mere human instinct. If Engadiners were made for anything, it was for bird-catching : no one did anything else, thought, spoke, or dreamt of anything else, in the Engadine. It was not a

pastime, or a caprice; it was not that the one was skilful,
or that the other was adroit at it, but the whole population felt that birds were their natural prey, and that the
business of their life was comprised in catching, feeding,
training, sending, and selling them all over the globe—
not only in Europe, but over the vast continent of America.
Wherever birds had fanciers, wherever men cared for the
tints of plumage or the warbling mellowness of their notes,
there an Engadiner was sure to be found. And who has
ever studied their nature like one of these mountaineers,
who knows all their habits and their tastes, their seasons
of migrating and returning, how they build their nests,
and all their likings and their antipathies—the causes
which influence their selection and abandonment of a
peculiar locality, the meaning of their songs—ay, and
they are full of meaning—of welcome, of sorrow, of love,
and of despair? None like an Engadiner for all this!
Few would have the patience, fewer still the requisite
gifts of acuteness, with uncommon powers of eye and ear
—of eye to discern the tints of plumage among the dark
leaves of the pine forest—of ear to catch and imitate the
notes of each tribe, so that birds themselves should answer
to the sounds.

The Engadiner stirred not from his hiding-place the
whole day; he watched the moving throng passing to
and from the village church; he saw the Bauers pass by,
some in the Sunday "waggons," their horses gaily capari-
soned, with huge scarlet tassels beneath their necks, and
great wide traces all studded with little copper nails;
and the more humble, on foot, the men dressed in their
light Bavarian blue, and the women clad in a coarser
stuff of the same colour, their wealth being all centered
in one strange head-dress of gold and silver filigree,
which, about the size and shape of a peacock's tail when
expanded, is attached to the back of the head—an un-
wieldly contrivance, which has not the merit of becoming-
ness ; it neither affords protection against sun or rain,
and is so inconvenient, that when two peasant women
walk together they have to tack and beat, like ships in a

narrow channel; and not unfrequently, like such craft,
run foul of each other after all.

The Engadiner watched these evidences of affluence,
such as his wild mountains had nothing to compare with,
and yet his heart coveted none of them. They were
objects of his wonder, but no more; while every desire
was excited to possess the little bird, whose cage hung
scarcely three yards from where he lay.

As evening drew nigh, the Engadiner became almost
feverish in excitement; each stir within the house made
him fear that some one was coming to take the bird
away; every step that approached suggested the same
dread. Twice he resolved to tear himself from the spot,
and pursue his journey; but each time some liquid note,
some thrilling cadence, fell like a charm upon his ear, and
he sank down spell-bound. He sat for a long time with
eyes rivetted on the cage, and then at length, stooping
down, he took from the ground beside him a long branch
of pine-wood; he measured with his eye the distance to
the cage, and muttered to himself an assent. With a
dexterity and speed which in his countrymen are instincts,
he fastened one handle of his scissors to the branch, and
tied a string to the other, making an implement like that
used by the grape gatherers in the wine season. He
examined it carefully, to try its strength, and even
experimented with it on the jessamine that grew over
the front of the cottage. His dark eyes glistened like
burning coals as the leaves and twigs were snapped off at
a touch. He looked around him to see that all was still,
and no one near. The moment was favourable : the
Angelus was ringing from the little chapel, and all the
Dorf was kneeling in prayer. He hesitated no longer,
but, lifting the branch, he cut through three of the little
bars in the cage; they were dry and brittle, and yielded
easily: in a moment more he had removed them, leaving
a little door wide enough for the bird to escape. This
done, he withdrew the stick, detached the scissors, and
in its place tied on a small lump of maple sugar—the food
the bird loves best. Starling, at first terrified by the
intrusion, soon gained courage and approached the bait.

He knew not that a little noose of horse-hair hung beneath it, which, no sooner had he tasted the sugar, than it was thrown over his neck and drawn tight. Less practised fingers than the Engadiner's could scarcely have enclosed that little throat sufficiently to prevent even one cry, and yet not endanger life.

Every step of this process was far more rapid than we have been in telling it. The moment it was effected, the Engadiner was away. No Indian ever rose from his lair with more stealthy cunning, nor tracked his enemy with a fleeter step ; away over the wide plain, down through the winding glens, among the oak-scrub, and into the dark pine-wood, who could trace his wanderings?—who could overtake him now ?

With all his speed, he had not gone above a mile from the Dorf when Fritz missed his treasure. He went to take his bird into the house for the night, when the whole misfortune broke full upon him. For a few seconds, like most people under sudden bereavement, his mind could not take in all the sorrow : he peered into the cage, he thrust his fingers into it, he tumbled over the moss at the bottom of it ; and then, at length, conscious of his loss, he covered his face with his hands, and sobbed as though his heart was breaking.

Men and women may find it hard to sympathize with such sorrow. A child, however, can understand a child's grief, for Fritz had lost everything he had in the world. This little bird was not only all his wealth, all his ambition, his daily companion in solitary places, his hope, his friend, but somehow it was linked mysteriously with the memories of his own home—memories that every day, every hour, was effacing—but these, Star still could call up in his heart : to lose him was, therefore, to cut the last slender cord that tied him to the past and linked him to the future.

His violent sobbing brought Grettl'a to him, but he could tell her nothing—he could only point to the cage, which now hung on its side, and mutter the one word,—

"Hin ! hin !"—Away ! away !

The little girl's grief was scarcely less poignant than his own. She wrung her hands in all the passion of sorrow, and cried bitterly.

The Bauer and his wife now came to the spot, the one to join in, the other to rebuke their affliction. How little the children noticed either! Their misery filled up every corner of their minds—their wretchedness was overwhelming.

Every corner of the little hut was associated with some recollection of the poor " Star." Here, it was he used to feed—here, he hopped out to greet Fritz of an evening, when the bad weather had prevented him accompanying him to the fields. There, he was accustomed to sit while they were at supper, singing his merry song; and here, would he remain silently while they were at prayers, waiting for the moment of their rising to utter the cry of " Maria, hülf uns!"

Each time the children's eyes met, as they turned away from looking at any of these well-known spots, they burst into tears: each read the other's thoughts, and felt his sorrows more deeply in the interchange.

What a long, long night was that! They cried themselves to sleep, to awake again in tears!—now, to dream they heard " Star " calling to them—now, to fancy he had come back again, all wayworn and ruffled, glad to seek his usual shelter, and be with friends once more—and then they awoke to feel the bitterness of disappointment, and know that he was gone!"

" And he told me, Grettl'a—he told me ' A good word brings luck!'" sobbed Fritz, whose despair had turned to scepticism.

Poor Grettl'a had no argument wherewith to meet this burst of misery—she could but mingle her tears with his.

We frequently hear of the hard-heartedness of the poor —how steeled they are against the finer affections and softer feelings of the world; but it might be as well to ask if the daily business of life—which to them is one of sheer necessity—does not combat more powerfully against the indulgence of sorrow than all the philosophy that mere wisdom ever taught?

Poor Fritzerl awoke with a heart almost weighed down with affliction, but still he went forth with his goats to the pasture, and tended and watched after them as carefully as ever. The next day, and the day after that again, he went about his accustomed duties; but on the third day, as he sat beside Grettl'a under the old linden-tree before the door, he whispered to her—

"I can bear it no longer, Grettl'a! I must away!— away!" And he pointed to the distance, which, vague and undefined as his own resolves, stretched out its broad expanse before them.

Grettl'a did her best to persuade him against his rash determination: she reasoned as well as she could reason; she begged, she even cried to him; and at last, all else failing, she forgot her pledge, and actually ran and told her father.

The Bauer, sorry to lose so faithful a servant as Fritz, added his influence to the little maiden's tears; and even the Bauer's wife tried to argue him out of his resolve, mingling with her wise suggestions about a "wide world and a cold one" some caustic hints about ingratitude to his friends and protectors.

Fritz was deaf to all: if he could not yield to Grettl'a's prayers and weeping eyes, he was strong against the old wife's sarcasms.

He cried all night through, and, arising before the dawn, he kissed Grettl'a as she lay sleeping, and, cautiously opening the latch, slipped out unheard. A heavy dew was on the grass, and the large, massive clouds rested on the mountains and filled the plain. It was cold, and gloomy, and cheerless—just such as the world is to the wanderer who, friendless, alone, and poor, would tempt his fortunes in it!

Fritz wandered on over the plain—he had no choice of paths—he had nothing to guide, no clue to lead him. He took this, because he had often gone it with "Star" when he was happy and contented. As he went along, the sun rose, and soon the whole scene changed from its leaden grey to the bright tint of morning. The hoar-frost glittered like thousands of spangles scattered over the grass; the earth sent up a delicious odour; the leaves, as they opened, murmured softly in the air; and the little brooks rustled among the stones, and rippled on with a sound like fairy laughter. There was gladness and joy everywhere, save in that heart which was now bereft of all.

"What could he mean?" said he, again and again to himself: "'A good word brings luck!' When had I ever misfortune till now?"

Oh, Fritzerl! take care lest you are not making the common mistake, and expecting the moral before the end of the story.

Were it my object to dwell on this part of my tale, I might tell you of Fritz's long conflict with himself—his doubts, his hesitation, and his reasonings, before he could decide on what course to take, or whither to bend his steps. The world was a very wide one to hunt after a Starling through it: that, he knew, though not very deeply skilled in geography.

Fritz had never heard of those wise inspirations by which knights-errant of old guided their wanderings; nor, perhaps, if he had, would he have benefited by them, seeing that to throw the rein loose on his charger's neck was a matter of some difficulty. He did, perhaps, what was the nearest thing in practice to this: he wandered along, keeping the straight path, and, neither turning right nor left, found himself at noon in the opening of the beautiful glen that leads to Reute. He looked up, and there were great mountains before him—not hills, but real mountains, with pine-forests beneath, and crags above that, and over them, again, snow-peaks and glaciers. They seemed quite near, but they were still many a mile off. No matter: the sight of them cheered and encouraged him; they reminded him of the old life among the Tyrol "Jochs," and the wild cattle sporting about, and the herdsmen springing from cliff to cliff, rifle in hand. Oh, that was a free and joyous life!

Fritz's musings on this head were suddenly put a stop to by a severe pang of hunger, in all likelihood suggested by the odour of a savoury mess which steamed from the open window of a little hut on the road-side.

The peasant family were about to sit down to their twelve o'clock dinner, when Fritz, unconsciously to himself, drew up at the window, and looked in at the tempting food.

There is one custom in Germany, which, simple as it is, it would be hard to praise above its merits : that is, the invariable habit of every one, so far as his means permit, to help the foot-traveller on his journey. By an old municipal law of most of the cities, the tradesmen cannot settle and establish themselves in their native town till they have travelled and lived in other places ; thus learning, as it is supposed, whatever improvements their several crafts may have obtained in different and distant cities. These wanderings, which are usually for one year or two, are accomplished during the period of apprenticeship ; so that you never travel on any of the high-roads without meeting these Lehr-Junkers, as they are called, who, with a knapsack on their back, and a spare pair of boots or two depending from it, are either smoking or singing to beguile the way. As it is not to be supposed that they are over-abundantly provided with means, it has grown into a recognized custom to assist them with some trifle : but the good habit ends not here ; it extends to the poor boy returning from the gymnasium, or school, to see his parents —the discharged or furloughed soldier—the wayfarer of every class, in fact, whose condition pleads to those more plenteously endowed than himself.

Fritz was now to reap the benefit of this graceful charity ; and scarcely had his wan features appeared at the window than a sign from the chief Bauer invited him to partake. Happily for poor Fritz—happily for all who give and all who accept such aid—there is no sense of humiliation in doing so. It is, in fact, less an almsgiving than a remnant of the ancient hospitality which made the stranger welcome beneath every roof—a custom that dates before railroads and giant hotels.

Fritz ate and drank, and was thankful. The few words he spoke were in answer to the common questions, as to whence he came—and whither he was going—and what was his handicraft ; inquiries which puzzled him sorely to reply to. His hesitations were not rendered more embarrassing by the curiosity of his questioners; they neither cared to push him closely, nor troubled their heads upon the matter.

"Farewell," said the Bauer's wife, as he thanked her gratefully; "farewell. Be good and pious, young lad; don't keep naughty company, nor learn bad ways; and remember 'A good word brings luck.'"

His eyes filled up with tears as she spoke. Who can tell the conflict of feelings they called up in his bosom?

"Where does this path lead to?" he asked, in a faint voice.

"To Reute, child."

"And then, after Reute?"

"To Zillerthal and Innspruck."

"To Innspruck!" said Fritz, while a sudden hope shot through him. "I'll go to Innspruck," muttered he, lower. "Good-bye, Bauer; good-bye, Frau. God bless thee." And with these words he set out once more.

How little they who roll on their journey with all the speed and luxury that wealth can purchase, defying climate and distance, know the vicissitudes that fall to the lot of the weary foot-traveller! From city to city, from kingdom to kingdom, the rich man glides on, the great panorama of life revealing itself before him, without an effort on his part. The Alps—the Pyrenees, scarcely retard him; the luxuries he requires meet him at every halting-place, as though difference of region should not trench upon even his daily habits; his patience, perhaps, not more tried than by the occasional stoppages where fresh horses meet him. And yet between two such stations a foot-traveller may spend the live-long day, wearied, foot-sore, heavy of heart. What crosses and trials are his! What strange adventures, too! and what strange companionships! Each day a new episode of life—but of life over which Poverty has thrown its shadow.

Fritz was now to experience all this; now, travelling with a company of wandering apprentices; now, keeping company with a group of peasants on the way to market; sometimes, partaking of a seat in a Bauer's waggon—

often, alone and weary, thinking over his future—a future that each day seemed to render more doubtful and gloomy.

As he penetrated deeper into the Zillerthal, the journeys of each day became longer, the resting-places for the night being further apart; sometimes he was obliged to stop a day, or even two days, at a village, to recruit strength sufficient for a long march; and then he would have to walk from before daylight to late in the night ere he reached his destination. His was not strength to endure fatigue like this with impunity; and if he did encounter it, it was from an enthusiasm that supplied energy, where mere bodily strength had failed. Two hopes buoyed him up, and carried him along through every opposing difficulty. Whether Star had escaped by accident, or been taken away by design, he was lame, and would surely be soon caught; and if so, what more likely than that he would be sent to Innspruck to be sold, for there was the greatest bird-market of all the world? at least, so Fritz believed. His second sustaining hope lay in the prospect of once again meeting the old priest, and learning from him how was it that a "good word" had not "brought luck" to him, and whether from any fault of his own.

These thoughts had so far obtained possession of his mind, that he became almost unconscious of every other; from dwelling on them so much, and revolving them so frequently and in so many different shapes and forms, he grew to think that he had no other object and aim than to reach Innspruck and solve these two doubts. Hunger, cold, and fatigue, every privation of a long and weary journey was unregarded by him; and although it was now late in the autumn, and snow was beginning to fall on the mountain passes, Fritz, poorly clad, and scarcely fed, trudged on, day after day, his own heart supplying the courage which his weak frame denied.

As winter drew near the days grew shorter; and the atmosphere, loaded with snow ready to drop, darkened the earth, and made night come on, as it seemed, many hours before sunset. This left very little time to Fritz for his long journeys, which, just at this very period, unfortunately, were longer than ever. The way, too, had become far more dreary and deserted, not only because it led through a little-travelled district, but that the snow being too deep for wheeled carriages, and not hard enough for sledges, the travellers were fain to wait till either rain or frost should come on, to make the road practicable. Hence it happened that not unfrequently, now, Fritz journeyed the livelong day, from dawn to dark, and scarcely met a single traveller. Sometimes, too, not a hut would be seen in a whole day's march, and he would never taste a morsel of food till he reached his halting-place for the night.

All this was bad enough, but it was not the only difficulty; the worst of all was, how to find out the way in the mountain passes, where the snow lay so deep, that the balustrades or parapets that flanked the road, and often guarded it from a precipice, were now covered, and no wheel-track could be seen to guide the traveller. Fritz, when he journeyed this road before, remembered the awe and terror with which he used to peep over the little stone railing, and look down hundreds of feet into the dark valley beneath, where a great river was diminished to the size of a mere brawling rivulet; and now, where was that parapet?—on which side of him did it lie? A deep gorge was near—that he well knew; the unfrozen torrent beneath roared like thunder, but a waving surface of untrodden snow stretched away on either side of him, without foottrack or aught to mark the way.

For a long time did the poor child stand uncertain which way to turn; now thinking he heard the heavy plash of wheels moving through the snow, and then discovering it was merely the sound of falling masses, which, from time to time, slipped from their places, and glided down the steep mountain sides. What desolate and heart chilling solitude was there! A leaden, greyish sky overhead—not a cloud, nor even a passing bird, to break its dreary surface—beneath, nothing but snow; snow on the wild fantastic mountain peaks; snow in waving sweeps between them. The rocks, the fir-trees, all covered.

Fritz stood so long, that already the thin drift settled on his head and shoulders, and clothed him in the same

wintry livery as the objects around; his limbs were stiff,
his fingers knotted and frozen; the little tears upon his
blue cheeks seemed almost to freeze; his heart, that till
now bore bravely up, grew colder and heavier. He felt
as if he would be happy if he could cry, but that even
grief was freezing within him. Despair was near him
then! He felt a drowsy confusion creeping over him.
Clouds of white snow-drift seemed to fall so thickly
around, that every object was hidden from view. Crashing branches and roaring torrents mingled their noises
with the thundering plash of falling snow-masses. Oh! if
he could but sleep, and neither hear nor see these wearying sounds and sights—sleep, and be at rest! It was just
at this instant his eye caught sight of a little finger-post,
from which a passing gust of wind had carried away the
snow. It stood at some distance beneath him, in the
midst of a waving field of snow. Had poor Fritz
remarked its leaning attitude, and the depth to which it
was covered, scarcely more than three feet appearing
above the surface, he would have known it must have
been carried away from its own appointed spot; but his
senses were not clear enough for such simple reasonings,
and with a last effort he struggled towards it. The snow
grew deeper at every step; not only did it rise above his
foot, and half his leg, but it seemed to move in a great
mass all around him, as if a huge fragment of the mountain had separated, and was floating downwards. The
post, too, he came not nearer to it; it receded as he
advanced; was this a mere delusion? had his weakened
faculties lost all control of sense? Alas! these sensations
were but too real! He had already crossed the parapet
which flanked the road—already was he in the midst of a
great "wraith" of fallen snow, which, descending from
the mountain peak, by a storm in the night, had carried
away the finger-post, and now only waited the slightest
impulse—the weight of that little child—to carry it
down, down into the depth below! And down, indeed,
it went; at first, slowly—moving like a great unbroken
wave; then growing more hurried as it neared the edge
of the precipice, thickening and swelling with fresh

masses : it rose around him — now, circling his waist,
now, enclosing his shoulders : he had but time to grasp
the little wooden cross, the emblem of hope and succour,
when the mass glided over the brink, and fell thundering
into the dark abyss.

I would not risk any little credit I may, perchance,
possess with the reader, by saying how deep that gorge
actually was; but this will I say, when standing on the
spot, in a very different season from this I have described
—when the trees were in full leaf, the wild flowers
blossoming, and both sky above and river beneath,
blue as the bluest turquoise; yet even then, to look
down the low parapet into the narrow chasm, was
something to make the head reel and the heart's blood
chill.

But to my story.—It was the custom in this season,
when the snow fell heavily on the high passes, to transmit
the little weekly mail between Reute and Innspruck by an
old and now disused road, which led along the edge of
the river, and generally, from its sheltered situation, continued practicable and free from snow some weeks later
than the mountain road. It was scarce worthy to be
called a road—a mere wheel-track, obstructed here and
there by stones and masses of rock that every storm
brought down, and not unfrequently threatened, by the
flooding of the river, to be washed away altogether.

Along this dreary way the old postilion was wending—
now, pulling up to listen to the crashing thunders of the
snow, which, falling several hundred feet above, might
at any moment descend and engulf him—again, plying
his whip vigorously, to push through the gorge, secretly
vowing in his heart that, come what would, he would
venture no more there that year. Just as he turned a
sharp angle of the rock, where merely space lay for the
road between it and the river, he found his advance
barred up by a larch-tree, which, with an immense fragment of snow, had fallen from above. Such obstacles
were not new to him, and he lost no time in unharnessing
his horse and attaching him to the tree. In a few minutes
the road was cleared of this difficulty; and he now

advanced, shovel in hand, to make a passage through the snow.

"*Saperlote!*" cried he; "here is the firger-post! This must have come down from the upper-road."

Scarcely were the words uttered, when a cry of horror broke from him. He trembled from head to foot; his eyes seemed bursting from their sockets: and well might they, for, close around the wood, just where it emerged from the snow, were two little hands clasped tightly round the timber.

He threw himself on the spot, and tore up the snow with his fingers. An arm appeared, and then the long yellow hair of a head resting on it. Working with all the eagerness of a warm and benevolent nature, he soon disinterred the little body, which, save one deep cut upon the forehead, seemed to have no other mark of injury; but it lay cold and motionless—no sign of life remaining.

He pressed the little flask of brandy—all that he possessed—against the wan, white lips of the child; but the liquor ran down the chin and over the cheek—not a drop of it was sucked. He rubbed the hands, he chafed the body, he even shook it; but, heavy and inert, it gave no sign of life.

"*Ach, Gott!*" muttered he, "it is all over!" But still, with a hope that asked no aid from reason, he wrapped the child's body in his fur mantle, and, laying him softly down in the cart, continued his way.

The lights, which were glittering here and there through the little village inns, had been gradually extinguished as the night grew later, till, at last, none remained, save those around the door of the post-house, where a little group of loungers was gathered. As they talked together, one or other occasionally would step out into the road and seem to listen, and then rejoin his companions. "No sign of him yet! What can keep him so late as this?" cried the Postmaster, holding up his watch, that the lamp-light should fall on it. "It wants but four minutes] to eleven—his time, by right, is half after nine."

"He is trying the upper road belike, and the deep snow has detained him."

"He threw himself on the spot, and tore up the snow with his fingers."

"No, no," said another, "Old Cristoph's too knowing for that: bad as the lower road is, the upper is worse; and with the storm of last night, there will be drift there deep enough to swallow horse and mail-cart twice over."

"There may be fallen snow on the lower road," whispered a third; "Cristoph told me last week he feared it would not be safe for another journey."

"He's a daring old fellow," said the Postmaster, as he resumed his walk up and down to keep his feet warm; "but he'll try that lower road once too often. He can't bear the upper road because it is a new one, and was not made when he was a boy. He thinks that the world is not half so wise, or so good, as it was some fifty years back."

"If he make no greater mistates than that," muttered an old white-headed hostler, "he may be trusted to choose his own road."

"What's that Philip is mumbling?" said the Postmaster; but a general cry of "Here he comes! Here he is now!" interrupted the answer.

"See how he drives full speed over the bridge!" exclaimed the Postmaster, angrily, "Potz-Teufel! if the Burgomaster hears it, I shall have to pay a fine of four gulden; and I would not wonder if the noise awoke him."

There was less exaggeration than might be supposed in this speech, for Old Christoph, in open defiance of all German law, which requires that nothing faster than a slow walk should be used in crossing a wooden bridge, galloped at the full stride of his beast, making every crazy plank and timber tremble and vibrate with a crash like small arms.

Never relaxing in his speed, the old man drove at his fastest pace through the narrow old Roman gate, up the little paved hill, round the sharp corner, across the Platz, into the main street, and never slackened till he pulled up with a jerk at the door of the post-house: when, springing from his seat, he detached the lamp from its place, and thrust it into the waggon, crying with a voice that excitement had elevated into a scream,—"He's alive still!—I'll swear I heard him sigh!　I know he's alive!"

It is hard to say what strange conjectures might have been formed of the old man's sanity, had he not backed his words by stooping down and lifting from the straw, at the bottom of the cart, the seemingly dead body of a boy, which, with the alacrity of one far younger, he carried up the steps, down the long arched passage, and into the kitchen, where he laid him down before the fire.

"Quick now, Ernest; run for the doctor!　Away, Johan; bring the Staats Physicus—bring two—all of them in the town!　Frau Hostess, warm water and salt —salt, to rub him with—I know he is alive!"

A shake of the head from the old hostess seemed to offer a strong dissent.

"Never mind that!　He is not dead, though he did fall from the Riesenfels."

"From the Reisenfels!" exclaimed three or four together in amazement.

"Who was it came galloping at full speed over the Bridge, and passed the grand guard on the Platz at the same disorderly pace?" said the deep voice of the Burgermeister, who arose from his bed to learn the cause of the tumult.

"It was I," exclaimed Cristoph, ruggedly; "there lies the reason."

"The penalty is all the same," growled the man of authority: "four gulden for one, and two gulden thirty kreutzers for the other offence."

Christoph either did not hear or heed the speech.

"Where's the mail-bag?　I haven't seen that yet," chimed in the Postmaster; who, like a wise official, followed the lead of the highest village functionary.

Old Cristoph bustled out, and soon returned, not only with the leathern sack in question, but with a huge fragment of a wooden cross over his shoulders.

"There's the bag, Herr Postmeister, all safe and dry," said he; "and here Herr Burgermeister, here's your fine finger-post that the Governor ordered to be stuck up on the Riesenfels.　I suppose they'll need it again when the snow melts and the road is clear: though to be sure," added he, in a lower tone, "he must have worse eyes than Old Christoph who could not see his way to Imst from that cliff without a finger post to guide him."

The Burgermeister was not disposed to suffer this irony in silence; but the occasion to exert his authority with due severity was not at that moment, when the whole attention of the bystanders was directed to the proceedings of the three village doctors—one of them no less a personage than the Staats Physicus—who, with various hard terms of art, were discussing the condition of the senseless form before them.

Were I to recount one half of the learned surmises and deep prognostications of these wise Esculapians, the chances are, my reader would grow as weary of the recital as did poor old Cristoph of the reality. For at last, unable to endure any longer active controversies about the pia mater and the dura mater, the vitreous table and the cerebellum, with vague hints of " congestion," " depression," " effusion," and so on, he broke in with, " In God's name, dear gentlemen, let him be kept warm and have a good glass of ' schnaps ' down his poor throat; and when he shows a chance of living, fight away about the name of the malady to your hearts' content."

I am far from defending Old Christoph's rude interruption. The learned faculties should always be treated with becoming deference; but he was a rude, unpolished old fellow, and the best one can say is, that he meant it well. Certain it is they seemed to acknowledge the force of his suggestion; for they at once removed the child to a warm bed, while they ordered the hostess to administer a very comfortable cordial of her own devising; and, to show their confidence in the remedy, had three likewise provided for their own individual comfort and support.

It is not my wish to dwell on the sad portions of our tale, wherever the recital would elicit nothing of our little hero's character: and such was the period which now ensued. Fritz was conveyed, early on the following morning, to the village hospital, where his case was pronounced of the very gravest nature. The dangers from cold, inanition, and exposure, were all inferior to the greater one resulting from some injury to the brain. I cannot be expected to be clearer and more explicit on this theme than were his doctors; and they, with proverbial propriety, did differ most amazingly: one advocating a fracture, another a concussion, and a third standing out for both, and something more. They agreed, however, on two points; one of which was, that he would die—and the other, that as he was evidently very poor and had no friends, his death was of less consequence. I would not be here understood, by any malevolent critic, as wishing to infer that the doctors' neglect of him was a strong point in Fritz's favour. I merely desire to relate a simple fact—that he continued to live from day to day, and from week to week, gaining in strength, but never once evidencing, by even the slightest trait, a return to his faculty of reasoning. Alas, poor child!—the intellect which, in all his sorrow and poverty, had been his happiness and his comfort, was now darkened, and he awoke from that long dream of death—an idiot!

Perhaps I may not have used the fitting word; but how shall I speak of his state? He seemed sad and sorrow-struck; never spoke, even to answer a question, moved listlessly and slowly about, as if in search of something, and muttering lowly to himself. No one ever saw him smile, and yet he did not weep. He looked more like one in whom reason was, by some terrible shock, suspended and held in abeyance, than actually routed or annihilated. Unlike most others similarly afflicted, he slept very little, remaining usually, the night long, sitting beside his bed, gesticulating with his hands in a strange way, and suddenly ceasing if observed.

His eye, for some minutes, would often seem bright with intelligence; but on looking more closely, it would be discovered that the gaze was fixed on vacancy, and it might be conjectured that no image of any near object was presented to the mind, since no expression of pain, pleasure, or astonishment would follow, when different substances were displayed before him. One might say, that the faculties were entirely absorbed by their own operations, and neither took note of those recorded by the senses, nor had any sympathy with their workings—volition was at a stand-still But why dwell on so sorrowful a picture?

Spring came, and Fritz, who ever obeyed each command of those over him, was suffered to walk daily in the little garden of the asylum. One day—it was the first bright one of the new season—the birds were singing sweetly in the trees when he went forth, and they who came some time after to fetch him to the house, found him in tears. His sorrow seemed, however, to have brought some sense of relief with it, for that night he slept more calmly and longer than usual. From this time out it was remarked that his appearance varied with the weather of each day. When the air was clear, and the sun shone bright, and the birds gathered together in the blossoming branches of the fruit-trees, he seemed happier ; but when dark skies or rain came on, he would walk impatiently from place to place—now, as if in search of some missing object—now, as if suddenly overwhelmed by his loss.

Thus did he continue till about the first week in May, when at the usual hour of recalling him to the house he was not to be found. Search was made everywhere— through the garden—about the neighbouring buildings— in all the Dorf—but all in vain. No one had seen him.

Poor and unfriended as he was, his little simple ways, his sinless innocence and gentleness, had made him friends among all who had any authority in the asylum ; and no pains were spared to track him out and discover him—to no end, however. He was seen there no more. Days and weeks long, with unwearying zeal, the search continued, aud was only abandoned when all hope seemed gone. By none was this sad termination of his suffering more poignantly felt than by old Cristoph. Every week he came to Imst, his first care was to ask after the little boy; and when he learned his fate, his grief was deep and heartfelt.

I know not if my reader has ever visited Innspruck.

Every one has been everywhere now-a-days; and so the chances are, that the Tyrol capital is as well known to them as to myself. At all the hazard of being tedious, however, I must mention one feature of that beautiful old city—a little street which leads out of the Old Market, and runs westward down a somewhat steep declivity towards the Inn. It is one of those narrow, old gloomy alleys a traveller would scarcely think of exploring. A low range of arches, supported on pillars of the most sturdy proportions, runs along either side, furnished with massive stone seats, worn smooth by the use of some centuries of gossips. The little shops within this dark arcade are undefended by windows of any kind, but lie open, displaying to the passer-by, not only the various wares exposed for sale, but frequently, as the wind, or chance, waves the folds of an old curtain at the back, the little household of the merchant himself.

The middle portion of this street, scarcely wide enough for three to walk abreast, grows even narrower as you look up, by the gradual encroachment of each storey on either side ; so that while the denizens of the first-floors have merely the neighbourly advantages of a near salutation, they who inhabit the garrets may embrace without any fear on the score of bodily danger. Our business is only with those beneath, however, and thither I must ask of your accompanying me.

If the two groined arches—dark with age as well as faint light—the narrow, gloomy-looking alley, might at first deter the stranger from entering, scarcely would he venture a few steps ere a strange fascination would lead him onward. Within these little dens—for such rather than shops do they seem—are objects to be found, the strangest and the most curious ever exposed for sale. In one, you find a collection of ancient armour the greatest Ritter Saal would be proud to choose from : weapons of every age and country—the chain-mail of Milan—the plate-armour of Venice—the heavy double-nailed suits of Regensbourg—the small conical helmet of the East—the massive but beautifully fashioned casque of Spanish mould —the blade of Damascus—the double-handled sword of

Appenzell—the jereed—the Crusader's lance—the old pike of the Tyrol, with daggers and poniards of every shape, that luxury or cruelty ever invented. Adjoining this, perhaps, lives one who deals in rare flowers and shrubs; and, strange as it may seem in such a place, the orange-tree, the cactus, the camellia, and the aloe, shed their bloom and perfume through these vaulted cells, where age, and rust, and decay would appear the most fitting denizens. Here, lives one who sells the rich brocaded silks and tabourets of a by-gone century—great flowering waistcoats, stiff and imposing as the once wearers—huge sweeping trains of costly embroidery—relics of a time when stateliness was cultivated, and dignified deportment the distinctive sign of birth. Right opposite to this is a store of ancient articles of furniture and *virtù*—marquetry and buhl—Dresden and Sèvres—carved oak and ebony—ivory and box-wood. All that ever fancy conceived uncomfortable to sit upon, or a diseased imagination ever inaugurated as the throne of nightmare to sleep in—are here to be had. Stools to kneel upon and altars to kneel at—Virgins in ivory and silver—idols of Indian adoration—ancient goblets, and most curiously carved treasure-boxes of solid-iron, massive little emblems of a time when men put slight faith in bankers.

A little further on you may meet with a jeweller's, where ornaments the most rare and costly are to be found: massive old necklaces of amethyst or emerald, in which the ungainly setting bears such a contrast to the value of the stone—rich clasps of pink topaz or ruby, for the collar of a cloak—sword-handles all paved with precious gems—and signet-rings, that have circled the fingers of proud Counts of the Empire, and, mayhap, sealed with their impress many a dark and gloomy record.

Some deal in old books and manuscripts, ancient rolls, and painted missals; some, in curious relics of horse-equipment, brass-mounted demi-piques and iron-strapped saddles of the sixteenth century, with spurs of a foot in length, and uncouth bits that would hold an elephant in check : and one little dusky corner-shop, kept by an old hunchback, contained the strangest of all stocks-in-trade, —an assemblage of instruments of torture : chains of every kind hung from the ceiling ; thumb-screws, back-bolts, helmets made to close upon the skull, and crushed by the action of a vice ; racks, hatchets, and pincers ; while conspicuous in the midst, as the support of an old iron lantern, is the block of a headsman, the surface bearing the shocking record of its usage. Just where this grim and ghastly cell stands, a little rivulet of clear water crosses the street, and seems to separate it from the remaining portion, which, by a steeper declivity, inclined towards the river.

Separate, indeed, I might well say, for the two portions are as unlike as the records of all man's vanity and cruelty are unlike the emblem of God's goodness and wisdom. You scarcely cross this tiny stream when the whole air resounds with the warbling of birds, bright in every tint and hue of plumage, golden and green, purple and crimson.

From the lordly eagle of the Ort'ler to the rich toned linnet of the Botzen valley, all are there. There, the paroquet of the Stelvio, gorgeous as the scarlet bustard in plumage ; and here, the golden jay of the Vorarlberg. Blackbirds, thrushes, finches of a hundred different races, "Roth kopfs," and woodpeckers, spring, chirp, flutter, and scream, on every side. The very atmosphere is tremulous with the sounds, lifelike and joyous as they are ! The very bustle and movement around is such a relief from the torpid stillness of the other end of the street, where nothing is heard save the low monotonous tones of some old Jew reading in his back-shop, or the harsh clank of an iron weapon removed from its place ; while, here, the merry twitter and the silvery-shake recall the greenwood and the grove, the bright fields and heath-clad mountains.

Here is the bird-market of Innspruck. It needs but one passing glance to show what attractions the spot possesses for the inhabitants. Every rank, from the well-salaried official of the government to the humblest burgher—from the richly clad noble in his mantle of Astracan, to the peasant in his dark jacket of sheep's skin—the field officer and the common soldier—the "Frau Gräfin" voluminous in furs—the "Stuben mädchen" in her woollen jerkin—the lounging sexagenarian from his coffee—the loitering school-boy returning from school—all jostle and meet together here; while the scantiest intimacy with the language will suffice to collect from the frequently uttered, "*Wie schön!*" "*Ach Gott!*" "*Wie wunder-schön!*" that admiration and delight are expressed by every tongue among them.

It is needless to say, that every corner of this little territory is familiar to all Innspruckers; not only each shop and its owner, but each separate treasure. The newly arrived bullfinch, or greywing, having the notoriety that a Parisian circulates about the last *débutante* of the ballet or the opera. If not exactly one of those "lions," that guide-books enforce among the duties of wandering sights-seers, it is at least a frequent resort of the town's-folk themselves, for whose gratification it supplies no small proportion of small-talk.

Among the well-known and familiar objects of this small world—for such the Juden Gasse in reality is—was a poor boy of some twelve years old, who, clad in the most wretched rags, and with want in every feature, used to sit the livelong day on one of the stone benches watching the birds. It needed but one glance at his bright but unsteady eye, his faint unmeaning smile, his vague and wild expression, to recognize that he was bereft of reason. Is it necessary to say this was poor Fritzerl?

Whence he came, who were his parents, how he journeyed thither, no one could tell! He appeared one morning, when the shop-people were removing the shutters, sitting close by a window, where the early songs of the birds were audible, his head bent down to listen, and his whole attitude betokening the deep attention. Though he offered no resistance when they bade him leave the spot, he showed such deep sorrow and such reluctance, that he was suffered to remain; and this was now his dwelling-place. He never quitted it during the day, and there did he pass the night, under the shelter of the deep arches, and protected by the fragment of a mantle, which some compassionate neighbour had given him. All endeavours to induce him to speak were in vain; a sickly smile was his only answer to a question; and, if pressed too closely, the tears would come, so that none liked to give him further pain, and the hope of learning anything about him, even his name, was given up. Equally fruitless was every effort to make him perform little services. If the shopkeepers gave him a bird to carry home for a purchaser, he would at once sit down beside the cage and gaze wistfully, delightedly, at the occupant; but he could not be persuaded to quit his abiding-place. Who could rob one so poor of all the happiness his life compassed? certainly not the good-natured and kindly folk who inhabited the bird-market.

He became then a recognized part of the place, as much as the bustard with one eye in the corner shop, or the fat old owl that had lived for fifty—some said seventy—years, in the little den with the low iron door. Every one knew him; few passed without a look of kindness towards him. It was of no use to give him money, for though he took money when offered, the next moment he would leave it on the stones, where the street children came and found it. It was clear he did not understand its meaning. The little support he needed was freely proffered by the neighbouring shopkeepers, but he ate nothing save a morsel of dry bread, of which it was remarked that he each day broke off a small portion and laid it by—not to eat later on, for it was seen that he never missed it if removed, nor took it again if suffered to remain. It was one of the secrets of his nature none could rightly account for.

Although many wealthy and benevolent people of the city wished to provide the poor boy with a more comfortable home, the shopkeepers protested against his removal. Some loved his innocent, childish features, and would have missed him sorely; others were superstitious enough to think, and even say, that he had brought luck to the bird-market—that every one had prospered since he came there; and some, too, asserted, that having selected the spot himself, it would be cruel to tear him away from a place where accustomed and familiar objects had made for him a kind of home. All these reasonings were backed by the proposal to build for him a little shed, in the very spot he had taken up, and there leave him to live in peace. This was accordingly done, and poor Fritz, if not a " Burgher of Innspruck," had at least his own house in the bird-market.

Months rolled on : the summer went by, and the autumn itself now drew to a close ; and the various preparations for the coming winter might be seen in little hand-barrows of firewood deposited before each door, to be split up and cut in fitting lengths for the stoves. Fur mantles and caps were hung out to air, and some prudent and well-to-do folks examined the snow-windows, and made arrangements for their adjustment. Each in his own way, and according to his means, was occupied with the cares of the approaching season. There was but one unmoved face in the whole street—but one who seemed to take no note of time or season—whose past, and present, and future, were as one. This was Fritz, who sat on his accustomed bench gazing at the birds, or occasionally moving from his place to peep into a cage whose occupant lay hid, and then, when satisfied of its presence, retiring to his seat contented.

Had the worthy citizens been less actively engrossed by their own immediate concerns, or had they been less accustomed to this humble dependent's presence amongst them, it is likely they would have remarked the change time had wrought in his appearance. If no actual evidence of returning reason had evinced itself in his bearing or conduct, his features displayed at times varieties of expression and meaning very different from their former monotony. The cheek, whose languid pallor never altered, would now occasionally flush, and become suddenly scarlet; the eyes, dull and meaningless, would sparkle and light up; the lips, too, would part, as if about to give utterance to words. All these signs, however, would be only momentary, and a degree of depression, even to prostration, would invariably follow. Unlike his former apathy, too, he started at sudden noises in the street, felt more interest in the changes that went on in the shop, and seemed to miss certain birds as they happened to be sold or exchanged. The most remarkable of all the alterations in his manner was, that, now he would often walk down to the river-side, and pass hours there gazing on the current. Who can say what efforts at restored reason were then taking place within him—what mighty influences were at work to bring back sense and intellect —what struggles, and what combats? It would seem as if the brain could exist in all its integrity—sound, and intact, and living—and yet some essential impulse be wanting which should impart the power of thought. Momentary flashes of intelligence, perhaps, did cross him; but such can no more suffice for guidance than does the forked lightning supply the luminary that gives us day. The landscape preternaturally lit up for a second, becomes darker than midnight the moment after.

Bright and beautiful as the river is, with its thousand eddies whirling along—now, reflecting the tall spires and battlemented towers of the town—now, some bold, projecting cliff of those giant mountains beside it—how does its rapid stream proclaim its mountain source, as in large sheets of foam it whirls round the rocky angles of the bank, and dashes along free as the spirit of its native home! Fritz came here, however, less to gaze on this lovely picture than on a scene which each morning presented to his eyes close by. This was a garden, where a little girl of some seven or eight years old used to play, all alone and by herself, while the old nurse that accompanied her sat knitting in a little harbour near.

The joyous river—the fresh and balmy air—the flowers flinging delicious odours around, and gorgeous in their brilliant tints, only needed this little infant figure to impart a soul to the scene, and make it one of ravishing enchantment. Her tiny footsteps on the ground—her little song, breathing of innocence and happiness—the garlands which she wove, now to place upon her own fair brow, now, in childish sport, to throw into the clear current—all imparted to the poor idiot's heart sensations of intense delight. Who can say if that infant voice did not wake to feeling the heart that all the wisdom of the learned could not arouse from its sleep?

Not only was Fritz happy while he sat and watched this little child, but, for the entire day after, he would appear calm and tranquil, and his face would display the placid expression of a spirit sunk in a pleasing trance.

It was not unusual with him, while he was thus gazing, for sleep to come over him—a calm, delicious slumber—from which he awoke far more refreshed and rested than from his night's repose. Perhaps she was present in his dreams, and all her playful gestures and her merry tones were with him while he slept. Perhaps—it is not impossible—that his mind, soothed by the calming influence of such slumber, recovered in part its lost power, and not being called on for the exercise of volition, could employ some of its perceptive faculties.

Be this as it may, this sleep was deep, and calm, and tranquillizing. One day, when he had watched longer than usual, and when her childish sport had more than ever delighted him, he dropped off almost suddenly into slumber. Motionless as death itself he lay upon the bank —a faint smile upon his parted lips, his chest scarcely seeming to heave, so soft and quiet was his slumber. The river rippled pleasantly beside him, the air was balmy as in the early spring, and fanned his hot temples with a delicious breath, the child's song floated merrily out—the innocent accents of infant glee—and Fritz seemed to drink these pleasures in as he slept.

What visions of heavenly shape—what sounds of angelic sweetness—may have flitted before that poor distracted brain, as with clasped hands and muttering lips he seemed to pray a prayer of thankfulness—the outpouring gratitude of a pent-up nature finding vent at last! Suddenly he awoke with a start—terror in every feature—his eyes starting from their sockets : he reeled as he sprang to his feet, and almost fell. The river seemed a cataract—the

mountains leaned over as though they were about to fall
and crush him—the ground beneath his feet trembled and
shook with an earthquake movement—a terrible cry rang
through his ears. What could it mean ? There!—there
again he heard it ! Oh, what a pang of heart-rending
anguish was that ! "*Hülf! hülf! hülf!*" were the words.
The infant was struggling in the current—her little hand
grasped the weeds, while at every instant they gave
way—the water foamed and eddied round her—deeper
and deeper she sank : her hair now floated in the stream,
and her hands, uplifted, besought, for the last time, aid.
"*Hülf uns ! Maria ; hülf uns !*" She sank. With a cry
of wildest accent, Fritz sprang into the stream, and seized
the yellow hair as it was disappearing beneath the flood :
the struggle was severe, for the strong stream inclined
towards the middle of the river, and Fritz could not swim.
Twice had the waves closed over him, and twice he
emerged with his little burden pressed to his heart; were
it not for aid, however, his efforts would have been vain.
The cry for help had brought many to the spot, and he
was rescued—saved from death : saved from that worse
than death—the terrible union of life and death.

He lay upon the bank. wearied and exhausted—but oh,
how happy ! How doubly bright the sky !—how inexpressibly soft and soothing the air upon his brow !—how
sweet the human voice, that not only sounded to the ear
but echoed in the heart !

In all his bright dreams of life he had fancied nothing
like the bliss of that moment. Friends were on every
side of him—kind friends, who never in a life-long could
tell all their gratitude ; and now, with words of affection,
and looks of mildest, fondest meaning, they bent over that
poor boy, and called him their own preserver.

Amid all these sights and sounds of gladness—so full
of hope and joy—there came one shrill cry, which,
piercing the air, seemed to penetrate to the very inmost
chamber of Fritz's heart, telling at once the whole history
of his life, and revealing the secret of his suffering and
his victory. It was Star himself; who, in a cage beneath
the spreading branches of a cheslnut-tree, was glad to

mingle his wild notes with the concourse of voices about him, and still continued at intervals to scream out "*Maria, hülf! hülf uns, Maria!*"

"Yes, child," said a venerable old man, as he kissed Fritz's forehead, "you see the fruits of your obedience and your trust. I am glad you have not forgotten my teaching —'A good word brings luck.'"

Every story-teller should respect those who like to hear a tale to its very end. The only way he can evince his gratitude for their patience is by gratifying all their curiosity. It remains for' me, then, to say, that] Fritz returned to the little village where he had lived with Star for his companion; not poor and friendless as before, but rich in wealth, and richer in what is far better—the grateful love and affection of kind friends. His life henceforth was one of calm and tranquil happiness. By his aid the old Bauer was enabled to purchase his little farm rent-free, and buy besides several cows and some sheep. And then when he grew up to be a man, Fritz married Gretl'a, and they became very well off, and lived in mutial love and contentment all their lives.

Fritz's house was not only the handsomest in the Dorf but it was ornamented with a little picture of the Virgin, with Star sitting upon her wrist, and the words of the golden letters were inscribed beneath,—

"Maria, Mutter Gottes, hülf uns!"

Within, nothing could be more comfortable than to see Fritz and Grettl'a at one side of the fire, and the old Bauer reading aloud, and the "Frau" listening, and Star who lived to a great age, walking proudly about, as if he was conscious that he had some share in producing the family prosperity; and close to the stove on a little low seat made on purpose, sat a little old man, with a long pigtail and very shrunken legs: this was old Christoph the postilion—and who had a better right?

Fritz was so much loved and respected by the villagers,

that they elected him Vorsteher, or rector of the Dorf ; and when he died—very old at last—they all, several hundreds followed him respectfully to the grave, and, in memory of his story, called the village Maria Hülf, which is its name to this day.

CHAPTER XV.

VARENNA, LAKE OF COMO.

ITALY at last! I have crossed the Alps and reached my goal, and now I turn and look at that winding road which, for above two thousand feet, traverses the steep mountain-side, and involuntarily a sadness steals over me—that I am never to recross it! These same "last-times" are very sorrowful things, all emblems as they are of that one great "last-time" when the curtain falls for ever! Nor am I sorry when this feeling impresses me deeply; nay, I am pleased that indifference—apathy—have no more hold upon me. I am more afraid of that careless, passionless temperament than of aught else, and the more as hour by hour it steals over me. Yesterday a letter, which once would have interested me deeply, lay half read till evening; to-day, a very old friend of my guardian's, Sir Gordon Howard, has left his card; he is in the inn, perhaps in the next room, and I have not energy to return his visit and chat with him over friends I am never to see again. And yet he is a gallant old officer—one of that noble class of Englishmen whose loyalty made the boldest feats of daring, the longest years of servitude, seem only as a duty they owed their sovereign. The race is dying out fast.

What can have brought him to Italy? Let me see. Here is the Travellers' Book; perhaps it may tell something.

"Sir Gordon Howard, Officier Anglais,"—simple enough for a Major-General and K.C.B. and G.C.H.—"de Zurich à Como." Not much to be learned from that. But stay! he is not alone. "Mademoiselle Howard." And who can she be? He never had a daughter, and his only son is in

India. Perhaps she is a granddaughter; but what care I? It is but another reason to avoid seeing him. I cannot make new acquaintances now. He wants no companions who must travel the road I am going! Antoine must tell me when Sir Gordon Howard goes out, and I'll leave my card then. I feel I must remain here to-day, and I am well content to do so. This calm lake, these bold mountains, the wooded promontory of Bellagio, and its bright villas seen amid the trees, are pleasant sights; while from the ever-passing boats, with their white arched awnings, I hear laughter and voices of happy people, whose hearts are lighter than my own.

If I could only find resolution for the task, too, there are a host of letters lying by me unanswered. How little do some of those " dear friends " who invite one to shoot grouse in the Highlands, or hunt in Leicestershire, think of the real condition of those they ask to be their guests! It is enough that you have been seen in certain houses of a certain repute. You have visited at B——, and spent a Christmas at G——; you are known as a tolerable shot and a fair average talker; you are sufficiently recognized in the world as to be known to all men of a very general acceptance, and no more is wanted. But test this kind of position by absence! Try, if you will, what a few years out of England effect! You are as totally forgotten as though you belonged to a past generation. You expect —naturally enough, perhaps—to resume your old place and among your old associates; but where are they? and what have they become? You left them young men about town, you find them now among the " middle ages; " when you parted they were slim, lank, agile fellows, that could spring into a saddle and fly their horse over a five-bar rail, or pull an oar with any one. Now, they are of the portly order, wear wider-skirted coats, trousers without straps, and cloth boots; their hats, too, have widened in the leaf, so as to throw a more liberal shade over broader cheeks; the whiskers are more bushy, and less accurate in curl. If they ride, the horse has more bone and timber under him; and when they bow to some fair face in a passing carriage there is no brightening of the eye, but in

its place a look of easier intimacy than heretofore.
These are not the men you left?—alas they are! A new
generation of young men about town has sprung up, who
"know not Joseph," and with whom you have few, if
any, sympathies.

So I find it myself. I left England at a time when
pleasure was the mad pursuit of every young fellow; and
under that designation came every species of extravagance
and all kind of wild excess. Men of five thousand a-year
were spending twelve! Men of twelve, thirty! Every
season saw some half-dozen cross the Channel, "cleared
out"—some never more to be heard of. Others, lingering
in Paris or Brussels to confer with their lawyer, who was
busily engaged in compromising, contesting, disputing,
and bullying a host of creditors, whose very rogueries had
accomplished the catastrophe they grumbled at. Lords,
living on ten or twelve hundred pounds a-year were to be
met with everywhere; countesses lodged in every little
town in Germany. The Dons of dragoon regiments were
seen a-foot in the most obscure of watering-places; and
men who had loomed large at Doncaster, and booked thousands, were now fain to risk francs and florins among the
flats of Brussels and Aix-la-Chapelle. The pace was
tremendous; few who came of age with a good estate held
out above two or three years. And if any listener should
take his place beside a group of fashionable-looking young
Englishmen in the Boulevard de Grand, or the Graben at
Vienna, the chances were greatly in favour of his hearing
such broken phrases as, " Caught it heavily ! "—"All wrong
at Ascot ! "—" Scott's fault ! "—" Cleared out at Crocky's !"
—"No standing two hundred per cent. ! "—" Infernal
scoundrel, Ford !"—" That villain Columbine ; "—" Rascal
Bevan !"—and so on, with various allusions to the Quorn
hounds, the Clarendon, and Houlditch the coachmaker.
Such was the one song you heard everywhere.

Now the mode—a better one I willingly own it—is
"Young Englandism." Not that superb folly of white
neckcloth and vest, that swears by Disraeli and the
Morning Post, but that healthier stamp, whose steps of
travel have turned eastward, towards the land of old-world

wonders, and who, instead of enervating mind and body
at Ems or Baden, seek higher and nobler sources of
pleasure among the cities and tombs of ancient Egypt.
Lord Lindsay, for instance, what a creditable specimen is
he of his age and class! and Warburton's book, the
" Crescent and the Cross," how redeeming is such a production among the mass of frivolity and flippancy the
magazines teem with ! These are the men who, returning
to England, more intensely national than they left it, cannot
be reproached with ignorance in this preference of their
native land above every other. Their nationality, not
built up of the leaders of the daily newspapers, is a conviction resulting from reflection and comparison.

They are proud of England ; not alone as the most
powerful of nations, but as that where personal integrity
and truth are held in highest repute—where character and
reputation stand far above genius—and where, whatever
the eminence of a gifted man, he cannot stand above his
fellows, save on the condition that he is not inferior in
more sterling qualities. The young man setting out to
travel can scarcely be sustained by a better feeling than
his strong nationality. He who sets a high store by the
character of his country will be slow to do aught that will
disgrace it. Of course I speak of nationality in its true
sense; not the affectation of John Bullism in dress,
manner, and bearing—not the insolent assumption of
superiority to the French and Germans, that some very
young men deem English; but a deep conviction that as
the requirements of England are higher in all that regards
fidelity to his word, consistency of conduct, and more
honourable employment of time and talents than prevail
abroad, he should be guardedly careful not to surrender
these convictions to all the seductions of foreign life and
manners.

I do not believe our country is superior to any foreign
land in any one particular so strikingly as in the capabili-
ties and habits of our higher orders. Such a class as the
titled order of Great Britain, taking them collectively,
never existed elsewhere.

A German, with anything like independence, lives a life

of tobacco-smoking and snipe-shooting. An Italian is content to eke out life with a *café* and a theatre—lemonade and a *liaison* are enough for him. The government of foreign states, in shutting out the men of rank and fortune from political influence, have taken the very shortest road to their degradation. What is to become of a man who has a Bureaucracy for a government and Popery for a religion ?

But what is the tumult in the little court-yard beneath my window? Ha! an English equipage! How neatly elegant that low-hung phaeton! and how superb in figure and style that pair of powerful dark-brown thoroughbreds! —for so it is easy to see they are, even to the smart groom, who stands so still before the pole, with each hand upon the bars of the bits. All smack of London. There is an air of almost simplicity in the whole turn-out, because it is in such perfect keeping. And here come its owners. What a pretty foot!—I might almost say, and ankle, too! How gracefully she draws her shawl around her! What! my friend Sir Gordon himself? So, this is Mdlle. Howard! I wish I could see her face. She will not turn this way. And now they are gone. How distinctive is the proud tramp of their feet above the shuffling shamble of the posters!

So, it is only a *piccolo giro* they are gone to make along the lake, and come back again, to dinner. I thought I heard him say my name to his valet, as he stepped into the carriage. Who knocks at the door? I was right; Sir Gordon has sent to invite me to dine at six o'clock. Shall I go? Why should I think of it? I am sick, low, weak, heart and body. Nay, it is better to refuse.

Well, I have written my apology, not without a kind of secret regret, for somehow I have a longing—a strange wish once more to feel the pleasant excitement of even so much of society; but, like the hero of the Peau de Chagrin, I dread to indulge a wish, for it may lead me more rapidly down to my doom. I actually tremble lest a love of life, that all-absorbing desire to live, should lie in wait for me yet. I have heard that it ever accompanies the last stage of my malady. It is better, then, to guard against whatever might suggest it. Pleasure could not—friendship, solicitude, kindness might do so.

CHAPTER XVI.

Villa Cimarosa, Lago di Como.

It is a week since I wrote a line in my notebook, and, judging only from my sensations, it seems like a year. Events rapidly succeeding, always make time seem longer in retrospect. It is only monotony is brief to look back upon. I expected ere this to have been at Naples, if not Palermo; and here I linger on the Lake of Como, as if my frail health had left me any choice of a resting-place. And yet, why should this not be as healthful as it is beautiful?

Looking out from this window, beneath which, not three paces distant, the blue lake is plashing—the music of its waves the only sound heard—great mountains rise grandly from the water to the very skies, the sides one tangled mass of olive, vine, and fig-tree. The dark-leaved laurel, the oleander, the cactus and the magnolia cluster around each rugged rocky eminence, and hang in graceful drapery over the glassy water. Palaces, temples, and villas are seen on every side; some, boldly standing out, are reflected in the calm lake, their marble columns tremulous as the gentle wind steals past; others, half hid among the embowering trees, display but a window or a portico, or perchance a deep arched entrance for the gondolas, above which some heavy banner slowly waves its drooping folds, touching the very water. The closed jalousies, the cloudless sky, the unruffled water, over which no boat is seen to glide, the universal stillness, all tell that it is noon—the noon of Italy, and truly the northern midnight is not a season of such unbroken repose. Looking at this scene, and fancying to myself the lethargic life of ease, which not even thought disturbs, of these people, I half wonder within me how

s 2

had it fared with us of England beneath such a sun, and in such a clime. Had the untiring spirit of enterprise, the active zeal and thirst for wealth, triumphed over every obstacle, and refused to accept, as a season of rest, the hours of the bright and glaring sunshine?

Here the very fishermen are sleeping beneath their canvas awnings, and their boats lie resting in the dark shadows. There is something inexpressibly calm and tranquillizing in all this. The stillness of night we accept as its natural and fitting accompaniment, but to look out upon this fair scene, one is insensibly reminded of the condition of life which leaves these busiest of mortal hours, elsewhere, free to peaceful repose, and with how little labour all wants are met and satisfied.

How came I here? is a question rising to my mind at every moment, and actually demanding an effort of memory to answer. The very apartment itself is almost a riddle to me, seeming like some magic transformation, realizing as it does all that I could ask or wish.

This beautiful little octagon room, with its marble "statuettes" in niches between the windows, its frescoed ceiling, its white marble floor, reflecting each graceful ornament, even to the silver lamp that hangs high in the coved roof; and then, this little terrace beside the lake, where under the silk awning I sit among a perfect bosquet of orange and oleander trees; it is almost too beautiful for reality. I try to read, but cannot; and as I write I stand up at each moment to peep over the balcony at the fish, as sluggishly they move along, or, at the least stir, dart forward with arrowy speed, to return again the minute after, for they have been fed here and know the spot. There is a dreamy, visionary feeling, that seems to be the spirit of the place, encouraging thought, and yet leading the mind to dalliance rather than moody reverie. And again, how came I here? Now for the answer.

On Tuesday last I was at Varenna fully bent on proceeding by Milan to Genoa and thence to Naples. I had not without some difficulty, resisted all approaches of Sir Gordon Howard and even avoided meeting him. What scores of fables did I invent merely to escape an interview with an old friend!

Well, at eight o'clock as I sat at breakfast I heard the bustle of preparation in the court-yard, and saw with inexpressible relief that his horses were standing ready harnessed, while my valet came with the welcome tidings that the worthy baronet was starting for Como, near which he had taken a villa. The Villa Cimarosa, the most beautiful on the lake—frescoes, statues, hanging gardens, I know not how many more charming items did my informant recite with all the impassioned eloquence of George Robins himself. He spared me nothing, from the news that Madamoiselle, Sir Gordon's granddaughter, who was a prodigious heiress, was ordered to Italy for her health, and that it was more than likely we should find them at Naples for the winter, down to the less interesting fact that the courier, Giacomo Bartoletti, was to proceed by the steamer and get the villa ready for their arrival. I could only stop his communications by telling him to order horses for Lecco, pay the bill, and follow me as I should stroll down the road and look at the caverns of rock which it traverses by the lake side.

I had seen Sir Gordon drive off—I had heard the accustomed "*Buon viaggio*" uttered by the whole household in chorus—and now I was free once more ; and so escaping this noisy ceremony of leave-taking, I sauntered listlessly forth and took my way along the lake. The morning was delicious ; a slight breeze from the north, the pleasantest of all the winds on the Lake of Como, was just springing up.

It is here opposite Varenna that the lake is widest ; but nothing of bleakness results from the greater extent of water, for the mountains are still bold and lofty, and the wooded promontory of Bellagio dividing the two reaches of the lake is a beautiful feature. Its terraced gardens and stately palaces peeping amid the leafy shade and giving glimpses of one of the sweetest spots the "Villeggiatura" ever lingered in.

I had got a considerable distance from the town of Varenna without feeling it. The enchanting picture ever presenting some new effect and the light and buoyant breeze from the water and a certain feeling of unusual lightness of heart all aiding, I walked on without fatigue; nor was I aware of the distance traversed till, at a little bend of the lake, I saw Varenna diminishing away—its tall poplars and taper spires being now the most conspicuous features of the town.

At a short distance in front of me lay a little creek or bay, from one side of which a wooden pier projected—a station for the steamers that ply on the lake. There now Sir Gordon Howard's phaeton was standing, surrounded with a most multifarious heap of trunks, packing-cases, portmanteaus, and other travelling gear—signs that some portion of his following, at least, were awaiting the arrival of the packet. Nor had they to wait long, for as I looked the vessel shot round the rocky point and darted swiftly across the smooth water, till she lay scarce moving, about a quarter of a mile from shore—the shoal water prevented her approaching nearer to the jetty.

With the idle curiosity of a lounger, I sat down on a rock to watch the scene.

I know no reason for it, but I ever take an interest in the movements of travellers. Their comings and goings suggest invariably some amusing pictures to my mind, and many a story have I weaved for myself from nothing but the passing glimpses of those landed hurriedly from a steamer.

I watched, therefore, with all my usual satisfaction, the launching of the boat laden heavily with luggage, on the top of which, like its presiding genius, sat a burly courier, his gold-banded cap glistening brightly in the sun. Then came a lighter skiff, in the stern of which sat a female figure shaded by a pink parasol. There was another parasol in the phaeton too—I thought I could even recognize Sir Gordon's figure in the last boat; but as I looked, the sky became suddenly overcast, and round the rocky point, where but a moment before the whole cliff lay reflected in the water, there now came splashing waves, tumbling wildly by, till the whole creek suddenly was covered by them; dark squalls of wind sweeping over the water,

tossing the two boats to and fro, and even heaving up the
huge steamer itself, till her bows were bathed in foaming
cataracts. The suddenness of the tempest—for such it
really was—was a grand and sublime " effect" in such a
scene ; but I could no longer enjoy it, as there seemed to
be actual danger in the situation of the two boats which,
from time to time, were hidden between the swelling waves.
At last, but not without a struggle, they reached the
packet, and I could plainly see by the signs of haste on
board that the captain had not been a very willing spec-
tator of the scene. The luggage was soon on board, and
the figures of the lighter boat followed quickly after.
Scarcely was this effected when the boats were cast off,
and again the paddle-wheels splashed through the water.
The gale at this instant increased, for no sooner was the
steamer's bow to the wind, than the waves went clean over
her, washing her deck from stem to stern, and dashing in
columns of spray over the dark funnel. A great stir and
commotion on deck drew off my attention from the boats ;
and now I heard a hoarse voice calling through a speaking-
trumpet to those in the boats. They, however, either
did not hear or heed the command, for they rowed boldly
towards the shore, nor once paid any attention to the sig-
nals which, first as a flag, and afterwards as a cannon-shot,
the steamer made for them.

While I was lost in conjecturing what possibly all this
might mean, the vessel once more rounded to her course,
and with full steam up breasted the rolling water, and
stood out towards the middle of the lake. A fisherman
just then ran his boat in to land, in a little creek beneath
me, and from him I asked an explanation of the scene.

" It's nothing, signor, but what one sees almost every day
here," said he jeeringly : that " *canaille* of Pellagino have
taken people out to the steamer, and would not wait to
bring them back again ; and now, they must go to Como,
whether they will or no."

This explanation seemed the correct one, and appeared
to be corroborated by the attitude of the party on shore,
for there stood the phaeton, still waiting, although all
chance of the other's returning was totally by-gone. Con-

cluding that, Sir Gordon thus carried off without his will, his servants might possibly need some advice or counsel—for I knew they were all English, except the courier—I hastened down to the jetty, to offer them such aid as I possessed. As I came nearer, I was more convinced that my suspicions were correct. About thirty ragged and not over-prepossessing looking individuals were assembled around the phaeton ; some busily pressing the groom, who who stood at the horses' heads, with questions he could not answer; and others imploring charity with all that servile tone and gesture your Italian beggar is master of. Making my way through this assemblage, I accosted the groom, who knew me to be an acquaintance of his master's, and instead of replying to me, at once cried out,—" Oh, Miss Lucy, here is Mr. Templeton ! You need not be afraid, now."   I turned at once, and instead of a lady's-maid, as I had believed the figure to be, beheld a very lovely but delicate-looking girl, who, with an expression of considerable anxiety in her features, was still following the track of the departing steam-boat. At the mention of my name she looked hurriedly around, and a deep blush covered her face as she said,—

" I am so happy to see Mr. Templeton ! Perhaps he will forgive me if I make the first moment of our acquaint-ance the burden of a request ? "   And then, in a very few words, she told me how her grandfather, having gone on board the steamer to give some particular orders and direc-tions about his baggage, was unwillingly carried off, leaving her with only a groom, who could speak no language but his own.   She went on to say, that they had taken the Villa Cimarosa on the lake, and were then proceeding thither by Lecco, when this *mésaventure* occurred.

" I now must ask Mr. Templeton's counsel how to act—whether to return to the inn at Varenna, and wait there till I can hear from my grandfather, or venture on to Como with the carriage ? "

" If you will take my carriage, Miss Howard, it will be here in a few minutes. My servant is a most experienced traveller, and will not suffer you to endure the slightest inconvenience ; and I will follow in yours."

" But perhaps you cannot travel in an open carriage ?
I have heard that your health is delicate."

" I prefer it greatly."

" And I too——"

She stopped suddenly, feeling that she was about to
utter what might seem an ungracious acknowledgment.
There was such an evident regret in the dread of having
offended me, that, without pausing to reflect, I said,—

" There is another alternative ; I am a very safe whip,
and if you would permit me to have the honour of accompanying you, I should be but too happy to be your
escort."

She tried to answer by a polite smile of acceptance, but
I saw that the proposition was scarcely such as she
approved of, and so at once I added,—

" I will spare you the pain of rejecting my offer; pray,
then, abide by my first suggestion. I see my carriage
coming along yonder."

" I don't know," said she, with a kind of wilfulness, like
that of one who had been long accustomed to indulgence ;
" it may seem very capricious to you, but I own I detest
post-horses, and cracking whips, and rope-harness. You
shall drive me, Mr. Templeton."

I replied by a very sincere assurance of how I esteemed
the favour, and the next moment was seated at her side.
As I stole a glance at the pale but beautifully-formed
features, her drooping eyelashes dark as night, and her
figure of surpassing symmetry and grace, I could not help
thinking of all the straits and expedients I had practised
for three entire days to avoid making her acquaintance.
As if she had actually divined what was then passing in
my mind, she said,—

" You see, Mr. Templeton, it was like a fate; you did
your utmost not to meet us, and here we are after
all."

I stammered out a very eager, but a very blundering
attempt at denial, while she resumed,—

" Pray do not make matters worse, which apologies in
such cases always do. Grandpapa told me that ill health
had made you a recluse and avoid society. This, and the

mystery of your own close seclusion, were quite enough to make me desirous to see you."

"How flattered I should have been had I suspected so much interest could attach to me! but, really, I dreaded to inflict upon a very old friend what I found to be so tiresome, namely, my own company."

"I always heard that you were fastidious about going into society; but surely a visit to an old friend, in a foreign country too, might have escaped being classed in this category?"

"I own my fault, which, like most faults, has brought its own penalty."

"If this be meant to express your deep affliction at not coming to us, I accept the speech in all it most complimentary sense."

I bowed in acquiescence, and she went on :—

"You must forgive me if I talk to you with a freedom that our actual acquaintanceship does not warrant, for, while *you* never heard of me before, *I* have been listening to stories and narratives about *you* I cannot say how long."

"Indeed! I scarcely suspected Sir Gordon had more than remembered me."

"I did not say that grandpapa was my informant," said she, laughing. "Lady Catherine Douglas—the Collingwoods—the Grevilles—and then that delightful person, Madame de Favancourt—all spoke of you . . . . For which of my catalogue was that blush intended, Mr. Templeton?"

"I was only yielding to a very natural sentiment—call it shame, pride or pleasure—that so many fair friends should have deemed me worthy a place in their memory. Is Mary Greville married?"

"Yes; about a month since she accepted the hand she had, it is said, some half-dozen times rejected."

"Sir Blake Morony?"

"The same : an intolerable bore, to my thinking; and, indeed, I believe, to poor Mary's, too. But, then, 'the' man did not offer. Some say he was bashful; some, that he dreaded what he need not have dreaded—a refusal; and so, Mary went out to the Cape when her father became

Governer there; and, like all governor's daughters, took a husband from the staff."

"She was very pretty, but——"

"Say on; we were never more than mere acquaintances."

"I was going to add, a most inveterate flirt."

"How I do detest to hear that brought as an accusation against a girl, from the very kind of person that invariably induces the error!—Young men like Mr. Templeton, who, entering life with the prestige of ability and public success, very naturally flatter the vanity of any girl by their attentions, and lead to a more buoyant character of mind and a greater desire to please, which are at once set down as coquetry. For my own part, I greatly prefer old men's society to young one's, from the very fact that one is permitted to indulge all the caprices of thought or fancy without incurring the offensive imputation of a design on his heart."

"I should not always give a verdict of acquittal even in such cases."

"Very likely not. There are old men whose manner and bearing are infinitely more attractive than the self-satisfied, self-relying composure of our modern young ones. Anything, however, even boyish awkardness, is preferable to your middle-aged gentleman, who with a slight bald spot on his head, and a very permanent flush on his cheek, adds the stately pomp of his forty autumns to a levity that has no touch of younger days."

"Heaven help us! what are we to do from thirty to fifty-five or sixty?"

"Marry and live in the country. I mean, do not be young men about town. *Apropos* to nothing—are we not, this instant, in the very scene of Manzoni's novel, 'I Promessi Sposi?'"

"Yes; the whole of our journey to-day lies through it from Lecco to Como; or rather, more to the northward again—what they call here, the 'Brianza.'"

"The scene deserves better actors, in my opinion. I have always thought it a very tiresome story, even among that most tiresome class—pure love tales."

" What say you to the ' Bride of Lammermoor ? ' "

"That it is only inferior to ' Romeo and Juliet.' But how many interests are there brought up before the reader in either of these—all subordinate to the great one—but all exciting mingled and conflicting emotions! The author, in neither case, was satisfied to dwell on the daily and nightly sighings of a love-stricken pair. He knew better than to weave his web of one tissue. In fact the Master of Ravenswood is more the slave of his own blighted ambition than of his love, which, at best, was only an element in his feeling of abasement."

"And yet, how faithfully was his love returned! Nothing short of a true passion meets such requital."

"If you said, that no heart incapable of feeling ever inspired such. I would agree with you; but I fancy that women are often imposed upon, by supposing that they possess the entire affection of those they know capable of strong attachments."

"That may possiby be true; but I suspect that in the world—in the middle of that life where we daily meet and form friendships—there is very little time or opportunity for anything above a passing feeling of admiration, that seldom reaches esteem. The Honourable Miss Tollemache meets Captain Fitzherbert of the Guards. They are introduced and dance together—the lady is pretty—the Captain amusing—they have a large number of mutual acquaintances, whom they quiz and praise by turns, with sufficient agreement to be mutually pleased. They separate; and the Captain asks if the lady really have " twenty thousand pounds fortune." Match-making aunts and mothers arrange preliminaries; and the young people have leisure to fall in love after the most approved fashion: that is, they meet very often, and talk more together, than common acquaintances are wont to do; but their talk is of Grisi and Lablache, of the Duke's *fête* at Chiswick, and Lord Donnington's yacht excursion to Malta. If the gentleman have a confidence to evoke, it is possibly, the state of his mind on the approaching ' Derby.' Now I would ask, how much of mutual esteem, or even knowledge grows out of all this ?"

"Pretty much the same amount as exists in a French marriage, where M. le Marquis having '*fait ses farces*,' is fain to marry, being somewhat too deep in debt to continue what his years admonish him to abandon. Mademoiselle is brought from the convent, or the governess's apartment, to sign the contract and accept her husband. There is enough in the very emancipation she obtains to be pleasurable, not to speak of a grand *trousseau*, diamonds, cashmeres, and the prettiest equipage in Paris."

Hence," said I, "we seem agreed, that one must not choose a wife or husband *à la mode Anglaise ni Française.*"

"I believe not," said she, laughing; "for if marriages be made in heaven, they are about the strangest employment for angels I ever heard of."

"It entirely depends on how you regard what are commonly called accidents and chances, as to the interpretation you give that saying. If you see, in those curious coincidences that are ever occuring in life, nothing more than hazard, you at once abandon all idea of governing human actions. If, on the other hand, you read them too implicitly, and accept them as indications for the future, you rush into fatalism. For my own part, I think less of the events themselves, than as they originate or evoke sentiments in two parties, who, though previously known to each, only discover on some sudden emergency a wonderful agreement in sentiment and feeling. In the ordinary detail of life they had gone on, each ignorant of the other's opinions: so long as the wheels of life revolved free and noiselessly, the journey had called for nothing of mutual interest; but some chance occurrence, some accidental rencontre occurs, and they at once perceive a most fortuitous similarity in taste or thinking. Like people who have suddenly discovered a long-persisted-in mistake, they hasten to repair the past by sudden confidences. Let me give an instance, even though it be almost too bold a one for my theory. A friend of mine, who had served some years with great distinction in the East, returned to England in company with a brother officer, a man of high family, knowing and known to every one of a certain standing in London. My friend, who, from a remote province, had no town acquaintances, was, however, speedily introduced by his friend, and, heralded by his reputation, was greatly noticed in society. He soon wearied of a round of dissipations, wherein the great, if not the only interest, lies in knowledge of the actors; and was one night stealing away from a large evening party, secretly resolving that it should be his last ball. He had, by dint of great labour and perseverance, reached the last salon, and already caught glimpse of the stair beyond, when his progress was suddenly arrested by a very sweet but excited voice, saying—'One moment, sir; may I beg you will release my scarf.' He turned and beheld a very handsome girl, who was endeavouring to disengage from her shoulders a rich scarf of lace, one end of which was caught in the star he wore on his breast—a decoration from the Nizam. He immediately began to detach the delicate tissue from its dangerous situation. But his address was inferior to his zeal, so that he continually received admonitions as to greater care and caution, with mingled laments over the inevitable mischief that must follow. Something abashed by his own awkwardness, his nervousness made him worse, and he muttered to himself in German, thinking it was a safe tongue for soliloquy—'Why will ladies wear such preposterous finery?—the spider's web is not so fragile.' To which at once the lady replied, in the same language,— 'If men are vain enough to carry a coat full of *crachats* and orders, ladies ought, at least, to be careful how they pass them.' He blushed at the tart rebuke, and in his eagerness he tore a little hoop or mesh of the scarf. 'Oh, pray sir, permit me! It is real Brussels!' and so saying, she at once began, with a skill very different from his, the work of disentanglement. My friend, however, did not desist, but gave what aid he could, their fingers more than once meeting. Meanwhile a running fire of pleasantry and smartness went on between them, when suddenly his brother officer came up, saying,—

"'Oh! Lydia, here is my friend Collyton. I have been so anxious you should know him; and he leaves to-morrow.'

"'I hope he will permit me to rescue my scarf first,' said the lady, taking no heed of the introduction.

"'I am so sorry—I really am in despair,' said Collyton, as the lady, growing at last impatient, tore the frail web in order to get free.

"'It was all your fault, sir, remember that—or rather that of your star, which I'm sure I wish the Sirdar, or the Nizam, had reserved for a more careful wearer.'

"'I never deemed it would have done me such service,' said Collyton, recovering courage; 'without it, I should have passed on, and you would never have taken the trouble to notice me.'

"'There, sir, I must leave you your prize,' said she, smartly, as, taking the arm of her partner, she joined the waltzers; while Collyton stood with the folds of a Brussels scarf draped gracefully on his arm.

"He went home; spent half the night disengaging the intricate web, and the next day called to restore it, and apologize for his misfortune; the acquaintance thus casually formed ripened into mutual liking, and, after a time, into a stronger feeling, and in the end they were married; the whole of the event, the great event of every life, originating in the porcupine fashion of the Nizam's star and the small loops of a Brussels-lace scarf! Here, then, is my case; but for this rencontre they had never met, save in the formal fashion people do as first acquaintances. Without a certain collision, they had not given forth the sparks that warmed into flame."

"I call that a pure chance, just as much as—as——"

"'Our own meeting this morning, you were about to say," said I, laughingly; and she joined in the mirth, but soon after became silent and thoughtful. I tried various ways of renewing our conversation; I started new topics, miles remote from all we had been talking of: but I soon perceived that, whether from physical causes or temperament, the eager interest she exhibited when speaking, and the tone of almost excited animation in which she listened, seemed to weary and exhaust her. I therefore gradually suffered our conversation to drop down to an occasional remark on passing objects; and so we travelled onwards

tin, late in the afternoon, we found ourselves at the gate
of a handsome park, where an avenue of trellised vines,
wide enough for two carriages to pass, led to a beautiful
villa, on the terrace of which stood my old friend, Sir
Gordon Howard himself.

For a few moments he was so totally engrossed by the
meeting with his granddaughter that he did not even perceive me.   Indeed, his agitation was as great as it might
reasonably have been had years of absence separated them,
instead of the few brief hours of a twenty miles' drive;
and it was only as she said, " Are you forgetting to thank
Mr. Templeton, papa ? " that he turned round to greet
me with all the warmth of his kindly nature.

It was to no purpose that I protested plans already
formed, engagements made, and horses written for; he
insisted on my staying, if not some weeks—some days—
and at last, hours, at the Villa Cimarosa.   I might still
have resisted his kind entreaties, when Miss Howard, with
a smile and a manner of most winning persuasiveness,
said, " I wish you would stay,"—and——here I am!

CHAPTER XVII.

La Villa Cimarosa, October.

How like a dream—a delicious, balmy, summer night's dream—is this life I am leading! For the first time have I tasted the soothing tranquillity of domestic life. A uniformity, that tells rather of security than sameness, pervades everything in this well-ordered household, where all come and go as if under the guidance of some ruling genius, unseen and unheard. Sir Gordon, too, is like a father; at least as I can fancy a father to be, for I was too early left an orphan to preserve my memory of either parent. His kindness is even more than what we call friendship. It is actually paternal. He watches over my health with all the unobtrusive solicitude of true affection; and if I even hint at departure, he seizes the occasion to oppose it, not with the warmth of hospitality alone, but a more deeply-meaning interest that sometimes puzzles me. Can it be that he recognizes in my weakened frame and shrunken cheek, greater ravages of disease than I yet feel or know of? Is it that he perceives me nearer the goal than as yet I am aware? It was yesterday, as we sat in the library together, running over the pages of an almanac, I remarked something about my liking to travel by moonlight, when, with a degree of emotion that amazed me, he said, "Pray do not talk of leaving us; I know that in this quiet monotony there may be much to weary you; but remember that your are not strong enough for the world, did you even care to take your place in it as of old. Besides,"—here he faltered, and it was with a great effort that he resumed—"besides, for *my* sake, if the

T

selfishness of the request should not deter you, for *my* sake remain with us some time longer."

I protested most warmly, as I had all reason to do, that for years past I had never known time pass on so happily; that in the peaceful calm we lived, I had tasted a higher enjoyment than all the most buoyant pleasures of healthier and younger days had ever given me. "But,"—I believe I tried to smile as I spoke,—"but recollect, Sir Gordon, I have got my billet: the doctors have told me to go, and die, at Naples. What a shock to science if I should remain, to live, at Como!"

"Do so, my dearest friend," said he, grasping my hands within both of his, while the tears swam in his eyes; "I cannot—I dare not—I have not strength to tell you, all that your compliance with this wish will confer on me. Spare me this anguish, and do not leave us." As he uttered these words he left me, his emotion too great to let me reply.

The sick man's selfishness would say, that his anxiety is about that wasting malady, whose ravages are even more plainly seen than felt.

Turn the matter over how I will, I cannot reconcile this eager anxiety for my remaining with anything but a care for myself. It is clear he thinks me far worse than I can consent to acknowledge. I do not disguise from myself the greater lassitude I experience after a slight exertion, a higher tension of the nervous system, and an earlier access of that night fever, which, like the darkness of the coming winter, creeps daily on, shortening the hours of sunlight, and ushering in a deeper and more solemn gloom; but I watch these symptoms as one already prepared for their approach, and feel grateful that their coming has not clouded the serenity with which I hope to journey to the last.

Kind old man! I would that I were his son, that I could feel my rightful claim to the affection he lavishes on me; but for *his* sake it is better as it is! And Miss Howard—Lucy, let me call her, since I am permitted so to accost her—what a blessing I should have felt such a sister to be, so beautiful, so kind, so gently feminine! for that is the true charm. This, too, is better as it is. How could I take leave of life, if I were parting with such enjoyments?

She is greatly changed since we came here. Every day seems to gain something over the malady she laboured under. She is no longer faint and easily wearied, but able to take even severe exercise without fatigue; her cheek has grown fuller, and its rosy tint is no longer hectic but the true dye of health; and instead of that slow step and bent-down head, her walk is firm and her air erect; while her spirits, no longer varying from high excitement to deep depression, are uniformly good and animated. Life is opening in all its bloom to her, as rapidly as its shadows are closing and gathering around me! Were it mine to bestow, how gladly would I give what remains of flickering life to strengthen the newly-sprung vitality, her light step, her brilliant smile and dark blue eye! That coming back to health, from out of the very shadow of death, must be a glorious sensation! The sudden outbursting of all this fair world's joys, on a spirit over which the shade of sickness has only swept, and not rested long enough to leave its blight. I think I read in that almost heroic elevation of sentiment, that exquisite perception of whatever is beautiful in Lucy, the triumph of returning energy and health. She is less fanciful and less capricious, too. Formerly, the least remark, in which she construed a difference of opinion, would distress or irritate her, and her temper appeared rather under the sway of momentary impulse than the guidance of right principle. Now, she accepts even correction mildly and gratefully, and if a sudden spark of former haste flash forth, she seems eager to check and repress it; she acts as though she felt that restored health imposed more restraint and less of self-indulgence than sickness. How happy if one were only to bring out of the sick chamber its teaching of submission, patience, and gratitude, and leave behind its egotism and its irritability! This she would appear to aim at; and to strive is to win.

And now I quit this chronicling to join her. Already

she is on her way to the boat, and we are going to see Pliny's villa ; at least the dark and shadowy nook where it once stood. The lake is still as a mirror, and a gorgeous mirror it is, reflecting a scene of faëry brilliancy and beauty. She is waving her handkerchief to me to come. "*Vengo, subito.*"

This has been a delightful day. We rowed along past Melzi till we came under the tall cliffs near Bellagio ; and there, in a little bay, land-locked and shaded by olive-trees, we dined. I had never seen Sir Gordon so thoroughly happy. When Lucy's spirits have been higher, and her fancy has taken wilder and bolder wings, he has usually worn a look of anxiety through all his admiring fondness. To-day, she was less animated than she generally is— almost grave at times—but not sad ; and I think that "grandpapa" loved her better in this tranquil mood, than in those of more eager enjoyment. I believe I read his meaning, that, in her highest flow of spirits, he dreads the wear and tear consequent on so much excitement ; while in her more sombre days he indulges the hope that she is storing up in repose the energies of future exertion. How it takes off the egotism of sickness to have some one whose ever-watchful care is busy for our benefit ! how it carries away the load of "self," and all its troubles ! while I . . . But I must not dwell on this theme, nor dis-turb that deep sense of gratitude I feel for all that I possess of worldly advantage, were it no more than this blessing, that on quitting life I leave it when my sense of enjoyment has mellowed into that most lasting and en-during one, the love of quiet, of scenery, of converse with old friends on by-gone events—the tranquil pleasures of age tasted without the repining of age !

Lucy bantered me to-day upon my inordinate love of ease, as she called it, forgetting that this inactivity was at first less from choice than complusion ; now, it is a habit, one I may as well wear out, for I have no time left to acquire new ones. She even tried to stimulate my ambition, by alluding to my old career and the rewards it might have opened to me. I could have told her that a father or an uncle at the " Council " was of more avail than a clever despatch or a well-concluded treaty; that some of our ablest Ministers are wasting life and energy at small, obscure, and insignificant missions, where their functions never rise beyond the presentation of letters of congratulation or condolence, attendance on a court ball, or a *Te Deum* for the sovereign's birthday ; while capacities that would be unnoticed, if they were not dangerous, have the destinies of great events in their keeping. True, there is always the Foreign Office as the " *Cour d' Appel ;* " and, whatever may be the objections—grave and weighty they certainly are at times—against those parliamentary interrogations by which the Minister is compelled to reveal the object and course of his dealings with foreign nations, there is one admirable result—our foreign policy will always be National. No Minister can long pursue any course in defiance of the approval of Parliament; nor can any Parliament, in our day, long resist the force of public opinion. While, therefore, Nicholas or Metternich may precipitate the nations they rule over into a war, where there is neither the sympathy nor the prejudices of a people involved, *we* never draw the sword without a hearty goodwill to wield it.

To what end all this in reference to Lucy Howard's question ? None whatever; for, in truth, I was half flattered by the notion that the shattered, storm-beaten wreck, could be supposed sea-worthy, and so I promised amendment. How pleasant it was, sitting Tityrus-like, to dream over high rewards and honours ! She, at least, seemed to think so ; for whether to stimulate my ardour, or merely following the impulse of her own, I know not, but she certainly dwelt with animation and delight on the advantages of a career that placed one almost *au pied d' égal* with sovereigns. " I am sure," said she, " that you cannot look upon those who started in the race with yourself, without some repinings that others, whom you know to be inferior to you, have passed you ; and that men whom you would never have thought of as competitors, are now become more than equals."

If I accede to this opinion to a certain extent, still I

must protest against any feeling of real regret when I think that success is much oftener obtained by what is called a "lucky hit," than by years of zealous and intelligent exertion. I have known a man obtain credit for stopping a courier—waylaying him, I might rather call it—and taking by force a secret treaty from his hand, while the steady services of a life-long have gone unrewarded. These things have an evil influence upon diplomacy as a "career;" they suggest to young men to rely rather on address and dexterity than upon "prudence and forethought." Because Lord Palmerston discourses foreign politics with a certain gifted and very beautiful Countess, or that M. Guizot deigns to take counsel from a most accomplished Princess of Russian origin, every small *attaché* thinks he is climbing the short road to fame and honours by listening to the *fadaise* of certain political *boudoirs*, and hearing "pretty ladies talk" about Spielberg and Monkopf. When the Northern minister sent his son to travel through the world, that he might see with his own eyes by what "commonplace mortals states were governed," he might have recommended to his especial notice Plenipos and Envoys Extraordinary. From time to time, it is otherwise. Lord Castlereagh, whatever detraction party hate may visit on his home politics, was a consummate ambassador. Not of that school which Talleyrand created, and of which he was the head, but a man of unflinching courage, high determination, and who, with a strong purpose and resolute will, never failed to make felt the influence of a nation he so worthily represented. With this, he was a perfect courtier; the extreme simplicity of his manner and address was accompanied by an elegance and a style of the most marked distinction. Another, but of a different stamp, was Lord Whitworth; one on whom all the dramatic passion and practised outrage of Napoleon had no effect whatever.

Sir Gordon remarked, that in this quality of coolness and imperturbability he never saw any one surpass his friend, Sir Robert Darcy. One evening when playing at whist, at Potzdam, with the late King of Prussia, his Majesty, in a fit of inadvertence, appropriated to himself several gold pieces belonging to Sir Robert. The King at last perceived and apologized for his mistake, adding, "Why did you not inform me of it?" "Because I knew your Majesty always makes restitution when you have obtained time for reflection." Hanover was then on the *tapis*, and the King felt the allusion. I must not forget a trait of that peculiar sarcastic humour for which Sir Robert was famous. Although a Whig—an old blue-and-yellow of the Fox school—he hated more than any man that mongrel party which, under the name of Whigs, have carried on the Opposition in Parliament for so many years; and of that party, a certain well-known advocate for economical reforms came in for his most especial detestation: perhaps he detested him particularly, because he had desecrated the high ground of Oppositional attack, and brought it down to paltry cavillings about the sums accorded to poor widows on the Pension List, or the amount of sealing-wax consumed in the Foreign Office. When, therefore, the honourable and learned gentleman, in the course of a continental tour, happened to pass through the city where Sir Robert lived as ambassador, he received a card of invitation to dinner, far more on account of a certain missive from the Foreign Office, than from any personal claims he was possessed of. The Member of Parliament was a *gourmand* of the first water; he had often heard of Sir Robert's *cuisine*—various travellers had told him that such a table could not be surpassed, and so, although desirous of getting forward, he countermanded his horses, and accepted the invitation.

Sir Robert, whose taste for good living was indisputable, no sooner read the note acceding to his request than he called his *attachés* together, and said, "Gentlemen, you will have a very bad dinner to-day, but I request you will all dine here, as I have a particular object in expressing the wish."

Dinner-hour came; and after the usual ceremony the party were seated at table, when a single soup appeared: this was followed by a dish of fish, and then, without *entrée* or *hors d'œuvre*, came a boiled leg of mutton, Sir Robert premising to his guest that it was to have no successor: adding, "You see, sir, what a poor entertainment I have provided for you; but to this have the miserable economists in Parliament brought us—next session may carry it further, and leave us without even so much." Joseph was sold, and never forgot it since.

I saw, that while Sir Gordon and I discussed people and events in this strain, Lucy became inattentive and pre-occupied by other thoughts; and on charging her with being so, she laughingly remarked that Englishmen always carry about with them the one range of topics; and whether they dine in Grosvenor Square, or beneath an olive-tree in the Alps, the stream of the table-talk is ever the same. "Now a Frenchman," said she, gaily, "had uttered I cannot say how many flat sentimentalisms about the place we are in; a German had mysticized to no end; and an Italian would have been improvising about everything, from the wire that restrained the champagne cork to the woes of enchained Italy. Tell us a story, Mr. Templeton."

"A story! What shall it be? A love story? a ghost story? a merry, or a sad one?"

"Any of these you like, so that it be true. Tell me something that has actually happened."

"That is really telling a secret," said I; "for while truth can be, and oftener is, stranger than fiction, it is so, rather from turning ordinary materials to extraordinary uses—making of every-day people singular instances of vice and virtue—than for any great peculiarity in the catastrophes to which they contribute."

"Well, I don't believe in the notion of every-day people. I have a theory, that what are so summarily disposed of in this fashion are just as highly endowed with individualities as any others. Do you remember a beautiful remark, made in the shape of a rebuke, that Scott one day gave his daughter for saying that something was 'Vulgar?' 'Do you know what is the meaning of the word vulgar? It is only common; and nothing that is common, except wickedness, can deserve to be spoken of in terms of contempt: and when you have lived to my years, you will be disposed to agree with me in thanking God that nothing really worth having or caring about in this world is *uncommon.*'"

" When I said ordinary, every-day people, don't mistake me! I meant only those who, from class and condition, follow a peculiar ritual, and live after a certain rubric of fashion; and who, hiding themselves under a common garment, whose cut, colour, and mode are the same, are really undistinguishable, save on great and trying occasions."

" Kings, for instance! whom great diplomatic folks are supposed to see a great deal of, and know in all the terms of an easy intimacy."

" But how do we see them ? In an armour of reserve and caution, never assumed to any one else. The ease you speak of is all assumed. It is the conventional politeness accorded to a certain station. Kings, so far as I have seen, are never really engaging, save to a great minister out of power. Then their manner assumes all its attractiveness; on the principle, perhaps, that Curran paid his homage to the antique Hercules— that *his* day might yet come uppermost, and he would not forget the friend who visited him in adversity."

" Well, to come back, tell us a story. Let it be what you will, or of where and whom you please, so that it last while we are rowing homeward. Monologue is always better than conversation by moonlight."

" But stay; what are the lights we see yonder, glancing from amid the trees ? And there, now, see the bright blaze that has sprung up, and is reflected red and lurid on the lake below. It is a ' *Festa* ' of the Church; for hear, the bells are ringing merrily from the mountain-top, and there go the people in procession, climbing the steep path towards the summit."

Wonderful superstition! that has fashioned itself to every phase and form of human nature—now sending its aid to the darkest impulses of passion, as we see in Ireland —now conforming to the most simple tastes of an unthinking people; for these peasants here are not imbued

with the piety of the Church—they only love its gauds.
It is to the Tyrol you must go to witness the real devotional feeling of a people.

"Well, shall 1 tell you a story?"

"No· I am weaving one now for myself!"

CHAPTER XVIII.

VILLA CIMAROSA, LAKE OF COMO.

GILBERT reminds me that I had arranged my departure hence for to-morrow; this was some weeks back, and now I have no intention of leaving. I cling to this "Happy Valley," as one clings to life. To me it is indeed such. These days of sunshine and nights of starry brilliancy—this calm, delicious water—these purpled mountains, glowing with richer tints as day wears on, till at sunset they are one blaze of gorgeous splendour—the very plash of those tiny waves upon the rocky shore are become to me like friendly sights and sounds, from which I cannot tear myself. And Lucy, too, she is to me as a sister, so full of kind, of watchful consideration about me; since her own health is so much restored, all her anxiety would seem for mine. How puzzling is the tone assumed by Sir Gordon towards me! It was only yesterday that, in speaking of his granddaughter, he expressed himself in such terms of gratitude to me for the improvement manifest in her health, as though I had really been the main agent in effecting it. I, whose power has never been greater than a heart-cherished wish that one so fair, so beautiful, and so good should live to grace and adorn the world she moves in! What a strange race, what a hard-fought struggle has been going on within me for some time back! Ebbing life contesting with budding affection; the calm aspect of coming death dashed by feelings and thoughts—ay, even hopes I had believed long since at rest. I feel less that I love, than that I should love if life were to be granted to me.

I believe it is the pursuit that in most cases suggests the passion; that the effort we may make to win exalts the object we wish to gain. Not so here, however. *If I do love*, it has been without any consciousness. It is so seldom that one who has never had a sister learns to know, in real intimacy, the whole heart and nature of a young and lovely girl, with all its emotions of ever-changing hue, its thousand caprices, its weakness, and its pride. To me this study—it has been a study—has given an inexpressible interest to my life here. And then to watch how gradually, almost imperceptibly to herself, the discipline of her mind has been accomplished—checking wild flights of fancy here, restraining rash impulses there, encouraging reflection, conquering prejudices—all these done without my bidding, and yet palpably through my influence. What pleasant flattery!

One distressing thought never leaves me. It is this— how will a nature so attuned as hers stand the rude jars and discords of "the world"? for, do how we will, screen the object of affection how we may from its shocks and concussions, the stern realities of life will make themselves felt. Hers is too impassioned a nature to bear such reverses, as the most even current sustains, without injury. The very consciousness of being mistaken in our opinions of people is a sore lesson; it is the beginning of scepticism, to end—who can tell where?

She smiles whenever I lecture her upon any eccentricity of manner, and evidently deems my formalism, as she calls it, a relic of my early teaching. So, perhaps, it may be. No class of people are so unforgiving to anything like a peculiarity as your *Diplomates*. They know the value of the impassive bearing that reveals nothing, and they carry the reserve of office into all the relations of private life. She even quizzes me about this, and says that I remind her of the old Austrian envoy at Naples, who never ventured upon anything more explicit than the two phrases—*C'est dure*, or *C'est sûre*, ringing the changes of these upon every piece of news that reached him. How altered am I, if this judgment be correct! I, that was headstrong even to rashness, led by every impulse, precipitate in everything, ready to resign all, and with one chance in my favour to dare nine full against me!

But why wonder if I be so changed? How has life
and every living object changed its aspect to my eyes,
rendering distasteful a thousand things wherein I once
took pleasure, and making of others that I deemed flat,
stale, and unprofitable, the greatest charms of my
existence? What close and searching scrutiny of motives
creeps on with years! what distrust, and what suspicion!
It is this same sentiment—the fruit of a hundred self-
deceptions and disappointments—makes so many men, as
they advance in life, abjure Liberalism in politics, and lean
to the side of Absolute Rule. The "Practical" exercises
the only influence on the mind tempered by long experience; and the glorious tyranny of St. Peter's is infinitely preferable to the miscalled freedom of Popular
Government. The present Pope, however our Radical
friends think of it, is no unworthy successor of Hilde-
brand; and however plausible be the assumed reforms in
his States, the real thraldom, the great slavery, remains
untouched! "Hands Free, Souls Fettered," is strange
heraldry.

Why have these thoughts crept over me? I would
rather dwell on very different themes; but already, far
over the mountains westward, comes the distant sound of
strife. The dark clouds that are hurrying over the lofty
summit of Monte Brisbone are wafted from regions where
armed hosts are gathering, and the cry of battle is heard;
and Switzerland, whose war-trophies have been won from
the invader, is about to be torn by civil strife. Even in
my ride to-day towards Lugano, I met parties of peasants
armed, and wearing the cockade of Ticino in their hats,
hastening towards Capo di Lago. The spectacle was a sad
one; the field labours of the year, just begun, are already
arrested; the plough is seen standing in the unfinished
furrow, and the team is away to share the fortunes of its
owners in the panoply of battle. These new-made
soldiers, too, with all the loutish indifference of the
peasant in their air, have none of the swaggering
effrontery of regular troops, and consequently present
more palpably to the eye the sufferings of a population
given up to conscription and torn from their peaceful

homes to scenes of carnage and bloodshed, and for what?
—for an opinion?—for even less than an opinion; for a
suspicion—a mere doubt.

Who will be eager in this cause on either side? None,
save those that never are to mingle in the contest. The
firebrand journalist of Geneva—the dark-intentioned
Jesuit of Lucerne; these are they who will accept of
no quarter, nor listen to one cry of mercy; such, at
least, is the present aspect of the struggle. Lukewarm-
ness, if not actual repugnance, among the soldiery;
hatred supplying all the enthusiasm of those who hound
them on.

The Howards are already uneasy at their vicinity to the
seat of war, and speak of proceeding southward; yet they
will not hear of my leaving them. I feel spell-bound, not
only to them but to the very place itself; a presentiment
is upon me, that, after this, life will have no pleasure left
for me—that I go hence to solitude, to suffering, and to
death!

A restless night, neither waking nor sleeping, but
passed in wild, strange fancies, of reality and fiction
commingled; and now, I am feverish and ill. The struggle
against failing health is at last become torture; for I feel
—alas that I must say it!—the longing desire to live.
Towards daybreak I did sleep, and soundly; but I dreamed
too—and how happily! I fancied that I was suddenly
restored to health, with all the light-heartedness and
spring of former days, and returning with my bride to
Walcott. We were driving rapidly up the approach,
catching glimpses at times of the old abbey—now a gable,
now some richly traceried pinnacle—some quaint old
chimney—some trellised porch. She was wild with
delight, in ecstasy at the sylvan beauty of the scene: the
dark and silent wood—the brown clear river, beside the
road—the cooing note of the wood-pigeon, all telling of
our own rural England. "Is not this better than ambition,
love?" said I. "Are not leafy groves, these moss-grown
paths, more peaceful than the high-roads of fame?" I
felt her hand grasp mine more closely, and I awoke—

awoke to know that I was dreaming—that my happiness was but a vision—my future a mere mockery.

Why should not Lucy see these scenes ? She will return well and in strength. I would that she would dwell, sometimes, at least, among the places I have loved so much. I have often thought of making her my heir. I have none to claim from me—none who need it. There is one clause, however, she might object to, nay, perhaps, would certainly refuse. My grand-uncle's will makes it imperative that the property should always descend to a Templeton. What if she rejected the condition? It would fall heavily on me were she to say " No."

I will speak to Sir Gordon about this. I must choose my time, however, and do it gravely and considerately, that he may not treat it as a mere sick man's fancy. Of course, I only intend that she should assume the name and arms ; but this branch of the Howards are strong about pedigree, and call themselves older than the Norfolks.

So there is no time to be lost in execution of my plan. The Favancourts are expected here to-morrow, on their way to Naples. The very thought of their coming is misery to me. How I dread the *persiflage* of the beauty " *en vogue ;*" the heartless raillery that is warmed by no genial trait; the spiritless levity that smacks neither of wit nor buoyant youth, but is the mere coinage of the *salons!* How I dread, too, lest Lucy should imitate her ! she so prone to catch up a trait of manner, or a trick of gesture! And Lady Blanche can make herself fascinating enough to be a model. To hear once more the dull recital of that world's follies that I have left, its endless round of tiresome vice, would be a heavy infliction. Alas that I should have gained no more by my experience than to despise it ! But stay—I see Sir Howard yonder, near the lake. Now for my project !

CHAPTER XIX.

ANOTHER month, or nearly so, has elapsed since last I opened this book; and now, as I look back, I feel like a convict who has slept soundly during the night before his doom, and passed in forgetfulness the hours he had vowed to thought and reflection. I was reading Victor Hugo's "Dernier Jour d'un Condamné" last evening, and falling asleep with it in my hand, traced out in my dreams a strange analogy between my own fate and that of the convicted felon. The seductions and attractions of life crowding faster and faster round one as we near the gate of death—the redoubled anxieties of friends, their kinder sympathies—how delightful would these be if they did not suggest the wish to live! But, alas! the sunbeam lights not only the road before us, but that we have been travelling also, and one is so often tempted to look back and linger! To understand this love of life, one must stand as I do now; and yet, who would deem that one so lonely and so desolate, so friendless and alone, would care to live? It is so, however: sorrow attaches us more strongly than joy; and the world becomes dearer to us in affliction as violets give out their sweetest odours when pressed.

Let me recall something of the last few weeks, and remember, if I can, why and how I am here alone. My last written sentence was dated "Como, the 29th October," and then comes a blank—now to fill it up.

Sir Gordon Howard was standing near the lake as I came up with him, nor was he aware of my approach till I had my hand on his arm. Whether that I had disturbed him in a moment of deep thought, or that something in my own sad and sickly face impressed him, I know not, but he did not speak, and merely drawing my arm within his own, we wandered along the water's edge. We sauntered slowly on till we came to a little moss-house, with stone benches, where, still in silence, we sat down. It belonged to the Villa d'Este, and was one of those many little ornamental buildings that were erected by that most unhappy Princess, whose broken heart would seem inscribed on every tree and rock around.

To me the aspect of the spot, lovely as it is, has ever been associated with deep gloom. I never could tread the walks, nor sit to gaze upon the lake from chosen points of view, without my memory full of her who, in her exile, pined and suffered there. I know nothing of her history, save what all others know; I am neither defender nor apologist—too humble and too weak for either. I would but utter one cry for mercy on a memory that still is dearly cherished by the poor, who dwelt around her, and by whom she is yet beloved.

Whatever were Sir Gordon's thoughts, it was clear the few efforts he made to converse were not in accordance with them. The rumours of disturbance in Switzerland— the increasing watchfulness on the Lombard frontier—the growing feeling of uncertainty where and how far this new discord might extend—these he spoke of, but rather as it seemed to mask other themes, than because they were uppermost in his mind.

" We must think of leaving this," said he, after a brief pause. "'Where to?' is the question. How would Genoa agree with *you* ?"

" With *me* ! Let there be no question of *me*."

" Nay, but there must," said he, eagerly. " Remember, first of all, that we are now independent of climate, at least of all that this side of the Alps possesses ; and, secondly, bethink you that *you* are the pilot that weathered the storm for us."

" Happily, then," said I, laughing, or endeavouring to laugh, " I may sing,—

' The waves are laid,
My duties paid.'

U

I must seek out some harbour of refuge and bo at rest.”

“But with us, Templeton—always with us,” said the old man, affectionately.

“Upon one condition, Sir Gordon—short of that I refuse.”

I fear me, that in my anxiety to subdue a rising emotion I threw into these words an accent of almost stern and obstinate resolution; for as he replied, “Name your condition,” his own voice assumed a tone of cold reserve.

It was full a minute before I could resume; not only was the subject one that I dreaded to approach from fear of failure, but I felt that I had already endangered my chance of success by the inopportune moment of its introduction. Retreat was out of the question, and I went on. As much to give myself time for a little forethought, as to provide myself with a certain impulse for the coming effort, as leapers take a run before they spring, I threw out a hasty sketch of the late events of my life before leaving England, and the reasons that induced me to come abroad. “I knew well,” said I, “better far than all the skill of physicians could teach, that no chance of recovery remained for me; Science had done its utmost: the machine had, however, been wound up for the last time —its wheels and springs would bear no more. Nothing remained, then, but to economize the hours, and let them glide by with as little restriction as might be. There was but one alloy to this plan—its selfishness; but when may a man practise egotism so pardonably as when about to part with what comprises it?

“I came away from England, then, with that same sentiment that made the condemned captain beg he might be bled to death rather than fall beneath the axe. I would, if possible, have my last days and hours calm and unruffled, even by fear—little dreaming how vain are all such devices to cheat one’s destiny, and that death is never so terrible as when life becomes dear. Yes, my friend, such has been my fate; in the calm happiness of home here—the first time I ever knew the word’s true meaning —I learned to wish for life, for days of that peaceful happiness where the present is tempered by the past, and hope has fewer checks, because it comes more chastened by experience. You little thought, that in making my days thus blissful my sorrow to part with them would be a heavy recompense. . . . Nay, hear me out; words of encouragement only increase my misery—they give not hope, they only awaken fresh feelings of affection, so soon to be cold for ever.''

How I approached the subject on which my heart was set I cannot now remember—abruptly, I fear; imperfectly and dubiously I know: because Sir Gordon, one of the most patient and forbearing of men, suddenly interrupted me by a violent exclamation, "Hold! stay! not a word more! Templeton, this cannot be; once for all, never recur to this again!" Shocked, almost terrified by the agitation in his looks, I was unable to speak for some seconds; and while I saw that some misconception of my meaning had occurred, yet, in the face of his prohibition, I could scarcely dare an attempt to rectify it. While I remained thus in painful uncertainty, he seemed, by a strong effort, to have subdued his emotion, and at length said, "Not even to you, my dear friend—to you, to whom I owe the hope that has sustained me for many a day past can I reveal the secret source of this sorrow, nor say why what you propose is impossible. I dreaded something like this—I foresaw how it might be; nay, my selfishness was such that I rejoiced at it, for her sake. There—there, I will not trust myself with more. Leave me, Templeton; whatever your griefs, they are as nothing compared to mine."

I left him, and, hastening towards the lake side, soon lost myself in the dark groves of chestnut and olive, the last words still ringing in my ears—" Whatever your griefs they are as nothing compared to mine." Such complete pre-occupation had his agitation and trouble over my mind, that it was long ere I could attempt to recall how I had evoked this burst of passion, and by what words I had stirred him so to address me. Suddenly the truth flashed boldly out; I perceived the whole nature of the error. He had, in fact, interrupted my explanation at a

point which made it seem that I was seeking his granddaughter in marriage. Not waiting to hear me out, he
deemed the allusions to my name, my family arms, and
my fortune, were intended to convey a proposal to make
her my wife. Alas! I needed no longer to wonder at his
repugnance, nor speculate further on the energy of his
refusal. How entertain such a thought for his poor child.
It were, indeed, to weave cypress with the garland of the
Bride!

Impatient any longer to lie under the misconception—
at heart, perhaps, vexed to think how wrongfully he must
have judged me when deeming me capable of the thought
—I hastened back to the Villa, determined at once to
rectify the error and make him hear me out, whatever
pains the interview should cost either.

On gaining the house I found that Sir Gordon had just
driven from the door. Miss Howard, who for two days
had been indisposed, was still in her room. Resolving,
then to make my explanation in writing, I went to my
room ; on the table lay a letter addressed to me, the
writing of which was scarcely dry. It ran thus :—

"My dearest Friend,
"If I, in part, foresaw the possibility of what your
words to-day assured me, and yet did not guard against
the hazard, the sad circumstances of my lot in life are all
I can plead in my favour. I have never ceased to re-
proach myself that I had not been candid and open with
you at first, when our intimacy was fresh. Afterwards,
as it became friendship, the avowal was impossible. I
must not trust myself with more. I have gone from
home for a day or two, that when we meet again the immediate memory of our last interview should have been
softened. Be to me—to her, also—as though the words
were never spoken ; nor withdraw any portion of your
affection from those you have rescued from the greatest
of all calamities.
"Yours ever,
"Gordon Howard,"

The mystery grew darker and more impenetrable; harassing, maddening suspicions, mixed themselves up in my brain, with thoughts too terrible for endurance. I saw that, in Sir Gordon's error as to my intentions, he had unwittingly disclosed the existence of a secret—a secret whose meaning seemed fraught with dreadful import; that he would never have touched upon this mysterious theme, save under the false impression my attempted proposal had induced, was clear enough; and, that thus I had unwittingly wrung from him an avowal which, under other circumstances, he had never been induced to make.

I set about to think over every word I had used in our last interview—each expression I had employed, torturing the simplest phrases by interpretations the most remote and unlikely, that thereby some clue should present itself to this mystery: but, charge my memory how I could, reflect and ponder as I might, the words of his letter had a character of more deep and serious meaning than a mere refusal of my proposition, taken in what sense it might, could be supposed to call for. At moments, thoughts would flash across my brain so terrible in their import, that had they dwelt longer I must have gone mad. They were like sudden paroxysms of some agonizing disease, coming and recurring at intervals. Just as one of these had left me, weak, worn out, and exhausted, a carriage, drawn by four post-horses, drew up to the door of the villa, and the instant after my servant knocked at my door, saying, "La Comtesse de Favancourt is arrived, sir, and wishes to see you."

Who was there whose presence I would not rather have faced?—that gay and heartless woman of fashion, whose eyes, long practised to read a history in each face, would soon detect in my agitated looks that "something had occurred," nor cease till she had discovered it. In Sir Gordon's absence, and as Lucy was still indisposed, I had no alternative but to receive her.

Scarcely had I entered the drawing-room than my worst fears were realized. She was seated in an arm-chair, and lay back as if fatigued by her journey; but on seeing me, without waiting to return my greeting of welcome, she asked, abruptly,—

"Where's Sir Gordon?—where's Miss Howard? Haven't they been expecting me?"

I answered, that Sir Gordon had gone over to the Brianza for a day; that Miss Howard had been confined to her room, but, I was certain, had only to learn her arrival to dress and come down to her."

"Is this said *de bonne foi?*" said she, with a smile where the expression was far more of severity than sweetness. "Are you treating me candidly, Mr. Templeton? or is this merely another exercise of your old functions as diplomatist?"

I started, partly from actual amazement, partly from a feeling of indignant shame, at the accusation; but recovering at once, assured her calmly and respectfully that all I had said was the simple fact, without the slightest shade of equivocation.

"So much the better," said she gaily; "for I own to you I was beginning to suspect our worthy friends of other motives. You know what a tiresome world of puritanism and mock propriety we live in, and I was actually disposed to fear that these dear souls had got up both the absence and the illness not to receive me."

"Not to receive you! Impossible!" said I, with unfeigned astonishment. "The Howards, whom I have always reckoned as your oldest and most intimate friends——"

"Oh, yes! very old friends, certainly: but remember that these are exactly the kind of people who take upon them to be severer than all the rest of the world, and are ten times as rigid and unforgiving as one's enemies. Now, as I could not possibly know how this affair might have been told to them——"

"What affair? I'm really quite in the dark to what you allude."

"I mean my separation from Favancourt."

"Are you separated from your husband, Lady Blanche?" asked I, in a state of agitation in strong contrast to her calm and quiet manner.

" What a question, when all the papers have been discussing it these three weeks!   And from an old admirer, too!   Shame on you, Mr. Templeton ! "

I know not how it was, but the levity of this speech, given as it was, made my cheek flush till it actually seemed to burn.

" Nay, nay, I didn't mean you to blush so deeply," said she.   " And what a dear, sweet, innocent kind of life you must have been leading here, on this romantic lake, to be capable of such soft emotions!   Oh dear ! " sighed she, weariedly.   " You men have an immense advantage in your affairs of the heart ; you can always begin as freshly with each new affection, and be as youthful in sentiment with each new love, as we are with our only passion. Now I see it all; you have been getting up a ' *tendre* ' here for somebody or other :—not Taglioni, I hope, for I see that is her Villa yonder.—There, don't look indignant. This same lake of Como has long been known to be the paradise of *danseuses* and opera-singers ; and I thought it possible you might have dramatized a little love-story to favour the illusion.   Well, well," said she, sighing, " so that you have not fallen in love with poor Lucy Howard——"

" And why not with her ? " said I, starting, while in my quick-beating heart and burning temples a sense of torturing pain went through me.

" Why not with her ? " reiterated she, pausing at each word, and fixing her eyes steadfastly on me, with a look where no affected astonishment existed; " why not with her ?—did you say this ? "

" I did ; and do ask, What is there to make it strange that one like her should inspire the deepest sentiment of devotion, even from one whose days are so surely numbered as mine are—so unworthy to hope to win her ? "

" Then you really are unaware !   Well, I must say this was not treating you fairly.   I thought every one knew it, however ; and I conclude they themselves reasoned in the same way.   Come, I suppose I must explain ; though, from your terrified face and staring eyeballs, I wish the task had devolved on some other.   Be calm and collected, or I shall never venture upon it.—Well, poor dear Lucy inherits her mother's malady—she is insane!"

Broken half-words, stray fragments of speech, met my ears, for she went on to talk of the terrible theme with the volubility of one who revelled in a story of such thrilling horror. I, however, neither heard nor remembered more; passages of well-remembered interest flashed upon my mind, but, like scenes lit up by some lurid light, glowed with meanings too direful to dwell on.

How I parted from her—how I left the Villa and came hither, travelling day and night, till exhausted strength could bear no more—are still memories too faint to recall; the realities of these last few days have less vividness than my own burning, wasting thoughts: nor can I, by any effort, separate the terrible recital she gave from my own reflections upon it.

I must never recur to this again—nor will I reopen the page whereon it is written: I have written this to test my own powers of mind, lest I too——

Shakspeare, who knew the heart as none, save the inspired, have ever known it, makes it the test of sanity to recall the events of a story in the same precise order, time after time, neither changing nor inverting them. This is Lear's reply to the accusation of madness, when yet his intelligence was unclouded,—" I will the matter re-word, which madness would gabble from."

CHAPTER XX.

Lerici, Gulf of Spezzia.

Another night of fever! The sea, beating heavily upon the rocks, prevented sleep; or worse—filled it with images of shipwreck and storm. I sat till nigh midnight on the terrace—poor Shelley's favourite resting-place—watching the night as it fell, at first in gloomy darkness, and then bright and starlit. There was no moon, but the planets, reflected in the calm sea, were seen like tall pillars of reddish light; and, although all the details of the scenery were in shadow, the bold outlines of the distant Apennines, and of the Ponto Venere and the Island of Palmaria, were all distinctly marked out. The tall masts and taper spars of the French fleet at anchor in the bay were also seen against the sky, and the lurid glow of the fires spangled the surface of the sea. Strange chaos of thought was mine! At one moment, Lord Byron was before me, as, seated on the taffrail of the *Bolivar*, with all canvas stretched, he plunged through the blue waters; his fair brown hair spray-washed and floating back with the breeze; his lip curled with the smile of insolent defiance; and his voice ringing with the music of his own glorious verse. Towards midnight the weather suddenly changed; to the total stillness succeeded a low but distant moaning sound, which came nearer and nearer, and at last a "Levanter," in all its fury, broke over the sea, and rolled the mad waves in masses towards the shore. I have seen a storm in the Bay of Biscay, and I have witnessed a "whole gale" off the coast of Labrador, but for suddenness, and for the wild tumult of sea and wind commingled, I never saw anything like this. Not in huge rolling mountains, as in the Atlantic, did the waves move along, but in short, abrupt jets, as though impelled by some force beneath; now, skimming each over each, and now, spirting up into the air, they threw foam and spray around them like gigantic fountains. As abruptly as the storm began, so did it cease; and as the wind fell, the waves moved more and more sluggishly; and in a space of time inconceivably brief, nothing remained of the hurricane save the short plash of the breakers, and at intervals some one, long, thundering roar, as a heavier mass threw its weight upon the strand. It was just then, ere the sea had resumed its former calm, and while still warring with the effects of the gale, I thought I saw a boat lying keel uppermost in the water, and a man grasping with all the energy of despair to catch the slippery planks, which rose and sank with every motion of the tide. Though apparently far out at sea, all was palpable and distinct to my eyes as if happening close to where I sat. A grey darkness was around, and yet at one moment— so brief as to be uncountable—I could mark his features, beautifully handsome and calm even in his drowning agony; at least so did their wan and wearied expression strike me. Poor Shelley! I fancied you were before me; and, long after the vision passed away, a faint, low cry, continued to ring in my ears—the last effort of the voice about to be hushed for ever. Then the whole picture changed, and I beheld the French fleet all illuminated, as if for a victory; the decks and yards crowded with seamen, and echoing with their triumphant cheers; while on the poop-deck of the *Souverain* stood a pale and sickly youth, thoughtful and sad, his admiral's uniform carelessly half-buttoned, and his unbelted sword carried negligently in his hand. This was the Prince de Joinville, as I had seen him the day before, when visiting the fleet. I could not frame to my mind where and over whom the victory was won; but disturbed fears for our own naval supremacy flitted constantly across me, and every word I had heard from the French captain who had accompanied me in my visit kept sounding in my ears: as, for instance, while exhibiting the Paixhan's cannons, he added,—"Now, here is an arm your ships have not acquired." Such impressions must have gone deeper than, at the time, I knew of, for they made the substance of a long and painful dream; and when, awaking suddenly, the first object I beheld was the French fleet resting still and tranquil in the bay, my heart expanded with a sense of relief unspeakably delightful.

So, then, I must hence. These Levanters usually continue ten or twelve days, and then are followed by the Tramoutana, as is called the wind from the Apennines; and this same Tramontana is all but fatal to those as weak as I am. How puzzling—I had almost said, how impossible—to know anything about climate! and how invariably, on this as on most other subjects, mere words usurp the place of ideas! It is enough to say "Italy," to suggest hope to the consumptive man; and yet, what severe trials does this same boasted climate involve! These scorching autumnal suns; and cold, cutting breezes, wherever shade is found; the genial warmth of summer, here; and yonder, in that alley, the piercing air of winter—vicissitudes that make up the extremes of every climate, occur each twenty-four hours. And he, whose frail system can barely sustain the slightest shock, must now learn to accommodate itself to atmospheres of every density; now vapour charged and heavy, now oxygenated to a point of stimulation that, even in health, would be felt as over-exciting.

There is something of the same kind experienced here intellectually: the every-day tone of society is trifling and frivolous to a degree; the topics discussed are of a character which, to our practical notions, never rise above mere levity; and even where others of a deeper interest are introduced, the mode of treating them is superficial and meagre. Yet, every now and then, one meets with some high and great intelligence, some man of wide reflection and deep research; and then, when hearing the words of wisdom in that glorious language, which unites Teutonic vigour with every Gallic elegance, you feel what a people this might be who have such an interpreter for their thoughts and deeds. In this way I remember feeling when first I heard Italian from the lips of a truly great and eloquent speaker. He was a small old man, slightly bowed in the shoulders—merely enough so to exhibit to more advantage the greater elevation of a noble head, which rose like the dome of a grand cathedral; his forehead, wide and projecting over the brows which were heavy, and would have been almost severe in their meaning save for the softened expression of his large brown eyes; his hair, originally black, was now grey, but thick and massive, and hung in locky folds, like the antique, on his neck and shoulders. In manner he was simple, quiet, and retiring, avoiding observation, and seeking rather companionship with those whose unobtrusive habits made them unlikely for peculiar notice. When I met him he was in exile. Indeed I am not certain if the ban of his offence be recalled; whether or not, the voice of all Italy now invokes his return, and the name of Gioberti is associated with the highest and the noblest views of national freedom.

Well, indeed, were it for the cause of Italy if her progress were to be entrusted to men like this — if the great principles of reform were to be committed to intelligences capable of weighing difficulties, avoiding and accommodating dangers. So late as the day before last I had an opportunity of seeing a case in point. It is but a few weeks since the good people of Lucca, filled with new wine and bright notions of liberty, compelled their sovereign to abdicate. There is no denying that he had no other course open to him; for if the Grand Duke of Tuscany could venture to accord popular privileges, supported as he was by a very strong body of nobles, whose possessions will always assure them a great interest in the state, the little kingdom of Lucca had few, if any, such securities. Its sovereign must either rule or be ruled. Now, he had not energy of character for the one—he did not like the other. Austria refused to aid him—not wishing, probably to add to the complication of Ferrara; and so he abdicated. Now comes *le commencement du fin*. The Luccese gained the day: they expelled the Duke — they organized a national guard — they illuminated, they protested, cockaded, and—are ruined!

Without trade, or any of its resources, this little capital, like almost all those of the German duchies, lived upon "the Court." The sovereign was not only the fount of honour, but of wealth! Through his household flowed the only channel by which industry was nurtured : it was his court and his dependants whose wants employed the active heads and hands of the entire city. The Duke is gone—the palace closed—the court-yard even already half grass-grown! Not an equipage is to be heard or seen ; not even a footman in a court livery rides past; and all the recompense for this is the newly conferred privileges of liberty, to a people who recognize in freedom, not a new bond of obligation, but an unbridled license of action. The spirit of our times is, however, against this. The inspired grocers, who form the Guardia Civica, are our only guides now ; it will be curious enough to see where they will lead us.

When thinking of Italian liberty, or Unity, for that is the phrase in vogue, I am often reminded of the Irish priest who was supposed by his parishioners to possess an unlimited sway over the seasons, and who, when hard-pushed to exercise it, at last declared his readiness to procure any kind of weather that three farmers would agree upon, well knowing, the while, how diversity of interest must for ever prevent a common demand. This is precisely the case. An Italian kingdom to comprise the whole Peninsula would be impossible. The Lombards have no interests in common with the Neapolitans. Venice is less the sister than the rival of Genoa. How would the haughty Milanese, rich in everything that constitutes wealth, surrender their station to the men of the South, whom they despise and look down upon ? None would consent to become Provincial ; and even the smallest states would stand up for the prerogative of separate identity.

"A National" Guard slowly paces before the gate, within which Royalty no longer dwells ; and the banner of their independence floats over their indigence ! Truly, they have torn up their mantle to make a cap of Liberty, and they must bear the cold how they may !

As for the Duke himself, I believe he deserves the epithet I heard a Frenchman bestow upon him—he is a *Pauvre Sire !*   There is a fatal consistency, certainly, about the conduct of these Bourbon Princes in moments of trying emergency !   They never will recognize danger till too late to avert it.   The Prince of Lucca, like Charles Dix, laughed at popular menace, and yet had barely time to escape from popular vengeance.   There was a ball at the palace on the very night when the tumult attained its greatest importance ; frequent messages were sent by the Ministers, and more than one order to the troops given during the progress of the entertainment.   A despatch was opened at the supper-table ; and as the Crown Prince led out his fair partner—an English beauty, by-the-by—to the *cotillon*, he whispered in her ear, " We must keep it up late, for I fancy we shall never have another dance in this *salle !* "   And this is the way Princes can take leave of their inheritance ; and so it is, the " divine right " can be understood by certain " Rulers of the people."

If the defence of monarchy depended on the lives and characters of monarchs, how few could resist Republicanism ! though, perhaps, everything considered, there is no station in life where the same number of good and graceful qualities is so certain to win men's favour and regard. Maginn used to say that we "admire wit in a woman as we admire a few words spoken plain by a parrot."

The speech was certainly not a very gallant one ; but I half suspect that our admiration of royal attainments is founded upon a similar principle.

Kings can rarely be good talkers, because they have not gone through the great training-school of talk—which is, conversation.   This is impossible where there is no equality ; and how often does it occur to monarchs to meet each other, and when they do, what a stilted, unreal thing, must be their intercourse !   Of reigning sovereigns, the King of Prussia is perhaps the most gifted in this way ; of course, less endowed with that shrewd appreciation of character, that intuitive perception of every man's bias, which marks the Monarch of the Tuileries ; but possessed of other and very different qualities, and with one especially which never can be over-valued—an earnest sincerity of purpose in everything. There is no escaping from the conviction that here is a man who reflects and wills, and whose appeal to conscience is the daily rule of life. The nationality of Germany is his great object, and for it he labours as strenuously—may it be as successfully! —as ever his "Great" predecessor did to accomplish the opposite. What a country would it be if the same spirit of nationality were to prevail from the Baltic to the Black Sea, and "Germany" have a political signification as well as a geographical one!

After all, if we have outlived the age of heroic monarchy, we have happily escaped that of royal débauchés. A celebrated civil engineer of our day is reported to have said, in his examination before a parliamentary committee, that he regarded "rivers as intended by Providence to supply navigable canals;" in the same spirit one might opine certain characters of royalty were created to supply materials for Vaudevilles.

What would become of the minor theatres of Paris if Louis XIV., and Richelieu, and the Regency were to be interdicted? On whose memory dare they hang so much of shameless vice and iniquitous folly? Where find characters so degraded, so picturesque, so abandoned, so infamous, and so amusing? What time and trouble, too, are saved by the adoption of this era! No need of wearisome explanations and biographical details of the *dramatis personæ*. When one reads the word "Marquis," he knows it means a man whose whole aim in life is seduction; while "Madame la Marquise" is as invariably the easy victim of royal artifice.

It might open a very curious view into the distinctive nature of national character to compare the recognized class to which vice is attributed in different countries; for while in England we select the aristocracy always as the natural subjects for depravity, in the Piedmontese territory all the stage villains are derived from the mercantile world. Instead of a lord, as with us, the seducer is always a manufacturer or a shipowner; and *vice* a captain of dragoons, their terror of domestic peace is a cotton-spinner or a dealer in hardware.

Let it not be supposed that this originates in any real depravity, or any actual want of honesty, in the mercantile world. No! the whole is attributable to the "Censor." By *his* arbitrary dictate the entire of a piece is often re-cast, and so habituated have authors become to the pre-vailing taste, that they now never think of occasioning him the trouble of the correction. Tradesman there stands for scoundrel, as implicitly as with us an Irishman is a blunderer and a Scotchman a knave. Exercised as this power is, and committed to such hands as we find it in foreign countries, it is hard to conceive any more quiet but effectual agent for the degradation of a national taste. It is but a few weeks back I saw a drama marked for stage representation in a city of Lombardy, in which the words "Pope" and "Cardinal" were struck out as irreverent to utter; but all the appeals—and most impious they were—to the Deity were suffered to remain unmutilated.

And now I am reminded of rather a good theme for one of those little dramatic pieces which amuse the public of the Palais Royal and the Variétés. I chanced upon it in an old French book, called "Mémoires et Souvenirs de Jules Auguste Prévost, premier Valet de Charge de S. A. le Duc de Courcelles." Printed at the Hague, anno 1742.

I am somewhat sceptical about the veraciousness of many of M. Prévost's recitals; the greater number are, indeed, little else than chronicles of his losses at *Ombre*, with a certain Mdlle. Valencay, or narratives of *petits soupers,* where his puce-coloured shorts and coat of amber velvet were the chief things worthy of remembrance. Yet here and there are little traits that look like facts, too insignifi-cant for fiction, and preserving something of the character of the time to which they are linked. The whole bears no trace of ever having been intended for publication; and it is not difficult to see where the new touches have been laid on over the original picture. It was in all probability a mere common-place book, in which certain circumstances of daily life got mixed up with the written details of his station in the Duke's household.

Neither its authenticity nor correctness, however, are of any moment to my purpose, which was to jot down—from memory if I can—the subject I believe to be invested with dramatic material.

M. Prévost's narrative is very brief; indeed it barely extends beyond a full allusion to a circumstance very generally known at the time. The events run somewhat thus, or at least should do so, in the piece. At the close of a brilliant *fête* at Versailles, where every fascination that an age of unbounded luxury could procure was assembled, the King retired to his apartment, followed by that prince of vaudeville characters, the Maréchal Richelieu. His Majesty was wearied and out of spirits; the pleasures of the evening, so far from having, as usual, elevated his spirits and awakened his brilliancy, had depressed and fatigued him. He was tired of the unvarying repetition of what his heart had long ceased to have any share in; and, in fact, to use the vulgar, but most fitting phrase, he was bored! Bored by the courtiers, whose wit was too prompt to have been unprepared; by the homage, too servile to have any sincerity; by the smiles of beauty, perverted as they were by jealous rivalry and subtle intrigue; and, above all, bored by the consciousness that he had no other identity than such as kingly trappings gave him, and that all the love and admiration he received were accorded to the monarch and nothing to the man.

He didn't exactly, as novel writers would say, pour his sufferings into Richelieu's ear, but in very abrupt and forcible expressions he manifested his utter weariness of the whole scene, and avowed a very firm belief that the company was almost as tired of him as he was of the company.

In vain the Maréchal rallies his Majesty upon successes which were wont to be called triumphs; in vain he assures him, that never at any period was the domestic peace of the lieges more endangered by his Majesty's condescensions: in fact, for once—as will happen, even with kings now and then—he said truth; and truth, however wholesome, is not always palatable. Richelieu was too subtle an adversary to be easily worsted; and after a fruitless

x

effort to obliterate the gloomy impression of the king, he, with a ready assurance, takes him in flank, and coolly attributes the royal dissatisfaction to the very natural weariness at ever seeing the same faces, however beautiful, and hearing the same voices, however gay and sparkling their wit.

"Your Majesty will not give yourself the credit due of winning these evidences of devotion from personal causes, rather than from adventitious ones. Happily, a good opportunity presents itself for the proof. Your Majesty may have heard of Madame de Vaugirarde, whose husband was killed at La Rochelle?"

"The pretty widow who refuses to come to court?"

"The same, sire. She continues to reside at the antique château of her late husband, alone, and without companionship; and, if report speak truly, the brightest eyes of France are wasting their brilliancy in that obscure retreat."

"Well, what is to be done? You would not, surely, order her up to Versailles by a ' *lettre de cachet?* '"

"No, sire, the measure were too bold; nay, perhaps my counsel will appear far bolder; it is, that since Madame de Vaugirarde will not come to court, your Majesty should go to Madame de Vaugirarde."

It was not very difficult to make this notice agreeable to the king. It had one ingredient pleasurable enough to secure its good reception—it was new—nobody had ever before dreamt of his Majesty making a tour into the provinces *incog.* This was quite sufficient; and Richelieu had scarcely detailed his intentions than the king burned with impatience to begin his journey. The wily minister, however, had many things to arrange before they set out; but of what nature he did not reveal to his master. Certain is it that he left for Paris within an hour, hastening to the capital with all the speed of post-horses. Arrived there, he exchanged his court suit for a plain dress, and in a *fiacre* drove to the private entrance of the Théâtre Français.

"Is M. Duroset engaged?" said he, descending from the carriage.

" He is on the stage, monsieur," said the porter, who took the stranger for one of the better *bourgeois* of Paris, coming to secure a good *loge* by personal intercession with the manager. Now, M. Duroset was at the very moment occupied in the not very uncommon task of giving a poor actor his *congé*, who had just presented himself for an engagement.

As was the case in those days—we have changed since then—the Director, not merely content with declining the proffered services, was actually adding some very caustic remarks on the pretension of the applicant, whose miserable appearance and ragged costume might have claimed exemption from his gratuitous lecture.

"Believe me, *mon cher*," said he, " a man must have a very different air and carriage from yours who plays ' Le Marquis ' on the Parisian boards. There should be something of the style and bearing of the world about him—his address should be easy, without presumption—his presence commanding, without severity."

"I always played the noble parts in the provinces. I acted the ' Regent '——"

" I've no doubt of it; and very pretty notions of royalty the audience must have gained from you. There, that will do. Go back to Nancy, and try yourself at valet's parts for a year or two—that's the best counsel I can give you! Adieu! adieu!"

The poor actor retired, discomfited and distressed, at the same instant that the graceful figure of Richelieu advanced in easy dignity.

" Monsieur Duroset," said the Maréchal, seating himself, and speaking in the voice so habituated to utter commands, " I would speak a few words with you in confidence, and where we might be certain of not being overheard."

" Nothing could be better than the present spot, then," said the manager, who was impressed by the style and bearing of his visitor, without ever guessing or suspecting his real rank. " The rehearsal will not begin for half-an-hour. Except that poor devil that has just left me, no one has entered this morning."

" Sit down, then, and pay attention to what I shall

say," said the Maréchal. The words were felt as a command, and instantly obeyed.

"They tell me, M. Duroset, that a young actress, of
great beauty and distinguished ability, is about to appear
on these boards, whose triumphs have been hitherto won
only in the provinces. Well, you must defer her *début*
for some days; and, meanwhile, for the benefit of her
health, she can make a little excursion to the neighbourhood of Fontainebleau, where, at a short distance from
the royal forest, stands a small château. This will be
ready for her reception; and where a more critical taste
than even your audiences boast will decide upon her
merits."

"There is but one man in France could make such a
proposition!" said the manager, starting back, half in
amazement, half in respect.

"And I am exactly that man," rejoined the Maréchal.
"There need never be secrets between men of sense. M.
Duroset, the case is this: your beauty, whose manners
and breeding I conjecture to be equal to her charms,
must represent the character of the widowed Countess of
Vaugirarde, whose sorrow for her late husband is all but
inconsolable. The solitude of her retreat will, however,
be disturbed by the accidental arrival of a stranger, who,
accompanied by his friend, will demand the hospitality of
the château. Grief has not usurped every faculty and
devoir of the fair Countess, who consents the following
morning to receive the respectful homage of the travellers,
and even invites them, weary as they seem by travel, to
stay another day."

"I understand—I understand," said Duroset, hastily
interrupting this narrative, which the speaker poured
forth with impetuous rapidity; "but there are several
objections, and grave ones."

"I'm certain of it," rejoined the other; "and now to
combat them. Here are a thousand louis; five hundred
of which M. Duroset will keep—the remainder he will
expend, as his taste and judgment may dictate, in the
costume of the fair Countess."

"But Mademoiselle Bellechasse?"

' Will accept of these diamonds, which will become her to perfection. She is not a blonde?"

" No; dark hair and eyes."

" This suite of pearls, then, will form a most graceful addition to her toilette."

" They are magnificent! " exclaimed the manager, who, with wondering eyes, turned from one jewel case to the other; "they are splendid! Nay "—then he added, in a lower accent, and with a glance, as he spoke, of inveterate cunning—" nay, they are a princely present."

" Ah, M. Duroset, *un homme d'esprit* is always so easy to treat with! Might I dare to ask if Mademoiselle Bellechasse is here ?—if I might be permitted to pay my respects ?"

" Certainly ; your Excell——"

" Nay, nay, M. Duroset, we are all *incog.*," said the Maréchal, smiling good humouredly.

" As you please, sir. I will go and make a brief explanation to Mademoiselle, if you will excuse my leaving you. May I take these jewels with me? Thanks."

The explanation, was, indeed, of the briefest; and he returned in a few seconds, accompanied by a young lady, whose elegance of mien and loveliness of form seemed to astonish even the critical gaze of Richelieu.

"Madame la Comtesse de Vaugirarde," said the Director, presenting her.

" *Ah, belle Comtesse!* " said the Maréchal, as he kissed the tips of her fingers with the most profound courtesy ; " may I hope that the world has still charms to win back one whose griefs should fall like spring showers, and only render more fragrant the soil they water! "

" I know not what the future may bring forth," said she, with a most gracefully affected sadness; "but for the present, I feel as if the solitude of my ancient château, the peaceful quiet of the country, would best respond to my wishes : there alone, to wander in those woods, whose paths are endeared to me——"

" Admirable !—beautiful !—perfect! " exclaimed Richelieu, in a transport of delight; "never was the tribute of affection more touching—never a more graceful homage rendered to past happiness! Now, when can you set out?"

"To-morrow."

"Why not to-day? Time is everything here."

"Remember, monsieur, that we have purchases to make —we visit the capital but rarely."

"Quite true; I was forgetting the solitude of your retreat. Such charms might make any lapse of memory excusable."

"Oh, monsieur! I should be, indeed, touched by this flattery, if I could but see the face of him who uttered it."

"Pardon me, fair Countess, if I do not respond to even the least of your wishes; we shall both appear in our true colours one of these days. Meanwhile, remember our proverb that says, 'It's not the cowl makes the monk.' When you shall hear this again, it will be in your château of Vaugirarde, and——"

"Is that the *consigne*, then?" said she, laughing.

"Yes, that is the *consigne*—don't forget it;" and, with a graceful salutation, the Maréchal withdrew to perfect his further arrangements.

There was a listener to this scene, that none of its actors ever guessed at—the poor actor, who, having lost his way among forests of pasteboard and palaces of painted canvas, at last found himself at the back of a pavilion, from which the speakers were not more than two paces distant. Scarcely had the Maréchal departed, than he followed his steps, and made all haste to an obscure *auberge* outside the barriers, where a companion, poor and friendless as himself, awaited him. There is no need to trace what ensued at this meeting. The farce writer might, indeed, make it effective enough, ending as it does in the resolve, that since an engagement was denied them at Paris they'd try their fortune at Fontainebleau, by personating the two strangers, who were to arrive by a hazard at the Château de Vaugirarde.

The whole plot is now seen. They set out, and in due time arrive at the château. Their wardrobe and appearance generally are the very reverse of what the fair

Countess expected, but as their stage experiences supply a
certain resemblance to rank and distinction—at least to
her notions of such—she never doubts that they are the
promised visitors, and is convinced by the significant
declaration, that if their wayworn looks and strange
costume seem little indicative of their actual position,
yet the Countess should remember, "It is not the cowl
makes the monk."

The constraint with which each assumes a new character
forms the second era of the piece. The lover, far from
suspecting the real pretensions he should strive to per-
sonate—the Countess, as much puzzled by the secrecy of
her guest's conduct, and by guesses as to his actual rank and
fortune. It is while these doubts are in full conflict, and
when seated at supper, that the King and Richelieu
appear, announced as two travellers, whose carriage being
overturned and broken, are fain to crave the hospitality of
the château.

The discomfiture of Richelieu and the anger of the
King at finding the ground occupied, contrast well with
the patronizing graces of the mock Countess, and the
insolent demeanour of the lover, who whispers in her ear
that the new arrivals are strolling players, and that he
has seem them repeatedly in the provinces. All Richelieu's
endeavours to set matters right, unobserved by the King,
are abortive ; while his Majesty is scarce more fortunate
in pressing his suit with the fair Countess, by whose
grace and beauty he is fascinated. In the very midst of
the insolent *badinage* of the real actors, an officer of the
household arrives, with important dispatches. Their
delivery brooks no delay, and he at once presents himself,
and, kneeling, hands them to the King. Shame, discomfiture, terror, and dismay, seize on the intruding players.
The King, however, is merciful. After a smart reproof
all is forgiven; his Majesty sagely observing, that although "the cowl may not make the monk," the ermine
has no small share in forming the monarch.

CHAPTER XXI.

WHAT did Shelley, what does any one, mean by their raptures about Florence? Never, surely, was the epithet of *La Bella* more misapplied. I can well understand the enthusiasm with which men call Genoa *Il Superbo*. Its mountain background, its deep blue sea, its groves of orange and acacia, the prickly aloe growing wild upon the very shore in all the luxuriance of tropical vegetation, indicative of an almost wasteful extravagance of production ; while its amphitheatre of palaces, proudly rising in terraced rows, are gorgeous remembrances of the haughty Republic. But Florence! dark, dirty, and discordant! Palaces, gaol-like and gloomy, stand in streets were wretchedness and misery seem to have chosen their dwelling-place—the types of feudal tyranny side by side with modern destitution. The boasted Arno, too, a shrunk-up, trickling stream, not wide enough to be a river, not clear enough to be a rivulet, winds along between hills hot and sun-scorched, where the brown foliage has no touch of freshness, but stands parched and shrivelled by the hot glare of eternal noon. The white-walled villas glisten in the dazzling heat, not tempered by the slightest shade, but reflecting back the scorching glow from rocks cracked and fissured by the sun !

How disappointing is all this ! and how wearisome is the endeavour, from the scattered objects here and there, to make any approach to that Florence one has imagined to himself ! To me the abstraction is impossible. I carry about with me, even into the galleries, before the triumphs of Raffaelle and the wonders of Michael Angelo, the sad discordant scenes through which I have passed. The jarred senses are rendered incapable of properly appreciating and feeling those influences that should diffuse their effect upon the mind; and even the sight of the "Guardia Civica," strutting in solemn mockery beneath the archways where the proud Medici have trod, are contrasts to suggest rather a sense of sarcasm than of pleasure.

Here and there you do come upon some grand and imposing pile of building, the very stones of which seem laid by giant hands; but even these have the fortress character, the air of strongholds, rather than of princely dwellings, as at Genoa. You see at once how much more defence and safety were the guiding principles, than elegance of design and beauty of proportion. No vestibule, peopled with its marble groups, opens here to the passerby a glimpse of a noble stair rising in spacious amplitude between walls of marble. No gate of gilded fretwork shows the terraced garden, with the plashing fountains, and the orange-trees bending with their fruit.

Like all continental cities where the English congregate, the inhabitants have a mongrel look, grafting English notions of dress and equipage upon their own, and, like most imitators, only successful in following the worst models. The Casciui, too, exhibits a very motley assemblage of gaudy liveries and dusky carriages, riding-grooms dressed like footmen, their masters no bad resemblance to the "Jeunes Premiers" of a vaudeville. The men are very inferior in appearance to the Milanese; they are neither as well-built nor well-grown, and rarely have any pretensions to a fashionable exterior. The women are mostly ill-dressed, and, in no instance that I have seen, even well-looking. They have the wearied look, without the seductive languor, of the South; they are pale, but not fair; and their gestures are neither plastic nor graceful. In fact, in all that I have seen here, I am sadly disappointed—all, save the Raffaelles; they are above my conception of them.

How much of this lies in myself I dare not stop to inquire; a large share, perhaps, but assuredly not all. This climate should be avoided by those of weak chest.

Symptoms of further "breaking-up" crowd upon me each day; and this burning sun and piercing wind make a sad conflict in the debilitated frame. But where to go, where to seek out a quiet spot to linger a few days and die! Rome is in all the agonies of its mock liberty—Naples in open revolt: here, where I am, all rule and government have ceased to exist; the mob have everything at their mercy : that they have not abused their power, is more owing to their ignorance than their honour. When the Irish rebels carried the town of Ross by storm, they broke into the grocers' shops to eat sugar! The Florentines having bullied the Duke, are only busied about the new uniforms of their Civic Guard!

Hitherto the reforms have gone no further than in organizing this same National Guard, and in thrashing the police authorities wherever found. Now, bad as this police was, it was still the only protection to the public peace. It exists no longer; and Tuscany has made her first step in liberty " *en Américaine*," by adopting "Lynch Law."

I was about to note down a singular instance of this indignant justice of the people, when the arrival of a letter, in a hand unknown to me, suddenly routed all my intentions. If I am able to record the circumstance here, calmly and without emotion, it is neither from that philosophy the world teaches, nor from any higher motive— it is merely on the same principle that one would bear with tolerable equanimity the break-down of a carriage when within a few miles of the journey's end! The fact, then, is simply this, that I, Horace Templeton, whose drafts a few days back might have gone far into the " tens of thousands," without fear of " dishonour," am now ruined! When we read this solemn word in the newspapers, we at once look back to the rank and station of him whose ruin is predicated. A Duke is " ruined" when he must sell three packs of hounds, three studs of horses, four of his five or six mansions, part with his yacht at Cowes, and his racers at Newmarket, and retire to the Continent with a beggarly pittance of some fifteen thousand per annum. A merchant is ruined when, by the sudden convulsions of mercantile affairs, he is removed from the unlimited command of millions to pass his days, at Leamington or Cheltenham, on his wife's jointure of two thousand a year.

His clerk is ruined when he drops his pocket-book on his way from the bank, and loses six hundred pounds belonging to the firm. His is more real ruin, for it implies stoppages, suspicion—mayhap loss of place, and its consequences.

But I have lost everything! Hamerton and Scott, my bankers, have failed; their liabilities, as the phrase is— meaning thereby what they are liable to be asked for, but cannot satisfy—are enormous. My only landed property is small, and so heavily mortgaged as to be worth nothing. I had only waited for the term of an agreement to redeem the mortgage, and clear off all encumbrances; but the "crash" has anticipated me, and I am now a beggar!

Yes, there is the letter, in all cold and chilling civility, curtly stating that "the unprecedented succession of calamities, by which public credit has been affected, have left the firm no other alternative but that of a short suspension of payment! Sincerely trusting, however, that they will be enabled——" and so forth. These announcements have but one burden — the creditors are to be mulcted, while the debtor continues to hope!

And now for my own share in the misfortune. Is it the momentary access of excitement, or is it some passing rally in my constitution? but I certainly feel better, and in higher spirits, than I have done for many a day. It is long since I indulged in my old habit of castle-building; and yet now, at every instant, some new notion strikes me, and I fancy some new field for active labour and exertion. To the present Ministers I am slightly known —sufficiently to ask for employment, if not in my former career, in some other. Should this fail, I have yet powerful friends to ask for me. Not that I like either of these plans—this playing *antichambre* is a sore penance at my time of life. Had I health and strength, I'd emigrate. I really do wonder why men of a certain rank, younger sons especially, do not throw their fortunes into the colonies.   Apart from the sense of enterprise, there is an immense gain, in the fact that individual exertion, be it of head or hand, can exercise, free from the trammels of conventional prejudices, which so rule and restrain us at home.   If we merely venture to use the pruning-knife in our gardens here, there, we may lay the axe to the root of the oak ; and yet, in this commonwealth of labour, the gentleman, if his claim to the title be really well founded, is as certain of maintaining a position of superiority as though he had remained in his own country.   The Vernons, the Greys, and the Courtenays, have never ceased to hold a peculiar place among their fellow-citizens of the United States ; and so is it observable in our colonies, even where mere wealth was found in the opposite scale.

But let me not longer dwell on these things, nor indulge in speculations which lead to hope !   Let me rather reflect on my present position, and calculate calmly by what economy I may be able to linger on, and not exhaust the means, till the lamp of life is ready to be quenched.

I am sure that most men of easy, careless temperament could live as well on one-half of their actual incomes, having all that they require, and never feeling any unusual privation ; that the other half is invariably *mangé* by one's servants, by tradespeople, by cases of mock distress, by importunity, and by indolence.   I well know how I am blamable upon each of these several counts.   Now, for a note to my banker here, to ascertain what sum he holds of mine ; and then, like the shipwrecked sailor on his raft, to see how long life may be sustained on half or quarter rations !

So, here is the banker's letter :—" I have the honour to acknowledge," and so on.   The question at issue is the sum—and here it stands : Three hundred and forty-two pounds, twelve shillings, and fourpence.   I really thought I had double the amount ; but here I find cheques innumerable.   I have, no doubt, given to many, now far richer than I am.   Be it so.   The next point is—How long can a man live on three hundred and forty pounds ?   One man would say, Three weeks—another, as many months—

and another, as many years, perhaps. I am totally ignorant what guidance to follow.

In this difficulty I shall send for Dr. Hennesy—he is the man in repute here—and try, if it may be, to ascertain what length of tether he ascribes to my case. Be it a day, a week, or a month, let me but know it. And now to compose myself, and speak calmly on a theme where the slightest appearance of excitement would create erroneous suspicions against me. If H. be the man of sense I deem him, he will not misconstrue my meaning, even should he guess it.

Gilbert reminds me of what I had quite forgotten—that yesterday I signed an agreement for a villa here : I took it for six months, expecting to live one ! It struck me, when driving out on the Bologna road, both for architecture and situation ; I saw nothing equal to it—an old summer-palace of the Medici, and afterwards inhabited by the Salviati, whose name it bears.

A princely house in every way is this; but how unsuited to ruined fortunes ! I walked about the rooms, now stopping to examine a picture or a carved oak cabinet; now to peep at the wild glens, which here are seen dividing the hills in every direction ; and felt how easy it would be to linger on here, where objects of taste and high art blend their influence with dreams of the long past. Now, I must address my mind to the different question—How to be released from my contract?

H. has just been here. How difficult it was to force him into candour ! A doctor becomes, by the practice of his art, as much addicted to suspicion as a police agent. Every question, every reply of the patient, must be a " symptom." This wearies and worries the nervous man, and renders him shy and uncommunicative.

For myself, well opining how my sudden demand, " How long can I live?" might sound, if uttered with abrupt sincerity, I submitted patiently to all the little gossip of the little world of this place—its envy, hatred, malice, and all uncharitableness — which certainly are prime features in an English colony on the Continent—

all, that I might at last establish a character for soundness of mind and calmness of purpose, ere I put my *quære*.

The favourable moment came at last, and I asked in full earnest, but with a manner that showed no sign of dread,—" Tell me, *Dottore mio*, how long may such a chest as mine endure ?   I mean, taking every possible care, as I do ; neither incurring any hazard nor neglect ; and, in fact, fighting the battle bravely to the last ?''

He tried at first, by a smile and a jocular manner, to evade the question ; but seeing my determination fixed, he looked grave, felt my pulse, percussed my chest, and was silent.

" Well,'' said I, after a very long pause, " I await my sentence, but in no mood of hope or fear.   Is it a month ? —a week ?—a day ?—nay, surely it can hardly be so near as that ?   Still silent !   Come, this is scarcely fair ; I ask simply——''

"That which is perfectly impossible to answer, did I concede that I ought to reply, as categorically as you ask.''

" Were I to tell my reasons, doctor, you might judge more harshly of my intelligence than I should like ; besides, you would certainly misinterpret my meaning. Tell me, therefore, in the common course of such changes as my disease involves, can I live a year?   You shake your head !   Be it so.   Six months ?—Three, then ?— Have I three?   The winter, you say, is to be feared.   I know it.   Well, then, shall I own that my convictions anticipate you at each negative ?   I feel I have not a month—nay, not half of one—a week will do it, doctor ; and now excuse scant ceremony, and leave me.''

Alone—friendless—homeless—ruined, and dying !   Sad words to write, each of them ; sadder when thus brought in brotherhood together.   The world and its pageants are passing fast by me, like the eddies of that stream which flows beneath my window.   I catch but one glimpse and they are gone, beneath the dark bridge of Death, to mingle in the vast ocean of Eternity.

How strange to see the whole business of the world going on, the moving multitude, the tumult of active minds and bodies—at the very moment when the creeping chill of ebbing life tells of days and hours numbered!

I am alone—not one to sit by me to combat thoughts that with the faintest help I could resist, but which unaided are too strong for me. In this window-seat where now I rest, who shall sit this day week? The youth, perhaps, in gushing pride of heart and buoyancy, now entering upon life, ardent and high-souled—or the young bride, gazing on that same river that now I watch, and reading in its circles wreathed smiles of happy promise. Oh, may no memories of him, whose tears fall fast now, haunt the spot and throw their gloom on others!

I am friendless—and yet, which of those I still call friends would I now wish beside me? To drink of the cup of consolation, I must first offer my own of misery—nay, it is better to endure alone!

Homeless am I, too—and this, indeed, I feel bitterly. Old familiar objects, associated with ties of affection, bound up with memories of friends, are meet companions for the twilight hours of life. I long to be back in my own chosen room—the little library, looking out on the avenue of old beeches leading to the lake, and the village spire rising amid the dark yew-trees. There was a spot there, too, I had often fancied—when I close my eyes I think I see it still—a little declivity of the ground beneath a large old elm, where a single tomb stood surrounded by an iron railing; one side was in decay, and through which I often passed to read the simple inscription—"Courtenay Templeton, Armiger, ætatis 22."

This was not the family burying-place—why he was laid there was a family mystery. His death was attributed to suicide, nor was his memory ever totally cleared of the guilt. The event was briefly this:—On the eve of the great battle of Fontenoy he received an insult from an officer of a Scotch regiment, which ended in a duel. The Scotchman fell dead at the first fire. Templeton was immediately arrested; and instead of leading an attack, as he had been appointed to do, spent the hours of the battle in a prison. The next morning he was discovered dead; a great quantity of blood had flowed from his mouth and nose, which, although no external wound was found, suggested an idea of self-destruction. None suspected, what I have often heard since from medical men, that a rupture of the aorta from excessive emotion—a broken heart, in fact—had killed him: a death more frequently occurring than is usually believed.

"Ruined and dying" are the last words in my record; and yet neither desirous of fortune nor life! At least, so faint is my hope that I should use either with higher purpose than I have done, that all wish is extinguished.

Seriously I believe that love of life is less general than the habit of projecting schemes for the future—a vague system of castle-building, which even the least speculative practises; and that death is thus accounted the great evil, as suddenly interrupting a chain of events whose series is still imperfect. The very humblest peasant that rises to daily toil has his gaze fixed on some future, some period of rest or repose, some hour of freedom from his life-long struggle. Now, I have exhausted this source; the well, that once bubbled with eddying fancies of days to come, is dry. High spirits, health, and the buoyancy that result from both, when joined to a disposition keenly alive to enjoyment, and yet neither cloyed by excess nor depraved by corrupt tastes, will always go far to simulate a degree of ability. The very freedom a mind thus constituted enjoys is a species of power; and its liberty exaggerates its range, just as the untrammelled paces of the young colt seem infinitely more graceful and noble than the matured regularity of the trained and bitted steed.

It was thus that I set out in life—ardent, hopeful, and enthusiastic: if my mental resources were small, they were always ready at hand, like a banker with a weak capital, but who could pay every trifling demand on the spot, I lived upon credit; and upon that credit I grew rich. Had I gone on freely as I began, I might still enjoy the fame of wealth and solvency, but with the reputation of affluence came the wish to be rich. I contracted my issues, I husbanded my resources, and from that hour I became suspected. To avoid a "run" for gold, I ceased to trade and retired. This, in a few words, is the whole history of my life.

Gilbert comes to say that the carriage is waiting to convey me to the villa—our luggage is already there. Be it so: still I must own to myself, that going to occupy a palace for the last few hours of life and fortune is very much like good Christopher Sly's dream of Lordliness.

CHAPTER XXII.

SOME REVERIES ABOUT PLACES.

WHAT would the old school of Diplomatists have said if they saw their secret wiles and machinations exposed to publicity as is now the fashion? When any "honourable and learned gentleman" can call for "copies of the correspondence between our Minister at the Court of —— and the noble Secretary for the Foreign Department;" and when the *Times* can, in a leader, rip up all the flaws of a treaty, or expose all the dark intentions of some special compact? The Diplomatic "Holy of Holies" is now open to the vulgar gaze, and all the mysteries of the craft as commonplace as the transactions of a Poor-law Union.

Much of the prestige of this secrecy died out on the establishment of railroads. The courier who travelled formerly with breathless haste from Moscow to London, or from the remotest cities of the far East, to our little Isle of the West, was sure to bring intelligence several days earlier than it could reach by any other channel. The gold greyhound, embroidered on his arm, was no exaggerated emblem of his speed; but now, his prerogative over, he journeys in "a first-class carriage" with some fifty others, who arrive along with him. Old age and infancy, sickness and debility, are no disqualifications— the race is open to all—and the tidings brought by "our messenger" are not a particle later, and rarely so full, as those given forth in the columns of a leading journal.

How impossible to affect any mysterious silence before the "House!"—how vain to attempt any knowledge from exclusive sources! "The ordinary channels of information," to use Sir Robert's periphrasis, are the extraordinary ones too, and not only do they contain whatever Ministers know, but very often "something more."

Time was when the Minister, or even the secretary at a foreign court, appeared in society as a kind of casquet of state secrets,—when his mysterious whispers, his very gestures, were things to speculate on, and a grave motion of his eyebrows could make "consols" tremble, and throw the "threes" into a panic. Now, the question is, Have you seen the city article in the *Times?* What does the *Chronicle* say? No doubt this is a tremendous power, and very possibly the enjoyment of it, such as we have it in England, is the highest element of a pure democracy. Political information of a very high order establishes a species of education, which is the safest check upon the dangers of private judgment, and hence it is fair to hope that we possess a sounder and more healthy public opinion in England than in any of the states of the continent. At least it would not be too much to infer that we would be less accessible to those sudden convulsions, those violent *coups de main* by which governments are overturned abroad; and that the general diffusion of new notions on political subjects, and the daily reference to such able expositors as our newspaper press contains, are strong safeguards against the seductive promises of mob-leaders and liberty-mongers.

In France, a government is always at the mercy of any one bold enough to lead the assault. The attempt may seem often a "forlorn hope"—it rarely is so in reality. The love of vagrancy is not so inherent in the Yankee as is the destructive passion in the Frenchman's heart; but it is there, less from any pleasure in demolition than in the opportunity thus offered for reconstruction. Mirabeau, Rousseau, Fournier, Lamennais are the social architects of French predilection, and many a clearance has been made to begin the edifice, and many have perished in laying the foundations, which never rose above the earth, but which ere long we may again witness undertaken with new and bolder hands than ever.

Events that once took centuries for their accomplishment are now the work of days or weeks. Steam seems to have communicated its impetuosity to mind as well as matter, and ere many years pass over, how few of the traces of Old Europe will remain as our fathers knew them !

I have scarcely entered a foreign city for the last few years without detecting the rapid working of those changes. Old families sinking into decay and neglect—time-honoured titles regarded as things that "once were." Their very homes, the palaces, associated with incidents of deep historic interests, converted into hotels or "*pensionnats.*"

The very last time I strolled through Paris I loitered to the *quartier* which in my young ambition I regarded with all the reverence the pilgrim yields to Mecca. I remembered the first *soirée* in which I was presented, having dined at the Embassy, and being taken in the evening by the ambassador that I might be introduced to the Machiavel of his craft, Prince Talleyraud. Even yet I feel the hot blush which mantled in my cheek as I was passing with very scant ceremony the round-shouldered little old man who stood in the very doorway, his wide black coat far too large for his figure, and his white hair trimly brushed back from his massive temples.

It did not need the warning voice of my introducer, hastily calling my name, to make my sense of shame a perfect agony. "Monsieur Templeton, Monsieur le Prince," said the ambassador; "the young gentleman of whom I spoke ;" and he added, in a tone inaudible to me, something about my career and some mention of my relatives.

"Oh, yes," said the Prince, smiling graciously, "I am aware how 'connection,' as you call it, operates in England ; but permit me, monsieur," said he, turning towards me, "to give one small piece of advice. It is this : ' If you can win by cards never score the honours.' " The precept had little influence on himself, however. No man ever paid greater deference to the distinctions of rank, or conceded more to the prestige of an ancient name. Neither a general, an orator, nor an author—not even the leader of a faction—this astonishing man stood alone, in the resources of his fertile intellect directing events which he appeared to follow, and availing himself of resources which he had stored up for emergency, but so artfully that they seemed to arise out of the natural current of events. Never disconcerted or abashed—not once thrown off his balance —not more calmly dignified when he stood beside Napoleon at Erfurth, then master of Europe itself, than he was at the Congress of Vienna, when the defeat of France had placed her at the mercy of her enemies.

It was in this same house, in the Rue Saint Florentin, that the Emperor Alexander lived when the Allies entered Paris, on the last day of March, 1814. His Majesty occupied the first floor; M. de Talleyrand, the *rez de chaussée.* He was then no more than ex-Minister for Foreign Affairs; neither empowered by the Bourbons to treat for the Restoration, nor by the nation for the conditions of a government—he was merely " one among the conquered ;" and yet to this man all eyes were turned instinctively, as to one who possessed the secret of the future. That *rez de chaussée* was besieged with visitors from morning till night; and even when, according to the custom of the French, he made his lengthened toilette, his dressing-room was filled by all the foreign ministers of the conquering monarchs, and Nesselrode and Metternich waited at these daily levées. In all these discussions M. de Talleyrand took the lead, with the same ease and the same *àplomb,* discussing kings to make and kingdoms to dismember, as though the clank of the muskets, which now and then interrupted their colloquy, came from the Imperial Guard of Napoleon, and not the Cossacks of the Don and the Uhlans of the Danube, who crowded the stairs and the avenues, and bivouacked in the court.

Here the Restoration was decided upon, and Talleyrand himself it was who decided it. The Emperor Alexander opposed it strongly at first, alleging that the old spirit and the old antipathies would all return with the elder Bourbons, and suggesting the Duc d'Orléans as king. Talleyrand, however, overruled the objection, asserting that no new agent must be had recourse to for governing at such a juncture, and that one usurpation could not be succeeded by another. It is said that when the news reached Vienna, in 1815, that Napoleon had landed from

Elba, the Emperor Alexander came hurriedly over to where Talleyrand was sitting, and informing him what had occurred, said, " I told you before, your plan would be a failure !" " Mais que faire ?" coolly retorted the calm *diplomate;* " of two evil courses it was the better—I never said more of it. Had you proclaimed the King of Rome you had been merely maintaining the power of Napoleon under another name. You cannot establish the government of a great nation upon a half measure. Besides that, Legitimacy, whatever its faults, was the only PRINCIPLE that could prove to Europe at large that France and Napoleon were parted for ever ; and, after so many barterings of crowns and trucklings of kingdoms, it was a fine opportunity of showing that there was still something— whether it be or be not by right divine—which was superior to sabres and muskets, generals and armies."

It was the sanctity of right—whether of kings, people, or individuals—which embodied Talleyrand's conception of the Restoration; and this is it which he so admirably expressed when arriving at the Congress of Vienna, the ambassador of a nation without wealth or army. " Je viens," said he to the assembled kings and ministers of conquering Europe—" Je viens, et je vous apporte plus que vous n'avez,—je vous apporte l'idée du droit !" This was happily expressed ; but no one more than he knew how to epigrammatize a whole volume of thought. In private life the charm of his manner was the most perfect thing imaginable : his consciousness of rank and ancient family divested him of all pretension whatever, and the idea of entering the lists with any one never occurred to his mind. Willingly availing himself of the talents of others, and their pens upon occasion, he never felt any embittering jealousy. Approachable by all, his unaffected demeanour was as likely to strike the passing observer as the rich stores of his intellect would have excited the admiration of a more reflecting one. Such was he who has passed away from amongst us—perhaps the very last name of the eventful era he lived in which shall claim a great place in history !

A singular picture of human vicissitude is presented to

us in the aspect of those places, but more particularly of
those houses wherein great events have once occurred,
but where time's changes have brought new and very different associations. A very few years in this eventful century we live in will do this. The wonderful drama of the
Empire sufficed to impress upon every city of Europe
some great and imposing reminiscence. A small unpretending little house, beside the ducal park at Weimar, was
Napoleon's resting-place for three days, when the whole
world was at his feet! The little *salon* where his receptions
were held at evening—and what receptions were they! the
greatest ministers and the most distinguished generals of
Europe!—scarcely more than an ordinary dressing-room
in size, remains to this hour as he left it. One arm-chair,
a little larger than the others, stands at the window, which
always lay open. A table was placed upon the grass-plot
outside, where several maps were laid. The *salon* itself
was too small to admit it, and here, from time to time, the
Emperor repaired, while, with eagle glance and abrupt
gesture, he marked out the future limits of the continental kingdoms, creating and erasing monarchies, fashioning
nations and peoples, in all the proud wilfulness of Omnipo-
tence! And now, while thinking of the Emperor, let me
bring to mind another local association.

In the handsomest part of the Chaussée d'Antin, surrounded on every side by the splendid palaces and gorgeous mansions of the wealthiest inhabitants of Paris,
stands a small, isolated, modest edifice, more like a Roman
villa than the house of some northern capital, in the midst
of a park; one of those pleasure-grounds which the
French—Heaven knows why—designate as "Jardin Anglais." The outer gate opens on Rue Chantereine, and
here to this hour you may trace, among the time-worn and
dilapidated ornaments, some remnants of the strange
figures which once decorated the pediment: weapons of
various ages and countries grouped together with sphinxes
and Egyptian emblems; the faint outlines of pyramids,
the peaceful-looking ibis, are there, among the helmets and
cuirasses, the massive swords and the death-dealing arms
of our modern warfare. In the midst of all, the number

52 stands encircled with a little garland of leaves; but even they are scarcely distinguishable now, and the number itself requires the aid of faith to detect it.

Within, the place speaks of neglect and decay; the shrubs are broken and uncared for; the parterres are weed-grown; a few marble pedestals rise amid the rank grass, to mark where statues once stood, but no other trace of them remains: the very fountain itself is fissured and broken, and the water has worn its channel along the herbage, and ripples on its wayward course unrestrained. The villa is almost a ruin, the sashes have fallen in in many places; the roof, too, has given way, and fragments of the mirrors which once decorated the walls lie strewn upon the floor with pieces of rare marble. Wherever the eye turns, some emblem of the taste of its former occupant meets you. Some fresco, stained with damp and green with mildew; some rustic bench, beneath a spreading tree, where the view opens more boldly; but all are decayed. The inlaid floors are rotting; the stuccoed ceilings, the richly-carved architraves, fall in fragments as your footsteps move; and the doomed walls themselves seem scarce able to resist the rude blast whose wailing cadence steals along them.

Oh, how tenfold more powerfully are the memories of the dead preserved by the scenes they inhabited while in life, than by the tombs and epitaphs that cover their ashes! How do the lessons of one speak home to the heart, calling up again, before the mind's eye, the very images themselves! not investing them with attributes our reason coldly rejects.

I know not the reason that this villa has been suffered thus to lapse into utter ruin, in the richest quarter of so splendid a city. I believe some long-contested litigation had its share in the causes. My present business is rather with its past fortunes; and to them I will now return.

It was on a cold dark morning of November, in the year 1799, that the street we have just mentioned, then called the Rue de la Victoire, became crowded with equipages and horsemen; cavalcades of generals and their staffs, in full uniform, arrived and were admitted within the massive gateway, before which, now, groups of curious and inquiring gazers were assembled, questioning and guessing as to the unusual spectacle. The number of led horses that paraded the street, the long lines of carriages on either side, nearly filled the way ; still there reigned a strange, unaccountable stillness among the crowd, who, as if appalled by the very mystery of the scene, repressed their ordinary tumult, and waited anxiously to watch the result.

Among the most interested spectators were the inhabitants of the neighbouring houses, who saw, for the first time in their lives, their quiet quarter the scene of such excitement. Every window was filled with faces, all turned towards that portal which so seldom was seen to open in general; for they who dwelt there had been more remarkable for the retirement and privacy of their habits than for aught else.

At each arrival the crowd separated to permit the equipage to approach the gate; and then might be heard the low murmur—for it was no louder—of " Ha ! that's Lasalle. See the mark of the sabre-wound on his cheek !" Or, " Here comes Augereau ! You'd never think that handsome fellow, with the soft eye, could be such a tiger." " Place there ! place for Colonel Savary !" " Ah, dark Savary ! we all know him."

Stirring as was the scene without, it was far inferior to the excitement that prevailed within the walls. There, every path and avenue that led to the villa were thronged with military men, walking or standing together in groups, conversing eagerly, and with anxious looks, but cautiously withal, and as though half fearing to be overheard.

Through the windows of the villa might be seen servants passing and repassing in haste, arranging the preparations for a magnificent *déjeûner*—for on that morning the generals of division and the principal military men in Paris were invited to breakfast with one of their most distinguished companions—General Buonaparte.

Since his return from Egypt, Buonaparte had been living

a life of apparent privacy and estrangement from all public
affairs. The circumstances under which he had quitted
the army under his command—the unauthorized mode of
his entry into France, without recall, without even permission—had caused his friends considerable uneasiness
on his behalf, and nothing short of the unobtrusive and
simple habits he maintained had probably saved him from
being called on to account for his conduct.

They, however, who themselves were pursuing the career
of ambition were better satisfied to see him thus, than
hazard anything by so bold an expedient. They believed
that he was only great at the head of his legions; and
they felt a triumphant pleasure at the obscurity into which
the victor of Lodi and the Pyramids had fallen when
measured with themselves. They witnessed, then, with
sincere satisfaction the seeming indolence of his present
life. They watched him in those *soirées* which Madame
Buonaparte gave, enjoying his repose with such thorough
delight—those delightful evenings, the most brilliant for
all that wit, intellect, and beauty can bestow; which
Talleyrand and Sièyes, Fouché, Carnot, Lemercier, and a
host of others frequented; and they dreamed that his hour
of ambition was over, and that he had fallen into the in-
glorious indolence of the retired soldier.

While the greater number of the guests strolled listlessly through the little park, a small group sat in the
vestibule of the villa, whose looks of impatience were ever
turned towards the door from which their host was
expected to enter. One of those was a tall, slight man,
with a high but narrow forehead, dark eyes, deeply buried
in his head, and overshadowed by long, heavy lashes; his
face was pale, and evinced evident signs of uneasiness, as
he listened, without ever speaking, to those about him.
This was General Moreau. He was dressed in the uniform
of a General of the day: the broad-skirted, embroidered
coat, the half-boot, the embroidered tricolour scarf, and a
chapeau with a deep feather trimming—a simple, but a
handsome costume, and which well became his well-formed
figure. Beside him sat a large, powerfully-built man,
whose long black hair, descending in loose curls on his

neck and back, as well as the jet-black brilliancy of his eye and deep olive complexion, bespoke a native of the South. Though his dress was like Moreau's, there was a careless jauntiness in his air, and a reckless *abandon* in his manner, that gave the costume a character totally different. The very negligence of his scarf-knot was a type of himself; and his thickly-uttered French, interspersed here and there with Italian phrases, showed that Murat cared little to cull his words. At his left was a hard-featured, stern-looking man, in the uniform of the Dragoons—this was Andreossy; and opposite, and leaning on a sofa, was General Lannes. He was pale and sickly; he had risen from a bed of illness to be present, and lay with half-closed lids, neither noticing nor taking interest in what went on about him.

At the window stood Marmont, conversing with a slight but handsome youth, in the uniform of the Chasseurs. Eugène Beauharnois was then but twenty-two, but even at that early age displayed the soldier-like ardour which so eminently distinguished him in after-life.

At length the door of the *salon* opened, and Buonaparte, dressed in the style of the period, appeared; his cheeks were sunk and thin; his hair, long, flat, and silky, hung straight down at either side of his pale and handsome face, in which now one faint tinge of colour marked either cheek. He saluted the rest with a warm shake of the hand, and then stooping down, said to Murat,—

"But Bernadotte—where is he?"

"Yonder," said Murat, carelessly pointing to a group outside the terrace, where a tall, fine-looking man, dressed in plain clothes, and without any indication of the soldier in his costume, stood in the midst of a knot of officers.

"Ha! General," said Napoleon, advancing towards him; "you are not in uniform. How comes this?"

"I am not on service," was the cold reply.

"No, but you soon shall be," said Buonaparte, with an effort at cordiality of manner.

"I do not anticipate it," rejoined Bernadotte, with an expression at once firm and menacing.

Buonaparte drew him to one side gently, and while he placed his arm within his, spoke to him with eagerness and energy for several minutes; but a cold shake of the head, without one word in reply, was all that he could obtain.

"What!" exclaimed Buonaparte, aloud, so that even the others heard him—"what! are you not convinced of it? Will not this Directory annihilate the Revolution? have we a moment to lose? The Council of Ancients are met to appoint me Commander-in-chief of the Army;—go, put on your uniform, and join me at once."

"I will not join a rebellion," was the insolent reply.

Buonaparte shrunk back and dropped his arm, then rallying in a moment, added,—

"'Tis well; you'll at least remain here until the decree of the Council is issued."

"Am I, then, a prisoner?" said Bernadotte, with a loud voice.

"No, no; there is no question of that kind: but pledge me your honour to undertake nothing adverse to me in this affair."

"As a mere citizen, I will not do so," replied the other; "but if I am ordered by a sufficient authority, I warn you."

"What do you mean, then, as a mere citizen?"

"That I will not go forth into the streets, to stir up the populace; nor into the barracks, to harangue the soldiers."

"Enough; I am satisfied. As for myself, I only desire to rescue the Republic; that done, I shall retire to Malmaison, and live peacefully."

A smile of a doubtful but sardonic character passed over Bernadotte's features as he heard these words, while he turned coldly away, and walked towards the gate. "What, Augereau! thou here?" said he, as he passed along, and with a contemptuous shrug he moved forward, and soon gained the street. And truly, it seemed strange that he, the fiercest of the Jacobins, the General who made his army assemble in clubs and knots to deliberate during the campaign of Italy, that he should now lend himself to uphold the power of Buonaparte!

Meanwhile, the *salons* were crowded in every part, party
succeeding party at the tables; where, amid the clattering
of the breakfast and the clinking of glasses, the conversation swelled into a loud and continued din.   Fouché,
Berthier, and Talleyrand were also to be seen, distinguishable by their dress, among the military uniforms; and
here now might be heard the mingled doubts and fears,
the hopes and dreads of each, as to the coming events;
and many watched the pale, care-worn face of Bourienne,
the secretary of Buonaparte, as if to read in his features
the chances of success; while the General himself went
from room to room, chatting confidentially with each in
turn, recapitulating as he went the phrase, "The country
is in danger!" and exhorting all to be patient, and wait
calmly for the decision of the Council, which could not,
now, be long of coming.

As they were still at table, M. Carnet, the deputation of
the Council, entered, and delivered into Buonaparte's
hands the sealed packet, from which he announced to the
assembly that the legislative bodies had been removed
to St. Cloud, to avoid the interruption of popular
clamour, and that he, General Buonaparte, was named
Commander-in-chief of the Army, and intrusted with the
execution of the decree.

This first step had been effected by the skilful agency
of Sièyes and Roger Ducos, who spent the whole of the
preceding night in issuing the summonses for a meeting of
the Council to such as they knew to be friendly to the
cause they advocated.   All the others received theirs too
late; forty-two only were present at the meeting, and by
that fragment of the Council the decree was passed.

· When Buonaparte had read the document to the end,
he looked around him on the fierce, determined faces,
bronzed and seared in many a battle-field, and said, "My
brothers in arms, will you stand by me here?"

"We will! we will!" shouted they, with one roar of
enthusiasm.

"And thou, Lefebvre, did I hear thy voice there?"

"Yes, General; to the death I'm yours."

Buonaparte unbuckled the sabre he wore at his side, and

placing it in Lefebvre's hands, said, "I wore this at the Pyramids; it is a fitting present from one soldier to another. Now, then, to horse!"

The splendid *cortége* moved along the grassy alleys to the gate, outside which, now, three regiments of cavalry and three battalions of the 17th were drawn up. Never was a Sovereign, in all his pride of power, surrounded with a more gorgeous staff. The conquerors of Italy, Germany, and Egypt, the greatest warriors of Europe, were there grouped around him—whose glorious star, even then, shone bright above him.

Scarcely had Buonaparte issued forth into the street than, raising his hat above his head, he called aloud, "Vive la République!" The troops caught up the cry, and the air rang with the wild cheers.

At the head of this force, surrounded by the generals, he rode slowly along towards the Tuileries, at the entrance to the gardens of which stood Carnet, dressed in his robe of senator-in-waiting, to receive him. Four colonels, his aides-de-camp, marched in front of Buonaparte, as he entered the Hall of the Ancients—his walk was slow and measured, and his air studiously respectful.

The decree being read, General Buonaparte replied in a few broken phrases, expressive of his sense of the confidence reposed in him; the words came with difficulty, and he spoke like one abashed and confused. He was no longer in front of his armed legions, whose war-worn looks inspired the burning eloquence of the camp—those flashing images, those daring flights, suited not the cold assembly, in whose presence he now stood—and he was ill at ease and disconcerted. It was only, at length, when turning to the generals who pressed on after him, he addressed the following words, that his confidence in himself came back, and that he felt himself once more,—

"This is the Republic we desire to have—and this we shall have; for it is the wish of those who now stand around me."

The cries of "Vive la République!" burst from the officers at once as they waved their *chapeaux* in the air, mingled with louder shouts of "Vive le Général!"

If the great events of the day were now over with the Council, they had only begun with Buonaparte.

"Whither now, General?" said Lefebvre, as he rode to his side.

"To the guillotine, I suppose," said Andreossy, with a look of sarcasm.

"We shall see that," was the cold answer of Buonaparte, while he gave the word to push forward to the Luxembourg.

This was but the prologue, and now began the great drama—the greatest, whether for its interest or its actors, that ever the world has been called to witness.

We all know the sequel, if sequel that can be called which our own days would imply is but the prologue of the piece

CHAPTER XXIII.

I HAVE had a night of ghostly dreams and horrors; the imagination of Monk Lewis, or, worse, of Hoffman himself, never conceived anything so diabolical. H., who visited me last evening, by way of interesting me, related the incidents of a dreadful murder enacted in the very room I slept in. There was a reality given to the narrative by the presence of the scene itself—the ancient hangings still on the walls—the antique chairs and cabinets standing as they had done when the deed of blood took place; but, more than all, by the marble bust of the murderess herself: for it was a woman, singularly beautiful, young, and of the highest rank, who enacted it. The story is this:—

The Villa, which originally was in possession of the Medici family, and subsequently of the Strozzi's, was afterwards purchased by Count Juliano, one of the most distinguished of the Florentine nobility. With every personal advantage—youth, high station, and immense wealth—he was married to one his equal in every respect, and might thus have seemed an exception to the lot of humanity, his life realizing, as it were, every possible element of happiness. Still, he was not happy; amid all the voluptuous enjoyments of a life passed in successive pleasures, the clouded brow and drooping eye told that some secret sorrow preyed upon him, and that his gay doublet, in all its bravery, covered a sad and sorrowing heart. His depression was generally attributed to the fact that, although now married three years, no child had been born to their union, or any likelihood that he should leave an heir to his great name and fortune. Not even to his nearest friends, however, did any confession admit this cause of sorrow; nor to the Countess, when herself lamenting over her childless lot, did he seem to show any participation in the grief.

The love of solitude, the desire to escape from all society, and pass hours, almost days, alone in a tower, the only admittance to which was by a stair from his own chamber, had now grown upon him to that extent, that his absence was regarded as a common occurrence by the guests of the castle, nor even excited a passing notice from any one. If others ceased to speculate on the Count's sorrow, and the daily aversion he exhibited to mixing with the world, the Countess grew more and more eager to discover the source. All her blandishments to win his secret from him were, however, in vain; vague answers, evasive replies, or direct refusals to be interrogated, were all that she met with, and the subject was at length abandoned—at least by these means.

Accident, however, disclosed what all her artifice had failed in—the key of the secret passage to the tower, and which the Count never entrusted to any one, fell from his pocket one day, when riding from the door; the Countess eagerly seized it, and guessing at once to what it belonged, hastened to the Count's chamber.

The surmise was soon found to be correct; in a few moments she had entered the winding stairs, passing up which, she reached a small octagon chamber at the summit of the tower. Scarcely had her eager eyes been thrown around the room, when they fell upon a little bed, almost concealed beneath a heavy canopy of silk, gorgeously embroidered with the Count's armorial bearings. Drawing rudely aside the hangings, she beheld the sleeping figure of a little boy, who, even in his infantine features, recalled the handsome traits of her husband's face. The child started and awoke with the noise, and looking wildly up, cried out, " Papa ; " and then suddenly changing his utterance, said, " Mamma." Almost immediately, however, discovering his error, he searched with anxious eyes around the chamber for those he was wont to see beside him.

"Who are you?" said the Countess, in a voice that trembled with the most terrible conflict of terror and jealousy, excited to the verge of madness. "Who are you?"

"Il Conte Juliano," said the child, haughtily; and showing at the same time a little medallion of gold embroidered on his coat, and displaying the family arms of the Julianos.

"Come with me, then, and see your father's castle," said the Countess; and she lifted him from the bed, and led him down the steps of the steep stairs into her husband's chamber.

It was the custom of the period that the lady, no matter how exalted her rank, should with her own hands arrange the linen which composed her husband's toilet, and this service was never permitted to be discharged by any less exalted member of the household. When the Count returned, toward night-fall, he hastened to his room—an invitation, or command, to dine at the Court that day compelling him to dress with all speed. He asked for the Countess as he passed up the stairs, but paid no attention to the reply, for as he entered his chamber he found she had already performed the accustomed office, and that the silver basket, with its snow-white contents, lay ready to his hand. With eager haste he proceeded to dress, and took up the embroidered shirt before him. When, horror of horrors! there lay beneath it the head of his child, severed from the body, still warm and bleeding—the dark eyes glaring as if with but half-extinguished life, the lips parted as if yet breathing! One cry of shrill and shrieking madness was heard through every vaulted chamber of that vast castle; the echoes were still ringing with it as the maddened father tore wildly from chamber to chamber in search of the murderess. She had quitted the castle on horseback two hours before. Mounting his swiftest horse he followed her from castle to castle; the dreadful chase continued through the night and the next day; a few hours of terrible slumber refreshed him again to pursue her; and thus he wandered over the Apennines and the vast plain byond them, days, weeks, months long, till in a wild conflict of his baffled vengeance and insanity he died! She was never heard of more!

Such is the horrid story of the chamber in which I sit; her bust, that of a lovely and gentle girl, fast entering into womanhood, is now before me; the forehead and the brows are singularly fine; the mouth alone reveals anything of the terrible nature within; the lips are firm and compressed—the under one drawn slightly—very slightly —backward. The head itself is low, and for the comfort of phrenologists, sadly deficient in "veneration." The whole character of the face is, however, beautiful, and of a classic order. It is horrible to connect the identity with a tale of blood.

With this terrible tragedy still dwelling on my mind, and the features of her who enacted it, I fell asleep. The room in which I lay had witnessed the deed. The low portal in the corner, concealed behind the arras, led to the stairs of the tower; the deep window in the massive wall looked out upon the swelling landscape over which she fled, and he, in mad fury, pursued her: these were enough to seize and hold the mind, and, blending the actual with the past, to make up a vision of palpable reality. Oftentimes did I start from sleep. Now, it was the fancy of a foot upon the tower stair; now, a child's fairy step upon the terrace overhead; now, I heard, in imagination, the one wild, fearful cry, uttered as if the reeling senses could endure no more! At last I found it better to rise and sit by the window, so overwrought and excited had my brain become. Day was breaking, not in the cold grey of a northern dawn, but in a rich glow of violet-coloured light, which, warmer on the mountain-tops, gradually merged into a faint pinkish hue upon the lesser hills, and became still fainter in the valleys and over the city itself. A light, gauzy mist tracked out in the air the course of the Arno; but so frail was this curtain that the sun's rays were already rending and scattering its fragments, giving through the breaches bright peeps of villas, churches, and villages on the mountain sides: the great dome, too, rose up in solemn grandeur; and the tall tower of Santa Croce stood, sentinel like, over the sleeping city. Already the low sounds of labour, awakening to its daily call, were heard; the distant rumbling of the heavy waggon, the crashing noise of branches, as the olive-trees beside the road brushed against the lumbering teams; and, farther off, the cheering voices of the boatmen, whose fast barques were hurrying along the rapid Arno;—all pleasant sounds, for they spoke of life and movement, of active minds and labouring hands, the only bulwarks against the corroding thoughts that eat into the sluggish soul of indolence.

For this fair scene—these fresh and balmy odours—this brilliant blending of blue sky and rosy earth, I could unsay all that I have said of Florence, and own that it is beautiful! I could wish to sit here many mornings to come, and enjoy this prospect as now I do. Vain thought! as if I could follow my mind to the contemplation of the fair scene, and so rove away in fancy to all that I have dreamed of, have loved and cared for, have trusted and been deceived in!

I must be up and stirring—my time grows briefer. This hand, whose blue veins stand out like knotted cordage, is fearfully attenuated; another day or two, perhaps, the pen will be too much fatigue; and I have still " Good-bye," to say to many—friends ?—ay, the word will serve as well as another. I have letters to write—some to read over once again; some to burn without reading. This kind of occupation—this " setting one's house in order" for the last time—is like a rapid survey taken of a whole life, a species of overture, in which fragments of every air of the piece enter, the gay and cheerful succeeded by the sad and plaintive, so fast as almost to blend the tones together; and is not this mingled strain the very chord that sounds through human life ?

Here, then, for my letter-box. What have we here?—a letter from the Marquis of D——, when he believed himself high in Ministerial favour, and in a position to confer praise or censure :

"CARLTON CLUB.

"DEAR TEMPY,

"Your speech was admirable—first-rate; the quotation from Horace, the neatest thing I ever heard; and astonishing, because so palpably unpremeditated. Every one I've met is delighted, and all say that, with courage and the resolve to succeed, the prize is your own. I go to Ireland, they say, or Paris. The latter if I can; the former if I must. In either case, will you promise to come with me? The assurance of this would be a very great relief to

"Yours truly,

"D——."

What have we pinned to the back of this? Oh, a few lines in pencil from Sir C—— S——, received, I see, the same evening.

"DEAR T.,

"Sir H—— is not pleased with your speech, although he owns it was clever. The levity he disliked, because he will not give D—— any pretence for continuing this system of personalities. The bit of Horace had been better omitted; Canning used the same lines once before, and the *réchauffé*—if it were such—was poor. The Marquis of D—— was twice at Downing Street, to say that he had 'crammed' you. This, of course, no one believes; but he takes the merit of your speech to himself, and aims high reward in consequence. He asks for an Embassy! This is what Lord L—— calls 'too bad.' Come over to-morrow before twelve o'clock.

" Believe me yours,

"C—— S——."

Another of the same date:—

" Go in and win, old boy! You've made capital running, and for the start too—distanced the knowing ones, and no mistake! The odds are seven to four that you're in the Cabinet before the Derby day. I've taken equal fifties that Tramp wins the Goodwood, and that you're in—double event. So look out sharp, and don't baulk

"Yours ever,

"FRANK LUSHINGTON."

A fourth, tied in the same piece of ribbon :—

"WILTON CRESCENT.

"DEAR FRIEND,

"We have just heard of your success. Brilliant and fascinating as it must be, do not forget those who long to share your triumph. Come over here at once. We waited supper till two; and now we are sitting here, watching every carriage, and opening the window at every noise in the street. Come then, and quickly.

"AUGUSTA BEVERLY."

And here is the last of the batch :—

"The D—— of B—— presents his compliments to Mr. Templeton, and begs to inform him that his 'ancestor was not the Marquis of T—— who conducted the negotiations at Malaga;' neither were 'thirty thousand pounds voted by the last Parliament to the family by way of secret service for parliamentary support,' but in compensation for two patent offices abolished—Inspectorship of Gold Mines, and Ordnance Comptrollership. And, lastly, that 'Infamous speech,' so pathetically alluded to, was made at a private theatrical meeting at Lord Mudbury's, in Kent, and not 'on the hustings,' as Mr. T. has asserted."

So much for one event, and in itself a trivial one! Who shall say that any act of his life is capable of exciting even an approach to unanimous praise or censure? This speech, which on one side won me the adhesion of some half-dozen clubs, the praise of a large body of the

Upper House, the softest words that the "beauty of the season" condescended to utter, brought me, on the other, the coldness of the Minister, the chilling civility of mock admiration, and lost me the friendship—in House of Commons parlance—of the leading member of the Government!

And here is a strange, square-shaped epistle, signed in the corner "Martin Haverstock." This rough-looking note was my first step in Diplomacy! I was a very young *attaché* to the mission at Florence, when, on returning to England through Milan, I was robbed of my trunk, and with it of all the money I possessed for my journey. It was taken by a process very well known in Italy, being cut off from the back of the carriage, not improbably, with the concurrence of the driver. However that might be, I arrived at the "Angelo d'Oro" without a sou. Having ordered a room, I sat down by myself, hungry and penniless, not having a single acquaintance at Milan, nor the slightest idea how to act in the emergency. My very passport was gone, so that I had actually nothing to authenticate my position—not even my name.

I sent for the landlord, who, after a very cold interview, referred me to the Consul; but the Consul had on that very morning left the city for Verona, so that his aid was cut off. My last resource—my only one, indeed—was to write to Florence for money, and wait for the answer. This was a delay of seven, possibly of eight, days, but it was unavoidable.

This done, I ordered supper—a very humble one too, and befitting the condition of one who had not wherewithal to pay for it. I remember still the sense of shame I felt as the waiter, on entering, looked around for my luggage, and saw neither trunk nor carpet-bag—not even a hat-box. I thought—nay, there could be no mistake about it, it was quite clear—he laid the table with a certain air of careless and noisy indifference that bespoke his contempt. The very bang of the door as he went out was a whole narrative of my purseless state.

I had been very hungry when I ordered the meal. I

had not tasted food for several hours, and yet now I could not eat a morsel; chagrin and shame had routed all appetite, and I sat looking at the table, and almost wondering why the dishes were there. I thought of all the kind friends far away, who would have been so delighted to assist me ; who, at that very hour perhaps, were speaking of me affectionately ; and yet I had not one near, even to speak a word of counsel, or say one syllable of encouragement. It was not, it may well be believed, the moneyed loss that afflicted me—the sum was neither large, nor did I care for it. It was the utter desolation, and the sense of dependence that galled me—a feeling whose painful tortures, even temporary as they were, I cannot, at this hour, eradicate from my memory.

Had I been left enough to continue my journey in the very humblest way, on foot even, it would have been happiness compared with what I felt. I arose at last from the table, where the untasted food still stood, and strolled out into the streets. I wandered about listlessly, not even feeling that amusement the newly seen objects of a great city almost always confer, and it was late when I turned back to the inn. As I entered, a man was standing talking with the master of the house, who, in his broken English, said, as I passed, "There he is !" I at once suspected that my sad adventure had been the subject of conversation, and hurried up the stairs to hide my shame. In my haste, however, I forgot my key at the porter's lodge, and was obliged to go back to fetch it. On doing so, I met on the stairs a large coarse-looking man, with a florid face, and an air of rough but of simple good-nature in his countenance. "You are a countryman, I believe ?" said he in English. "Well, I've just heard of what has happened to you. The rascals tried the same trick with me at Modena ; but I had an iron chain around *my* trunk, and as they were baulked, and while they were rattling at it, I got a shot at one of them with a pistol—not to hurt the devil, for it was only duck-shot ; not a bullet, you know. Where's your room ?—is this it ?"

I hesitated to reply, strange enough ; though he showed that he was well aware of all my loss. I felt ashamed to show that I had no baggage, nor anything belonging to me. He seemed to guess what passed in my mind, and said,—

"Bless your heart, sir, never mind me. I know the rogues have stripped you of all you had; but I want to talk to you about it, and see what is best to be done."

This gave me courage. I unlocked the door, and showed him in.

"I suspected how it was," said he, looking at the table, where the dishes stood untouched; "you could not eat by yourself, nor I either: so come along with me, and we'll have a bit of supper together, and chat over your business afterwards."

Perhaps I might have declined a more polished invitation; whether or not, it was of no use to refuse him, for he would not accept an excuse; and down we went to his chamber, and supped together. Unlike my slender meal, his was excellent, and the wine first-rate. He made me tell him about the loss of my trunk, twice over, I believe; and then he moralized a great deal about the rascality of the Continent generally, and Italy in particular, which, however, he remembered, could not be wondered at, seeing that three-fourths of the population of every rank did nothing but idle all day long. After that he inquired whether I had any pursuit myself; and although pleased when I said "Yes," his gratification became sensibly diminished on learning the nature of the employment. "I may be wrong," said he, "but I have always taken it that you diplomatic folk were little better than spies in gold-laced coats—fellows that were sent to pump sovereigns and bribe their ministers." I took a deal of pains, "for the honour of the line," to undeceive him; and, whether I perfectly succeeded or not, I certainly secured his favour towards myself, for, before we parted, it was all settled that I was to travel back with him to England, he having a carriage and a strong purse, and that he was to be my banker in all respects till I reached my friends.

As we journeyed along through France, where my knowledge of the language and the people seemed to give the greatest pleasure to my companion, he informed me that he was a farmer near Nottingham, and had come abroad to try and secure an inheritance bequeathed to him by a brother, who for several years had been partner in a great silk factory near Piacenza. In this he had only partly succeeded, the Government having thrown all possible obstructions in his way; still he was carrying back with him nearly twenty thousand pounds—a snug thing, as he said, for his little girl, for he was a widower with an only child. Of Amy he would talk for hours— ay, days long! It was a theme of which he never wearied. According to him, she was a paragon of beauty and accomplishments. She had been for some time at a boarding-school at Brighton, and was the pride of the establishment. "Oh, if I could only show her to you!" said he. "But why couldn't I? what's to prevent it? When you get to England and see your friends, what difficulty would there be in coming down to Hodley for a week or two? If you like riding, the Duke himself at Retton Park has not two better bred ones in his stable than I have!" No need to multiply his arguments and inducements: I agreed to go, not only to, but actually with, him—the frank good-nature of his character won on me at every moment, and long before we arrived at Calais I had conceived for him the strongest sentiments of affection.

From the moment he touched English ground his enthusiasm rose beyond all bounds; delighted to be once back again in his own country, and travelling the well-known road to his own home, he was elated like a school-boy. It was never an easy thing for me to resist the infectious influence of any temperament near me, whether its mood was grave or gay, and I became as excited and overjoyed as himself; and I suppose that two exiles, returning from years of banishment, never gave themselves up to greater transports than did we at every stage of our journey. I cannot think of this without astonishment, for, in honest truth, I was all my life attached to the Continent—from my earliest experience I had preferred the habits and customs to our own, and yet, such was the easy and unyielding compliance of my nature, that I actually fancied that my Anglo-mania was as great as his own.

At last we reached Hodley, and drove up a fine, trimly-kept gravel avenue, through several meadows, to a long comfortable-looking farmhouse, at the door of which, in expectant delight, stood Amy herself. In the oft-renewed embraces she gave her father I had time to remark her well, and could see that she was a fine, blue-eyed, fair-haired, handsome girl—a very flattering specimen of that good Saxon stock we are so justly proud of; and if not all her father's partiality deemed as regarded ladylike air and style, she was perfectly free from anything like pre-tension or any affectation whatever. This was my first impression: subsequent acquaintance strengthened it. In fact, the Brighton boarding-school had done no mischief to her; she had not learned a great deal by her two years' residence, but she had not brought back any toadying subserviency to the more nobly born, any depreciating sense of her former companions, or any contempt for the thatched farmhouse at Hodley and its honest owner.

If our daily life at the farm was very unvarying, it was exceedingly pleasurable; we rose early, and I accompanied Martin into the fields with the workmen, where we remained till breakfast. After which I usually betook myself to a little brook, where there was excellent fishing, and where, her household duties over, Amy joined me. We dined about two; and in the afternoon we—that is, Amy and myself—rode out together; and as we were admirably mounted, and she a capital horsewoman, usually took a scamper "cross country," whenever the fences were not too big and the turf inviting. Home to tea, and a walk afterwards through the green lanes and mossy paths of the neighbourhood, filled the day; and however little exciting the catalogue of pursuits, when did I feel time pass so swiftly? Let me be honest and avow that the position I enjoyed had its peculiar flattery. There was through all their friendship a kind of deferential respect —a sense of looking up to me, which I was young enough to be wonderfully taken by: and my experiences at

Foreign Courts—which Heaven knows were few and meagre enough—had elevated me in their eyes into something like Lord Whitworth or Lord Castlereagh; and I really believe that all the pleasure my stories and descriptions afforded was inferior to the delight they experienced in seeing the narrator, and occasionally the actor, in the scenes described, their own guest at their own table.

It was while revelling in the fullest enjoyment of this pleasant life that I received a Foreign Office letter, in reply to an application I had made for promotion, rejecting my request, and coolly commanding my immediate return to Florence. These missives were not things to disobey, and it was in no very joyful mood I broke the tidings to my host.

"What's it worth?" said Martin, abruptly.

"Oh, in point of money," said I, "the appointments are poor things. It is only that there are some good prizes in the wheel, and, whether one is lucky enough to gain them or not, even Hope is something. My salary is not quite two hundred a year!"

Martin gave a long, low whistle, and said,—

"Why, dang it! my poor brother George, that's gone, had six hundred when he went out as inspector over that silk factory! Two hundred a year!" mused he; "and what do you get at your next promotion?"

"That is not quite certain. I might be named *attaché* at Vienna, which would, perhaps, give me one hundred more—or, if I had the good fortune to win the Minister's favour, I might be made a secretary at some small legation and have five hundred—that is, however, a piece of luck not to be thought of."

"Well, I'm sure," sighed Martin; "I'm no judge of these matters; but it strikes me that's very poor pay, and that a man like myself, who has his ten or twelve hundreds a year—fifteen in good seasons—is better off than the great folk dining with kings or emperors."

"Of course you are," said I; "who doubts it? But we must all do something. England is not a country where idleness is honourable."

"Why not turn farmer?" said Martin, energetically; "you'd soon learn the craft. I've not met any one this

many a year picks up the knowledge about it like yourself.
You seem to like the life too."

"If you mean such as I live now, I delight in it."

"Do you, my dear boy?" cried he, grasping my hand,
and squeezing it between both his own. "If so, then
never leave us. You shall live with us—we'll take that
great piece of land there near the haugh—I've had an eye
on it for years back; there's a sheep run there as fine as
any in Europe. I'll lay down the whole of those two
fields into meadow, and keep the green crops to the back
altogether. Such partridge-shooting we will have there
yet. In winter, too, the Duke's hounds meet twice a-week.
I've got such a strapping three-year-old—you haven't seen
him, but he'll be a clipper. Well, don't say nay. You'll
stay and marry Amy. I'll give her twenty thousand
down, and leave you all I have afterwards."

This was poured forth in such a voluble strain that an
interruption was impossible; and at last, when over, the
speaker stood with tearful eyes gazing on me, as if on my
reply his very existence was hanging.

Surprise and gratitude for the unbounded confidence he
had shown in me were my first sensations, soon to be followed by a hundred other conflicting and jarring ones. I
should shame—even now, after years have gone by—to
own to some of these. Alas! our very natures are at the
mercy of the ordinances we ourselves have framed; and
the savage red man yields not more devotion to the idol
he has carved than do we to the fashion we have made
our Deity! I thought of the Lady Georginas and Caro-
lines of my acquaintance, and grew ashamed of Amy
Haverstock! If I had loved, this I am sure would not
have been the case, but I cannot acquit myself that
principle and good feeling should not have been sufficient
without love! Whether from the length of time in which
I remained without answering, or that in my confusion he
read something adverse to his wishes, but Martin grew
scarlet, and in a voice full of emotion said,—

"There, Mr. Templeton, enough said. I see it will
not do—there's no need of explaining. I was a fool,
that's all!"

"But will you not let me, at least, reflect?"

"No, sir; not a second. If my offer was not as frankly taken as made—ay, and on the instant too—I am only the more ashamed for ever making it: but there's an end on't. If you would be as good friends parting with me as we have been hitherto, never speak of this again." And so saying, Martin turned on his heel and walked hastily away. I followed him after a second, but he waved me back with his hand, and I was forced to comply.

That day Amy and I dined alone together. Her father, she said, "had got a bad headache;" and this she said with such evident candour, it was clear she knew nothing of our interview. The dinner was to me, at least, a very constrained affair; nor were my sensations rendered easier as she said, "My father tells me that you are obliged to leave us this evening, Mr. Templeton. I'm very sorry for it; but I hope we'll meet soon again."

We did not meet soon again, or ever. I left the farm that night for London. Martin came to the door from his bed to wish me good-bye. He looked very ill, and only spoke a few words. His shake-hands was, however, hearty; and his "God bless you," uttered with kind meaning.

I have never seen that neighbourhood since.

It was about two years after that I received a letter—the very one now before me—superscribed Martin Haver-stock. It was brief, and to this effect:—The Secretary for Foreign Affairs being a candidate for the representation in Parliament of the county in which Martin held a large stake, had, in acknowledgment of his friend Mr. Haverstock's exertions in his support, been only too happy to consider the application made respecting Mr. H.'s young friend, who, by the next *Gazette*, would be announced for promotion.

And thus I was made Secretary of Legation at Studtgart!

There was a postscript to Martin's letter, which filled me with strange and varying emotions:—"Amy is sorry that her baby is a little girl; she'd like to have called it 'Horace.'"

This packet I need not open. The envelope is super-scribed, "Hints and Mems for H. T. during his Residence at the Court of M——." They were given in a series of letters from old Lord H——, who had long been a resident Minister there, and knew the people thoroughly. I followed, very implicitly too, the counsels he gave, and was said to have acquitted myself well, for I was *chargé d'affaires.* But what absurdity it is to suppose that any exclusive information is ever obtainable by a Minister, except when the Government itself is disposed to afford it! I remember well, the spy we employed was also in the pay of the French Embassy. He was a Sardinian, and had spent some years of his life an Austrian prisoner in a fortress. We all believed, whatever the fellow's sentiments on other subjects, that he was a profound hater of Austria. Well, it turned out that he sold us all to Metternich.

Old Sir Robert W—— used to say to his *attachés,* "Never tell me secrets, but whenever anything is publicly discussed in the clubs and cafés, let me hear it." In the same way, he always rejected the authenticity of any revelations where Talleyrand, or Metternich, or Pozzo di Borgo's names appeared. "These men," he always used to say, "were their own confidants, and never leaked save to serve a purpose." It was from Sir Robert I heard a story first, which has since, I believe, been fully corroborated. An under-secretary of Talleyrand, during the Prince's residence as French ambassador at St. James's, informed his Excellency one morning that a very tempting offer had been made to him if he would disclose the contents of his master's writing-desk. He had not accepted nor altogether declined the proposal, wishing to know from the Prince how it might be made available to his plans, and whether a direct accusation of the author, a person of high station, would be deemed advisable. Talleyrand merely said, "Take the money; the middle board of the drawer in my secretary is removable by a very simple contrivance, which I'll show you. I had it made so at Paris. You'll find all the papers you want there. Take copies of them."

" But, Monsieur le Prince——"

"Pray make your mind at ease. I'll neither compro-
mise myself nor you."

The Secretary obeyed ; the bargain was perfected, and
a supposed "secret correspondence between Talleyrand
and Arnim," deposited in Lord T——'s hands. About a
week afterwards Lord T—— invited the Prince to pass
some days at his seat in Herefordshire, where a distinguished party was assembled. The ambassador accepted ;
and they met like the most cordial of friends. When the
period of the visit drew to its conclusion, they were walking one morning in the grounds together, engaged in a
conversation of the most amicable candour, each vying
with the other by the frankness and unreserve of his communications.

"Come now, Prince," said Lord T——, "we are, I
rejoice to find, on terms which will permit any freedom.
Tell me frankly, how do you stand with Prussia? Are
there any understandings between you to which we must
not be parties ? "

"None whatever."

"You say this freely and without reserve ? "

"Without the slightest reserve or qualification."

Lord T—— seemed overjoyed, and the discussion con-
cluded. They dined that day together, and in the evening
a large company was assembled to meet the Prince before
his departure for London. As usual at T—— House, the
party contained a great show of distinguished persons,
political and literary. Among the subjects of conversation started was the question of how it happened that
men of great literary distinction so rarely could shine as
statesmen, and that even such as by their writings
evinced a deep insight into political science, were scarcely
ever found to combine practical habits of business with
this great theoretical talent.

The discussion was amusing, because it was carried on
by men who themselves occupied the highest walks in
their respective careers.

To arrest a somewhat warm turn of the controversy,
Lord T——, turning to the Prince, said, "I suppose,

Monsieur le Prince, you have seldom been able to indulge in imaginative composition?"

"Pardon me, my lord, I have from time to time dissipated a little in that respect; and, if I must confess it, with a very considerable degree of amusement."

The announcement, made with a most perfect air of candour, interested at once the whole company, who could not subdue their murmured expressions of surprise as to the theme selected by the great diplomatist.

"I believe," said he, smiling, "I am in a position to gratify the present company; for, if I mistake not, I have actually with me at this moment a brief manuscript of my latest attempt in fiction. As I am a mere amateur, without the slightest pretension to skill or ability, I feel no reluctance at exposing my efforts to the kind criticism of friends. I only make one stipulation."

"Oh, pray, what is it? anything, of course, you desire!" was heard on every side.

"It is this. I read very badly, and I would request that T——, our kind host, would take upon him to read it aloud for us."

Lord T—— was only too much flattered by the proposal, and the Prince retired to fetch his papers, leaving the company amazed at the singularity of a scene which so little accorded with all they had ever heard of the deep and wily Minister; some of the shrewdest persons significantly observing, that the Prince was evidently verging on those years when vanity of every kind meets fewest obstacles to its display.

"Here are my papers, my lord," said the Prince, entering with his manuscript. "I have only to hope that they may afford to the honourable company any portion of the amusement their composition has given me."

The party seated themselves round the room, and Lord T——, disposing the papers on the table before him, arranged the candles, and prepared to begin. "The title of the piece is missing," said he, after a pause.

· "Oh, no, my lord; "you'll find it on the envelope," replied Talleyrand.

"Ah, very true; here it is!—' Secret Correspon-

dence'——" Lord T—— stopped—his hands trembled
—the blood left his face—and he leaned back in his
chair almost fainting.

"You are not ill!—are you ill?" broke from many
voices together.

"No; not in the least," said he, endeavouring to
smile; "but the Prince has been practising a bit of
plaisanterie on me, which I own has astounded me."

"Won't you read it, my lord; or shall I explain?"

"Oh, Monsieur le Prince," said Lord T——, crushing
the papers into his pocket, "I think you may be satisfied;" and with this, to the company, very mysterious
excuse, his lordship abruptly retired; while Talleyrand
almost immediately set out for London.

The nature of the mystification was not disclosed till
long afterwards; and it is but justice to both parties to
say, not by Talleyrand, but by Lord T—— himself.

With what facility men whose whole daily life is artifice can be imposed on, is a very remarkable feature in
all these cases. The practice of deceit would actually
appear to obstruct clear-sightedness and dull the ordinary
exercise of common sense. Witness that poor Dutch
ambassador Fabricius, who, a few years ago, was imposed
on at Paris by Bouffé, the comedian, representing himself
to be the first Secretary of the Minister for Foreign
Affairs, and offering, for a sum of money, to confide to
him the secret negotiations between M. Guizot and the
Belgian Government! Fabricius, deceived by the great
resemblance of Bouffé to the person he represented,
agreed, and actually wrote to the King of Holland a
triumphant despatch, announcing his own diplomatic
dexterity. Every post saw a huge packet of letters to
the king, containing various documents and papers;
some assuming to be in the handwriting of Guizot
—some, of Nothomb—some, of the Duke of Wellington—and two or three of King Leopold himself. The
task of undeceiving the unhappy dupe was taken by his
Majesty Louis Philippe, who having, at an evening reception at Neuilly, exposed his attempted corruption, coolly
turned his back and refused to receive him.

Another dive into this chaotic mass of reminiscence! A letter from poor Granthorpe, whose sad suicide remains the unexplained and unexplainable mystery of all who knew him. A man whose mind was remarkable for its being so deeply imbued with sentiments of religious truth—whose whole life was, so to say, devotional—is found dead, the act being by his own hand! No circumstance of domestic calamity, no pecuniary difficulty, not even a passing derangement of health, to account for the terrible event. Here is his note; we were but new acquaintances at the time, and it begins,—

"Dear Sir,
"From the conversation we held together lately at Lord N——'s table, I believe I shall not misinterpret your sentiments by supposing that any new fact connected with Waterloo will interest you strongly. I therefore enclose you a memoir, drawn up a few evenings back at W——. It was begun by way of a regular refutation of Alison, whose views are so manifestly incorrect; the idea of publication is, however, abandoned, and I am at liberty merely to show it to such of my friends as take a more than common interest in the transaction.

"Truly yours,
"S. GRANTHORPE."

The memoir which accompanied this is curious for two reasons: first, from its authenticity; and, secondly, from the fact that, being dictated from beginning to end, it is as clear, as consecutive, as free from unnecessary, and as full of all necessary, detail as if the events were of a few days' back, and that no recital of them had yet been given to the world. Two or three anecdotes (new to me, at least) were interspersed here and there, not for themselves, but as circumstantially evidencing facts of some importance.

One, I remember, alluded to a Prussian statement by a Captain Hahnsfelder, who stated that two British guns, placed on the height above La Haye Sainte, were captured

by the French as early as eleven o'clock. The passage in
the memoir is this:—" Untrue; these guns were in the
field at seven in the evening, in the same position in which
they stood at the beginning of the battle. They are in
advance of Adam's left, and were so far unprotected that
the artillerymen who served them had to retire after each
discharge. The Cuirassiers made several attempts to
carry them off, but as orders were given that, after each
fire, one wheel should be taken off each gun, the cavalry
failed in their object. They tried to lasso them, but this
also failed, besides losing them some men."

Alison's strategy, for he went so far as to plan a campaign of his own, is very ably exposed, and the necessity
of posting troops in particular districts clearly explained
from circumstances peculiar to the localities, such as
stationing the cavalry at Enghein, where alone forage was
procurable. The controversy, if it can be so called, is
worthless. They whose opinions are alone valuable are
exactly the persons who will not speak on the subject.

A strange-looking letter is this from C——, enclosing
the proof of a paper I wrote on Irish Educational matters,
very laconic and editorial :—

     " Dear T.,
"You are all wrong: as blue and yellow, when mixed,
form green, so will your Protestant and Papist League
make nothing but rampant infidelity. In any great State
scheme of education there must be one grand standard of
obedience—the Bible is the only one I've heard of yet.
Keep this one, then, till you hear of better.

                    " Yours,
                       " H. C."

Another of the same hand :—

"H—— desires me to inclose you these two letters :
One I know is an introduction to Guizot ; the other, I
suppose, to be 'Ein empfehlungs Brief' to the 'Gräfin.'
Take care to say as little as possible to the one, and to

have, in Irish parlance, as little as possible ' to say ' to the
other. At Paris you want no guidance; and at Vienna
the Abbé Discot is your man. Coloredo is out of favour
for the moment; but he can afford to wait, and, waiting,
to win. Be assiduous in your visits at B——y's; and
when the Countess affects ignorance, let us always hear
from you.

" Yours ever,

" H. C."

This is a very rose-coloured and rose-odoured document :—

" Dear Mr. Templeton,
" I have to make two thousand excuses ; one each for
two indiscretions. I believed I had your box at the
Opera for last evening; and I also fancied—think of my
absurdity!—that the bouquet of camellias left there was
meant for me. Pray forgive me; or, rather, ask the fair
lady who came in at the ballet to forgive me. I never can
think of the incident without shame and self-reproach;
du reste, it has given me the opportunity of knowing that
your taste in beauty equals your judgment in flowers.

" Very much yours,

" HELEN COLLYTON.

" Sir H—— bids me say that he expects you on Wednesday. We dine earlier, as the Admiral goes on board
in the evening."

This was an absurd incident; and, trivially as it is
touched on here, made of that same Lady Collyton a very
dangerous enemy to me.

This is not a specimen of caligraphy, certainly :—

" If you promise neither to talk of the Catholic Question, the Kildare Place Society, nor the ' Glorious
Revolution of 1688,' P—— will have no objection to

meet you at dinner. Hammond, you've heard, I suppose, has lost his election; he polled more voters than there were freeholders registered on the books: this was proving too much, and he must pay the penalty. Y—— is in, and will remain if he can; but there is a hitch in it—'as the man who lent him his qualification is in gaol at Bruges.' Write and say if you accept the conditions.

"Yours,

"FREDERICK HAMILTON."

There are some memorials of a very different kind—they are bound up together; and well may they, they form an episode quite apart from all the events before or after them! I dare not open them; for, although years have passed away, the wounds would bleed afresh if only breathed on! This was the last I ever received from her. I have no need to open it—I know every line by heart! —almost prophetic, too!——

"I have no fear of offending you now, since we shall never meet again. The very thought that the whole world divides us, as completely as death itself, will make you accept my words less as reproof than warning. Once more, then, abandon the career for which you have not health, nor energy, nor enduring strength. Brilliant displays, discursive efforts, however effective, will no more constitute statesmanship than fireworks suffice to light up the streets of a city. Like all men of quick intelligence, you undervalue those who advance more slowly, forgetting that their gleaning is more cleanly made, and that, while you come sooner, they come more heavily laden. Again, this waiting for conviction—this habit of listening to the arguments on each side, however excellent in general life, is inapplicable in politics. You must have opinions previously formed—you must have your mind made up, on principles very different and much wider than those a debate embraces. If I find the person who guides me through the streets of a strange city stop to inquire here, to ask this, to investigate that, and so on, I at once conceive—and very reasonably—a doubt of his skill and intelligence; but if he advance with a certain air of assured knowledge, I yield myself to his guidance with implicit trust: nor does it matter so much, when we have reached the desired goal, that we made a slight divergence from the shortest road.

"Now, if a constituency concede much to your judgment, remember that you owe a similar debt to the leader of your party, who certainly—all consideration of ability apart—sees farther, because from a higher eminence, than other men.

"Again, you take no pleasure in any pursuit wherein no obstacle presents itself; and yet, if the difficulty be one involving a really strong effort, you abandon it. You require as many conditions to your liking as did the commander at Walcheren—the wind must not only blow from a particular quarter, but with a certain degree of violence. This will never do! The favouring gale that leads to fortune is as often a hurricane as a zephyr; some are blown into the haven half-shipwrecked, but still safe.

"Lastly, you have a failing, for which neither ability, nor address, nor labour, nor even good luck, can compensate. You trust every one—not from any implicit reliance on the goodness of human nature—not that you think well of this man, or highly of that, but simply from indolence. 'Believing' is so very easy—such a rare self-indulgence! Think of all the deception this has cost you—think of the fallacies, which you knew to be fallacies, that found their way into your head, tainting your own opinions, and mingling themselves with your matured convictions. Believe me, there is nothing but a strict quarantine can prevail against error!"

Enough of these,—now for an incremation: would that, Hindoo-like, I could consume with them the memory to which they have been wedded!

*   *   *   *   *

Dr. H—— has been here again; he came in just as the last flicker was expiring over the charred leaves; he guessed readily what had been my occupation, and seemed to feel relieved that the sad office of telling bad tidings of my case was taken off his hands. Symptoms seem now crowding on each other—they come, like detached battalions meeting on the field of battle when victory is won, only to show themselves and to proclaim how hopeless would be resistance. The course of the malady would, latterly, appear to have been rapid, and yet how reluctant does the spirit seem to quit its ruined temple!

I wish that I had more command over my faculties; the tricks Imagination plays me at each moment are very painful: scarcely have I composed my mind into a calm and patient frame, than Fancy sets to work at some vision of returning health and strength—of home scenes and familiar faces—of the green lanes of Old England, as seen at sunset of a summer eve, when the last song of the blackbird rings through the clear air, and odours of sweet flowers grow stronger in the heavy atmosphere.

To start from these, and think of what I am—of what so soon I shall be!

What marvellously fine aspirations and noble enterprises cross the sick man's fancy! The climate of health is sadly unfavourable to the creatures begot of fancy—one tithe of the strange notions that are now warring in my distracted brain would make matter for a whole novelist's library. Thoughts that are thus engendered are like the wines which the Germans call " Ausgelesene," and which, falling from the grape unpressed, have none of the impurities of fabrication about them. After all, the things that have been left undone by all of us in this life, would be far better and greater than those we have done.

> Oh, the fond hearts that have never been smitten,
>   And all the hot tears that have never been shed!
> Not to speak of the books that have never been written;
>   And all the smart things that have never been said!

*   *   *   *   *

Weaker and weaker!—the senses fail to retain impressions, and, like cracked vases, let their contents ooze out by slow degrees. Objects of sight become commingled with those of sound; and I can half understand the blind man Locke tells us of, who imagined "the colour scarlet to be like the sound of a trumpet."

Mesmerism affects the power of transferring the operations of one sense to the organs of another; can it be that, in certain states of the brain, the nervous fluids become intermixed?

It is night—calm, still, and starlit! How large are the stars compared with what they appear in northern latitudes! And the moonlight, too, is pale as silver, and has none of the yellow tint we see with us. Beautifully it lies along that slope of the mountain yonder, where the tall dark yew-trees throw their straight shadows across the glittering surface. It is the churchyard of St. M——and now in the church I can perceive the twinkle of lights —they are the candles aroun l the coffin of him whose funeral I saw this morning. The custom of leaving the body for a day in the church before consigning it to the grave is a touching one. The dimly-lighted aisles, and the solemn air of the place, seem a fitting transition from Life to the sleep of Death.

I have been thinking of that very old man, who came past the window yesterday, and sat down to rest himself on the stone-bench beside the door. Giordano never took a finer head as a study: lofty and massive, with the temples deeply indented; and such a beard, snow-white and waving! How I longed for strength enough to have wandered forth and seated myself beside him! A strange mysterious feeling was on me—that I should hear words of comfort from his lips! This impression grew out of his own remarkable story. Yes, poor and humble as his dress, lowly as his present condition may seem, he was a " Captain of the Imperial Guard "—a proud title once! He was taken prisoner during the retreat from Moscow, and, with hundreds more, sent away to eternal exile in Siberia At that period he was in all the pride of manhood, a true specimen of his class—gay, witty, full of daring, and a sceptic; a Frenchman of the Revolution grafted on a gentleman of the old *régime!* The Fatalism that sustained them—it was their only faith—through long years

of banishment, brought many in sadness to the grave!
It was a gloomy religion, whose hope was but chastened
despair! He himself lived on, the reckless spirit of a
bold heart hardening him against grief as effectually as
it excluded memory. When, at length, as time went on,
and his companions dropped off around him, a severe and
cheerless melancholy settled down upon him, and he lived
on in a state of dreamy unreality, less like sleep than
death itself! And yet, through this dense cloud a ray of
light pierced and fell upon his cold and darkened spirit,
like day descending into some cleft between the mountains!

He was sitting at the door of his hut one evening, to
taste the few short moments of sunset, when, unwrapping
the piece of paper which surrounded his cigar—the one
sole luxury the prisoners are permitted—he was proceeding to light it, when a thought occurred that he would
read the lines, for it was a printed paper. He opened the
bit of torn and ragged paper, and found there three verses
from the Gospel of St. John. Doubtless he had often sat
in weariness before the most heart-stirring appeals and
earnest exhortations; and yet these few lines did what
years of such teaching failed to do. The long-thirsting
heart was refreshed by this one drop of clear water! He
became a believer, firm and faithful! His liberation,
which he owed to the clemency of the Emperor Alexander,
set him free to wander over the world as a missionary,
and this he has been ever since. How striking are his
calm and benevolent features among the faces which pass
you in every street!—for we live in times of eager and
insensate passion. The volcano has thrown forth ashes,
and who knows how soon the flame may follow!

How long this night appears! I have sat, as I believe,
for hours here, and yet it is but two o'clock! The dreary
vacuity of weakness is like a wide and pathless waste. I
see but one great spreading moorland, with a low, dark
horizon: no creature moves across the surface—no light
glimmers on it. It is the plain before the Valley of the
Shadow of Death.

Poor Gilbert!—how soundly he sleeps, believing that I

am also sunk to rest! The deep-drawn breathings of his strong chest are strange beside the fluttering hurry of my respiration. He was wearied out with watching—wearied, as I feel myself: but Death comes not the sooner for our weariness; we must bide our time, even like the felon whose sentence has fixed the day and the hour.

Three o'clock! What a chill is on me! The fire no longer warms me, nor does the great cloak with which I braved the snows of Canada. This is a sensation quite distinct from mere cold—it is like as though my body were itself the source from which the air became chilled. I have tried to heap more wood upon the fire, but am too weak to reach it. I cannot bear to awaken that poor fellow. It is but enduring a little—a very little longer—and all will be over!

There was a man upon the terrace below the window, walking slowly back and forwards. What can it mean, so late? It has made me nervous and irritable to watch his shadow as it crosses before me. There!—how strange! —he has beckoned to me! Is this real? Now I see no one! Some trick of imagination; but how weak it has left me! My hand trembles, too, with a strange fear.

It has struck again! It must be four; and I have slept. What a long night it has been! O Life! Life! how little your best and highest ambitions seem to him who sits, like me, waiting to be released! Now and then the heart beats full and strong, and a momentary sense of vigour flashes across my mind; and then the icy current comes back, the faint struggle to breathe shaking the frame as a wrecked vessel trembles with each crashing wave!

Day breaks at length—that must be the dawn! But my eyes are failing, and my hands are numbed. Poor Gilbert! how sound is his sleep! He has turned—and now he dreams! What is he muttering? Good night! good night! Even so—good night!

*   *   *   *   *
*   *   *   *   *

How cold—how very cold I feel! I thought it had been over! Oh, for a little longer of this dalliance here!

—ay, even here, on the last shores of life! Inexpressibly
sweet the odours are, and the birds! How I drink in
those strains!—they will float with me along the journey
I am going! Weaker and weaker. This must be death!
Farewell!

Envoy.

THE circumstances which have placed these papers in
my hands afford me the only apology I can offer for making
them public. They were bequeathed to me, in some sort,
as a recompense for services which my poor master had
long intended to have rewarded very differently; nor, save
under the pressure of an actual necessity, should I devote
them now to the purpose of personal assistance. I neither
understand how to correct nor arrange them. I have no
skill in editorship, and send them to the printer without
the addition of a letter by any hand except his who wrote
them. It is true, some pages have been withheld—I am
not sure whether necessarily or not—for I have no com-
petent judgment to guide me. I would, however, hope
that what I here give to the world may, while benefiting
the servant, leave no stain upon the memory of the best of
masters.

GEORGE GILBERT,

Valet to the late H. Templeton, Esq.

DOVER, January, 1848.

Postscript to Envoy.

A word may be necessary as to the political allusions.
As they were all written in the autumn of the past year,
many are, of course, inapplicable to countries whose con-

dition the wonderful events lately occurring have modified : many are, however, almost correct in every detail of prophetic foresight; and, it is not necessary that I should repeat, have neither been changed nor added to since penned by my late master.

THE END.

Woodfall and Kinder, Printers, Milford Lane, Strand, London, W.C.

THE BOOK OF BRITISH BALLADS. Edited by S. C. HALL, F.S.A. With Illustrations by E. M. WARD, R.A., Sir J. NOEL PATON, JOHN TENNIEL, Sir JOHN GILBERT, R.A., T. CRESWICK, R.A., and others. 21s.

DRAWING FROM NATURE : a Series of Progressive Instructions in Sketching. By GEORGE BARNARD. Illustrated with 18 Plates in Tints and Colours, and more than 100 Woodcuts. 21s.

THE THEORY AND PRACTICE OF LANDSCAPE PAINTING IN WATER COLOURS. By GEORGE BARNARD. Illustrated with 26 Drawings and Diagrams in Colours, and numerous Woodcuts. 21s.

HEADS OF THE PEOPLE ; or, Portraits of the English. Drawn by KENNY MEADOWS. With Descriptive Sketches by W. M. THACKERAY, DOUGLAS JERROLD, Mrs. GORE, WILLIAM HOWITT, LEMAN REDE, NIMROD, Mrs. S. C. HALL, and others. With 110 Illustrations. 2 vols., 15s.

LAMB'S TALES FROM SHAKESPEARE. A New Drawing-room Edition. With Illustrations by Sir JOHN GILBERT, R.A. 10s. 6d.

SIR WALTER SCOTT'S POETICAL WORKS. A New Edition, with the Author's Notes and 8 full-page Illustrations. Red Line Edition. 7s. 6d.

A THOUSAND AND ONE GEMS OF POETRY. Edited by CARLES MACKAY. With Illustrations by J. E. MILLAIS, R.A., Sir JOHN GILBERT, R.A., and BIRKET FOSTER. 7s. 6d.

POETS' CORNER : Selections from the Works of the greatest British Poets, with Biographical Sketches. Red Line Edition. 7s. 6d.

FIFTY "BAB" BALLADS. By W. S. GILBERT. New Edition, embodying the Two Series. With many Illustrations by the Author. 7s. 6d.

MODERN MAGIC. A Complete Manual of Conjuring. By Professor HOFFMANN. With 300 Illustrations. 7s. 6d.

SCIENCE IN SPORT MADE PHILOSOPHY IN EARNEST. Edited by ROBERT ROUTLEDGE, Author of "Discoveries and Inventions of the Nineteenth Century." With many Illustrations. 7s. 6d.

LONDON AND NEW YORK: GEORGE ROUTLEDGE AND SONS.

A MANUAL OF DOMESTIC ECONOMY. Suited to Families Spending from £150 to £1500 a year. By J. H. WALSH, F.R.C.S. Illustrated with Coloured Plates by KRONHEIM, and numerous Woodcuts. 10s. 6d.

NAOMI: or, The Last Days of Jerusalem. By MRS. WEBB. A New Edition, Reprinted from larger type with Illustrations. 7s. 6d.

MOTHER GOOSE'S NURSERY RHYMES AND FAIRY TALES. With 400 Illustrations. 7s. 6d.

THE YOUNG LADY'S BOOK: a Manual of Exercises, Amusements, &c. By Mrs. HENRY MACKARNESS. With many Illustrations and Coloured Plates. 7s. 6d.

ROUTLEDGE'S EVERY BOY'S ANNUAL FOR 1878. With Full-page Plates and Coloured Illustrations. 6s.

THE SECRETS OF CONJURING; or, How to Become a Wizard. By ROBERT HOUDIN. Translated and Edited with Notes, by Professor HOFFMANN. Illustrated. 6s.

FROM CADET TO COLONEL: the Record of a Life of Active Service. By Major-General Sir THOMAS SEATON, K.C.B. With Illustrations. 5s.

LITTLE WIDE-AWAKE FOR 1878. A Story Book for Good Children. By Mrs. SALE BARKER. With 400 Illustrations and a Coloured Frontispiece. 5s.; and in boards, 3s.

MOTHER GOOSE'S FAIRY TALES. A Complete Collection of Popular Fairy Tales. With 230 Illustrations by Eminent Artists, and a Coloured Frontispiece. 5s.; and in boards, 3s.

BABY'S OPERA: a Book of Old Rhymes, with New Dresses, by WALTER CRANE. Engraved and Printed in Colours by EDMUND EVANS. The Music by the Earliest Masters. 5s.

LITTLE BLUEBELL'S PICTURE BOOK. With 400 Illustrations by Sir JOHN GILBERT, R.A., J. D. WATSON, HARRISON WEIR, and other Artists. 5s.; and in boards, 3s.

LITTLE LAYS FOR LITTLE FOLK. Selected by JOHN G. WATTS. Illustrated by W. SMALL, E. M. WIMPERIS, R. BARNES, and others. 5s.; and in boards, 3s.

LONDON AND NEW YORK: GEORGE ROUTLEDGE AND SONS.

(4)

BUCKMASTER'S COOKERY. A New Edition, thoroughly revised, and for the most part re-written by the Author. 2s. 6d.

THE FLORAL BIRTHDAY BOOK. With Pictures of Flowers, printed in Colours by EDMUND EVANS. Fancy boards, 2s.

THE BOYS OF WESTONBURY. By the Rev. H. C. ADAMS. With Illustrations by A. W. COOPER. 5s.

THE ARABIAN NIGHTS. Selected and Revised for Family Use. With Illustrations and Coloured Plates. 5s.

UNCLE TOM'S CABIN. With Illustrations printed in Colours by KRONHEIM. 5s.

LEILA. By Miss A. F. TYTLER. Containing 'Leila; or, the Island'—'Leila in England'—and 'Leila at Home.' With 9 Illustrations. 5s.

THE CHRISTIAN YEAR. With Illustrations of Flowers, designed by W. FOSTER, and printed in Colours by EDMUND EVANS. 18mo, cloth. 5s.

NAPIER'S HISTORY OF THE PENINSULAR WAR. Vol. I. 1807-1810; Vol. II. 1810-1812. With Maps and Plans. 3s. 6d. each.

MONSTRELET'S CHRONICLES OF ENGLAND AND FRANCE. From the Text of Colonel JOHNES. With Notes and upwards of 100 Woodcuts (uniform with Froissart). 2 vols., super-royal 8vo, Roxburghe, 24s.

THE RISE OF THE DUTCH REPUBLIC. By J. LOTHROP MOTLEY. In 3 vols., crown 8vo, 18s.

Do.   Do.   New Edition, Complete in One volume, crown 8vo, cloth, gilt edges, 6s.

A HISTORY OF BRITISH INDIA, from the Earliest Period of British Intercourse to the Present Time. By CHARLES MACFARLANE. With Additions to the Year 1858 by a late Editor of the *Delhi Gazette.* Illustrated with numerous Engravings. Post 8vo, cloth gilt, 5s.

FROISSART'S CHRONICLES OF ENGLAND, FRANCE, AND SPAIN, &c. New Edition, from the Text of Colonel JOHNES. With Notes, a Life of the Author, an Essay on his Works, and a Criticism on his History. Embellished with 120 beautiful Woodcuts, illustrative of the Manners, Customs, &c. 2 vols., super-royal 8vo, Roxburghe, 25s.

THE FALL OF ROME AND THE RISE OF NEW NATIONALITIES. Showing the connection between Ancient and Modern History. By the Rev. JOHN G. SHEPPARD, D.C.L. Post 8vo, cloth, 750 pages, 7s. 6d.

BANCROFT'S HISTORY OF THE UNITED STATES, from the Discovery of the American Continent to the Declaration of Independence, in 1776. 7 vols., fcap. 8vo, Roxburghe, 15s.

THE HISTORY OF FRANCE, from the Invasion of the Franks under Clovis to the Present Time. Including the War of 1870–71. By EMILE DE BONNECHOSE. A New Edition. Post 8vo, cloth, 7s. 6d.

HISTORY OF FRANCE, from the Conquest of Gaul by the Romans to the Peace of 1856. By AMELIA B. EDWARDS. 1s.

SHAKESPEARE.

ROUTLEDGE'S ILLUSTRATED SHAKESPEARE. Edited by HOWARD STAUNTON, with 850 Illustrations by Sir JOHN GILBERT, R.A., and a Steel Portrait. 3 vols., super-royal, cloth, £2, 16s.

" The pen, the pencil, and the printer have striven together in honourable rivalry, combining clearness of text, elegance of illustration, and beauty of type. The result is worthy of the labour, and we can say with a safe conscience to all who wish to receive or present the bard in a becoming dress, buy ' Routledge's Picture Shakespeare.' "—*The Times.*

" One of the most important additions to the mass of Shakespearian literature which has appeared for many years."—*The Critic.*

LONDON AND NEW YORK: GEORGE ROUTLEDGE AND SONS.

(6)

CHARLES KNIGHT'S GUINEA SHAKSPERE. With 340 Illustrations by Sir JOHN GILBERT, R.A. 2 vols., super-royal 8vo, cloth extra, 21s.; gilt edges, 25s.; or in 1 volume, gilt edges, 21s.

THE WORKS OF SHAKESPEARE. Edited by HOWARD STAUNTON. With Notes, Glossary, and Life. A beautiful Library Edition, in large type. 6 vols., demy 8vo, Roxburghe binding, £1, 11s. 6d.

SHAKSPEARE'S WORKS. Edited by THOMAS CAMPBELL. With Life, Portrait, and Vignette, and 16 page Illustrations, by Sir JOHN GILBERT, R.A. Bound in cloth, 10s. 6d.; gilt edges, 12s.

SHAKSPERE. Red Line Edition, Edited by CHARLES KNIGHT. With Steel Portrait, cloth extra, 7s. 6d.

THE BLACKFRIARS SHAKSPERE. Edited by CHARLES KNIGHT. Crown 8vo, cloth, 3s. 6d.

CHARLES KNIGHT'S SHAKSPERE. Complete, with the Poems, 768 pages, with Illustrations, cloth, extra gilt, 3s. 6d.

SHAKSPEARE'S DRAMATIC WORKS. A New Edition, with Notes and Life. Printed in a new Type from the Text of Johnson, Stevens, and Reed. Edited by W. HAZLITT. 5 vols., fcap. 8vo, cloth gilt, 18s.

THE BOOK OF SHAKESPEARE GEMS. A Series of Landscape Illustrations to the most Interesting Localities in Shakespeare's Plays. In 45 Steel Plates. 8vo, cloth, gilt edges, price 12s. 6d.

LAMB'S TALES FROM SHAKESPEARE. With Illustrations by Sir JOHN GILBERT, R.A. 3s. 6d.

DODD'S BEAUTIES OF SHAKESPEARE. With Illustrations by Sir JOHN GILBERT, R.A. 3s. 6d.

THE MIND OF SHAKESPEARE AS EXHIBITED IN HIS WORKS. By the Rev. A. A. MORGAN. With Illustrations by Sir JOHN GILBERT, R.A. 3s. 6d.

LONDON AND NEW YORK: GEORGE ROUTLEDGE AND SONS.

THE OLD DRAMATISTS AND THE OLD POETS.

WITH BIOGRAPHICAL MEMOIRS, &c.

These Volumes are beautifully printed on fine paper, with Steel Portrait and Vignette, and are each, with one exception, complete in ONE VOLUME.

THE OLD DRAMATISTS.

SHAKSPEARE. With Remarks on his Life and Writings by THOMAS CAMPBELL; and Portrait, Vignette, Illustrations, and Index. In 1 vol., 8vo, price 10s. 6d., cloth.

WYCHERLEY, CONGREVE, VANBRUGH, AND FARQUHAR. With Biographical and Critical Notices by LEIGH HUNT; and Portrait and Vignette. In 1 vol., 8vo, price 16s., cloth.

MASSINGER AND FORD. With an Introduction by HARTLEY COLERIDGE; and Portrait and Vignette. In 1 vol., price 16s., cloth.

BEN JONSON. With a Memoir by WILLIAM GIFFORD; and Portrait and Vignette. In 1 vol., 8vo, 16s., cloth.

BEAUMONT AND FLETCHER. With Introduction by GEORGE DARLEY; and Portraits and Vignettes. In 2 vols., 8vo, price £1, 12s., cloth.

JOHN WEBSTER. With Life and Notes by the Rev. ALEXANDER DYCE. In 1 vol., 8vo, price 12s., cloth.

LONDON AND NEW YORK : GEORGE ROUTLEDGE AND SONS.

MARLOWE. With a Memoir and Notes by the Rev. ALEX-ANDER DYCE; and Portrait and Vignette. In 1 vol., 8vo, price 12s., cloth.

PEELE AND GREENE'S DRAMATIC WORKS. Edited by the Rev. ALEXANDER DYCE. In 1 vol., 8vo, price 16s., cloth.

THE OLD POETS.

SPENSER. With Selected Notes, Life by the Rev. H. J. TODD, M.A.; Portrait, Vignette, and Glossary Index. In 1 vol., price 10s. 6d., cloth.

CHAUCER. With Notes and Glossary by TYRWHITT; and Portrait and Vignette. In 1 vol., price 10s. 6d., cloth.

DRYDEN. With Notes by the Revs. JOSEPH and JOHN WARTON: and Portrait and Vignette. In 1 vol., price 10s. 6d., cloth.

POPE. Including the Translations. With Notes and Life by the Rev. H. F. CARY, A.M.; and Portrait and Vignette. In 1 vol., price 10s. 6d., cloth.

---

(9)

The "Harry Lorrequer" Edition

OF

CHARLES LEVER'S NOVELS.

Price 3s. 6d. each Volume, with Illustrations.

HARRY LORREQUER.
JACK HINTON.
CHARLES O'MALLEY. **2 vols.**
ARTHUR O'LEARY.
TOM BURKE. **2 vols.**
THE O'DONOGHUE.
THE KNIGHT OF GWYNNE. **2 vols.**
ROLAND CASHEL. **2 vols.**
THE DALTONS. **2 vols.**
THE DODD FAMILY ABROAD. **2 vols.**
SIR JASPER CAREW.
MAURICE TIERNAY.
CON CREGAN.
THE FORTUNES OF GLENCORE.
DAVENPORT DUNN. **2 vols.**
THE MARTINS O' CRO MARTIN. **2 vols.**
ONE OF THEM.
BARRINGTON.
A DAY'S RIDE.
LUTTRELL OF ARRAN.
TONY BUTLER.
CORNELIUS O'DOWD.
SIR BROOKE FOSBROOKE.
THE BRAMLEIGHS.
A RENT IN A CLOUD.
THAT BOY OF NORCOTT'S.
LORD KILGOBBIN.

LORD LYTTON'S NOVELS.

KNEBWORTH EDITION.

Handsomely printed in crown 8vo, from new type, and bound in green cloth, with frontispiece.

Price 3s. 6d. each Volume.

EUGENE ARAM.
NIGHT AND MORNING.
PELHAM.
ERNEST MALTRAVERS.
ALICE.
THE LAST DAYS OF POMPEII.
THE CAXTONS.
DEVEREUX.
THE DISOWNED.
GODOLPHIN.
HAROLD.
PAUL CLIFFORD.
A STRANGE STORY.
THE LAST OF THE BARONS.
LEILA, AND THE PILGRIMS OF THE RHINE.
LUCRETIA.
MY NOVEL, Vol. I.; MY NOVEL, Vol. II.
RIENZI.
WHAT WILL HE DO WITH IT? Vol. I.
WHAT WILL HE DO WITH IT? Vol. II.
ZANONI.
THE COMING RACE.
KENELM CHILLINGLY.
THE PARISIANS, Vol. I.; THE PARISIANS, Vol. II.
FALKLAND AND ZICCI.
PAUSANIAS THE SPARTAN.

LONDON AND NEW YORK: GEORGE ROUTLEDGE AND SONS.

LORD LYTTON'S
MISCELLANEOUS WORKS.
KNEBWORTH EDITION.

Volumes already Issued, price 3s. 6d. each.

QUARTERLY ESSAYS.
PAMPHLETS AND SKETCHES.
SCHILLER AND HORACE, TRANSLATED.
KING ARTHUR.
THE NEW TIMON, ST. STEPHEN'S, AND **THE LOST**
    TALES OF MILETUS.
DRAMATIC WORKS, Vol. I.
ENGLAND AND THE ENGLISH.
ATHENS: ITS RISE AND FALL.
CAXTONIANA.
THE STUDENT; AND ASMODEUS AT LARGE.

" Poet, Essayist, Orator, Statesman, Dramatist, Scholar, Novelist—
he had been all these, and this not like the fickle profligate satirised by
Pope, who tried all things and never finished any; for whatever the
character Lord Lytton essayed to fill, he worked at the object he put
before himself with conscientious thoroughness until he had completed
his design. . . . . The vigour, wit, and polish of 'St. Stephens'
entitled him to high rank in the masculine school of Dryden and Pope;
the 'Lost Tales of Miletus' have charmed scholars with their playful
fancy, and the translations from Schiller have been vouched by Mr.
Carlyle as the versions an English reader should consult who wishes to
know the lyrics of the great German author. Those who are most
familiar with Lord Lytton's essays are most fond of them, and are most
persuaded that they have never received fit recognition. Certain it is,
that among the earliest collected of his writings of this kind—'The
Student'—are some papers of singular power and beauty which have
never been adequately appreciated. The author of the 'Lady of
Lyons' was flattered by the preference of every actress on the stage for
the part of Pauline; and the audience in the most fastidious of our
theatres have welcomed ' Money' every night for more than six months
past."—*Times*, Jan. 20, 1873.

LONDON AND NEW YORK : GEORGE ROUTLEDGE AND SONS.

BOOKS ON NATURAL HISTORY, FARMING, SPORTING, ETC.

NATURAL HISTORY.

ROUTLEDGE'S ILLUSTRATED HISTORY OF MAN. Being an Account of the Manners and Customs of the Uncivilized Races of Men. By the Rev. J. G. WOOD, M.A., F.L.S. With more than 600 Original Illustrations by ZWECKER, DANBY, ANGAS, HANDLEY, and others, engraved by the Brothers DALZIEL. Vol. I., Africa, 18s. ; Vol. II., Australia, New Zealand, Polynesia, America, Asia, and Ancient Europe, 20s. Two Vols., super-royal 8vo, cloth, 38s.

ROUTLEDGE'S ILLUSTRATED NATURAL HISTORY. By the Rev. J. G. WOOD, M.A. With more than 1500 Illustrations by COLEMAN, WOLF, HARRISON WEIR, WOOD, ZWECKER, and others. Three Vols. super-royal, cloth, price £2, 14s. The volumes are also sold separately, viz. :—Mammalia, with 600 Illustrations, 18s. ; Birds, with 500 Illustrations, 18s. ; Reptiles, Fishes, and Insects, 400 Illustrations, 18s.

THE IMPERIAL NATURAL HISTORY. By the Rev. J. G. WOOD. 1000 pages, with 500 Plates, super-royal 8vo, cloth, gilt edges, £1, 1s.

AN ILLUSTRATED NATURAL HISTORY. By the Rev. J. G. WOOD, M.A. With 500 Illustrations by WILLIAM HARVEY, and 8 full-page Plates by WOLF and HARRISON WEIR. Post 8vo, cloth, gilt edges, 6s.

A PICTURE NATURAL HISTORY. Adapted for Young Readers. By the Rev. J. G. WOOD. With 700 Illustrations by WOLF, WEIR, &c. 4to, cloth, gilt edges, 12s. 6d.

THE POPULAR NATURAL HISTORY. By the Rev. J. G. WOOD. With Hundreds of Illustrations, 7s. 6d.

SKETCHES AND ANECDOTES OF ANIMAL LIFE. By the Rev. J. G. WOOD. Illustrated by HARRISON WEIR. Fcap. 8vo, cloth, 3s. 6d.

THE POULTRY BOOK. By W. B. TEGETMEIER, F.Z.S. Assisted by many Eminent Authorities. With 30 full-page Illustrations of the different Varieties, drawn from Life by HARRISON WEIR, and printed in Colours by LEIGHTON Brothers; and numerous Woodcuts. Imperial 8vo, half-bound, 21s.

LONDON AND NEW YORK : GEORGE ROUTLEDGE AND SONS.

THE STANDARD OF EXCELLENCE IN EXHIBI-
TION POULTRY. By W. B. TEGETMEIER, F.Z.S. Fcap., cloth, 2s. 6d.

PIGEONS. By W. B. TEGETMEIER, F.Z.S. Assisted by many
eminent Fanciers. With 27 Coloured Plates drawn from Life by HARRISON
WEIR, and printed by LEIGHTON Brothers; and numerous Woodcuts.
Imperial 8vo, half-bound, 10s. 6d.

THE HOMING OR CARRIER PIGEON; its History,
Management, and Method of Training. By W. B. TEGETMEIER, F.Z.S.
1s. boards.

BRITISH BIRDS' EGGS AND NESTS. By the Rev.
J. C. ATKINSON. With Original Illustrations by W. S. COLEMAN, printed
in Colours. Fcap., cloth, gilt edges, 3s. 6d.

BRITISH BIRDS' EGGS. By R. LAISHLEY. With 20
Pages of Coloured Plates, embracing 100 subjects. Cloth, 5s.

WANDERINGS IN SOUTH AMERICA. With Instruc-
tions for the Preservation of Birds for Cabinets. By CHARLES WATERTON.
Fcap., cloth gilt, 3s. 6d.

WHITE'S NATURAL HISTORY OF SELBORNE.
New Edition. Edited by J. G. WOOD, and Illustrated with above 200
Illustrations by W. HARVEY. Fcap. 8vo, cloth, 3s. 6d.

DOGS AND THEIR WAYS. Illustrated by Numerous
Anecdotes, from Authentic Sources. By the Rev. CHARLES WILLIAMS.
With Illustrations. Fcap. 8vo, cloth, 3s. 6d.

THE COMMON OBJECTS OF THE COUNTRY. By
the Rev. J. G. WOOD. With Illustrations by COLEMAN, containing 150 of
the "Objects" beautifully printed in Colours. Cloth, gilt edges, 3s. 6d.
. Also a Cheap Edition, price 1s., in fancy boards, with plain Plates.

COMMON BRITISH BEETLES. By the Rev. J. G. WOOD,
M.A. With Woodcuts and Twelve pages of Plates of all the Varieties,
beautifully printed in Colours by EDMUND EVANS. Fcap. 8vo, cloth, gilt
edges, 3s. 6d.

WESTWOOD'S (PROFESSOR) BRITISH BUTTER-
FLIES AND THEIR TRANSFORMATIONS. With numerous Illustrations, beautifully coloured by hand. Imperial 8vo, cloth, 12s. 6d.

BRITISH BUTTERFLIES. Figures and Descriptions of
every Native Species, with an Account of Butterfly Life. With 71 Coloured
Figures of Butterflies, all of exact life-size, and 67 Figures of Caterpillars,
Chrysalides, &c. By W. S. COLEMAN, Fcap., cloth, gilt, 3s. 6d.
. A Cheap Edition, with plain Plates, fancy boards, 1s.

THE COMMON MOTHS OF ENGLAND. By the Rev.
J. G. WOOD, M.A. Twelve plates printed in Colours, comprising 100
Objects. Cloth, gilt edges, 3s. 6d.
. A Cheap Edition, with plain Plates, boards, 1s.

LONDON AND NEW YORK: GEORGE ROUTLEDGE AND SONS.

THE COMMON OBJECTS OF THE MICROSCOPE.
By the Rev. J. G. Wood. With 12 pages of Plates by Tuffen West, embracing upwards of 400 Objects. The Illustrations printed in Colours. Fcap. 8vo, price 3s. 6d., cloth, gilt edges.

⁎ A Cheap Edition, with plain Plates, price 1s., fancy boards.

BRITISH ENTOMOLOGY. Containing a Familiar and
· Technical Description of the Insects most common to the localities of the British Isles. By Maria E. Catlow. With 16 pages of Coloured Plates. Cloth, 5s.

THE COMMON OBJECTS OF THE SEA-SHORE.
With Hints for the Aquarium. By the Rev. J. G. Wood. The Fine Edition, with the Illustrations by G. B. Sowerby, beautifully printed in Colours. Fcap. 8vo, cloth, gilt edges, 3s. 6d.

⁎ Also, price 1s., a Cheap Edition, with the Plates plain.

THE FRESH-WATER AND SALT-WATER AQUA-
RIUM. By the Rev. J. G. Wood, M.A. With 11 Coloured Plates, containing 126 Objects. Cloth, 3s. 6d.

⁎ A Cheap Edition, with plain Plates, boards, 1s.

THE MICROSCOPE: Its History, Construction, and Appli-
cation. By Jabez Hogg, F.L.S., F.R.M.S. With upwards of 500 Engravings and Coloured Illustrations by Tuffen West. Crown 8vo, cloth, 7s. 6d.

BRITISH FERNS AND THE ALLIED PLANTS.
Comprising the Club-Mosses, Pepperworts, and Horsetails. By Thomas Moore, F.L.S. With 20 pages of Coloured Illustrations, embracing 51 Subjects. Cloth, 5s.

OUR WOODLANDS, HEATHS, AND HEDGES. A
Popular Description of Trees, Shrubs, Wild Fruits, &c., with Notices of their Insect Inhabitants. By W. S. Coleman, M.E.S.L. With 41 Illustrations printed in Colours on Eight Plates. Fcap., cloth, gilt edges, 3s. 6d.

⁎ A Cheap Edition, with plain Plates, fancy boards, 1s.

BRITISH FERNS AND THEIR ALLIES. Comprising
the Club-Mosses, Pepperworts, and Horsetails. By Thomas Moore. With 40 Illustrations by W. S. Coleman, beautifully printed in Colours. Fcap. 8vo, cloth, gilt edges, 3s. 6d.

⁎ A Cheap Edition, with Coloured Plates, price 1s., fancy boards.

AGRICULTURE AND FARMING.

MECHI'S SYSTEM OF FARMING.

HOW TO FARM PROFITABLY; or, The Sayings and
Doings of Mr. Alderman Mechi. A New Edition, with Additions. Half-bound, 5s.

London and New York: George Routledge and Sons.